THE
STOLEN
CHILD

Carmel Harrington

THE
STOLEN
CHILD

REVIEW

First published in 2025 by Headline Review
An imprint of HEADLINE PUBLISHING GROUP LIMITED

1

Cataloguing in Publication Data is available from the British Library

Hardback ISBN 978 1 0354 2550 1
Trade paperback ISBN 978 1 0354 2138 1

Typeset in 12/15pt Sabon LT Std by Jouve (UK), Milton Keynes

Printed and bound in Great Britain by Clays Ltd, Elcograf S.p.A.

Headline's policy is to use papers that are natural, renewable and recyclable products
and made from wood grown in well-managed forests and other controlled sources.
The logging and manufacturing processes are expected to conform to the
environmental regulations of the country of origin.

HEADLINE PUBLISHING GROUP LIMITED
An Hachette UK Company
Carmelite House
50 Victoria Embankment
London EC4Y 0DZ

The authorised representative in the EEA is Hachette Ireland, 8 Castlecourt
Centre, Dublin 15, D15 XTP3, Ireland (email: info@hbgi.ie)

www.headline.co.uk
www.hachette.co.uk

For my son Nate, my inspiration.

Prologue

The woman never lets her gaze waver from the boy. She greedily takes in the soft curve of his cheeks and the dimple in his chin. Even from this safe distance, she sees the steel blue of his eyes as he looks up to his mother adoringly – eyes so like his father's.

The mother reaches over to brush damp blond curls from his forehead, warm from the afternoon sun. The tenderness of the moment catches the woman off guard. A surge of pain, sharp and intrusive, hits her, and it takes all her willpower not to shout, '*Stop!*'

She closes her eyes momentarily and breathes in and out until the pain subsides. The woman looks again at the little boy and focuses only on him, not the mother. A resolute smile forms on her lips as she observes his plump, pink hands cradling his bottle. She knows, with unwavering certainty, what she must do to protect the boy and keep him safe from his father.

The woman's smile widens, her heart aching with the intensity of her love for this boy whom she can only watch from afar. She commits to memory every extraordinary detail, her mind painting a vivid picture of what it will feel like to hold him. Her arms ache with the intensity of her longing, a longing that will consume her if she does not make it happen.

Soon.

PART ONE

Come away, O human child!
To the waters and the wild
With a faery, hand in hand
For the world's more full of weeping than you can understand.

'The Stolen Child', William Butler Yeats

THEN

July 1983

Kimberly

The Carousel, *Spanish Coast*

Kimberly lay back on a blue plastic sun lounger, sighing as the warmth of the late afternoon sun washed over her. Her husband, Jason, stood in the shallow water of the kiddies' pool of the *Carousel*, a cruise ship with the Blue Wave line. He was playing with their two children, Robert and Lily. She took in Jason's toned and tanned physique. As a young girl, Kimberly and her best friend had dreamed of marrying stereotypical tall, dark and handsome men. They'd have two children each, a boy and a girl, and live happily ever after.

'Two out of three, ain't bad,' Kimberly sang softly, tears filling her eyes again. She bit the inside of her cheek, and the unbidden emotion obeyed the command, staying hidden.

It was five days into their two-week family cruise around the Mediterranean. A delayed honeymoon, they'd called it. Kimberly had been pregnant with Lily when they'd got married last year. Between chronic morning sickness and taking care of her then eighteen-month-old son Robert, now Jason's stepson, they'd decided to wait.

Today had been a sea day, a chance to relax by the pool and recharge their batteries, before they arrived in the Spanish port of Barcelona the following morning. Kimberly fidgeted on her sun lounger, keeping her attention on her family. She grabbed a scrunchie and pulled her blonde, shoulder-length hair into a ponytail. Her eyes darted to each child, back and forth. Lily was now six months old, wearing bright orange armbands and giggling as she tried to escape her father's hold. With her light-brown hair pulled into two tiny bunches on top of her head, Lily was undoubtedly adorable. Quick to smile, their daughter was a big hit with the eight hundred passengers on board the *Carousel*.

Kimberly turned her attention to Robert, who was two and a half years old, and slight for his age. He'd progressed to a floating ring round his tummy, which had cute dolphins etched on it. His face was scrunched in determination as he tried to swim from one side of the pool to the other. He'd do it too, Kimberly knew. He kicked his legs furiously behind him, but in doing so water splashed over Lily's face, and she squealed in protest.

'Hey!' Jason snapped to Robert, pulling Lily closer to him protectively and wiping her eyes gently with his hand. 'Watch what you're doing, buddy. Your little sister is only a baby.'

Kimberly pulled her Wayfarer mirror sunglasses off in irritation. She moved to the pool's edge and swung her legs into the shallow water.

'He's playing. Please remember that he's only a wee baby too,' Kimberly hissed to Jason. She waded closer to Robert and then said to her little boy in a softer tone, 'It's okay, little lamb. Daddy didn't mean to shout.'

Robert looked at his stepfather from under his dark eyelashes, his bottom lip trembling. 'It was a abbident.'

Kimberly sighed as she pulled him in for a reassuring hug. 'Of course it was. You didn't do anything wrong.'

'I don't think I shouted,' Jason said, looking from his wife to his stepson, confusion clouding his eyes.

'People are watching; must you make a scene?' Kimberly hissed, feeling the stare of an older couple seated close by, taking it all in. Her breath quickened, and despite the vast ocean around them she felt claustrophobic. 'I'm going back to the cabin with the children.'

Kimberly scooped up both kids with ease, wrapping them in fluffy blue-and-white towels. Jason joined them, pulling a towel round his waist. He lifted Lily into his arms to dry her off.

Why couldn't he have picked up Robert to let the boy know that he wasn't cross with him, that the moment was already forgotten?

Her baby girl was oblivious to any worrying family dynamics and squealed again, but this time in delight, as her daddy tickled her.

'Tickle me too, Daddy,' Robert asked, raising his arms upwards.

Jason and Kimberly swapped children so Jason could tickle Robert, and peace was restored for the Murphy family.

When Kimberly had met Jason two years previously, the last thing on her mind was dating. Her only thought was taking care of Robert. But she hadn't bargained on the love she would feel for her new beau, fast and all-enveloping. From the moment he'd knocked on the door of her flat in Dublin, she'd felt an instant attraction to him. And it wasn't only a physical reaction to his good looks. It was a meeting of two like-minded souls, who both instantly knew that the other was to be an essential part of their future. Jason had proposed shortly after she found out she was expecting Lily. And here Kimberly was, twenty-eight years old, with that perfect family she'd always dreamed of having.

Looks are often deceiving, though.

'Hey, Kimberly, no sad faces are allowed on holiday,' Jason said, looking over Robert's shoulder, a frown creasing his forehead.

'Ignore me,' Kimberly said, folding the towels into her large poolside bag. 'I'm being overly sentimental, that's all.' She pointed to Robert, who was now snuggled in his stepfather's arms. 'It's nice to see you two together like that, father and son. I'm sorry I snapped a minute ago. I know I can be a little overprotective.'

Jason's frown disappeared instantly, and he leaned in to kiss his wife. 'Forgiven! I can't stay mad with someone as bonnie as you.' Jason's Irish accent changed to Scottish as he mimicked Kimberly's soft lilt.

'I couldn't love him any more if he were my own; you know that, don't you?' Jason asked in a low voice as they began their short walk back to their family cabin.

'Yes. I know that,' Kimberly replied.

Jason's face relaxed into an easy smile. 'Don't judge me, but I'm glad we have the kids' club booked for later tonight. I'm looking forward to having a drink with my beautiful wife.'

Kimberly accepted a kiss from Jason as a tension headache began to thump in her temples. She pushed it aside, and within an hour all four of them were showered, bathed, dressed and ready for the evening buffet.

'You've caught the sun – it suits you!' Jason complimented Kimberly as they waited for the lift. 'Doesn't Mama look lovely tonight?' he said to Robert, who nodded enthusiastically in agreement. 'In fact, I think we all scrub up well.'

Kimberly took a moment to take their family in. There were striking, dressed in their holiday best, bright colours against sun-kissed skin. Robert and her, blonde and blue-eyed, Jason and Lily, dark with brown eyes.

They found a table at the *Carousel* buffet, taking turns choosing from the delicacies offered that evening. But as Kimberly spoon-fed Lily her mashed potatoes, she felt the tension headache that had niggled her all day tighten its claws into her.

'You okay?' Jason asked, a forkful of stroganoff held in midair. 'You've gone pale.'

'Headache,' Kimberly admitted. She steeled herself for an argument, continuing, 'I'm going to take a sleeping tablet and go to bed early, once the children are asleep. Knock it on its head.'

Jason's eyes dropped, and his jaw clenched. 'But the talent show is on tonight in the main theatre. We were going to go. A night for just the two of us.'

Kimberly picked up a napkin and wiped Lily's face clean, then turned her attention to Robert, who was about to throw a piece of chicken onto the floor. 'I know that was the plan. And I'm sorry to miss it. I need to sleep this headache off. But there's no reason why you can't go alone.'

'I can't do that,' Jason answered warily.

'Yes, you can. You've been looking forward to it. So go. Have a couple of beers. I'll wake up a new woman, and tomorrow we can have a nice family day in Barcelona.'

Jason needed little encouragement. Kimberly knew she'd been snappy all day, and while her husband was a patient man he was ready for the escape and comfort a cold pint could offer. Jason offered to help her get the kids into bed, but Kimberly insisted he leave immediately. She needed time to herself, without his watchful eyes on her and the children.

If he looks back, I'll call out and ask him to stay, Kimberly thought after he'd kissed them all goodbye. But he carried on purposefully and disappeared out of sight into the busy atrium of the ship without a backwards glance.

Back in their cabin, once Lily had drunk her bottle, and was drifting off to sleep in her crib, Kimberly turned her attention to Robert, who sat cross-legged on the floor watching TV. Cartoon Tom chased Jerry menacingly around the garden, and a shiver ran down Kimberly's back as she picked up Robert's empty night-time bottle of milk from the floor beside him.

'I drank it all, Mama,' her little boy said proudly.

'You are such a good boy. Come here to me,' Kimberly said, holding her hand out to him.

'I sleepy, Mama,' Robert replied, wiping his eyes with his hands. He clasped his beloved Peter Rabbit soft toy in his right hand.

Kimberly picked him up and gently placed him in his sofa bed. Then, climbing in beside him, she read him his favourite bedtime story, *Goodnight Moon*.

Even before Kimberly was halfway through, the quiet poetry had lulled Robert asleep in her arms. She lay beside him until her eyes became heavy too, the power of her sleeping tablet taking effect. Kimberly almost stayed there, her little boy wrapped up in her arms.

Safe, the two of them together.

The temptation to hold on to him and never let go was overwhelming. But then Lily stirred in her cot, and the sound brought Kimberly back from the brink of sleep. She kissed Robert one last time, breathing in his scent, then carefully placed Peter Rabbit under the crook of his arm.

'I love you more than the moon,' Kimberly whispered. Slowly, she made her way back to her double bed, her legs heavy and uncooperative, falling on to the mattress with one last, 'Goodnight, moon. Goodnight, Lily. Goodnight, Robert . . .'

Her eyes closed, and all was dark.

Lily's cries woke Kimberly. She sat up, groggily looking around the small cabin in surprise. Her head thumped as if she'd been partying late into the night and she could smell stale beer. It took her a moment to remember that they were on a cruise ship, not at home in Dublin.

'What time is it?' Jason mumbled from beneath the bedclothes.

Kimberly looked down at her watch and answered, 'Seven.'

She pulled Lily from her cot and held her close, instantly soothing her cries. The sound of a vehicle rumbling nearby drifted up to their cabin from outside.

'We must be docked in Barcelona,' Jason said, stretching his arms above his head. 'God, I feel rough! I drank way too much last night.' He made his way towards Robert's sofa bed. 'Wake up, sleepy head. Come on, buddy, let's go out to the balcony and take a look at Barcelona.'

Jason pulled back the white duvet to reveal an empty bed.

'He must be in the bathroom,' Jason said. He opened the en suite door, his expectant smile turning to a frown. 'Robert's not in here either.' Jason's voice rose as he called out, 'Buddy, where are you hiding?'

With Lily in her arms, Kimberly joined Jason, and they both searched for their son in the small cabin. Kimberly moved slowly, her legs immobilised with terror. The cabin was only one hundred and forty square feet, so the search was over as quickly as it began.

'He's not here. He's gone . . .' Jason said, his face white, sweat glistening on his forehead. He ran to the cabin door and opened it, running out into the hallway and calling out their son's name desperately.

Kimberly clutched her chest, dread twisting her gut and heart. Then she began to scream.

THEN

July 1983

Kimberly

The Carousel, *Port of Barcelona, Spain*

Two hours had raced by since the chilling realisation that Robert was not in their cabin. As soon as Jason had raised the alarm, everything happened at double speed. Captain Phillipe swiftly imposed an emergency lockdown on the *Carousel*, halting all pre-arranged shore visits to Barcelona. The crew began scouring every inch of the ship in a desperate search for the missing boy.

It felt as if they were actors in a play, being directed to move from one room to the next as the captain and his staff took charge. Kimberly, Jason, and Lily were eventually shepherded to one of the small bars, which had been cordoned off to become the search headquarters. Kind staff, who had become familiar faces during the voyage so far, placed tea and water on the table before them, along with boxes of tissues.

'La Policía has arrived,' Captain Phillipe announced, ushering in a plain-clothes officer. Slight, the man had jet-black hair, olive skin, and piercing green eyes. He was young, no more than thirty. He stubbed a cigarette into an ashtray on a nearby table, and then approached the Murphys.

Kimberly clasped Jason's hand. It was clammy and damp, like her own, but they clutched to each other all the same. She watched the officer's face, desperately trying to decipher his thoughts. But his expression remained inscrutable, offering no clue to the news he carried. A surge of bile threatened to rise in Kimberly's throat, and she quickly covered her mouth as her anxiety mounted.

'Are you going to be sick?' Jason asked. Kimberly waved aside his concern and managed to control her heaving stomach. She felt the police officer's eyes on them both, looking them up and down as he weighed them up.

'Hello, Mr and Mrs Murphy. My name is Inspector Hugo Ortega. I'm with the Guardia Civil, in the Spanish police. And I'm here to help you find your son.' He reached over to shake their hands in turn.

His English was almost perfect, his handshake firm. Kimberly could smell the faint odour of nicotine and cologne lingering in the air between them. But the banality of shaking hands and uttering pleasantries with the Spanish police while her little boy was missing from her arms made her body tremble and rage. Kimberly fought back another scream.

'I am so sorry that you are dealing with this upset,' Inspector Ortega continued.

'Our son is missing. That's hardly an upset!' Jason spluttered, two dots of red appearing on his cheeks.

Inspector Ortega raised a hand in apology. 'Of course. My English does not always translate well. I assure you that I am treating this with utmost urgency. Please, go through everything, from the last time you saw Robert to this morning when you realised he was missing from your cabin.'

He reached into his jacket pocket and pulled out a small notebook and pencil. He licked the tip of the lead, then looked at them both expectantly.

Jason cleared his throat and said, 'After our evening meal, I went for a drink. It was after seven o'clock. My wife went back to our cabin with the children.' His voice caught. 'I kissed them all goodbye, the kids and Kimberly, outside the lift in the main atrium.' Jason breathed in deeply and gathered himself to continue. 'I got back to the cabin at midnight. Everyone was asleep when I arrived.'

Lily made a sound as she dreamed. They all glanced over to the double red buggy, one side now poignantly empty, the other with a sleeping Lily, who was thankfully unaware of the drama unfolding around her. Kimberly reached over and pulled the buggy closer to her, placing a hand protectively on the handlebar.

'I can see how hard this is for you.' Inspector Ortega said gently to Kimberly, his eyes still looking at Lily. 'She's a beautiful little girl.' He cleared his throat, then continued. 'You didn't join your husband for a drink? Perhaps leave the children unattended?'

'No!' Kimberly exclaimed, shaking her head in shock at the suggestion. 'I would never leave the children alone. As it happens, we had booked a spot in the children's club . . .' She paused to gather herself, then explained, 'But we didn't need to use that service. I had a headache brewing all day. So I insisted that Jason go for a drink without me. Lily fell asleep a little after eight o'clock, and then I read Robert his bedtime story. *Goodnight Moon*. It's his favourite.' Kimberly's voice cracked, and she felt tears dampen her cheeks.

Jason handed her a tissue and tightened his grip on her spare hand.

'I have a little girl who loves story-time too,' Inspector Ortega replied gently. 'Did you notice anything amiss as you put the children to bed? Anything out of the ordinary?'

Kimberly thought for a moment, then shook her head sadly. 'No. Robert fell asleep in my arms, and I almost dozed off on his little sofa bed with him. But then Lily stirred, and I made my way to our double. Her cot is beside ours, on my side. That way, I can reach her, if she wakes at night.'

Kimberly lightly touched her daughter's cheek. Thank goodness she was too young to understand that her big brother was missing. And then Robert's face entered her mind, and she knew that, wherever he was, he must be crying and calling out for her, his mama. A sharp pain edged its way beneath her rib cage. She couldn't bear it.

'And what time did you go to sleep?' Inspector Ortega asked Kimberly, and she knew that she had to find the strength to bear this.

'It was almost nine. I remember looking at the bedside clock before I closed my eyes.'

'And were you asleep when your husband returned to the cabin?'

Kimberly bit her lip, and tears filled her eyes. She had cried so much since she'd woken this morning that she should have no tears left. 'I didn't hear Jason return. I took a sleeping tablet. I get these headaches. My doctor prescribed them.' Kimberly's hands began to tremble, and she covered her face as she wept. 'You think it's my fault . . . if I'd been awake . . .'

Kimberly couldn't finish the sentence. Jason pulled her into his arms, denying it was true, but her guilt made her push him away.

Then Kimberly looked around the room, listening acutely. It was the strangest thing, but she was sure she could hear Robert crying out for her.

'Can you hear that? It sounds like Robert's cries.' She looked from Jason to Captain Phillipe, then to Inspector Ortega. They quietened and listened, then shook their heads, sympathy etched on each face.

'Nobody is blaming you, Mrs Murphy,' Inspector Ortega said softly. 'We are simply trying to work out the chain of events to narrow down what happened.' He turned to Jason. 'When you returned to the cabin, was Robert in his bed?'

Jason's jaw tightened, then he replied, 'Yes.'

But his voice didn't sound sure. Inspector Ortega's eyes travelled to Jason's hand, which was twitching on his knee.

'I'm sure my husband tucked him in when he returned to the cabin. He sometimes drops his favourite toy – Peter Rabbit – we always put it in his arms, so if he wakes up he's not distressed,' Kimberly said. She looked at her husband, nodding encouragingly for him to confirm this. But his face coloured and he shook his head.

'I went straight to bed. I'd had more to drink than I normally would and felt a bit worse for wear. I didn't go over to either of the children's beds. Not last night.' His eyes pleaded with Kimberly to forgive him.

But she looked away, unable to offer him any solace. Her only thought was for her beloved little boy.

'Robert might have been gone from the cabin before you returned, no?' Inspector Ortega asked, looking from one to the other.

'He can't have been gone since then,' Jason replied, paling at the thought. 'That would be hours ago.' His eyes widened and darted from the sleeping Lily to the bar entrance. 'Why isn't there any news on the search? Somebody must have seen something. Robert can't have disappeared off the face of the earth!'

Captain Philippe stood up, saying, 'I shall gather an update on the search.' Then, with a slight bow, he walked away.

'Would Robert leave the cabin on his own?' Inspector Ortega asked.

Kimberly and Jason looked at each other and shook their heads simultaneously.

'If he woke up, perhaps he decided to explore outside alone, no? Boys are adventurous,' Inspector Ortega insisted, twisting his pencil round his fingers one by one.

'He's only two and a half years old,' Kimberly whispered, wringing her hands in her lap until Jason reached over to still them beneath his own.

'If he woke up, he'd go straight to our bed. He's a mama's boy. Most nights, he ends up in our bed anyhow,' Jason insisted as Kimberly nodded in agreement.

Inspector Ortega raised an eyebrow, scribbling a note in his notebook. 'And how did that make you feel, Mr Murphy? I'm sure it was irritating to have a small child jump into your bed, between you and your wife.'

Jason looked at him quickly, his face flushing at the veiled insinuation. 'On the contrary. I love having cuddles with our children.'

Kimberly reached over and squeezed her husband's hand. 'Jason bought a king-size bed for our bedroom at home, so there is space for everyone when the children climb in with us.'

Inspector Ortega acknowledged this with a slight incline of his head, then looked down to his notebook.

'I've been to see your cabin. And it struck me how heavy the door was. Could a two-year-old open the door to the cabin himself?' He made a face as he shrugged.

'No! Robert can't even reach the handle!' Kimberly said, her voice raising with every word.

'I suppose he could if he used a chair,' Jason mused.

Kimberly looked at him open-mouthed. 'As if Robert would ever do that.'

'You didn't let me finish. I was about to say that it doesn't make sense that he would, though,' Jason said, his voice now thin and brittle.

Inspector Ortega gazed at Jason with a perplexed expression on his face, then jotted a few more notes onto his notepad. In a calm tone, he asked, 'Did you remember to close the cabin door after returning, Jason?'

The question seemed routine, but to Kimberly it felt as if a bolt of lightning had struck her. A fresh wave of terror surged through her veins as she waited for Jason's response.

'Yes. I think so. I'm sure I did,' Jason replied hesitantly, but his lack of confidence was palpable.

Then Captain Phillipe strode into the room and gestured to Inspector Ortega, who joined the captain for a hushed conversation.

Kimberly felt her heart pound against her chest as her stomach twisted into new knots. She strained her neck to get a better view of what was happening, and that's when she saw it.

In Captain Phillipe's hand was a soggy stuffed toy – it was Robert's Peter Rabbit.

NOW

July 2023

Lily

Phibsborough, Dublin

Lily glanced at her father's house, which looked calm from the outside. But she also knew that this didn't necessarily mean that all was peaceful inside. Spotting a space, she brought her car to a halt, switching her indicators on and mentally high-fived herself as she managed to parallel park in one go. As she got out of the car, Michael rang.

'Hi, love. I'm visiting Dad this afternoon, remember? You're picking Ben up from crèche, aren't you?' Lily clicked the lock on her key fob and walked back up the street.

'I remember. I called to wish you luck – that's all. I know Jason can be . . . difficult, especially this time of year, with the anniversary looming,' Michael replied.

It was like her husband to be so thoughtful and, not for the first time, Lily thanked the stars that she'd been lucky enough to marry such a good man. 'Thank you. I won't be long. I'll be home for dinner. Bye.'

It took three hard raps of the brass door knocker before she heard footsteps approaching. Her dad had lived in this two-bedroom, mid-terraced redbrick house since his separation from her mother nearly forty years ago. They were first in line to get a divorce in 1998, once it became legal in Ireland. She remembered him saying that the house would be a doer-upper as it needed a lot of modernising. But, of course, that never happened. It remained trapped in a 1980s time-warp, which was apt, as that's where her father was too.

The door opened, and Lily's father looked around her, his eyes darting up and down the street, checking for goodness knows what. Only when satisfied that all was clear did he turn to his daughter and say warmly, 'Hello, Lily. You look well.'

Lily's heart immediately swelled at the love in her father's voice, then fell again when she took in his appearance. His once-dark hair was now steel grey, thinning at the top, and he needed a shave. Her eyes ran over his joggers and T-shirt combo, which hung too loose on his lean frame. She moved in for a quick hug and breathed in his typical aroma of caffeine and cigarettes.

'Time for a coffee?' her dad asked as he shuffled along the hallway to the kitchen. His back was rounded, stooping too early for his age. He was sixty-eight years old, the same age as her mother. But, unlike her mum, who still looked ten years younger than she was, the lines and wrinkles on his face were a roadmap to the hard life he'd been dealt. Lily felt another rush of emotion for him – this time, sympathy.

'Coffee would be lovely, Dad. Black, but with one sugar. I need the boost,' Lily replied. She looked around the open-plan living space for a spot to sit. Every surface was covered in boxes of paperwork, which was the norm in this house. She peered into the nearest box, which was full of flyers.

'That's a kid from Leeds. Bobby. Only eight years old. Disappeared from outside his home twenty years ago. His family are convinced he's in Ireland. Family abduction. It's thought that his father might have brought him here. I've been distributing the flyers around the city,' Jason said in a rush.

'Hmmm . . .' Lily murmured, pushing the box to one side. She didn't have it in her to hear one more heartbreaking tale of a lost child. While her father had made it his life's work to support

19

StolenChild, an international missing children's network, Lily longed for one day with her dad where he focused on her – the child who had never left.

'I've had a call from Mary Wilson.' When her dad looked blankly at her, Lily added, 'Your neighbour.'

As he stirred sugar into Lily's coffee, he looked over, an eyebrow raised in question.

'Mary said you've been playing music late again.'

'Ah, she's always got to have something to moan about.'

'Perhaps. But, to be fair, she did say that it was four in the morning.'

Her father was an insomniac. He'd call it a win if he got three hours a night, but he had to be reminded often that the rest of the world didn't share his schedule.

'The music helps me think. You know that. I've been working on a new article for *StolenChild* about your brother.'

This was of no surprise to Lily. She ignored that too, and instead reminded her dad she'd bought him AirPods the previous year. 'You need to wear them. That way, I don't get phone calls to my office. Please.'

Her dad handed her a chipped blue-and-white mug filled with steaming coffee. 'Hungry? I've got a packet of Jaffa cakes here somewhere. And I'll try to remember about the music. Promise.'

'Thank you. I'll skip the biscuits – I'll get dinner with Michael and Ben when I get home.'

Lily waited to see if her dad would ask about his grandson, but she should have known better. He was already rifling through a towering pile of paperwork on the kitchen table, his mind back to *StolenChild*.

'Dad, Mum said to remind you that you need to call in to the office to sign paperwork.'

He paused his search, a small smile appearing at the mention of his ex-wife. 'I meant to do that last week, but I got sidetracked. I'll go in tomorrow. Take her for lunch. It's a difficult time for Kimberly, what with the anniversary coming up.'

If Lily lived to be a hundred, she would never understand the dynamics of her parents' relationship. And, with her years of experience as a psychotherapist, she had lost hours trying to work out what made them tick. They could be loving and warm towards each other, and within moments be at each other's throat. But, despite their divorce, they'd managed to run their letting agency together for over forty years. Her father took a back seat, as he became more and more obsessed with finding Robert. And it had thrived under her mother's leadership, who proved herself to be a shrewd businesswoman.

Her dad continued looking through folders on the table, muttering under his breath. Lily reached over and touched his arm.

'Are you okay, Dad? You look a little . . . wired.'

'I've got something to show you,' he replied, grinning triumphantly as he found what he was looking for. 'Take a look at this!'

Lily took the A4 paper sheet he proffered, which had two photographs printed on it, side by side. On the left was her brother Robert, aged two and a half. Blond curls, steel-blue eyes that looked almost grey, rosy cheeks – the quintessential cute baby. She knew every inch of this face off by heart – they all did. It was all they had of him. The photo was taken on the first night of their cruise. In his little hand, clutched lovingly, was his stuffed toy, Peter Rabbit.

On the right-hand side of the A4 paper was a photograph of a stranger. He had mousy brown hair cut short, blue eyes and was clean shaven. Fine lines hovered around his mouth, eyes and forehead.

'It's the latest age-progression photograph,' her dad said triumphantly, his eyes dilated with excitement.

'I know what it is, Dad.' Lily replied softly, then looked away.

Jason frowned. 'You could at least take a proper look at it.'

Lily had seen many versions of Robert over the years. She had watched her brother grow up courtesy of age progressions, created by forensic artists. At first, her family clung to the images, seeing them as beacons of hope. But now Lily found the photographs unbearable to look at.

'It's been five years since the last one. I've made a poster with the heading "Missing for Forty Years, Time for Answers". And earlier today I had a chat with a producer on *IrelandA M*. They want to have me on the show again, on the anniversary next week.'

It took all Lily's strength not to scrunch the A4 sheet into a ball. Bile rose to her mouth at the thought of her father speaking to TV cameras again, rehashing it all.

'To what end, Dad?' Lily said in a clipped voice. 'Robert went missing on a cruise ship in Spain. He's not in Ireland . . . He's probably not even . . .' Lily paused, leaving the thought unfinished.

'To what end?' Her dad began to pace the kitchen. 'I'll tell you to what end. Someone might recognise Robert. Or, better still, Robert could see his photograph and recognise himself. It happens. Did I tell you about that baby who was only two months old when he was abducted, but he was found when he was twenty-two? He saw an age-progression photograph and thought, that's me!'

Lily sighed and tried again with a gentler tone. 'How accurate are the age progressions, though, Dad? The forensic team don't have any photographs of Robert's biological father. So they can only use Mum's image, and that of a two-year-old boy, to guess what he might look like today.' Lily's stomach flipped and turned as she tried to find the courage to ask a difficult question. 'It's been forty years, Dad. Isn't it possible that too much time has passed?'

'I know how long it's been. Don't you think I know that?' Her dad sat back down again, pushing his hands through his thinning hair.

'You can't keep doing this to yourself. I think it's time that you accept—'

Her father slammed his fist on the table, startling Lily. Then, seeing the hurt in her eyes, his face softened. His shoulders slumped as his anger dissipated, and he said with a weary tone, 'You don't understand. You couldn't.'

'Try me,' Lily replied.

'People think I had something to do with Robert's disappearance. Do you have any idea what that does to a man?'

Lily bit back a sigh. 'Yes, Dad, I do. I've been here, with a front-row seat to it all.'

Her dad's eyes became glassy. 'I'm sorry. But I can't stop until we find him.'

They'd had this conversation so many times over the years. And each time she was met with this same resolute determination to continue on the same path. Lily wished that her father could leave a little of himself for the family members that were still here. But she didn't say that to him. Instead she squashed her own feelings down, and tried for the umpteenth time to ease her father's pain.

'There will always be a few who believe the worst in people. But most know the truth. You've spent decades searching for Robert. If that's not love, I don't know what is.'

'I did love him; I truly did. I never saw him as anything but my own.' Jason's eyes pleaded with Lily's to understand.

'I know. Please don't upset yourself. Everything will be okay. I promise.' Lily stood up and embraced her father, her gut wrenching at his obvious pain.

What happened to you, Robert? Where did you go?

If they knew the truth, maybe it would finally set them all free. Because Robert's disappearance had changed them. Her father was locked in a world of constant questioning and doubt, trying to escape the lingering suspicion that he'd played a part in Robert's disappearance. Her mother was trapped in a world of grief and pain, refusing to accept the truth of what had most likely happened to Robert, instead immersing herself in work.

As for Lily?

She had spent most of her life trapped in a cycle of feeling invisible, until Michael and Ben had come along – who both needed her, loved her. *Saw* her.

But even their love couldn't stop Lily feeling confused about her position in the Murphy family. Because in moments like these, Lily felt that she might as well have disappeared alongside her brother forty years ago.

NOW

July 2023

Lily

Phibsborough, Dublin

Lily quickly ran down the hallway in their Edwardian house, picking up strewn toys and a laundry basket that belonged upstairs. She couldn't deny that working from home had its benefits. For one thing, the commute was peachy. But its charms always faded on Monday mornings as she tried to hide family life from the communal area through which her clients passed.

However, as she tidied up, it gave Lily time to further process her father's interview on *IrelandAM* Friday morning. The anniversary of Robert's disappearance was always a problematic milestone for the Murphy family, but seeing their story on a forty-two-inch TV screen while eating breakfast was both surreal and heartbreaking. Lily had asked her mother if she wanted to join them to watch the interview. But she'd declined, saying she had no intention of tuning in and would be in the office by that time.

The presenters, Muireann and Tommy, had treated her dad with gentle respect as they asked him to relive the horror of Robert's disappearance. Her dad had shaved at least, and looked smart, wearing a navy suit and an open-necked white shirt. He spoke eloquently and passionately about the importance of continuing to shine a light on stolen children, no matter how many years had passed. At the end of the interview, a short slideshow of family snaps, interspersed by various age-progression shots of Robert, was shown on screen.

'A copy of Jason's flyer is available to download from our website. Please share it, and who knows, maybe someone will recognise Robert.' Tommy had said to the camera.

And then Muireann finished the interview by sadly adding, 'What would life be like for the Murphy family if Robert had *not* gone missing forty years ago today?'

And that was the million-dollar question that Lily had asked herself for years. Would her parents have stayed together? Or were they doomed to fall apart at some point over the years, their differences waiting to be picked apart by life's stresses? Would Lily and Robert have grown up to be close, each other's ally and best friend? Robert now a doting uncle to little Ben?

Tomorrow was Ben's third birthday, a milestone that they had not got to share with Robert. How would things play out tomorrow, when her parents came to help blow his birthday candles out? Would they be happy to be in their grandson's company or allow the shadow of Robert to dampen their happiness? In fairness, Lily's mother *did* spend a lot of time with Ben. He was the only person that could divert her attention from her phone and work.

The doorbell rang, pushing a blessed pause on the questions that raced through her mind. Lily looked at her watch, seeing that her first appointment was eight minutes early. She threw the laundry basket and toys inside the living room. Then, with a quick smoothing of her hair, she opened the front door.

'Hello. Lily Coogan? I'm Zach Brady. I called on Friday. I'm a little early for our nine-thirty appointment. Should I wait outside?' Zach said in a rush from underneath a large black umbrella, dripping with rainwater.

'Not at all. You are welcome, Zach.' Lily shook his hand after she'd ushered him inside.

As they walked into the consultation room, Lily ran through the notes she'd taken on Friday afternoon when Zach had made the appointment. He'd told her he had recently relocated to Ireland from New York. And that he had sleep issues. His accent wasn't entirely American, though. Or, at least, she felt it had shades of somewhere European mixed in there too.

She glanced at him, quietly assessing him from veiled eyes. Her initial thought was that everything about this man was on trend. He had light-brown hair, cut short on the back and sides but wavy and longer on top. And a tight beard and moustache framed his broad chin and strong jaw. His features were angled. She couldn't determine his eye colour because they were behind matt black round glasses. He had perfectly straight white teeth, the kind that always made her want to keep her own mouth closed, and make an appointment with the dental hygienist. Zach wore faded straight-leg jeans with navy runners and a white T-shirt peeped out from under a light-blue sweater. She'd hazard a guess it was cashmere. Her eyes finally rested on his hands, which were manicured. This man had money, and every inch of him announced that fact.

'This is nice,' Zach said, admiring the room with its high ceilings, white decorative coving and a picture rail that framed green embossed wallpaper, which reflected onto a polished wooden floor. 'What a cool place to work and live.'

Lily glanced at him quickly. How did he know she lived here too? It was a lucky guess, she surmised.

'One of the great things about these old houses is the two reception rooms. It meant we could turn one into my office and still have lots of space for the family.' Lily sighed in satisfaction as her eyes swept around it. 'This is one of my favourite rooms. I love the original windows.'

They both looked over to the large bay window, painted white, which flooded the room with light, even on grey and wet days like today.

'It's got a lot more charm than the apartment on the docks I'm renting, that's for sure. Where should I sit?' Zach asked.

Lily's desk and chair were at one end, and a few feet away were two large armchairs. She pointed towards them, and they both made themselves comfortable. She noted that while his voice was assured, there were tells that he was nervous. His eyes darted around the room. But this was all normal for a new client. It could be intimidating walking into therapy.

'Thank you for seeing me so quickly,' Zach said.

Lily shrugged. 'Well, you were lucky, as it happened. I am fully booked for three months in advance, but a client finished up with me last week so his spot became free.'

'That *was* lucky,' Zach said. Then he added, in a whisper, 'As if it is meant to be . . .' He watched her intently, his gaze steady.

'As this is our first session, I'll take some notes, okay?' Lily said, thinking that this guy was intense.

Zach nodded his consent to the note-taking, and Lily smiled warmly at him as she asked, 'How are you settling into Dublin?'

'I love it here. I like the vibe at the Docklands. I can see why so many visit and never leave.'

'Ireland of the thousand welcomes. We're a friendly bunch, for sure. And your job, is that a new position for you?'

'No. It's the same job, but in a different location. I'm a risk advisor for a multinational company, Ace Funds. They have divisions all over the world. When the offer to work here for twelve months came up, I decided, why not?' He shrugged and smiled warmly at her.

He was charming, and easy company to be around, Lily thought. 'Where were you based before here?'

'London. Before that, New York, the Netherlands, Spain . . . I suppose I'm what you might call a bit of a nomad.'

Lily scribbled notes as Zach spoke. 'That's impressive! Do you speak many languages?' she asked, her curiosity piqued.

'Five.' He shrugged as if it were no big deal.

'Wow. I never managed to conquer Irish at school, never mind French. Languages were not my thing.'

Zach looked at the four framed certificates on the wall behind her desk. 'I think you did okay without them.' He nodded in their direction.

She acknowledged this with another smile.

'Tell me a little about yourself. Where did you grow up?' Lily asked, so she could continue to build a picture of his life before they got to the real issue.

'I grew up in Westport, which is a suburb about forty minutes outside of New York. We lived close to Lake Champlain. I practically grew up on the water. Our family likes to boat.'

'Can you tell me a little about your life there? Describe your family for me if you feel comfortable doing that.'

'Sure. My mom is from London, but she married a New Yorker when I was five. My stepdad is born and bred in Westport. They had three girls, so I have three younger sisters.' His face relaxed, and he smiled as he spoke. 'Jenny, Ally and Issy. We're close.'

'And do they all still live in Westport?'

'Jenny and Ally are married and settled there, with their own families now. Issy is currently in London. She's a chef. Single like me. But I think she might be seeing someone new. She's gone quiet.'

Lily could tell that his family meant a great deal to him.

'And are your mom and stepdad both alive?'

'Yep. Thankfully, both are in great health. Mom retired last year. She sold her hairdressing salon, which was the best place in town for a blowout,' Zach boasted with a smile.

His face changed when he spoke about his mom; there was warmth in every recollection. They were especially close.

'My dad is a third-generation plumber. And he refuses to retire. My mom says he'll die with a wrench in his hand, head under a U-bend.'

Again, the same warmth for his stepdad. Who he called Dad, Lily noted. She leaned forward and asked gently, 'And your biological father, is he in the picture?'

A shadow passed over Zach's face. His shoulders tensed, and it was obvious that this subject was difficult for him.

29

'I've never met him. Or, at least, not that I can remember. My mother left my biological father when I was a baby.'

'Have you ever been curious to meet him?' Lily asked, watching Zach closely as his jaw tightened.

'He put my mother through hell before she found the courage to leave him. So no. I never wanted to meet him.' His voice caught as he continued. 'Dom, my stepdad, is the only father I've known or want to know. He is the best of men, and if I can live a life as good as his I'll be doing well.'

Lily poured a glass of water for each of them, then passed the drink to Zach. This gave him a beat before they moved on, allowing Lily to scribble more detailed notes. She drew a circle round the word 'Father'.

'Do *you* have siblings?' Zach asked, surprising Lily. Occasionally, clients wanted to know more about her life, but in the main she made it a point to keep her private life private.

'We're here to discuss you, Zach,' Lily said gently, then quickly diverted back to him. 'You said when you made the appointment that you wanted to discuss your difficulty sleeping. Please tell me more about this. When did the issue begin?'

'I can't remember a time when I didn't have problems sleeping.' Zach began picking at a thread on his blue shirt. 'I had bad dreams on and off until I was in my twenties.' He paused, swallowed, then said, 'I used to have an imaginary friend when I was a kid.'

Lily noted that he'd found this admission more difficult than the bad dreams. 'Can you remember from what age both things began?'

'I've been seeing therapists since I was four years old, so I guess at least since then.'

'How did you find therapy? Did it help?'

'Yes. Or at least it didn't *not* help. But since I arrived in Dublin I've not been sleeping well again. I don't know.' His eyes darted around the room, glancing at Lily for a second, then moving on again. 'Maybe it's the stress of a new job. The move. But something feels off,' Zach said, blinking rapidly.

Lily noticed a hint of unease in Zach's demeanour, suggesting he might be withholding something. But there was plenty of time to unpack whatever that was, remove his mask. For now she wanted to reassure him.

'We'll figure all this out. Together. What age are you, Zach?'

'Forty-two.'

'Entering our forties can be a significant milestone for some people. Before we dive deeper into what is stressing you out right now, can we talk a little more about your imaginary friend? Which I hope you know is normal and healthy for many children. Especially if they don't have siblings or friends to play with. Would you feel comfortable sharing a little more about this friend with me? Was he – or she – the same age as you?'

Zach locked eyes with Lily as he spoke. 'Oh, my imaginary friend wasn't a child. It was a woman.' Zach paused. 'I called her my other mother.'

BEFORE

September 1963

Sally

Sunshine House Orphanage, Hammersmith, London

Sally felt the car come to a juddering halt. She lay in the back seat of the vehicle, paralysed with fear. Where was she? And why had her mummy told her to get into this car without her? Sally placed her thumb in her mouth and sucked hard, trying to keep tears at bay.

'Time to see your new home,' Mrs Burton said in a high-pitched sing-song voice.

'Is my mummy here?' Sally asked, sitting up to peek out of the window. They were on a gravel driveway in front of an imposing redbrick house. It was bigger than any house she'd ever seen before.

Mrs Burton turned round and faced her. She tilted her head and sighed. 'No, poppet. Your mother isn't here. This is an orphanage, especially for little girls like you who need a new home.'

This confused Sally. 'But I don't need a new home. I have one. I'd like to go back there now.'

'Your mother can't take care of you right now. So she asked me to bring you here. Come on now. Be a good girl.'

Mrs Burton exited the car and opened the back door, holding

her hand out to Sally. Sally inched her way along the car seat, then took the woman's hand. It felt scratchy and clammy, unlike her mummy's hand, which was soft and cool. Sally pulled her hand out of Mrs Burton's grasp and, instead, clung on to the small brown case that her mother had packed for her.

Sally concentrated on the sound of the gravel under her black patent shoes as she walked up the driveway, and tried to block the fear that was racing through her little body. Mrs Burton rapped a large black knocker loudly on a bright yellow door, and the door opened.

'This is Sister Jones,' Mrs Burton said. 'She is one of the staff who will care for you now.'

Sally looked upwards. Sister Jones was tall and much older than her mummy, with wiry grey hair that peeked out from beneath a black veil. She wore a black cardigan, buttoned up, over a crisp white blouse and a long black skirt. Her cheeks were round and red, and she had small dark eyes that peered down at her now, making Sally shiver.

'Hello, Sally. We've been expecting you. Welcome to Sunshine House,' Sister Jones said. 'Come on inside. Let's see if we can find where the girls are.'

'You sound funny,' Sally said. She pronounced 'house' as 'hoose' and 'about' as 'aboot'.

Sister Jones smiled. 'Aye, I bet I do. I'm from Scotland, Sally. You'll get used to me soon enough. You, however, have a lovely little accent.'

She walked down a hallway, her black shoes clip-clopping on the black-and-white tiled floor. Mrs Burton gave Sally a little nudge forward, and they both followed the nun into a large room with the highest ceiling Sally had ever seen. A dozen girls were in there, all wearing dark-green gym slips, a square-necked yellow blouse, and black stockings that reached their knees. Some were playing board games, and others were curled up reading books. The girls all turned and stared in her direction. Their hair was cut identically into a short, blunt bob. Sally reached up to touch her long blonde tresses, which her mummy had always told her was her best feature.

'Elsie Evans,' Sister Jones called out.

A tall, lanky girl who looked a few years older than Sally uncurled herself from a brown couch, where she was reading a Ladybird book to a group of girls who looked no more than two or three years old. She had bobbed brown hair and blue eyes that sparkled.

'Yes, Sister,' she answered in a cockney accent that sounded like Sally's mother.

Sally inched closer to the girl, feeling an instant camaraderie with her.

'You are a good girl. Always taking care of the younger ones. Can you bring Sally up to her dormitory. She's in Four B, same as you,' Sister Jones said. 'Then bring her to the dining hall and get her something to eat. I'll send the housemother to collect her from there.' She sighed as she touched Sally's golden hair. 'Such a shame.'

Sally wasn't sure what was a shame, but was afraid to ask, so she followed Elsie out of the room.

'Goodbye, Sally. I hope you'll be happy here,' Mrs Burton called out.

'Here, let me take that,' Elsie said, reaching down to grab Sally's case as they began to climb up the dark mahogany staircase. A few moments later, Elsie opened a heavy wooden door to reveal a large, gloomy square room with eight single beds, four on either side. The beds had a grey steel frame and were neatly dressed with a white sheet, single white pillow and grey woollen bedspread. A grey steel locker sat beside each bed.

'I wondered who was gonna be my new neighbour. Maria turned eighteen last week and left,' Elsie said, patting the second bed from the door on the right-hand side. 'This is you. And I'm here, right beside you.'

Sally hoisted herself up onto the bed. The blanket scratched her bare legs. Elsie opened the locker. 'You can put all your bits

and bobs in there. Housemother will go through it all and confiscate anything that isn't regulatory. If there's something special
that you don't want to go missing, stick it under your mattress
for safekeeping.'

Sally didn't know what 'confiscate' meant. She shivered, her
eyes wide and fearful as she looked around the room. She spied
a daddy long legs crawling its way up the wall in the far corner
and almost cried out. Elsie helped Sally take her items out of the
case, and put them into the locker. Then she grabbed Sally's
hand and led her back downstairs again.

The dining hall was another high-ceiling room painted in mag-
nolia. It had three long tables adjacent to each other and wooden
benches running on either side. Sally took a seat at the end of one
of the tables, and then Elsie disappeared into the kitchen, returning a few moments later with a steaming bowl of soup.

'You're lucky – it's tomato soup today. Vegetable soup is
horrible.'

'I'm not hungry,' Sally said, looking down into the white
bowl. Her mummy usually gave her sandwiches for lunch, with
the crusts cut off. She felt an ache move from her heart all the
way into her tummy.

'It gets easier. Promise,' Elsie said, watching her closely. 'I've
been here nearly three years now. I remember how scared I was
that first day.' Her eyes narrowed. 'What age are you? Four?'

'I'm five,' Sally said, reeling at the thought that Elsie had been
in this awful place for three years.

'You're small for five. I'm eight,' Elsie said, standing tall.

'Where is your mother?' Sally asked as she stirred the soup.

A shadow passed over Elsie's face, and her eyes glistened, but
she replied stoically, 'Dead.'

Sally looked at Elsie in horror. Was her mummy dead too? Is
that what happened when you arrived here? She closed her eyes
and thought about her mother that morning as she'd brushed
her shiny red hair and got dressed. No. Her mummy was alive
and well. And she would come and get her from here soon.

Sally reached over and squeezed Elsie's hand because she felt sad for the older girl, whose mother was dead and could never come get her from this gloomy place.

'Try to eat a little. By the looks of it in there, dinner is boiled bacon and cabbage today.' Elsie made a face and pretended to gag.

Sally managed to get half of the soup into her before the door opened with a crash and a thin woman marched in. She was dressed in a white starched uniform, with a grey apron over the front. Her hair was pulled back in a tight bun.

'You must be Sally,' the woman said. 'I'm your housemother. You may call me Mother.'

Sally's eyes widened. She couldn't call her that. 'I can't do that. I have a mummy at my home.'

Housemother laughed out loud as if she'd told the funniest joke. 'If you are at Sunshine House, you don't have a mother any more. Come on, let's be having you. I dread to think what's lurking in your long hair.' Her hand grasped Sally's arm, bony fingers pinching her skin, making her grimace.

Housemother half dragged Sally back upstairs into a bathroom where a claw-footed bath was filled with water.

'Take those clothes off and get in,' Housemother said.

'My mother gave me a bath this morning,' Sally protested.

Housemother threw her eyes upwards and began peeling Sally's clothes off. She picked Sally up and threw her into the bath. Then she began ladling water from a plastic bowl over her head. Housemother washed her hair with a foul-smelling disinfectant shampoo, pulling her hair this way and that as she searched for nits. She seemed almost disappointed to find Sally's hair didn't have any. After her bath, Housemother scrubbed her dry with a threadbare towel that scratched her skin. Then she dressed Sally in the same uniform Elsie wore. As hot tears trailed Sally's face, Housemother cut her long blonde hair into a short bob. Her mummy would be so cross.

'That's better,' Housemother declared once she'd finished.

'Dinner is at five o'clock sharp. You are excused from chores this afternoon as it's your first day. Off you go.'

Sally walked into the dark hallway and looked up and down, trying to figure out what to do next. She couldn't face the other girls; she wanted her mummy. But she wouldn't be coming to rescue her – not today, at least. Sally returned to the dorm and climbed onto her bed, slipping under the scratchy blanket and sheet. Curling herself into a ball, she sobbed into the pillow.

Sally felt a hand on her shoulder and looked up to see Elsie standing by her bed. Elsie climbed in beside Sally and pulled her into her arms.

'Shush there, treacle. It's going to be okay. I'll take care of you. I promise.'

But this kindness only made Sally's sobs grow.

'When I was sad, my mum used to sing to me. And then I'd feel better. Would you like me to sing to you?' Elsie asked.

Sally nodded mutely in between her sobs.

Elsie began to sing the prettiest song Sally had ever heard about sunshine making you happy when skies were grey. And with Elsie's arms wrapped round her, Sally stopped crying and fell into a fitful sleep.

BEFORE

November 1970

Sally

Sunshine House Orphanage, Hammersmith, London

Elsie placed a finger on her lips, indicating to Sally that she should remain quiet. Moving towards them across the wooden floor, heavy footsteps echoed around the damp, dark hallway. They were hiding behind a large armoire that stood under the oak staircase. Sally held her breath as Elsie reached over to clasp her hand in her own. It felt clammy to touch, and Sally cursed herself for letting the time get away from her. They knew that either Sister Jones or Housemother always did their rounds at eleven o'clock.

Sally's heart raced so fast inside her chest that it felt like a wild animal trying to break free. She could still hear the *clip-clop* of feet approaching. It was Housemother, she decided. She recognised the heavy footfall of her steel-tip brogue boots. Sally's mind raced with anticipation and dread. Would House-mother look under the stairs or go straight to the dormitory? She heard the footsteps pause and saw the flash of a lantern moving up and down the hallway.

She and Elsie had got into countless scrapes together over the past seven years, and this year alone they had been caned half a dozen times by Housemother. The memory of the last punishment still stung on the back of her legs, a constant reminder of the risks they took.

Elsie looked stricken, but Sally scowled back at her, unwilling to let her off the hook. Her face was ashen, but her lips were pink and bruised from all the kissing with her boyfriend. Elsie now had curves that rivalled Marilyn Monroe, and she loved the attention this got her, whereas Sally still looked young for her twelve years, and was invisible to boys, but that was okay. She was in no rush.

Sally saw Housemother's sensible black boots move to the first step of the staircase. And she knew that they were done for.

Then Sister Jones's voice called out from the staff den. 'Are you playing this round of sevens or not? I'm dealing the cards now.' The nun moved into the hallway, joining Housemother on the stairs, looking in their direction and spotting the girls hiding. She shook her head, her forehead creased in a frown.

Mercifully, Sister Jones called out to the Housemother, 'There's not a sound coming from any of the dorms. They must all be out like a light. Come on back to the cards.' Then she led Housemother back towards the staff den.

Only when they heard the door close, did Sally and Elsie exhale.

'I thought we were goners . . .' Elsie whispered, her blue eyes still wide with fright.

Sally faced the girl who had become her surrogate older sister in everything but blood. She knew she had only herself to blame, agreeing to go along with Elsie's latest escapade. After years of moments like these, Sally should know better. But the problem was that Sally could never say no to Elsie. Because life was always more exciting with Elsie around.

'Good old Sister Jones. "I'm dealing the cards now!"' Elsie said, mimicking the nun's Scottish accent perfectly.

Tomorrow Sally would find Sister Jones and thank her for saving them. Over the years, for every dark moment in the orphanage, Sister Jones had found a way to counteract it with an act of kindness. Along with Elsie, the nun had become like family to Sally.

'I am sorry,' Elsie whispered. 'I should have gone out to meet Reggie on my own.'

Reggie was also a resident of their orphanage, but lived in the boy's block across the courtyard. The staff did an admirable job keeping the boys and girls separate, but they were no match for hormonal teenagers in the first flush of love. Plus, when Elsie decided to do something, there was little that anyone could do to deter her. No matter the consequence.

They'd sneaked out earlier tonight once it was lights out in their dormitories. Sally's job was to keep watch while Elsie and Reggie stole thirty minutes together.

'We need to get back to bed,' Elsie whispered, and they moved silently to the staircase and began creeping to their dormitory, one step at a time. Elsie warned Sally to avoid the loose step halfway up, which always told tales. It was only when they were in the safety of their dormitory that Sally relaxed. Soft snores filled the room from the six other girls who they shared with. They quickly undressed, climbing into their regulation fleeced nightdresses.

'That was too close,' Sally said, still holding on to her annoyance. She shivered as her body hit the cold sheets. The weather had turned icy this week, and the temperatures had dropped to almost freezing. Elsie climbed in beside Sally as she'd done most nights since arriving at the orphanage.

Elsie smiled weakly at her friend, and pulled the blankets tightly over them.

'I'm sick of always being the sensible one, looking out for you when you mess up. It's not fair, Elsie. You are alone if you decide to have more moonlit rendezvous. I mean it. You can count me out,' Sally whispered crossly. Then she continued, softer now, 'You do know that you are not the first to fall for Reggie's charms. He broke Rebecca's heart last month. You heard her crying into her pillow every night. Honestly, it would be best to stay away from him.'

Elsie's face slid into a smile, and she sighed dreamily. 'If you had been kissed like I was tonight, you wouldn't have asked me to make that promise.' Then she winked and added, 'Plus, who can blame Reggie for dumping Rebecca. She gave him a headache with all her moaning. It's too cold. I don't like the rain. It's too dark.' Elsie mimicked Rebecca's nasal twang to perfection. She had an ear for accents and could copy most.

Sally's lips curled into a smile as she tried to suppress a giggle. She couldn't help it – she had no choice but to forgive Elsie immediately.

'I knew you'd understand, Sally. I swear, I'll lose my mind if I have to do one more day in this existence without the prospect of a fun diversion,' Elsie declared.

Life in the orphanage was bleak, from when the bell rang out to wake the residents to when the bell rang for the last time, signalling lights out.

Then Elsie propped her head up on her arm and whispered, 'And don't worry about me. I know that Reggie and I ain't no Romeo and Juliet. I have no intention of falling for him. He's fun – that's all. A stopgap until I meet the *right* man when I leave this dump.'

'Do you think I'll meet someone one day too?' Sally asked, her eyes glistening dreamily as she bought into the fantasy of life outside the orphanage. Unlike Elsie, Sally had only read about romance in books and magazines.

Elsie cupped Sally's chin in her hand. 'You are so pretty, Sally Fox. The boys will be falling at your feet. We'll marry two brothers, or best friends at least, and we can live in houses next door to each other.'

'The brothers will be tall, dark and handsome,' Sally added.

'Wouldn't want them any other way,' Elsie agreed.

'Will we have children?' Sally asked.

'You'll have at least four children. You're born to be a mother.'

'What about you, Elsie?' Sally asked, watching her friend closely.

Elsie's eyes glistened. 'I'll have a baby boy. With sparkling blue eyes, and a mop of curly blond hair. He'll be my everything.' She ended on a whisper. Then, sitting up straight, she added in a stronger voice, 'And you'll have your own hairdressing salon, Sally. I'll work in one of those skyscrapers. The ones with plush offices in London.'

Sally smiled as she listened to their favourite daydream. And while Sally didn't know what her future would turn out like, she knew one thing for sure. She would never follow in her mother's footsteps. Falling for every wrong un who looked in her direction before becoming pregnant with a child she could never care for. Dumping them in an orphanage without a backwards glance.

Her anger at her mother caught her off-guard some days. And occasionally her grief and loss pierced her heart into so many tiny pieces that she didn't think it could ever be remade.

'We'll give our children the life we never had,' Sally said firmly. 'And they'll grow up to be as close as you and I are.'

Elsie clasped her hand and nodded fervently. 'That's right, treacle.' Then she shivered in the icy room. 'I don't want to get into my own bed.'

'Housemother doesn't like us to share a bed,' Sally said, worried, her brow furrowed as she glanced at the closed door, half expecting it to open. 'We were lucky to get away with tonight.'

'You're right,' Elsie said. 'I'll get out in a minute. Tell you what, how about I sing our song before I go?'

It had been years since Elsie had sung to her, and Sally knew her friend was trying to make amends for their near miss tonight, but Sally didn't mind. She loved hearing Elsie's pretty voice in her ear, singing 'you are my sunshine' until Sally fell asleep, dreaming of a life outside the orphanage with love, marriage and a family.

THEN

July 1983

Kimberly

The Carousel, *Port of Barcelona, Spain*

Every bone in Kimberly's body ached. She felt weighed down by her desperate worry and dread of how Robert was. Jason suggested that she go back to their cabin to lie down. And for a brief moment she was tempted to do that and take another of her sleeping pills. Anything to find temporary relief from this living nightmare. But there could be no respite. Kimberly had to find her inner strength for her children's sake.

'Please let one of my staff take that and dry it for you,' Captain Phillipe said, his eyes drifting to the wet stain on Kimberly's T-shirt, left by the sodden soft toy she'd been clinging to.

Peter Rabbit had been lying near a lifeboat on deck ten, in a puddle of seawater.

'I appreciate your offer, Captain, but this toy . . . it's all I have of Robert.' Kimberly's voice trembled with emotion as she clutched the damp toy. 'He slept with Peter Rabbit since I bought it for him, when he was six months old.' She leaned down and breathed in Robert's scent that lingered in the fabric. Kimberly decided that she would only let it go if she got to return it to him. She closed her eyes and prayed once again for a miracle.

43

Bring him back to me. Realise that he should be with me, his mama.

Her daughter's laughter rippled through the room as she played peek-a-boo a few feet away. It had been suggested earlier that Lily be sent to the onboard crèche while they navigated the search for Robert, but Kimberly had scooped up her daughter and said firmly, 'She stays with me.'

So, Pamela, a young nanny from Wales, who worked in the children's club, was sequestered to join them and help care for Lily while they all waited for updates from the search parties.

'There must be news by now,' Kimberly said, looking at her watch. It was almost midday.

'I know it must be torture to wait. From the moment you raised the alarm this morning, the ship was placed on lockdown. I can assure you that between the ship's staff and the Policia, if Robert is onboard the *Carousel*, we shall find him,' Captain Phillipe responded gently. 'Are you sure I cannot get you something to drink or eat? You look so pale.'

Kimberly shook her head. Her stomach had been so clenched in terror that she could scarcely sip water, never mind eat. She wished Jason would come back too. He'd insisted on joining the search, convinced he'd find Robert curled up in a hidden corner, asleep or maybe too scared to call out for help.

The door opened, and Kimberly looked up, hoping it was her husband. But it was the inspector again.

'I'm afraid we've not found Robert,' he said quickly before she had a chance to ask. 'I'd like to speak with you privately, if possible.' He turned to Pamela and said, 'Please take Lily to her father; he's waiting outside.'

'Lily stays with me,' Kimberly insisted again. The mere thought of not being able to see her daughter made her half mad with terror.

'As you wish,' Inspector Ortega said, and asked Captain Phillipe and Pamela to leave the room. Inspector Ortega opened his cigarette box, tapped one out, then put it back when Kimberly gave him a look of reproach.

'Force of habit. I apologise.'

'It's fine. I'm on edge. I feel so useless. I should be doing something,' Kimberly said, wringing her hands in her lap.

'I know this is an impossible situation for you. But trust me, Mrs Murphy, the most critical thing you can do for your son is answer my questions. This may give me crucial information which will help me find him.'

Kimberly watched Lily on the play mat beside her, where the little girl was playing with soft toys, and breathed in deeply. She sat up straight in her chair and told the inspector she was ready.

'Your husband is Irish, but your accent is different, no?' Ortega asked.

'I'm from Scotland. I met Jason while visiting Ireland.'

'How long have you and Jason been married?'

'One year.'

If this surprised the inspector, he didn't show it. 'Your children were born before you got married?'

'Robert was,' Kimberly said, feeling her scalp prickle. 'He was six months old when I met Jason. I was pregnant with Lily before we got married.'

This did get a reaction. Inspector Ortega leaned in closer and asked, 'Jason is Robert's stepfather?'

'Yes.' Kimberly bristled at the question.

'And how was their relationship?' Inspector Ortega asked. His eyes narrowed, and his pencil tapped his notebook as he watched her.

Kimberly's mouth went dry. She sipped her water and replied, 'They are as close as any father and son could be.'

The inspector shrugged. 'We have spent the morning calling cabin to cabin, interviewing your fellow passengers and the crew. And one couple mentioned that there was an incident at the pool yesterday. They witnessed a situation where Jason shouted at Robert.'

Kimberly looked at him sharply. 'That was nothing. He splashed his sister, and Jason reprimanded him for it.'

Inspector Ortega looked down at his notebook, flipped back two pages, and then said, 'The couple said you seemed upset with your husband.'

Kimberly took a steadying breath, trying to avoid the obvious direction of this conversation. 'I had a headache. If I was snappy with Jason, it was because of that.'

'I understand,' Inspector Ortega said, writing some more notes.

'Why can't Jason be in here with me?' Kimberly asked, her eyes darting to the door. She missed her husband's solid and calming presence.

'Because I need to talk to you on your own. I plan to question Jason next.'

Another ripple of unease ran through Kimberly.

'Where is Robert's father?' the inspector asked.

Kimberly felt her hackles rise. She did not like the inspector's tone and direction of questioning. 'Standing outside this room, no doubt waiting impatiently to return to our side.'

The inspector almost smiled. 'I meant, where is the child's biological father, as I suspect you know.'

'Why do you want to know that?' Kimberly asked, every fibre in her body recoiling at the question.

Inspector Ortega leaned in. 'I'm trying to determine if Robert has been abducted. Often, a family member is involved in situations like this. An ex-husband, crazy boyfriend, occasionally a grandparent.'

Kimberly's heart began to race so fast that she was sure the inspector could hear it. She looked him squarely in the eye and responded, 'The father is not in the picture. He couldn't have taken Robert.'

'Why is that?'

'Because he doesn't know that Robert even exists. And, before you ask, I can't give you a name. It was a one-night stand,' Kimberly said, feeling colour flood her face.

More notes were scribbled. 'And are there any other family members who might have taken Robert?'

'I'm an only child, and both my parents are dead. Other than Jason and my children, I am alone.' Her voice choked, and tears began to roll down her cheeks. She tried to control her emotions, but it was too much to bear. 'I'm sorry. I can't seem to stop them.'

Inspector Ortega handed her a pressed white handkerchief from his jacket pocket. 'It's okay. A mother's love knows no bounds. Let's leave it for now. Either way, I have some questions for your husband.'

Kimberly stood up. 'I think I'll return to our cabin with Lily to freshen up while you speak to Jason.' Since their nightmare began this morning, she'd not even brushed her teeth or combed her hair. Lily was still in her sleepsuit, and the early afternoon sun was getting even hotter. She should change her into something lighter, at least.

But Inspector Ortega interrupted her. 'I'm afraid you can't return to your cabin. But Captain Phillipe has assigned you a new cabin in the interim, and transferred your clothes there.'

'Why on earth not?' Kimberly asked.

'Your cabin is now a crime scene.' Ortega's eyes bore into Kimberly as he spoke, his tone stern and unwavering. 'I believe it was impossible for Robert to leave the cabin alone. Which means that someone took him. And, until our investigation is complete, the cabin must be protected and preserved for evidence.' His eyes now moved to Robert's Peter Rabbit. 'I will have to take the soft toy too for biological analysis. We'll check for hair samples, and I promise to return the toy as soon as possible.'

Crime.

Evidence.

Investigation.

Kimberly's mind was in turmoil as the words taunted her, intensifying her feelings of helplessness and vulnerability.

How had it come to this?

BEFORE

March 1973

Sally

Sunshine House Orphanage, Hammersmith, London

Sally placed the card into the white envelope and licked the gum
to seal it. Tomorrow was Elsie's eighteenth birthday. And the day
that Elsie would leave Sunshine House forever. Sister Jones would
provide a cake after their tea, as she did for every girl in her care.
Everyone would sing 'Happy Birthday' while Elsie blew out her
candles and made a wish. And then Mrs Burton would come one
final time for Elsie.

Sally sighed as she thought about the many birthday wishes
she'd made over the years in Sunshine House. At first, she truly
believed in the magic of birthday candles. Each year, Sally made
the same wish – *Come get me, Mum. Take me home again.* But
she'd long since realised that wishes were not for girls like her.

Sally closed her eyes and tried to bring her mum's face back
into focus. It had been almost ten years since she'd last seen
her. Her mother's face, voice, smell and touch had faded like
an out-of-focus Polaroid snap. Occasionally, she'd hear the
Beatles on the radio, and the lyrics would bring her mum back
to her. 'I Want to Hold Your Hand' had always been one of her
mother's favourite songs. Her mum would reach over as she
sang along off-key to the tune. Then she'd beckon Sally to her

48

and together they'd hold hands, sing about love and dance around their tiny flat.

There were other memories, too, that she thought were long buried but which could surprise her occasionally. Only a few weeks back, Sister Jones had arrived at the common room with a punnet of peaches. Round and plump, their soft flesh was juicy and fragrant. She'd cut them into quarters so each girl could have a share and an image had hit Sally so sharply that it winded her.

Her mother's perfume – Avon's Pretty Peach, Eau de Cologne – had an ornate peach cap on the bottle. Sally was obsessed with it, begging her mum to let her try it. But her mother wasn't one for sharing. She'd shake her head and say it was for big girls only. But one day she'd made an exception and squirted it onto Sally and herself. It was the same day that she'd sent Sally away. While many of Sally's early memories were clouded by the fog of time, that day was crystal clear.

She'd turned to Elsie, her confidante and shared the memory. 'Peaches always make me think of Mum.'

Elsie had replied sadly, 'You're lucky – it's rotten eggs for me.'

And Sally had giggled, thinking this was funny, and though Elsie smiled along, she had tears in her eyes, so Sally gave her an extra-big hug.

Now, Sally started when Elsie appeared in the doorway. 'What are you up to, hiding away in here?' Elsie asked, as she walked inside. She'd had another growth spurt, and her knee-length black stockings only reached halfway up her leg.

Sally stuffed the card and small gift behind her back. But Elsie didn't miss a thing and smiled knowingly.

She sat crosslegged on the bed beside Sally. 'You looked sad when I walked in.'

Sally's eyes met hers, and the words came tumbling out. 'I was thinking about Mum,' she admitted, her voice barely above a whisper.

Elsie shook her head, a deep frown creasing her forehead. 'Not that again, Sally. Nothing good comes from dwelling on the past. Your mum is gone. Same as mine. You've got to forget she ever existed.' Elsie's lips pursed, and her eyes took on a distant look, as they always did when the subject of mothers came up.

'Do you think my mum is dead too?' Sally asked softly. And her face flushed because she'd worried about this for some time. When her mind brought her to dark places late at night, Sally wondered if this was why her mum had never come back for her. She felt wicked for thinking this, but it was easier to bear the thought of a dead mother than one who did not love her.

Elsie sighed deeply, then shrugged. 'I don't know that, treacle. But I know that if she is alive you're better off without her.'

'Because she doesn't want me,' Sally replied, her voice barely above a whisper.

'Yeah,' Elsie agreed, her eyes softening with sympathy.

Sally hesitated momentarily, then decided to be brave and ask Elsie a question once more that she'd dodged for years. 'How did your mum die?'

'What does it matter how? She's dead; that's all you need to know.'

The air was thick with unspoken weight, and the room was filled with uncertainty and discomfort. A couple of moments passed, stretching endlessly as both girls tried to find the right words.

Then Elsie saved the day by pointing behind Sally's back. 'What you got there, then?'

And because Sally didn't want to think about mothers and the heartbreaking choices they'd made, she happily pulled the gift and card out of its hiding space behind her back.

'Oh, all right then. I was going to give it to you tomorrow. But I know what you're like! I'll turn my back for five minutes, and you'll be searching our bedroom for it.'

Elsie's laugh tinkled through the room, magically dispersing all sad thoughts. She picked up the card and ran her finger along the seal, opening it carefully without damaging the envelope.

Sally watched her fondly. When it was her birthday, she'd always rip the paper off the gift first and foremost. Not Elsie. She pulled out the card, taking in every detail. So Sally had taken her time choosing it, knowing it was important to her friend. The card had a sketch of two girls, one blonde and one brunette, wearing pretty tea dresses as they drank from blue-and-white china cups.

'I thought they looked like us two,' Sally said shyly.

'May the blessings of love, joy and peace be yours throughout the year,' Elsie read out loud. Then, with a smile that lit up her face, she said, 'With all my love, your best friend forever, Sally. Oh, I love this card. I'll keep it always.'

Then Elsie unwrapped the brown paper, revealing a small black jewellery box. Sally held her breath as Elsie opened the lid, only exhaling when she saw the genuine surprise and delight flood her best friend's face.

'It's the prettiest thing I've ever owned,' Elsie said breathlessly, taking it out of its box to look closer at the silver ring, with a large oval black stone set into an ornate silver clasp.

'It's a mood ring. The stone will change colour in response to how you feel. And there's a card that tells you what each colour means. Put it on!'

Elsie obliged, slipping the ring onto the middle finger of her right hand. They leaned in and watched the ring as the colour slowly morphed from inky black to light blue.

Sally pulled the small card out from the ring box and said with delight, 'That means you are calm, comfortable and relaxed!'

'Well, it's perceptive because that's how I feel. You know, I've always wanted one of these, but how could you afford one?' Elsie's pretty face crumpled into a frown.

'I got it in the British Red Cross charity shop on Old Bond Street.' Sally hadn't wanted to admit this fact. She continued in a rush, 'But the shopkeeper said that the ring is new. It was an unwanted gift, donated.'

Elsie's eyes glistened with unshed tears. 'It's my favourite gift that I've ever received. I love it. I really do.' Then Elsie pulled Sally into her embrace, hugging her tightly, letting her go with a squeal. 'It's changed colours again! Now it's violet! What does that mean?'

Sally quickly checked the card and said, 'It means you are happy.'

She reached under the bed and pulled out another bag. 'I got something else when I was in the second-hand shop.' Sally opened the bag and pulled out a plastic doll's head, with long blonde hair. 'It's the Super Girl's World styling head. You can change the length of the hair, and the colour too.'

She stopped speaking, feeling self-conscious. She glanced up at Elsie, half expecting her to laugh.

But Elsie understood immediately. 'You can practise hairstyles on this. Genius. And it will give you something to do when I'm gone. You'll be bereft without me,' she finished with a wink.

Sally felt a rush of happiness for her best friend, the only person who understood Sally's dreams, followed quickly by despair that Elsie would soon be gone – because she *would* be bereft.

Elsie's eyes narrowed as she saw her friend's bottom lip quiver. She quickly joked, 'You can't let Housemother see it, though. She'll have her shears out and will give it a bloody bob like the rest of us!'

The following afternoon, the time came for Elsie to leave. Sally found her friend in their bedroom, packing her suitcase.

'I hope you've packed your plaid pyjamas with their matching quilted dressing gown,' Sally joked as she leaned against the door frame with a cheeky grin.

'Naturally. I wouldn't leave home without them. Because, after all, these beauties are . . .' Elsie replied, pausing so that she and Sally could scream in unison, 'flame retardant!'

Elsie and Sally clutched each other as they squealed with laughter at their inside joke at Housemother's expense, who had been most excited when she'd handed out the new night attire to everyone the previous Christmas, repeatedly saying that she'd bought them especially because they were flame retardant.

'I mean . . . at least you won't spontaneously burst into flames . . .' Sally said, which caused another round of almost hysterical laughter.

'Nor will I ever attract a husband, the state of me in them!' Elsie replied, holding up the pyjamas with disdain. 'When I earn my first pay cheque, I will buy a slinky, silky nightgown in bright fuchsia or scarlet red. And I'll get you one too, so it's waiting for you as soon as you leave here.'

'I don't want you to go,' Sally admitted in a small voice. All traces of her merriment were gone now, and a deep furrow creased her forehead. The prospect of three long years without her best friend was daunting. 'I can't see why they won't let you stay here a bit longer. It's cruel sending you off on your own.'

Elsie sighed. 'You know that's not how the system works. You turn eighteen, and it's bye-bye, care home – hello, big bad world. But I do wish you could come with me.' A bittersweet smile played on her lips as she looked at her friend. 'I can't get my head around the fact that I won't wake up to see your mug opposite me every morning.' Then her face softened, and tears glistened in her eyes. 'We've done everything together, haven't we, since that day you arrived here.'

Sally knew that she had to be brave, because, despite Elsie's bravado, she could see how scared she was. So she tried to offer some solace. 'We have, but we will again when I leave here too. The time will go by so fast. You'll see. And you have to write to me every day,' Sally said, her pink lips now pouting prettily.

'I'm not much of a writer – you know that – but I'll try to send a letter every week if I can.'

And Sally knew that next year, on her birthday, she'd make a new wish, that Elsie and she would remain best friends forever, just as the card had said they would.

NOW

July 2023

Lily

Phibsborough, Dublin

The room sang 'Happy Birthday' to Ben, who sat in his high chair, clapping his hands with delight. Lily's throat constricted, and her body swelled with love for her little boy.

'Blow the candles out,' Lily said, holding the caterpillar cake closer to him.

'Be careful, Lily. He'll burn himself,' Lily's mother commanded, her hands reaching out to protect him.

Lily rechecked her son's position. Ben was perfectly safe. She took a deep breath and answered her mother as calmly as possible: 'I'm out of his reach, Mum.'

And, even though Lily knew that her mother's micro-managing came from a place of love, it still hurt. From the moment Ben had arrived in all their lives, her mum had become overly zealous in keeping him safe from perceived dangers. Her mother's constant reminders to keep him safe more often felt intrusive rather than helpful.

In an over-the-top bright voice, Michael said, 'Three cheers for the big boy. Hip, hip, hooray . . .'

They all joined in, but there was tension in the room now. Lily smiled weakly, feeling her husband's worried gaze on her.

'I'll go make the tea and cut this up,' Lily said, walking out to the kitchen, muttering under her breath. Her mother was either absent, or excessively supervising Lily, as if she was a member of her staff. She didn't know which aggravated her more.

Michael followed her into the kitchen and put the kettle on while Lily sliced the cake into eight pieces and placed them on a prepared tray. As the kettle whistled its way to boiling point, Lily took several calming breaths. She always promised herself she wouldn't let her mother trigger her, but her mum had a knack of undoing all her resolve with one cutting comment. And Lily didn't blame her. She understood that it wasn't only love that made her interfere. It was fear too. Because Lily knew that when her mother looked at her little grandson, she saw her beloved Robert too.

Michael moved closer to her and said, 'I can't believe he's three years old. Our little lockdown baby. It feels like a nano-second ago that I drove you home from the hospital.'

'That ten-minute journey took nearly an hour; you drove so slowly!' Lily teased.

'Precious cargo. I have no regrets. I wasn't taking any risks getting you home in one piece,' Michael replied with ease.

Lily blew a kiss to her husband, whispering a thank-you. He always found a way to calm her down and make her feel better. She glanced back towards the living room. 'Do I have to go back in there?'

'Nah. I'll grab Ben, and we can make a run for it,' Michael joked. 'I reckon we can make it to the M50 before they notice we're gone. Try not to worry. It's going great. They'll behave.'

Lily wasn't so sure. Her parents had form. At Ben's christening, her father had to leave early because they'd got into round nine-hundred-and-ninety-nine of why their marriage had ended. It never came to any fruitful conclusion, because neither wanted to discuss the elephant in the room – the little boy who they couldn't forget.

Michael placed the teapot on the tray and then moved closer to Lily. 'How are you doing? Truthfully.'

Lily shrugged. 'I grew up hating birthdays. All family occasions.' Feeling her husband's eyes on hers, she continued, 'The focus was never on the special occasion. It was on Robert. Mum and Dad would buy another gift and place it in a box for him. Frozen in time for when he came home. But he never came, did he?'

Michael shook his head sympathetically, as Lily bit the inside of her cheek to counteract the rush of emotion she felt.

'Let's say that birthdays have always been difficult for our family.' Lily paused, then looked at her husband, her face softening with gratitude. 'Until I met you, that is. You persuaded me that all milestone moments deserve cake.'

'Always cake,' Michael agreed solemnly.

'And now that Ben is here it's even easier.'

'How so?'

Lily thought back to this morning when the alarm went off and smiled. 'I woke up today thinking about Ben. Only him.'

'He's hard to ignore. I never imagined I could love anyone that small this much,' Michael replied, using his arms to draw a large round circle.

'I wish it could be the same for Mum and Dad as it is with us two.' Lily bit back a sigh. 'I was never enough for them.'

'You can't change your childhood, but they are good with Ben, aren't they? Your mother dotes on him,' Michael pointed out.

And Lily knew this was true. It was joyful watching Ben with his grandmother. Lily walked over to the sink and washed the cake frosting from her hands.

'But it always comes back to Robert. You'll see. Before the day is over, he'll be centre stage again. For someone I can't remember, he sure makes his presence felt,' Lily said, then she put her face in her hands. 'God, that makes me sound like such a bitch.'

'It makes you sound human,' Michael replied. 'You love your brother and miss him. But you've lived in the shadow of his disappearance your entire life. That's a lonely spot at times.'

Lily looked at her husband with gratitude that he understood her position. And Michael was right. She should give herself a pass. She *did* love Robert. It was the mystery of where he was that she hated. She glanced back in the direction of the living room and frowned.

'Dad is crushed that there have been no leads since his TV interview. He was sure someone would come forward.'

'In fairness, I can understand why he clings to that. Someone must know what happened to Robert.'

A shiver of unease ran down Lily's spine. She hated it when family or friends began speculating about what had happened that night, because among that speculation were fingers of doubt, often pointed in her father's direction.

'Stop worrying,' Michael said, sensing his wife's unease. 'Today is Ben's day, and we'll ignore everything else.'

But, now that the subject had been broached, Lily couldn't shut it down. She touched her husband's arm and whispered, 'I could see it happening when I was a kid.'

'See what?' Michael asked.

'Their gradual breakup. It was . . .' Lily wrinkled her nose as she grappled for the right words to explain, 'as if they were making nicks in their love. They couldn't stop themselves. Each time they fought, another dent was cut. Mum became obsessed with the family business, and Dad with finding Robert. It was inevitable that their love would snap irreparably one day.' Lily shivered, and her eyes glistened as she looked at Michael. 'It's so sad. And unnecessary. Because I think, underneath it all, they still love each other.'

Michael cupped her chin with his hand, kissing her lightly, then promised, 'No nicks, dents or cuts allowed for us.'

'That I can happily agree to,' Lily replied.

'I vote we forget all the sad stuff and try to relax and enjoy Ben's day.'

'That gets my vote too.'

Returning to the sitting room, Lily found her mother singing

'Old McDonald Had a Farm' with Ben in her arms. Ben loved making the *moo moo* and *oink oink* noises. Her dad was joining in too, a big goofy grin on his face.

Michael looked at her with a smug I-told-you-it-would-be-okay look on his face. And she felt the tension begin to disappear as she took in the happiness on her parents' faces.

No shadows. No pain. No aches from a fateful night decades before.

And it caught Lily, making her throat constrict again, bringing tears to her eyes. She looked at her father and saw that he was watching her mother too, a look of such tenderness on his face as she sang to their grandson.

Why couldn't love have been enough for them?

Then, mercifully saving Lily from her maudlin thoughts, Ben reached his two arms towards her, calling out, 'Mama, Mama.' Lily took him from his grandmother's arms and pulled her son close. She breathed in his sugary scent and laughed loudly when his hands grabbed her cheeks.

'My special boy,' she whispered, kissing his forehead, cheeks and lips.

Was it any wonder her own mother had become an overly protective, at times a control freak, when she'd lost Robert? For years, Lily had been so angry with her mum. But she was finally beginning to understand.

When Robert had become a ghost in their family, her mother had become one too, faded to half herself, with one part in the past and the other in the now.

Lily looked over her son's shoulder at her mother and father. She turned to them both, her voice trembling with emotion, 'I love you, Mum. And you too, Dad.'

And they both responded with their own declarations of love. At that moment, all was well with the fractured Murphy family. Ben was their glue, bringing them back together again and offering balm to their open wounds.

*

After cake and tea, Lily put Ben down for his afternoon nap. As Lily descended the stairs, she found Michael hovering in the hall.

'I'm sorry. I tried to divert them, but I'm afraid you were right. It's going to kick off.'

'What this time?' Lily asked as her stomach plummeted. She felt so stupid for ever allowing herself a moment to hope that things would ever change.

'Your dad brought up the interview on *IrelandAM*. He has the latest age progression photo with him,' Michael said.

They found her mother putting on her jacket. Her face was tight, and her eyes flashed in anger.

'I'll give you a call tomorrow,' Her mum said in clipped tones, the inference in every word that Lily had allowed this to happen.

'Please don't go. Not like this. We've had a nice day.'

'I'll go. Your mum can stay,' her dad said, pulling his coat on too. He turned to his ex-wife. 'I thought you'd want to see Robert. I can see so much of you in this photo, around his mouth in particular. He has the same oval face as you. Look.'

Lily's mother omitted an anguished groan and said in a strangled voice, 'It's cruel. I can't bear to look at him. Don't you see? I don't recognise this man. He's a stranger to me.' Then her voice disintegrated to a sob. 'I want my baby boy back. The two-year-old Robert who loved the moon, chocolate buttons and Peter Rabbit.'

'I didn't mean to upset you,' her dad said helplessly to her mum.

Michael stepped closer to him and patted Jason's shoulder in solidarity. Lily was stuck in familiar ground: standing in the middle of her parents whilst they fired shots at each other, unable to offer comfort to either one, as it would be seen as taking a side.

'It's not just me who finds the photographs upsetting. Tell him,' her mother demanded of Lily, pulling her to her side.

'That's not true!' her dad responded. 'Tell her, Lily.'

Michael and her parents looked over to her, waiting for a response.

Lily wanted to run back upstairs to Ben's nursery, sit on the rocking chair and close her eyes to pretend all was okay. But she knew that she had to be honest.

'I tried to tell you this last week, Dad. I find the photographs difficult to look at too.' Lily took a deep breath and looked at her parents one by one. 'And, while we're on this subject, I think it's time we let Robert go. Let him rest in peace.'

A stunned silence descended into the room. Because Lily had broken a cardinal Murphy rule. Nobody was allowed to say out loud what they all must have thought privately hundreds of times – that Robert was dead.

Her dad was the first to respond, his face flushed with anger. 'Why would you say that?' His voice raised, and he almost shouted, 'You all think I'm crazy! Don't you? But from where I'm standing, it's you who are crazy.'

Michael once again placed a hand on his father-in-law's shoulder, but this time in warning. 'You'll wake Ben. Remember, it's his birthday. Let's not ruin his day.'

The anger dissipated from her father's face. 'I'll let myself out.' With one last look of regret at each of them, he left the house, softly closing the front door behind him.

'I'm worried about him,' Lily said, sinking to the sofa.

'He needs to speak to a professional. Get some support,' Michael agreed. 'He's a man on the brink.'

'You don't understand,' her mother muttered, almost to herself.

'What don't we understand?' Michael asked.

Her mother joined Lily on the sofa, pulling a cushion into her lap, embracing it like a child. 'You said we should let Robert go Lily. But, the thing is, guilt never allows you to let go.'

'But it wasn't your fault. Or Dad's,' Lily said firmly.

'What if it was?' her mother asked in a whisper.

Lily's breath quickened. 'What do you mean by that?' She'd had enough of tip-toeing around this subject.

'I can't . . .' Her mother began, then stopped mid-sentence.

'Yes, you bloody can. You will not clamp up and leave me with more unanswered questions. Tell me.'

'I ask myself every day what we could have done differently,' her mum whispered.

'You took a sleeping pill like millions do every night. Dad had a drink. Ditto. You can't keep blaming yourself.'

'I'm not talking about any of that!' her mum replied loudly, her nostrils flaring.

Lily's mouth dried up. She swallowed, wetting her lips with her tongue. 'What *do* you mean then, Mum?'

Fear filled her mother's face, and she began to rock back and forth, clasping the pillow between her arms.

'Mum!' Lily cried, looking at her mother in horror. 'What did you do?'

Time stretched between them. The air felt dense with tension as Lily watched her mother's face twitch in pain.

'I didn't do anything! That's the problem. I knew that something bad was going to happen, but I did *nothing*!' Her mother slumped further into the sofa. 'I should have taken the children and run. I'll never forgive myself that I didn't do that.'

Lily looked over at Michael, who seemed as baffled by her mother's words as she was. 'You are not making any sense, Mum.'

Her mother placed her hands over her face, and when she took them down a moment later she'd composed herself. 'That will teach me to have a glass of wine. Makes me neurotic. Ignore me. I was overwrought. Talking nonsense.'

Then she stood up and with a quick goodbye walked out, leaving Lily more confused than ever before.

THEN

July 1983

Kimberly

The Carousel, *Port of Barcelona, Spain*

Kimberly wrapped a towel around herself as she exited the tiny shower. She had wedged the en suite door open with one of her espadrille sandals. Her eyes never left Lily, who was also freshly washed and sitting in her pram, wearing a pretty yellow sundress. The colour seemed incongruous with the manic fear Kimberly felt, rattling its way around her body and mind. Then the cabin door burst open, and Jason ran in, his face red and sweating, as if he'd sprinted the whole way to them.

'He thinks I hurt Robert,' Jason exploded.

Kimberly moved to her husband's side, forgetting her own torment as she saw how distressed Jason was. 'Sit down. Tell me what's happened,' she said.

Her calm and gentle tone seemed to do the trick. Jason complied and sank onto the double bed.

'That . . . that . . . bloody inspector. He interviewed me when you came back here to freshen up.' He paused, looking down. 'He asked me if I'd ever thought about hurting Robert. He kept pushing and pushing, trying to get me to admit guilt.'

'That's outrageous!' Kimberly said. 'You are such a gentle man – you'd never hurt anyone!'

Jason looked up, and his lips quivered. His body began to shake. She'd never seen her husband break down like this before, and it frightened her. She fought the urge to fire questions at him, but instead let Jason take a moment to compose himself.

'I got so angry about him suggesting that I'd ever lay a hand on my child. But that only seemed to fuel the fire I was guilty. He'd give me a scathing look, then go back to scribbling in his bloody notebook. They found Robert's passport in the safe, along with ours. So whoever took him didn't take his passport too.'

Kimberly understood her husband's annoyance. She'd felt her hackles rise every time Inspector Ortega had picked up his pencil as she'd spoken too. She wished she knew *what* he'd been writing.

Jason stood up, his hands curling into fists by his side. 'Then he changed tactics. Acted like we were best buddies and asked me to go over how much I had to drink last night.'

Kimberly could hardly believe that it was only the previous evening that Jason left them to go out. It felt like a lifetime had passed since that moment.

'The inspector asked me if I might have been so drunk that I accidentally hurt Robert. He suggested that when I returned, Robert awoke and got into our bed. That I shook him too hard or smothered him with a pillow to stop him crying.' Seeing Kimberley's shocked face, he added quickly, 'Don't worry. He thinks that you slept through it all because you'd taken a sleeping tablet.' Tears were now streaming down Jason's face, and any anger he felt disappeared again as he recounted the horror of the accusations made to him. He finished in a terrified whisper, 'He thinks I killed Robert.'

Kimberly fought a rising panic. She bit her lip hard until she felt blood reach her tongue. She must keep calm and rational if they were ever to get through this ordeal. It was clear that Jason was falling apart. And was it any wonder, faced with Inspector Ortega's accusations?

'I'm going back to see the inspector. I'll tell him that his supposition is ridiculous.' Then, taking in a whiff of her hus-band's body odour, she added gently, 'Take a shower. It helps. I promise.'

Jason nodded numbly.

Kimberly took the brake off the buggy and moved it towards the cabin door, but Jason called out to her, 'Leave Lily here with me.' Kimberly hesitated a fraction too long, and he slumped even further onto the bed. 'You think I'm guilty too. You're afraid to leave our daughter with me.'

'Of course not. It's just . . . I can't be without her. It's nothing to do with you, I promise.'

Jason's shoulders dropped in defeat, and he walked to the bathroom, kicking her sandal aside and closing the en suite door between them.

Kimberly returned to the bar area, where she found Inspector Ortega smoking. Lily's face broke into a smile when she saw the childminder Pamela again, so Kimberly left them together to play.

'How could you accuse my husband of something so mon-strous?' Kimberly snapped, anger dancing its way through her now.

Inspector Ortega narrowed his eyes, and he asked, 'We must rule out all avenues to find out the truth. You want to know what happened to your son, no?'

'Yes, of course! But I do not want you to waste time run-ning down the wrong avenue!' Kimberly said, feeling heat rush into her cheeks. She sighed, then apologised for her out-burst. 'I'm sorry. I'm so scared.'

The inspector's face softened in sympathy. 'I understand. And I assure you that I am looking at all avenues, as you put it.' He leaned in a little closer. Looking back, can you think of any-thing suspicious that you noticed in the lead-up to Robert's disappearance? Was anybody watching your family?'

Ortega noticed Kimberly blanching at his words. 'There was something?' he asked quickly.

Kimberly held her hands up. 'No. It's the thought of someone watching my children, plotting, planning . . . I can't bear to think of that.'

Ortega accepted this. 'You need to know that we've searched the ship several times. Robert is not onboard.' Inspector Ortega let that sit with her for a moment, then continued, 'We've interviewed all staff, particularly those who were on duty last night and early this morning. Nobody saw Robert or indeed anything suspicious. We've reviewed the security footage taken on the cameras in the public areas. Looked at all personnel as they entered or left the ship. They shed no light on where your son might be. La Policia have now issued an amber alert, and checkpoints are already in place as they search for Robert.'

He drummed his fingertips against his unopened cigarette packet. 'But I have to be honest, Mrs Murphy, it is unlikely that Robert could have left the ship alone. He's a child no more than two years old. Which brings me back to Jason.'

'Jason would never hurt our son. I'm sure of that,' Kimberly said firmly.

'I believe that to be true. Under normal circumstances.' He sucked in air between his teeth. 'But what if it were an accident?'

Kimberly was struck dumb as the inspector outlined a possible truth. 'Jason, by his own admission, was drunk last night. We've interviewed the bar staff who served him, and he had, by their reckoning, several beers followed by several shots of whiskey.'

'My husband can handle his alcohol,' Kimberly stated, although this wasn't strictly true. Jason didn't drink much at all. He was a self-confessed lightweight. She felt another wave of guilt flood her because she knew that Jason had only drunk as much as he had last night because he'd had a stressful day, to which she had contributed.

'Maybe,' Inspector Ortega said with another of his shrugs, 'but he might have unintentionally hurt Robert.'

Kimberly felt stars dance across her eyes, and her body swayed as she imagined her son dead. She shook her head, desperately trying to ward off the images that taunted her.

'Your husband loves Robert,' continued the inspector. 'So, of course, he would have panicked. Add alcohol, and he would not be thinking straight. He might think that his only course of action was to hide Robert's body.'

Kimberly held a hand up to stop the inspector from continuing. She couldn't bear it. But the inspector would not be deterred and finished with a damning supposition. 'And maybe it's possible that Jason would throw Robert overboard in the hope that it looked like an accidental drowning.'

Fresh terror reared up through Kimberly's body as she imagined her little boy falling from the deck, plunging into cold, dark waters. Kimberly could understand the inspector's logic, even if it horrified her. If Jason had accidentally killed Robert, he would have done anything to make sure that he didn't lose Lily too. He *would* cover up his actions.

'Exactly,' the inspector said, and Kimberly realised in dismay that she'd spoken her traitorous thoughts out loud.

'Jason couldn't . . . h-he would never . . .' Kimberly stammered in a shaking voice, breaking off mid-sentence. But it was too late. The damage was done.

BEFORE

April 1976

Sally

Sunshine House Orphanage, Hammersmith, London

Sally had been waiting for this day to arrive for years. In fact, she'd thought about it almost every day, at least once, since her thirteenth birthday. Over the past five years, it felt as if time had moved at half speed. Especially since Elsie had left. But, as the days neared towards her eighteenth birthday, to her surprise everything had moved too fast for her liking.

There were increased visits with her case worker, Mrs Burton, to discuss the next steps. There were details of a flat for Sally in Battersea. Sister Jones said several other ex-residents of the orphanage had moved there.

Sister Jones had taken Sally out for lunch the previous week as a special treat.

'What do you want to do when you leave here?' Sister Jones asked as she buttered a fruit scone.

Sally shrugged, unsure how to answer.

'Yes, you do know. Don't think I haven't seen that doll's head you are always working on. And I've seen you give the girls make-overs in the common room when Housemother isn't on duty.'

Sally's eyes widened in surprise. 'You know about my Super Girl's World?'

'Of course. I know everything.' Sister Jones pointed to the side of her nose and winked. 'I thought it best not to tell House-mother, though.'

Sally felt a rush of warmth for Sister Jones.

'You have to get a job, I know, but who says that job can't be one in a hair salon? I have faith in you, Sally. You can do any-thing you want if you set your mind to it.'

When Sister Jones put it like that, Sally believed she *could* reach for the stars.

She'd been given a small allowance to help her, until she found a job. Now, Sally sat on the edge of her bed and looked at her small grey suitcase, which lay open beside her. Inside, folded neatly, was everything she owned. Two midi skirts, one grey, one navy, both hideous. Two shirts, both plain white with over-sized collars. A cream peasant blouse with a pair of green bell-bottom trousers, that she liked. And a bright red cowl-neck jumper that she could just about bear. Seven pairs of knickers, one spare bra, stockings, a slip and two pairs of socks. And a pair of sensible court shoes, in black.

Her stomach flipped, and she felt a wave of nausea hit her as she closed the case with two clicks, and stood up. Her legs felt like a wobbling plate of jelly, and she could not move. Why did she falter when she was minutes away from saying goodbye to it all? She'd longed for the independence that this milestone birthday would bring. But, now that it was almost upon her, her body trembled in fear.

Sally looked around the bedroom. Would she miss it? This morning she was sure she'd happily walk away from here with-out a backward glance. But now?

Her mind went back to Elsie again. At first, Elsie had done as she'd promised. A new letter arrived every week, written in Elsie's large round script. She'd shared how she was looking for work and eating cereal for dinner. How she was scouring the markets for trinkets to brighten up her flat. But the letters had dwindled to once every few weeks, until they eventually stopped. Sally continued to write to Elsie every week until one day, about six months after she'd left, the letters came back with 'Return to sender' printed on them.

Elsie had left and moved on. Everyone did that in the end.

Sighing, Sally stood up and manoeuvred herself to see her reflection in the small mirror on the dressing table. Did she look okay? She'd been planning what to wear today for months. She'd lost hours trying on different outfits from her small selection of clothes that she'd been given in preparation for her life outside the orphanage. In the end, she opted for her favourite blue denim jeans, which had a white embroidered flower on the wide bell bottoms, matched with her favourite tie-dyed orange-and-white blouse.

Sally touched her bobbed hair and made a face at herself in the mirror. She vowed not to cut her hair again until it fell into long waves down her back, like Lynda Carter's did. She twirled in a perfect Wonder Woman circle. She'd been practising.

A voice called up from downstairs for her. 'Mrs Burton is here!'

To her surprise, a shiver of excitement ran down Sally's spine. Maybe she was ready after all. She walked back to her bed and, with one last check that she'd not forgotten anything, she made her way downstairs.

Sister Jones, Housemother, Mrs Burton and Sally's friends were gathered at the end of the dark staircase, watching her silently as she walked down. Sally held her chin high, swishing hips as she moved. She saw Sister Jones smile and Housemother raised an eyebrow in disapproval. But Sally winked back at her, and in return she got a wry grin. Years of reprimands for being too sassy were about to end. Would she miss them? Maybe, a little.

'You look like you are ready to face the world head-on,' Mrs Burton said warmly as she grabbed Sally's suitcase from her. Sally liked her. Mrs Burton seemed to genuinely want to help the girls under her care. If hairdressing didn't work out, then one day Sally could work in this field too, helping young girls like herself who found themselves in care. That was a nice thought.

Sister Jones moved towards Sally and placed her hands lightly on her shoulders. 'This is a landmark day for you. I know you are desperate to grow up and experience all that eighteen offers. But please don't forget that you don't have to do everything all at once. Don't be in such a rush to leave behind your childhood, dear. Be the good girl that I know you truly are. And remember what I said last week. Go chase those dreams of yours.'

Sister Jones's words didn't feel like an unwanted lecture. She heard the sincerity behind them, and Sally felt an unfamiliar lump in her throat. But she pushed it down, because she no longer allowed herself to shed a tear about her lot in life. The last tears she'd cried were when Elsie had left. Sally had learned first-hand that it got you nowhere, feeling sorry for yourself.

'Thank you for all you've done for me,' Sally managed to say.

'It wasn't all bad, then?' Sister Jones asked.

'No. It was a lot of good,' Sally replied as a rush of memories came back to her.

Hot-chocolate Saturdays, watching TV with all the girls, curled up on the worn but comfy sofas in the common room. Jigsaw puzzles so big that they took up the entire dining-room table, but that sense of achievement when, together, they all managed to complete it. Watching *Wonder Woman*. Singing and dancing to the Rolling Stones, Cilla Black, Cliff Richard and the Bee Gees, David Bowie and – Sally's favourite – Carly Simon on *Top of the Pops*.

'You've all been my family,' Sally said tremulously, looking around at her friends. 'And I'll never forget you. Come find me when your get-out-of-jail card arrives . . .' She smiled as she said this part, so Sister Jones didn't think she was having a go at her or the home.

Sister Jones.

The kind-hearted and caring nun who had been like a mother

to her, reached out and touched Sally's arm gently. 'You are always welcome if you want to come back to visit. And if you need me, if you find yourself in a bother, you call, okay?'

Sally nodded her thanks, but deep down she knew that she would never return. She knew that, like every other girl who had left before her, she was embarking on a new journey, a new life. There was a rush of hugs from her friends.

'Hush now. We'll all see each other again one day soon.' Sally promised through her tears, which now fell, despite her heroic efforts to quell them.

Sister Jones put a comforting arm round Sally, and with one last wave she knew it was time to leave. Sally climbed into the front seat of Mrs Burton's chocolate-brown Austin Allegro, the car that would take her away from the only real home she had ever known.

As she drove away, with the cries of well-wishes from her friends echoing behind her, Sally couldn't help but feel the weight of the unknown, and the beginning of a new, uncertain chapter of her life.

NOW

July 2023

Lily

Phibsborough, Dublin

Lily's last client of the morning was Zach Brady. And ever since he'd arrived for his appointment she could see that he was like a coiled spring. His eyes darted around the room and his left leg shook so much she could feel the vibrations from her seat across from him. Was it the lack of sleep, she wondered? Or perhaps he was taking something. She looked at his eyes to see if there was any telltale evidence that he had taken drugs. But, while they looked troubled, they were unglazed and clear.

'Can we get back to your childhood again, Zach?'

They'd had three sessions over the past couple of weeks, and Lily was convinced that the key to unlocking the issues he grappled with, lay with his formative years and his absent father.

'What do you want to know?'

'You've spoken a lot about your relationship with your siblings and love of the outdoor life on the lake your family enjoyed. What do you remember or know about your life before your mother married your stepfather?'

'I don't remember that time. I was too young. Why are you interested in that, anyhow?' Zach asked, his eyes narrowing.

'I know. It's a terrible cliche, delving into a person's childhood in therapy. You wait and see. Next, I'll be blaming the parents,' Lily teased.

He smiled warily in return, but said, 'I told you several times. I have good parents. I had a great childhood. Whatever is going on with me isn't their fault.' But he started to blink rapidly, in what Lily now recognised as one of Zach's tells that he was lying.

'I want to talk about the past, in particular, the time when you had nightmares and bad dreams. I'd like to see if we can find a connection between those back then and your insomnia now.'

Zach looked unsure, and he frowned.

'Our childhood can be highly influential on our adult years,' Lily continued, then paused as she felt a stab of pain under her rib cage. There was nothing physically wrong with her. She knew that. But whenever her mind drifted back to Ben's birthday and her mother's confusing statement about guilt, she'd had a physical reaction.

'Are you okay?' Zach asked, his own eyes narrowing as he watched Lily.

'Sorry. Yes. I'm fine.' She shifted her position to sit up straight. 'When you were a child, and something went wrong, who did you go to for help?'

'My dad,' Zach answered immediately.

'Not your mother?'

His nose scrunched up for a moment as he pondered this. 'If I fell or hurt myself, I'd always go to Mom. She's loving. A nurturer . . .' His face clouded, and he paused, leaving his thought unsaid.

Lily knew she had to push him a little further on this. 'There's a but there. I can hear it.'

'Ha! Not much gets past you.' Zach smiled. 'Let's say that I worked out young that there was no point in asking my mother about certain subjects. She'd get this look . . .'

'Like what?'

'My biological father was a no-go. I wanted to know his name when I was about eleven. I mean, I always knew that I was Dom's stepson. But, honestly, we never did the whole step thing. He was just Dad. But then a kid in school reconnected with his birth father, who he'd been estranged from. He was full of stories about how alike they were, and it made me curious. So I asked my mother about my birth father. She shut it down immediately. Refused to discuss him with me. Dad took me aside that evening and explained why.'

'Can you share that with me?' Lily asked.

'Dad told me that my father . . .' Zach's face darkened, 'was abusive to my mother.'

Lily could see so much pain on Zach's face. 'I'm sorry. That must have been difficult to learn. How did it make you feel?'

'Honestly, I was angry at first. The thought of anyone laying a hand on my mom made me want to hit something. But afterwards, once Dad had calmed me down, I felt grateful.'

'For what?'

'For my mom's strength to leave that asshole. For giving us both a better life.'

'That's astute from one so young. Looking back, can you understand why she found it difficult to talk to you about it?'

Zach nodded. 'Of course.' Then he said flatly, 'He's dead now anyhow. My birth father.'

This was new information. 'When did you find that out?'

'At the same time, when I was eleven. After I approached Dad about my father, he looked him up. Said he wanted to see what he was up to. He discovered that he'd died a few years previously. He was young. Prostate cancer.'

'That must have been difficult to hear. How did it make you feel?'

'That I needed to get my prostate checked.' Zach's joke landed awkwardly between them.

Lily raised an eyebrow, giving him time to answer her more honestly.

'Truthfully, I was relieved that he was dead. It meant that I didn't have to face him. Otherwise, by now, I would have had to have looked him up, I suppose. And that would have hurt my mother. Perhaps me too. It's better this way.'

'Does your mom know about this?'

'Not as far as I know. Dom and I decided we'd tell her if she ever brought him up to us.' A shadow passed over his face. He leaned in a little closer to Lily. 'Mom never wanted to talk about my other mother either.'

'Did she tell you why *that* subject was difficult for her?' Lily asked.

Zach shook his head. 'She'd pretend she was all cool and happy to talk about anything, but, like with my birth father, I could see that any mention of my other mother distressed her.'

'She may have thought you created this imaginary friend because you were unhappy with her. Her existence might have been hurtful for her. I think if my son created another mother, despite my head knowing that it was normal, it might sting.'

'Yeah, I can see how hard it would be for you if Ben did that.'

Lily looked at Zach sharply. 'How do you know my son's name?'

'You mentioned it was his birthday last week. You said his name then,' Zach said, blinking again.

Lily felt a trickle of unease run down her back. She couldn't say for sure that she *hadn't* mentioned Ben by name, but it was unlike her to do so. She had rules that she stuck by about sharing her personal life.

Zach continued in a rushed voice, 'My therapist said the same to me when I was a kid. My mom probably couldn't talk about my other mother because she was jealous. And I believed that to be true throughout my entire life.'

'You don't believe that now?'

Zach's leg began to jitter and shake again. He looked around the room as if half expecting someone to jump out at him.

'You seem agitated today, Zach. Ever since you walked in, you've looked upset. Has something specific happened you want to share?'

He shrugged. And something about the almost scowl on his face made Lily uneasy. An echo of something or someone.

'What if my other mother wasn't imaginary?' Zach asked. 'What if she was real?'

He stood up abruptly, causing his chair to topple backwards. His hands were balled into tight fists by his sides, and his breathing was erratic. Lily watched him carefully, trying to gauge his mood and level of distress. She'd dealt with demanding clients before, and she knew how to handle situations when they became agitated or angry. Sympathise, empathise, listen.

'Sit down, Zach,' Lily said firmly. He made no move to return to his chair, though. 'I'm sorry you are feeling so upset, Zach. But, please, I need you to sit down.'

'I lied about why I came to see you,' Zach whispered, his voice barely audible. 'I wanted to tell you, every time I've been here. But I thought you might throw me out. Say I was crazy.'

Lily felt another pang of concern. She had sensed that Zach had been holding something back. Were they finally going to get to the truth? She smiled encouragingly at him. 'Nothing you can tell me will shock me, Zach. This is a safe place for you. And I want you to be honest with me. There should be no secrets.'

His face turned ashen, and Lily realised that Zach wasn't angry. He was scared.

'It's going to be okay,' she said gently, pointing to the chair again. 'Please sit down.'

He stopped pacing, but remained standing, his eyes fixed on something behind Lily. She swivelled round to follow his gaze to a bookshelf, where a framed graduation photograph of her and her parents sat amongst the books.

Before she had a chance to process this, he continued. 'I saw the interview. While eating granola and yoghurt, I saw Jason Murphy – your dad.'

Lily stood up. Backing away from the man in front of her, every part of her was now on high alert. Zach reached behind

76

him, and for one horrifying moment Lily thought he was going to pull out a weapon.

Instead, he grabbed a folded page from his jeans pocket. Lily watched silently, her heart hammering in her chest as he unfolded the sheet and placed it on the table between them.

The words *Missing for Forty Years and Time for Answers* were emblazoned across the top in bold, black letters.

Zach locked eyes with Lily once again. His lips trembled, and his eyes filled with tears as he said seven words that would forever change their lives, 'I think I'm your older brother, Robert.'

PART TWO

Eyes of the innocent
Lies of the guilty
Float around like loose atoms
Ready to collide
Ready to explode in my mind

Dave Alan Walker

THEN

July 1983

Kimberly

Hotel Miramar, Barcelona, Spain

Kimberly and Jason stood side by side on the edge of the bustling Barcelona portside, watching the *Carousel* sail out of the harbour. They were lost in their thoughts, still reeling from the news that the cruise ship would continue without them. With the captain's help, they had booked a hotel in Barcelona, and their luggage had already been transferred there.

People jostled by them, laughing and joking as they posed for photographs, but Kimberly barely noticed. Holding on to Lily's buggy, they stood like statues, staring out to sea. It was as if their feet had become concreted to the pier, and they could not move.

Each lost in the horror of the past seventy-two hours.

She heard Jason sigh heavily beside her. And her hand moved a few inches to her right, to offer him support. But paused, before her hand made contact with his, dropping back to her side again. She felt sweat trickle down the small of her back in the stifling summer heat.

Only when the white ship became a dot on the horizon did Jason speak.

'I suppose we should head to the hotel. It's only a few minutes' walk from what I can make out.' He held up a small map given to him by one of the ship's stewards.

'That was the last place I held my baby boy in my arms,' Kimberly said in a strangled voice, tears welling up in her eyes.

'They've searched the entire ship over and over. He's not there,' Jason replied, his voice devoid of emotion.

Kimberly felt irritation nip at her, and she fought to bite back a sarcastic response. Did he think she was that stupid that she thought Robert was hidden in a dusty corner of the ship? Wherever her boy was, it wasn't there – that much she knew.

Kimberly released the brake on the buggy, reaching down to adjust the bonnet on Lily's head. Lily smiled happily up to her mama, happy to be out and about. It had been a trying few days for their daughter too. Her holiday had come abruptly to an end. No more splashes in the pool. No more games of peek-a-boo with her older brother. Kimberly felt another wave of terror run over her. But she couldn't allow it to take hold. Not here. So she pushed the buggy and followed Jason as he pointed to a street on their right. They walked through narrow cobbled streets leading them to lively squares lined with tall coconut trees and water fountains.

A few moments later, they arrived at their hotel. A manager was ushered to them when they gave their name at check-in.

He tilted his head in sympathy as he spoke. 'The Miramar is here to help in any way we can at this difficult time. Please do not hesitate to ask me personally if you need anything. Anything at all.' He pressed a card into Jason's hand.

'As it happens, there is something you can help me with,' Jason replied. 'Can you reserve a room for my father, please? He is travelling from Dublin later today. Kevin Murphy.'

Kimberly looked sharply at her husband. When had that been decided? He shuffled uneasily beside her. Jason knew that she had a strained relationship with his father. He had been suspicious when Jason had introduced Kimberly to Kevin. She could read his thoughts as he'd looked her up and down disdainfully.

What on earth did Jason see in a single mother, with very little to her name?

'Of course,' the manager replied, smiling for the first time. He looked relieved to be given something to do. 'For how many nights? I've held the reservation for your room for one week already, but we can extend or reduce that, depending on how . . .' He struggled to find the right words to complete that sentence.

'On if we find our son?' Kimberly said, her voice tight with emotion. When she saw a flush run across the manager's face, she softened and added, 'We don't know how long we'll be here.'

'We'll be here until they find Robert,' Jason said firmly. 'As long as it takes.'

The manager called a sombre porter, who led them down a plush carpeted hallway. They all stood in awkward silence in the lift as it moved to the fifth floor. The porter opened the door to their room and backed out, leaving them to it.

'It looks nice,' Jason said, again in that same voice that was starved of any joy. She took in the growing stubble on his face, the dark circles under his eyes all in stark contrast to how rested and tanned he'd looked only a few days ago.

He'd aged since Robert was taken. She supposed she had too. Kimberly looked around the spacious room with a crib assembled beside a large queen-sized bed. Plush bedspreads in burnt orange-and-gold matched the curtains that framed a large window overlooking the ocean. A few days ago, Kimberly would have been giddy at the opulence had they stepped into this beautiful room. But now it left a bitter taste in her mouth. She guessed that they had been given this superior room because their child had been snatched from them. Consolation for their loss. Kimberly wanted none of it; every luxurious inch of the space insulted her missing son.

Jason unclipped Lily from her buggy, and she cooed with delight to be free from her restraint. There was a lot to explore in this new space. As he cuddled their little girl, Kimberly kicked her sandals off and entered the bathroom. She told Jason that she would have a shower, locking the door from the inside. She'd never done that before. They were not the kind of family to turn keys between themselves. But everything had changed three nights ago, and she was sure they would never be the same again.

Kimberly peeled off her T-shirt and shorts and stepped into the large shower cubicle. She turned the water on, and only when it cascaded over her, hot and sharp, stinging her body, did she allow herself to cry out. She pounded her hands against the tiled walls of the shower and screamed as sobs overcame her.

She had always been a good mother to Robert and Lily, giving her life to them and putting them above all else. Every single moment of every single day was in service to her children.

Unlike her own mother.

And yet this was what she got in return.

Why has this happened to me? she thought to herself, feeling the shame rise from her toes upwards, through her heaving stomach, to her flushed face. She knew why it had happened. She had let her guard down, and now the unimaginable had happened.

THEN

July 1983

Kimberly

Hotel Miramar, Barcelona, Spain

It had been seven long days, which translated to one hundred and sixty-eight hours of agony and uncertainty, since Robert went missing. Ever since then, Kimberly had been living in a state of perpetual fear and anxiety,

Her hand rested on the side of Lily's cot. Kimberly had got into the habit of sleeping like that, always with a hand ready to reach out and catch her daughter if she should need her. Or to clasp an unknown predator between her fingers before they ran away with another child. Kimberly sat up and massaged her shoulder, which ached from its unusual position.

Jason's side of the bed was empty, but that didn't surprise her. However little Kimberly slept, he managed less every night. He'd taken to walking the streets of Barcelona at all hours of the day and night in the hope he'd spot Robert. She missed him, but she understood why he had to do this.

Her father-in-law, Kevin, was by his side for every trek. Together, they were determined to knock on every door and leave no stone unturned. Kevin, a retired civil servant, had come prepared for battle. His hotel room became the headquarters for their unofficial 'Find Robert' operation. He'd created a missing-child poster, with a photograph of Robert, centre, under a large headline, 'Help us bring Robert home.' Over the past couple of days, they had distributed over a thousand of these posters throughout Barcelona.

Inspector Ortega had updated them daily, but, unfortunately, there were no genuine leads for him to go on. The lack of progress made it difficult for them to maintain any hope.

Lily stirred in her sleep. She'd be awake soon. So Kimberly washed and dressed quickly.

The hotel room, which had appeared spacious and luxurious during check-in, now looked cluttered and cramped. Kimberly couldn't help but long for the comfort of their home in Dublin.

Maybe this was her hell – to stay in this room, neither living nor dead – a purgatory for her sins.

At seven o'clock, like clockwork, Lily reached her two chubby arms upwards, calling for her mama. Twenty minutes later, Kimberly made her way down to the dining room with Lily in her arms. She was directed to an empty table in the corner of the room by a member of the waiting staff. A highchair appeared, and Kimberly busied herself, settling Lily into it. All the while, she was studiously avoiding eye contact with any of the guests, who she knew were all watching her as they ate their bacon and eggs.

Kimberly had heard their whispers as she'd passed them by in the lobby over the previous week.

'There's the mother of that missing child.'

'How could you sleep through someone taking your child?'

'Something suspicious about all of this.'

'I heard the dad isn't the dad, but the stepdad.'

Kimberly wanted to scream at them all to mind their own business, to shut up, shut up, shut up. But she had to find the strength to keep going and stay sane. Robert's disappearance had been covered by the local and national press here in Spain. They'd had several requests for interviews that, up to now, they'd refused to give. And the story had broken at home in

Ireland too. Her family's nightmare had become the source of sensationalist headlines.

'Good morning,' Kevin said as he approached the table. He gave Kimberly a polite nod, and then his face broke into a happy smile as he looked down at his granddaughter.

Lily babbled in delight when she saw him. He kissed the top of her head, saying, 'Whose my best girl?'

'Where is Jason?' Kimberly asked, looking around the room for him. She didn't like being in her father-in-law's company without her husband. Kevin had a way of looking right through her, and it felt as if he were uncovering all her secrets.

'He's done in. Barely able to move one foot in front of the other. I wanted him to go to sleep, but he insisted he must see you and Lily. So he's splashing cold water on his face before he comes in to eat.' His brown eyes scrutinised Kimberley, a frown creasing his forehead. 'This cannot continue, you know.'

It appeared that *this*, whatever *this* was, was all Kimberly's fault.

'He needs to get some rest,' Kevin insisted.

Ah, that's what *this* was. 'I begged him to stay in our hotel room last night,' Kimberly said. She sighed and added, 'Wherever Robert is, he'll be long gone from Barcelona.'

Kevin nodded his agreement as he poured himself a cup of coffee. 'I'm going to hire a car today so we can take our posters further afield. We've got Barcelona a hundred per cent covered.'

'Thank you for all you're doing,' Kimberly said. She reached over to pat her father-in-law's hand awkwardly. 'I appreciate everything you've done for us since you arrived.'

'I wish I could do more.'

A pot of tea and coffee arrived at the table, along with a silver tray of toast. They ordered bacon and eggs for them all, including Jason. Kimberly had little appetite, though. She'd nibble on a square of buttered toast and devote her energy to spoon-feeding porridge to Lily.

But then Kevin's eyes narrowed. 'Jason blames himself. For

going out for a few drinks. For not being there to protect his family. That kind of guilt can eat away at a person. And it's unfair to put this at this feet.'

'I don't blame him!' Kimberly said truthfully.

'That's good. After all, it was you who insisted he go out. And you took a sleeping pill while in charge of the children.'

Kimberly felt a flush rise to her cheeks. 'I wish I could go back and do it all differently.'

Tears came once again. She was incredulous that she still could produce them, having shed so many over the past week.

Kevin's eyes never left her as he sipped his coffee.

'It's clear that you hold me accountable, Kevin. Well, I can assure you that I do too. I'll never forgive myself for taking that pill.'

Jason arrived, took one look at Kimberly's face and rushed to her side. He handed her a napkin and asked, 'Are you okay?'

She noted that he didn't put his arms round her, though. Rot had crept into their marriage. It had caused their love to shrink day by day, and now it was crumbling in front of her eyes, splintering, piercing, failing. And she didn't know what to do to prevent it.

She wiped her eyes, telling Jason all was fine. They both looked towards Lily. An unspoken promise moved between them: they would not allow themselves to fall apart in front of their daughter. Jason took a seat on the other side of Lily. Kevin passed him a cup of coffee, which he gulped down in two large swigs.

'You look tired,' Kimberly said, noticing the bags under Jason's eyes. His lips were chapped and blistering. She reached into her handbag and pulled out a ChapStick, handing it to him. He half smiled at her, and for a moment it was as it used to be.

He slicked it onto his lips and said, 'That's better. Thanks.' Then he cleared his throat before turning to Kimberly. 'We've had a call from Inspector Ortega. He'd like us both to call down to the station.'

'Is there news?' Kimberly asked, her stomach clenching at the thought.

'I don't know. But he did say he'd like to see us this morning.' Kevin lowered his voice and leaned in. 'Should you take a lawyer with you?'

'Why would we do that?' Kimberly asked, her eyes wide.

'If we take a lawyer, surely that will make the authorities think we look guilty?' Jason asked, his knee jiggling up and down.

'Not for one moment do I believe that either of you had anything to do with Robert's disappearance. But there's been chatter. You've heard it yourselves. And speculation in the press too. That article in the *Independent* hinted that you were a possible suspect, Jason,' Kevin said.

'They always blame the parents,' Kimberly murmured.

'Or the wicked step-parent,' Jason added bitterly.

'We have to box clever here, son. I've been talking to one of my contacts in the Irish embassy, and they have suggested a lawyer for you. He's a local lad, but excellent at this type of thing.'

Kimberly felt bile rush its way into the back of her throat. She held a napkin to her mouth and closed her eyes to ward off nausea.

'I will not allow them to pin this on you,' Kevin said firmly to Jason.

'Or Kimberly,' Jason added.

'Absolutely. This one needs you both,' Kevin said, pointing to Lily. 'This can't be the right environment for Lily. Living out of a suitcase, with none of her toys and things. We have to think about when it's time to go home.'

'No!' Kimberly snapped loudly, banging her hand on the table so hard that her teacup rattled in the saucer. Several diners turned in their direction. 'I'm sorry. I didn't mean to snap. But we can't go.' She reached over to Jason, clasping his hand between her own. 'What if they bring Robert back to us? What if they realise they've made a mistake when Robert keeps asking for us, his mama and daddy? We have to be here, waiting for him.'

'It's okay, honey. Don't get upset. We'll stay,' Jason reassured her.

Kevin raised his hands in defeat. 'Fair enough. But in the meantime think about the lawyer. If this inspector starts making any accusations when you go down this morning, you immediately call a halt and say you need your lawyer present. Give me a call here, and I'll get it sorted.'

NOW

July 2023

Lily

Phibsborough, Dublin

Lily looked back and forth between the photograph of Robert, aged forty-two, and at Zach, comparing the two, as her mind raced. There was little more than a passing resemblance between them. Zach was clearly delusional. So why say it? Had he fixated on Lily maybe and wanted to establish a connection? That didn't sit right with her, though. They'd only had a couple of sessions, hardly enough time for him to have an unhealthy obsession with her.

'Are you okay?' Zach asked, moving closer.

Lily took a step backwards.

'Sorry,' Zach said, holding his hands up as if in surrender.

Lily sat down, her breath ragged, as if she'd run a three-minute mile.

'It's the shock,' Zach said kindly. He poured two glasses of water, mirroring the trick Lily often used with her clients when they became overcome with emotion.

She took the glass offered and gulped the water down. As she composed herself, she looked at Zach, wondering what to do next. She was the professional, and it was clear that this man had issues. He had convinced himself that he was her brother, attaching himself to her family because his own was unhappy. Was he a fantasist or simply confused? She knew it was her job to help him, but first of all she needed to confirm whether he was dangerous.

'Zach, why do you think you are my missing brother?'

He pointed to the flyer, to the two photographs and then back to his own face as if this explained everything.

'But you look nothing like Robert. You've got a square jaw; Robert has an oval face. And your nose is different. Yours is much smaller than his.'

'We have the same eyes.' Zach removed his glasses and presented himself to Lily in a Clark Kent/Superman reveal.

She studied his face and then looked down to Robert's eyes. 'Okay. Your eyes are similar. But the rest, sorry, I don't see it.'

'I've been researching age progression technology. I assume they've used your mother, your image, and this one of Robert at two years old to create forty-two-year-old Robert.'

Lily nodded warily. She didn't like to think that anyone was researching her family. It felt intrusive, and every antenna in her body screamed stranger danger.

'But the forensic artist is missing one half of Robert – of me – for the progression: my father's face. So it stands to reason that without that there would be differences in the final result.'

Lily could not deny the logic in this argument. But the way Zach was referring to himself as Robert so emphatically made her deeply uncomfortable.

Then Zach reached into his pocket again and pulled out a bundle of photographs. 'Can I show you something?'

Lily figured that there was little point in saying no. Zach was clearly on a mission.

He passed the snaps to her as he said, 'These were taken on my third birthday and the others, later that year.'

Lily looked down and felt her body tremble as she took in every detail of the first image. A little boy, sitting in a high chair with a big smile on his face, looked at a cake with three candles on it. Blonde curl and sparkling steel-blue eyes smiled up at the camera.

That boy, whoever he was, could be Robert's double.

'You see it too, right?' Zach asked, his voice little more than a whisper.

Lily couldn't speak. The air in her body had vanished, and she couldn't breathe. Tiny dots danced in front of her eyes, and the room swam around her. She felt arms round her, steadying her. The dots disappeared, bringing sharp focus. Lily reached her hand up to touch Zach's solid and muscular arm. And she caught a sob before it escaped.

'Robert . . .'

'I think so.'

'Your other mother,' Lily whispered, thinking about the discussions she'd shared with Zach about his imaginary childhood friend.

'I know. It's all starting to make sense now,' Zach said grimly.

Lily pulled back from Zach's arms. For goodness' sake, he was still her client. She took a steadying breath and signalled for him to sit opposite her. Then, using every ounce of her inner resolve, she asked him, 'Can you start at the beginning? You said you saw the interview on *IrelandAM*.'

'Yes!' Zach answered enthusiastically. His shoulders dropped, and Lily thought that this was the first time he looked relaxed since he'd started seeing her. 'By pure chance. I'm normally out of my apartment before seven. I use a gym in the office complex before I start my day. But I pulled a muscle in my thigh the day before, so I was taking a day off from my usual workouts.'

Lily had to stifle a scream of frustration. She wanted Zach to stop waffling and get to the point.

'I flicked through the TV channels, then stopped in my tracks when they announced the next guest coming up after the break was a man who was looking for his stepson, who'd gone missing forty years ago. And then they showed a photograph of me . . .' Zach paused when he heard a snort from Lily. 'Of Robert, I should say, taken on a cruise ship in 1983. I recognised that child's face. Lily, I promise you, that child is me.'

Lily counted to ten in her mind, only responding when she was sure her voice was steady enough. 'Did you call your mother to ask her to explain?'

Zach shook his head. 'I told you. She doesn't do well with conversations about our past,' he said.

Maybe because she snatched you. The thought sneaked into her mind, but she pushed it aside, refusing to let it stay. 'But surely, if you think you are Robert, you have to confront your mother?' She leaned in and said gently, 'Is it possible that you don't want to do that because you know, deep inside you, that this is a . . . fantasy?'

Now Zach sighed, looking at Lily in disappointment. 'You think I'm crazy. Of course you do.'

'You're not crazy, Zach. I believe you have a lot of unresolved childhood trauma, though. And because of that—'

Zach interrupted her before she could finish. 'I know what it must look like. And I know that I don't look much like the progression photograph, but how can you explain the similarity between my childhood photograph and Robert's?' He pointed to the photographs again so she could examine the likeness.

Lily took in every detail, from the matching curl of the two boys' hair to the cow's lick at their crown. Their eyes were the exact same shape and colour. And their noses were slightly upturned at the end. Freckles scattered across their cheeks, almost in mirroring patterns. Yes, they could be brothers. Or twins.

'I read an article recently about doppelgängers. Unrelated people, yet they look like siblings or, in some cases, like twins,' Lily said. 'There were two women – one from India, one from Eastern Europe. And, oh boy, they looked identical, other than their height, which was mismatched. Honestly, the similarity was uncanny. But they were not related in any way. There were dozens of cases, all similar to those two women.' Lily touched the flyer once more with her forefinger. 'I can't explain why

Robert's and your DNA made your features similar; no more than those two women could explain why their looks were mirrors, especially from different ethnicities. But it happens.'

Zach listened to Lily and, for a moment, uncertainly flashed into his eyes. He stiffened on the chair, shoulders hunched up again, and his jaw clenched with tension.

'You think I'm making this up? If so, for what purpose?'

'I don't know why, Zach. And I want to help you understand that. Answer me this. Does your mother have any photographs of you as a newborn?'

'Yes,' Zach answered warily. 'There are some of her in hospital in London. And of my baptism.'

'And does she have any of you as a young baby?'

'Only a few. But I've seen some of them. She said that when she left my father she could only take a small bag and left most of her photographs behind her.'

'That makes sense. Don't you agree?'

Zach shrugged.

'And do you look like the newborn infant in those photographs?' Lily asked gently.

'Impossible to say. I'm wrapped up in blankets.' But when Lily raised her eyebrows at him, he conceded. 'Some of the photographs I believe are me.'

'Okay, let's look at this logically. Why does your mother have photographs of you as a newborn if she only abducted you when you were two and a half years old?'

'Photoshop.' But even Zach didn't believe this, judging by the quiver in his voice.

'Do you believe your mother is capable of abducting you and pretending you are hers for forty years?' Lily asked.

Zach's face crumpled. He didn't need to reply to the question. Then Lily's watch buzzed as her alarm notified her that Zach's time was up. Her mind raced with questions that she needed the wherewithal to answer. But, for now, she wanted this man out of her house.

95

'We've come to the end of our session, Zach. I think it's time we wrap this up.'

He stood and looked at Lily with such longing it made her shiver. 'I know this doesn't make sense. And I know how crazy I sound. But I believe that I'm your brother. I truly do. From in here.' He thumped his gut. Then he reached up and touched his heart. 'And in here too. I'll go, because I know I've given you a shock, but, please, Lily, I beg of you. Please think about what I've said. Allow yourself to acknowledge the possibility that I'm right.'

Lily looked into his eyes, and, try as she might, she could not look away. For a few moments, the rest of the world disappeared, and it was just the two of them. She swallowed rapidly, wrapping her arms round her body, until he walked out of the room with one last shy glance in her direction.

And only when she heard the front door shut did she allow herself to think the unthinkable.

What if he was right? What if his mom had crept into their cabin forty years ago, and stolen Zach? Could that man be her long-lost brother Robert?

NOW

July 2023

Lily

Phibsborough, Dublin

Lily felt as if she was on the edge of a cliff, and every time Zach had looked at her, his eyes pushed her closer to a fall. Her skin felt clammy, and her body ached as if she was coming down with the flu. She ran to the kitchen, turned the tap on and splashed cold water onto her face. It made her mascara run, and the black inky make-up stung her eyes. She grabbed a tea towel and wiped her face clean.

What should she do?

She'd call her husband. He'd know what to do.

Pick up, please, Lily thought as she called his mobile, but it rang without answer. Should she leave a voicemail?

'Can't talk. All okay?' Michael's voice asked breathlessly as she was about to hang up.

Lily felt a sob escape. She took a deep breath, knowing she would only scare Michael if she began to cry. 'Ben is fine. But I need you to come home.'

'What's wrong?' His voice was curt. He could never handle Lily or Ben being sick, and worry made him seem cold and unfeeling when it was the opposite of how he felt.

'I can't tell you on the phone, but I need you here, please.'

Michael didn't waste further time asking questions, and she could not have loved him more. He said so calmly that she instantly felt a weight lift from her shoulders, 'I'm on my way. I love you.'

While waiting for her husband to get home, Lily cancelled and rescheduled the rest of her appointments that afternoon. She knew it would be impossible to give herself entirely to her clients after the bombshell she'd had thrown at her. And she respected them and their time too much to see them when her head was not on straight.

Once her day was clear from all obligations, she made a pot of coffee. Michael arrived as she plunged the filter. Relief flooded his face when he saw that she was – physically, at least – in one piece. Shrugging his jacket off, he moved quickly to her side and took her in his arms. She allowed herself a moment to take solace from this embrace. Touch had always been their love language. Then she took his hand and led him to their kitchen table, pouring the coffee into two mugs.

How often had they sat in this spot to discuss their lives' essential and mundane moments? They held weekly diary scheduling sessions, they debated niggles over Ben missing a significant milestone – he sure took his time at walking – they worried about their budget as they discussed if they could afford a holiday. And, of course, they often spoke about their families too.

About Robert.

Well, once again, they were about to discuss him . . . but she was pretty sure Michael would never guess in what context.

'Okay, tell me what's going on,' Michael said once they'd both taken their first sip of coffee.

'I took a new client on recently. An American called Zach Brady.'

Michael raised his eyebrows in surprise. Lily never divulged information about her work.

'At our session this morning, Zach told me that he believes he is Robert.'

Lily watched Michael's face register shock, then surprise, then back to shock again as he whispered her words to himself.

'That face. That's how I felt,' Lily said, waving a finger in her husband's direction.

'How . . . w-what . . .' Michael stammered. His hand reached over to cup hers, the warmth steadying her, giving her the strength to continue.

'Zach said he watched Dad's interview on *Ireland A M*. And when he saw Robert's photograph, he couldn't believe his eyes. One sec.' She reached behind the countertop to retrieve the photographs Zach had given her earlier. 'These are of Zach when he was three years old.'

Michael's eyes darted between Robert's and Zach's baby photograph. 'They could be twins,' he acknowledged. He pointed to the age-progression photograph now. 'Does he look like this?'

'Nope. Not at all. Well, maybe the eyes. I honestly can't see the resemblance to the age-progression photo, but that might not mean anything because—'

'It can never be an accurate portrayal without both parents' photographs,' Michael interrupted. It was impossible to spend time with the Murphy family and not become an expert on missing children.

'Your father was right all along. He said the photographs and interviews would pay dividends,' Michael said in wonder.

Lily had shared the same thought earlier, but she still couldn't trust this information to be true. Discussing this possibility felt surreal, dreamlike.

'Zach said his mother met and married an American when he was five. He's close to his stepfather, and he has three younger sisters. He's on a temporary contract with his firm here in Ireland. It was pure chance that he saw that interview.'

They both took a sip of their coffee, their eyes locked.

'Where's his biological father?' Michael asked.

'He never had a relationship with him. His stepfather looked him up a few years ago and found out that he'd died.'

'Okay, but I'm still missing something here,' Michael said, his eyes narrowing as he looked at the photographs again. 'Why does he think he's Robert? Just because he looks like this? That sounds fishy to me.'

Lily frowned. Now that Michael was questioning it, she realised it seemed preposterous. But it wasn't only the photographs.

'He used to have an imaginary friend as a young child.' She exhaled deeply. 'He called her his other mother.'

Michael raked his hands through his hair and swore softly under his breath.

'I know. It's a lot,' Lily said.

'What does he want from you?' Michael's eyes narrowed. 'Did he ask for anything?'

Lily shook her head quickly. 'He looked stressed by it all too. He wanted to talk it through, but I asked him to leave. I couldn't handle him being here. I suppose I'll have to get in touch, once I've had a chance to think about it all.'

Michael stood up and grabbed a notebook and pen from a drawer on the kitchen island. Then he flipped open their laptop and switched it on. 'Right. I'd like to know more about what or who we are dealing with before we invite this Zach dude back into our home. Can you start by listing everything you know about this man? Let's regain some power and ensure he's been telling the truth about the basics. For all we know, this is some kind of shakedown. A scam to get money.'

Lily jumped up, her heart pounding. She had never been more grateful for her husband than she was right now. She knew he'd have a plan.

'I'll get his file. It has his address and date of birth in it,' Lily replied, sprinting to the office.

It took Michael only a few moments to find confirmation that Zach did work for the firm he'd given her. He was listed in their employee section. And his image was included in a recent fundraiser on their Instagram page. He'd cycled from Dublin to Wexford with twenty colleagues, who'd raised over fifty thousand euros for a children's charity. Lily took in his bright, wide smile as he posed for a photograph, sitting on his bike. And she fancied she could see a resemblance to her mother around his mouth and chin.

'Let's see if he's been tagged in any of the photos, then we can do a deeper dive into his online profile,' Michael said. He tapped away on the screen for a few minutes, then whooped when he found his personal account. He had 412 followers and followed 155 accounts, most of which were brand and sports-related accounts. They scrolled through his grid, clicking on each photograph. The most recent images were posted in June, with the caption 'June photo dump'. Ten shots, which included the charity cycle run, a night out in a bar and a barbecue at a friend's house.

'This feels intrusive,' Lily said, nibbling her bottom lip.

'You think he's not had a good look through all of your socials?' Michael muttered.

A shiver ran down Lily's spine. She remembered Zach mentioning Ben by name and how odd it had felt. Now she had never felt more vulnerable.

'Open that one.' Lily pointed to an image of Zach standing in the middle of three girls, his arms looping over their shoulders. 'I think that could be him with his sisters. He's the eldest of four.'

They both peered closely at the image as Michael zoomed in on it. They looked tanned and happy, standing before a grey lake beneath a blue cloudless sky.

'He looks more like them than me,' Lily said firmly.

'Hmm,' Michael replied. 'These two sisters are alike. And Zach has a similar colouring to this one. They do look like siblings, I suppose.' He turned and scrutinised Lily. 'There are similarities between you and Zach too. You have the same smile, chin . . .'

Damn it, Lily thought. Michael saw that too. Her stomach began to cramp in protest again. She decided to ignore her husband's comment. If Lily allowed herself to believe, to hope, that Zach was her brother . . . Her body trembled at what that might mean for her and her family.

'Location says this is Lake Champlain,' Michael added.

'Again, this rings true with what he's shared with me. His family lives in Westport, about an hour from New York. They are a boating family, always on the lake. Are there any photos of his parents?'

Michael moved the mouse again and stopped when he saw an image of Zach sitting around a fire pit beside an older woman and a man. The caption read simply, 'Good times with the folks.' His parents were both smiling as they looked in Zach's direction. The photograph captured him mid-story, both his hands gesturing, his face glowing with excitement as he spoke. A happy moment frozen forever.

'Zoom in again,' Lily whispered.

Zach's parents looked to be in their sixties. Lily could not take her eyes from the woman's face. She was tanned, with faint lines embedded around her eyes and mouth, and her ash-blonde hair was streaked with grey and worn loose to her shoulder. It framed a pretty face. Lily guessed that she'd been stunning when she was younger. The kind of beauty that could stop traffic. There was a kindness in her face. She looked normal, not like a crazy person who would snatch a child in the dead of night.

Michael moved on, and they spent over an hour clicking and zooming in on the family's online memories that were special enough for them to share with the world.

'He didn't lie about his background and family,' Michael said. 'I reckon we have to at least give him a chance to explain further.'

Lily's intuition told her that he was right. However, she couldn't shake the fear of the consequences that may follow.

'We also need to consider whether we should tell your mum and dad,' Michael added.

Lily's reaction was visceral and quick. 'No!' She steadied,

then continued, 'Not until we find out more. We cannot put them through another false alarm.'

'Fair enough. But I think you should give this Zach a call,' Michael said, pushing her mobile closer.

'Now?' Lily said, her voice little more than a high-pitched squeak.

'Ben is in the crèche, safe and sound. I'm here. I do not want this guy catching you off guard when I'm not around. So let's do it now. Call him and see if he'll return to talk now.'

NOW

July 2023

Lily

Phibsborough, Dublin

They sat at the kitchen table, Zach on one side, his eyes nervously darting from Lily to Michael, who were opposite, their shoulders almost touching. Lily's heart beat so fast that she was sure Zach could hear it from a few feet away.

'Thank you for seeing me again,' Zach said. 'I was scared I'd frightened you off, and you wouldn't call again.'

He'd arrived ten minutes after their call, admitting that he'd been in a nearby café for the past hour, hoping to hear from her.

'It's a pretty big bombshell you threw at Lily, bud,' Michael said evenly.

Zach licked his lips and then sipped his water. He was nervous, but so was Lily. It didn't mean he was doing anything wrong.

'I didn't know what to do,' Zach replied. 'I planned to say it to you at our first session, but I chickened out. It seemed ludicrous to say it out loud.'

'It felt pretty ludicrous to hear it,' Lily replied softly.

Michael picked up the age-progression flyer that Jason had produced. 'I'm still struggling with how you went from this photograph to deciding you are Robert.'

104

Zach nodded and licked his lips again. 'I can't explain it. But when I saw Robert's photograph, I knew it was me. In my gut.' He looked down to his stomach, then back to Lily and Michael.

Then his eyes moved to three large canvas prints that hung on the kitchen wall. In the centre was Lily and Michael on their wedding day, gazing into each other's eyes. On the left, Michael stood between his mum and dad. And, on the right, Lily stood between her parents, Kimberly and Jason.

'I told you I had an imaginary friend when I was a child,' Zach said. 'If you'd asked me to describe what she looked like, I would have struggled, because her face had become blurred and vague over the years.' His lips quivered as his eyes closed for a brief second.

Lily's mouth was dry, and she couldn't speak. Her eyes now locked on the family photograph too.

Zach raised his hand and pointed to Kimberly. 'But her face became clear again, when I saw this photograph. She looked exactly like her.'

Lily heard a gasp. Then she realised that it was she who'd emitted it.

Zach turned back to Lily and said, 'That's my other mother.'

Lily felt Michael's hand move towards hers and clasp it between his own. Her body trembled as Zach's words sunk in.

'Before you got here, we looked you up on Instagram,' Michael said evenly.

'I would assume nothing less,' Zach replied.

'I saw your family – your parents, your sisters, your work colleagues. There is a lot of information on social media, available within a few quick clicks of a mouse.'

Zach locked eyes with Michael. 'You think I looked up Lily's socials and am here for . . . for what exactly?'

'That's what I'd like to understand,' Michael said. 'What do you want from my wife?'

'Nothing. Everything. I don't know.' Zach placed his face in his hands and took a deep breath.

Lily's heart constricted, and she felt sympathy wash over her. He'd spoken about his gut and, right now, her gut told her that this man truly believed he was her brother. But that didn't mean he was right.

'I have a good family and a good life. I don't need money; I have a job that pays me more than I could ever spend. My parents are independently wealthy too. So, if you think I'm here for some kind of a shakedown, please know that is not what this is about.'

Michael's fingers drummed on the table in front of him. 'What do you remember about your early childhood?'

'Bits and pieces. I remember Spain, the sunshine, the hills, the people. We lived there for two years until Mom met and married my stepdad. However, most of my early memories are those from Westport in America.'

Spain. A trickle of sweat ran down Lily's back. She looked at Michael and saw that this had thrown him too.

'Where in Spain?' Michael asked.

'Ronda.'

Lily had never heard of it and raised an eyebrow in query.

'It's one of the most beautiful places in Andalusia. It sits atop the edge of a mountain. And locals say it's so high that it rains upwards. I spent a month there a few years ago, and birds flew beneath my feet as I leaned out over the El Tajo gorge.'

'Is your mother Spanish?' Lily asked, confused, because she was sure he'd said she was English.

A shake of his head. 'She moved to Spain from London when I was a baby.'

'Is your biological father English too?' Lily continued her probing.

'Yes.'

'But you never met him.' Lily re-stated.

'No, I didn't.'

'Why?' Michael asked.

'He was abusive to my mother. That's why we ended up in rural Spain. We were hiding from him.'

Hiding. The word hung in the air between them all. Lily couldn't help but wonder what else Zach's mother might be hiding. She felt as if she was looking at a giant, unmade jigsaw puzzle with half the pieces missing.

'And he's dead now,' Lily stated.

'Yes. 2015.'

'Cancer,' Lily said, remembering Zach telling her.

'Yep.'

They sat silently for a moment, each lost in their thoughts.

Lily thought about the woman sitting around the campfire, gazing at Zach so adoringly. 'Your mother. Is she a good woman?' Lily asked.

Zach's answer was immediate. 'The best.'

'Do you believe she would be capable of kidnapping a child? Because that's what you're accusing her of, if you truly believe you are Robert,' Lily said.

Zach winced. And tears glistened in his eyes. He inhaled deeply, then said, 'I cannot comprehend a world where my mother would cause pain to another human. She's an incredible mother. A good wife. A pillar of our community in Westport. To think she could live that life, knowing she'd taken me from your parents . . . it's unthinkable.'

'Yet you *do* think it,' Lily whispered.

Zach nodded.

'When did you move to Spain?' Michael asked.

'My mother told me she left my father and moved there in 1982.'

'Robert went missing in 1983,' Lily stated, and to her surprise, a stab of disappointment pierced her ribcage. This would mean that Zach couldn't be her brother.

Zach inhaled profoundly and looked from Michael to Lily. 'I know that doesn't add up. There's something else that is niggling me. It might be nothing but . . .'

'Go on,' Michael urged.

'Mom left my dad when I was six months old. I was born in

1981. And she brought me to Ronda in Spain, where we lived until Mom married Dom, and we relocated to America.'

Lily nodded along, committing the dates to her memory.

'I went back to Ronda a few years ago. And I visited the villa we'd rented as a baby. It's carved inside a huge gash in the mountains. Still owned by the same couple that rented it to my mother, Señor and Señora Alvarez.' He smiled wistfully. 'I had this romantic notion of tracing my early years. The couple remembered Mom and me.' His face softened at the memory. 'They said they babysat me when my mum went into town, shopping. And they had photographs of us all sitting on deckchairs in their back garden.' His smile disappeared and he frowned. 'They were the kind of photographs that always have the date imprinted on them.' He paused, and then finished. 'I remember thinking that it was weird that every photograph they had was taken in 1983 – nothing before that.'

Lily and Michael exchanged a worried glance.

Lily's head pounded as she took in Zach's words. She was beginning to understand why he had so many questions.

'Maybe they didn't have a camera until 1983. My parents have hardly any snaps of me and my brother when we were kids,' Michael said, with a shrug.

But Zach looked doubtful.

'Do you think your mother took you from my family in 1983 and created this whole story about your abusive father as a ruse to cover that . . .' Lily said, her jaw dropping open at the thought.

Zach's mouth quivered, and he looked so vulnerable as he turned to Lily. 'I feel like I'm losing my mind, Lily. And I'm asking you to help me. Please help me uncover the truth. Help me find out if my life has been a lie and I'm truly your brother.'

BEFORE

April 1976

Sally

Doddington Estate, Battersea Park Road, London

Sally tried to cling to sleep for a few more minutes. But the sound of a train trundling by nudged her awake. Her nose was numb, cold from the damp flat. And her stomach rumbled, reminding her that she'd gone to bed hungry the night before. She'd have cereal. She didn't have any milk, but she'd got used to hot water over her Ready Brek. And, if she closed her eyes, she could even trick herself into thinking that it was the same breakfast she'd had in the orphanage throughout her childhood.

In the distance, Sally heard the faint sound of a child's cry. The thumping of feet on the floor above her shook the ceiling, and a door slammed shut, followed by a man's voice reverberating through the walls. These sounds were not unusual, given that over seven thousand people lived in the blocks of council flats near Wandsworth railway station. However, despite the hustle and bustle of the surrounding environment, Sally had never felt so alone.

She climbed out of bed, putting her feet into her slippers before they hit the cold floor. How it felt damp despite being carpeted was a mystery. Sally pulled her dressing gown round herself. Was it her imagination, or did the belt cinch in tighter now? She made her way to the kitchen and put the kettle on. Sally retrieved a used teabag from a saucer and placed it in a mug. She'd been so excited on her first full day here, walking to the local grocer's to shop. She was a grown-up, in charge of what and when she ate, no longer at the beck and call of the staff in the orphanage. But that excitement disappeared as fast as her allowance did when she had to pay for a basket of groceries. As the kettle slowly began to heat up, Sally looked around. Mustard wallpaper and chequered blue-and-black tiles should have brightened up the tiny galley kitchen, but they only seemed to make the room darker. She'd washed the net curtains when she'd arrived, but that hadn't made a difference. Sally's stomach fell when she opened her kitchen cupboard and saw it was bare, save for the box of Ready Brek. She prepared breakfast and took it with her into the sitting room.

She sighed when she sat at the small dining-room table in the corner of the sitting room. This room wasn't much better than the kitchen. Lime-green wallpaper was beginning to peel above the brown wooden door. A damp patch stained the grey ceiling tiles. Sally avoided looking too closely at the murky brown shag-pile carpet. She glanced at the two-bar electric heater as she shivered in the cold morning air.

'No point hankering over something you can't have,' Sally said out loud, mimicking Sister Jones's soft Scottish brogue.

She blew on the hot cereal and took a mouthful. One day, she would have all the money she needed to live a life with every luxury she could ever want.

Loneliness hit her again as she thought about her old friend. If Elsie were here, they'd find a way to make this place a happier one. And if they were hungry, well, at least they wouldn't be alone. Sally turned her radio on, smiling when Cilla Black's voice filled the room. There was something comforting about *our Cilla*.

She'd not seen *Top of the Pops* since she'd moved in here. The flat had minimal furniture, and luxuries like a television were not included. The radio had been a lucky and much-needed find in the local charity shop, along with the bed linen for her bed.

She washed up once she'd finished her food, trying to bite down another wave of emotion as she saw her single spoon, bowl and mug sitting on the draining board.

She decided it was too cold to shower, so she did a quick top and tail in the bathroom, which was another dark room with an avocado suite and a black-and-white linoleum tiled floor. A single tear escaped her and trailed down her cheek. Sally had never felt so low in her entire life. And she'd had some bleak moments in her eighteen years.

Then she heard Sister Jones's voice again, reprimanding her for feeling sorry for herself. She dressed and decided that today was the day she'd find a job.

She'd long since given up the dream of finding a position in a hair salon. Her first week here, Sally had spent hours poring through the Yellow Pages directory to list the hair salons in the general area, then visiting them one by one, only to be refused a job even to sweep floors, never mind train as a stylist.

Today, Sally decided to go back to every business within walking distance, in the hope that a position may have opened up since the last time she'd tried. Four hours later, as she made her way over the concrete walkway back to the tower block of flats, dread made her legs move at half speed. She'd called into every shop within a four-mile radius. Most took one look at her and said no. Others muttered various excuses when she begged for a chance.

She was too young.

They needed someone with more experience.

They didn't need any staff. This was from a shop that had a sign in the window stating it had vacancies.

Sally slowed down as she approached the bins outside the block of flats. A sickening feeling crept over her as she drew closer, but she pressed on, because she hoped there might be food in one of them. She heard a rustle, and jumped back with a start when a massive black rat darted its way out from behind the bin, pausing to look at her with mournful eyes, before scurrying off into the alleyway.

'Things that bad, treacle?' a voice called out from behind her.

Sally felt a shiver run down her entire body. She knew that voice. Could it be? She turned round slowly and blinked three times to ensure she wasn't imagining the person standing a few feet away, watching her.

'Elsie,' Sally cried out, her voice cracking with emotion. Then she felt shame rise through her body. Her friend had witnessed how low she'd allowed herself to go. She stepped away from the bins, trying to regain her composure.

'It's good to see you,' Elsie said warmly, her eyes taking in Sally's dishevelled appearance.

Sally wanted to run into her arms and feel her warm embrace of comfort. But she felt anger nip at her, rooting her to the ground.

'You stopped writing,' she eventually accused, feeling her bottom lip wobble, betraying her emotion.

Elsie nodded. 'I know. I'm sorry. But I'm glad to see you now.' She paused, looking to the bins again, then back to Sally. 'You look hungry.' Her voice was full of concern.

'I'm fine,' Sally lied. She wasn't sure why, but she didn't want to show weakness to Elsie. She might have thought they were as close as sisters once upon a time, but sisters wouldn't abandon each other.

Another damning thought snaked its way into her mind.

Mothers were not supposed to do that either. But look what had happened there.

'I knew you'd have left Sunshine House by now. So I've been keeping an eye out for you, in case Burton placed you in these flats too,' Elsie said.

And Sally felt a glimmer of hope return. Maybe Elsie still cared, after all.

'You look good,' Sally said, taking in her friend properly. Elsie's mousy-brown hair now fell to her shoulders in soft waves.

Her skin was still pale, with a dusting of freckles across the bridge of her nose. She wore a navy jumper over bell-bottomed jeans. Elsie was attractive rather than beautiful, but she still had an air of confidence that could sometimes intimidate Sally.

'I'm in number eighteen, at the end of the fourth-floor landing. Come over in ten minutes for something to eat,' Elsie said.

It wasn't an invitation but a firm direction. With that, Elsie turned and walked away, leaving Sally feeling shell-shocked and uncertain in her wake. Where had Elsie been for the past three years? And, now she was back, was she here to stay?

BEFORE

April 1976

Sally

Doddington Estate, Battersea Park Road, London

'It's nothing fancy, but it'll fill ya up all the same,' Elsie said, placing a bowl of steaming hot vegetable soup before Sally. 'Go on. Dig in, and don't be shy.'

Sally didn't wait to be told twice. She blew on her spoon, but was too impatient to let the liquid cool down. It was too hot, but so good.

'Best soup I've had,' Sally gushed as she dived in for a second spoonful.

'Not sure that's true, but when you're Hank Marvin everything tastes good.'

Elsie buttered two slices of bread with margarine, opened a tin of spam and cut a thick slice off, placing it between the bread. 'Here. Have this too. And slow down, treacle. There's no rush.'

'Did you make this?' Sally asked.

Elsie nodded. 'If you go down to the Co-op in the evenings, they reduce all the fresh produce to half price. I grab whatever vegetables they have, throw them in a pot with a stock cube, and Bob's your uncle. That's dinner for a couple of days.'

'I'll try that too. Thanks for the tip,' Sally said.

She felt nostalgia hit her as she remembered hundreds of

bowls of soup eaten in the dining room at the orphanage. She'd not appreciated the hot meals she'd always had in front of her back then.

'Do you miss Sunshine House?' Sally asked. She wanted to ask her friend so many questions, but, more than anything, Sally needed to know why Elsie had disappeared from her life. For now, though, she decided to stick with the easy ones.

Elsie cut her sandwich in half and dunked a piece into her soup. Her brow furrowed for a moment. 'I never thought I'd say this, but I missed the food. And I missed you, Sally.'

Sally reached down and pinched her thigh. She felt like she was dreaming, sitting here with Elsie again. Elsie cocked her head to one side as if waiting for a difficult question. But Sally couldn't find the words, and the moment passed.

'How you coping out here?' Elsie asked, nodding towards the world outside their flats.

'It's not what I thought it would be like when I left the home.' Sally admitted.

'Never is. Bet you thought you'd be the bee's knees, living it large in the big bad world. But instead, you're skulking around bins, looking for scraps.' Elsie said, not unkindly.

'I've almost run out of money.' Sally admitted in a small voice, realising there was little point in bravado.

Elsie nodded in sympathy. 'I remember that feeling. It took me less than a week to run out of cash when I arrived here. You're barking up the wrong tree if you think I can help you with that. I barely have enough to make ends meet myself,' Elsie said. 'But I won't see you hungry. I promise you that.'

Sally quickly raised her hands. 'You've done more than enough with this. I'm not begging, I swear. I want to work, but nobody wants me. I thought I had a shot in a hardware shop earlier today in Wandsworth – until they asked me my address.'

Elsie rolled her eyes. 'Nobody wants the residents of the Battersea slums.'

'I've been to the dole office and filled out an application for unemployment benefit. But it will be a couple of weeks before it comes through. I don't know what to do.' Sally whispered. 'Should I call Mrs Burton?'

Elsie snorted, 'There's no point doing that, Treacle. Once she dropped you here, that's her job done. Now the rest is up to you.' She looked Sally up and down. 'Have you ever thought about cleaning?'

'We all had jobs in the orphanage. I know how to mop a floor.'

'I'm not promising anything, but I'll see if I can get you a few shifts with my cleaning crew. One of the girls is pregnant and went into labour last night. With a bit of luck, they won't have replaced her yet. Fair warning: money is a pittance. And it's back-breaking, all-night work.'

Sally felt her heart flutter as hope danced its way around her. 'I don't mind that. I'll happily do it.' She placed her spoon in the empty bowl and licked her lips. 'That's the first time I've felt full in weeks.'

Elsie smiled. 'I'm glad of that. And I promise you won't be hungry at least, not with me around.'

Sally smiled shyly and found the courage to ask, 'Elsie, why did you stop writing?'

Elsie sighed and looked out of the flat window, avoiding eye contact. 'It's a long and sorry story that maybe I'll tell you one day. I suppose the easiest way to explain it is that things got dark for me for a while. And you're a pure bright white light, Sally. Always have been. I had to step back, so I didn't spread my darkness to you. But I never stopped thinking about you. And I'm happy to see you today. Truly.'

Sally's eyes glistened, thinking about the possible hardships her friend had encountered without her. She reached over and squeezed her friend's hand, and for a moment they sat there, looking at each other happily.

'Right, you need to get some rest. Me too. Then meet me here at six this evening. I'll have something ready for us both before I bring you to meet my gaffer. Cyril's all right, as it goes.'

A few hours later, after a supper of Fray Bentos steak-and-kidney pie in a tin, served with a large scoop of Smash potato, Sally and Elsie walked into a tall office block. A stocky man operated a floor cleaner, moving it slowly in circular movements over the marbled floor. He nodded a hello at Elsie, who waved back. Sally's eyes took in the plush building. She'd never been anywhere like this before. As she passed the glossy receptionist's desk, Sally glanced at Elsie, her heart sinking a little. Elsie had always dreamed of taking her secretarial exams once she'd left school.

'It wasn't meant to be like this, I know,' Elsie said, reading Sally's mind, 'but no point dwelling on that.'

Elsie moved through double grey doors and then took a right into a long corridor. They passed a men's and a ladies' toilets, then Elsie opened another door, that led into a small room with lockers on one wall and cupboards and shelves filled with cleaning products on the other. Three women were putting on light-grey overalls over their clothes. They glanced at Sally with interest as they said hello to Elsie.

'Where's the gaffer?' Elsie asked.

'Ask, and he shall appear,' a small round man replied as he walked into the room. He removed his glasses and began cleaning them with the edge of his shirt, which had come untucked from his brown trousers.

'Hey, Cyril,' Elsie said, moving closer. 'Have you got a replacement yet for Mary?'

'The agency is to send someone over next week,' Cyril said, looking over Elsie's shoulder at Sally, who nervously bit her lip as he took her in.

'I've saved them the bother. Sally is here, ready to start now.'

'That's not how this works, Elsie,' Cyril said, putting his glasses back on, pulling a packet of Embassy cigarettes from his shirt pocket, and tapping one out.

'I know. But she's a tough one – a hard worker – and ready to do a shift on trial. If you like what she does, you pay her. If you don't, she'll go home, no questions asked.'

'Can't say fairer than that gaffer,' one of the women called out as she filled a steel mop bucket with water.

Cyril moved closer to Sally and walked around her, inspecting her like a piece of meat in a market. 'Scrawny. I've seen more fat on a stray cat.'

'I'm strong, sir,' Sally said. She guessed the man would like to be addressed formally, and she was right. His gratified expression suggested that he liked the respect.

'You can start with the toilets. Mind you, I want to eat my dinner off the floors,' Cyril told Sally.

'Thank you, sir,' she quickly said, half curtseying to him, making him laugh out loud.

Elsie sorted her out with an overall, and they both buttoned their uniforms over their clothes. Then, with her own bucket, mop and a plastic basket of cleaning products, Elsie ushered her into the men's toilet and left her there.

The smell hit her first of all. The stench of urine made her gag. But she didn't have time for that. She had a job to do. One hour later, she had bleached and scrubbed every cubicle and urinal and washed down the sinks, skirtings and mirrors before mopping the tiled floor. Cyril poked his head in several times, but didn't say a word to her. She wasn't sure if that was a good or a bad sign. Once Sally determined she couldn't do any more, she moved to the ladies' toilet and did the same again. She had a moment of satisfaction when she'd completed the second room, which was dashed when Elsie told her that she had to repeat the same thing on every floor of the office block. Twenty floors in total.

At the end of her shift, a little after four thirty in the morning, she returned to the cleaning room. There, she found Elsie sitting on a bench, rubbing her feet, beside the other three cleaning ladies – Carys, Sandra and Noreen – who'd introduced themselves at their tea break at midnight.

'You look done in, treacle,' Elsie said in sympathy, taking in Sally's flushed and sweating face.

Sally's shoulders ached as muscles that had never been used before complained. 'I'm okay.'

Cyril walked in, a cigarette dangling from his lips, and walked over to Sally. 'We'll make a charwoman of you yet. You did well tonight.'

Sally's pains disappeared at that compliment. 'Do I get the job?'

Cyril regarded her for a moment. 'What age are you?'

'Eighteen.'

He shook his head with a deep sigh. 'I've a daughter a year younger than you.' He looked over to Elsie and back again to Sally. 'Five nights a week, Monday to Friday. Seven thirty p.m. on the button. If you're late, you get one strike. Two strikes, you're out. Eight pounds per shift. You can start Monday.'

'Thank you,' Sally said, relief making her shoulders sag.

Cyril reached into his jacket's inside pocket, pulled out four envelopes, and then handed one to Elsie, Carys, Sandra and Noreen. 'Right, let's lock up and get out of here. Thank Christ it's the weekend.'

Elsie stood up and placed her hands on her hips as she regarded Cyril. 'Aren't you forgetting something? Sally worked hard tonight. So she'll need paying. Cash.'

'Don't push it, Elsie.' His voice hardened in warning. 'Like the rest of them, you're a charlady, not a gaffer. You don't tell me what to do.'

Carys, Sandra and Noreen busied themselves at the lockers, pulling on their coats, then walking out with their heads down. Sally got it. They didn't want to get involved in any trouble. And she didn't want Elsie to get into strife either, not on her behalf.

'It's fine,' Sally whispered to her.

Elsie ignored her and moved closer to Cyril. 'I mean no disrespect, but you'd want your daughter to be treated fairly, wouldn't you?' Her voice softened. 'Please, gaffer. It's the weekend, and she hasn't a bob to her name.'

Cyril sighed and pulled a five-pound note from his wallet. 'This is all you're getting. So don't ask for a penny more. Don't make me regret being this generous.'

Elsie's response was to rush over to Cyril and kiss him loudly on his cheek.

'Get off me, woman,' he complained, but a big smile broke out over his face.

As they walked the two miles home, arm in arm, while Sally was exhausted, she could not stop grinning. She'd found a job, had enough money to buy some groceries and, more important than anything else, she had found her best friend again.

THEN

July 1983

Kimberly

The Guardia Civil, Barcelona, Spain

'The posters you've been distributing and the media we've already had in the Spanish local and national press have brought forward another set of leads,' Inspector Ortega said.

'What are they?' Jason interrupted, his face alight with excitement.

Ortega held his hand up. 'We are working our way through them. Rest assured, we will make sure everything is followed up. Now is the time to amplify. I've arranged for a press conference in one hour. Kimberly, we need you to make a televised plea for Robert.'

Kimberly gagged, her reaction visceral and raw. 'I can't.'

Kimberly felt Jason's hand reach over and touch her back, but she shrugged it off. She felt too warm, and his hand felt like a red-hot poker.

'Can I do it on my own?' Jason asked, casting a worried look in Kimberly's direction. 'I don't think my wife is up to it.'

Inspector Ortega inched his chair towards Kimberly. 'Both parents must be at the press conference. I will be there too. You will only have to make a statement, which our team will help you prepare now. I'll handle all questions.'

Kimberly's stomach flipped at the thought of speaking publicly in front of cameras. She'd always shied away from the limelight and didn't do well in large groups. When she joined the local mother and toddler group with Robert two years ago, she'd only managed one visit. As soon as the mothers began questioning her about her life, she felt panicky and under a too-bright spotlight.

'I don't mind answering questions,' Jason said. 'I have nothing to hide.'

An edge had crept into his voice as he said that. A couple of media reports had speculated about his relationship with Robert, questioning his love for his stepson.

'Very well, but we need Kimberly too,' Ortega insisted.

Kimberly's mind raced as she contemplated doing this. The more she thought about it, being on display, the whole world watching her, the more her body trembled and shook. She felt nausea rise through her in waves until she had no choice but to bolt for a bathroom, where she was violently ill.

An hour later, with Kimberly still unable to stop retching, it was conceded that the interview would go ahead without her. Inspector Ortega and Jason sat on a platform about five or six inches high in front of a desk. Several TV crews were filming, with a dozen photographers and at least thirty press, their Dictaphones and microphones pointed towards them. As soon as they walked out, the cameras began flashing, paps snapping.

Inspector Ortega began by addressing the room and sharing the rules of engagement. He'd make a short statement, followed by a statement from Jason, and then he would answer any questions.

Kimberly knew that Ortega was disappointed in her. He'd insisted that it was crucial for the public to see Kimberly's pain at the press conference. But she knew Ortega and her husband could never understand why she couldn't endure it.

'And now I'll ask you all to be respectful and remain quiet as Mr Murphy addresses the room,' Inspector Ortega said. He turned to Jason and nodded.

Jason picked up her handwritten statement and began to read, keeping his eyes down. The room became deathly quiet, with the only sound the occasional click of a camera lens. He cleared his throat, took a sip from his water and looked to his left, towards Kimberly. She wasn't sure he would be able to continue, and she felt a further flash of pain, seeing the agony that was evident on her husband's face.

This wasn't fair to anyone, but Jason had it worse than the lot of them. He was dealing with so much more than a missing child. She closed her eyes momentarily and thought of her little boy in her arms as she read a story to him. And she knew she had to continue being brave and get through these next moments without causing further scenes.

'Hello. My name is Jason Murphy. I am Robert's daddy. Kimberly wanted to speak to you all too, but she's too upset, so she has asked me to do this on our behalf. He is two and a half years old, with blond curls just like his mum. He has her blue eyes too, but they look grey sometimes. He is such a smart little boy – quiet and thoughtful, but he has a mischievous side too. He had so much fun in the swimming pool every day, splashing us all.'

Kimberly heard a ripple of quiet laughter in the room. Glancing towards the audience, she saw faces looking at her husband in sympathy. She felt their support, that they wanted to help her family find her son.

Kevin continued, 'I'd like to thank Inspector Ortega and the crew on *Carousel*, who helped search for Robert. And I want to plead with you all, anyone with information, *anything*, no matter how small the detail, to please come forward. Help us bring our little boy back to where he belongs.' Jason licked his lips and breathed in deeply. 'We have such a happy family. Robert sleeps in the room next door to mine and Kimberly's, which he shares with his sister. He adores her. He only has to make a face, and Lily starts to giggle. Hearing them both laugh together is my favourite sound in the world. I wish I had a recording of it. I'd play it for you. It's special . . .' Jason broke off as a sob caught up with him. Cameras flashed again, and Kimberly saw the TV cameras zoom in closer to him. 'Kimberly has asked me to say this. To whoever has Robert, I'm begging you, please bring him back to us. His only memories are of her – his loving mama – and Lily and me. He loves us all, as we love him. And keeping us from each other is cruel.'

Inspector Ortega handed Jason a tissue. Kimberly wanted desperately to go to her husband and comfort him, but she couldn't move, the cameras terrifying her.

Jason looked up and directly faced the camera lens. 'Please. I beg of you. Please. I'm not asking you to bring Robert back for me. I know you don't owe us anything. But do it for our son. Do it for that little boy who must miss us all so much. I can't bear to think how confused he must be . . . Please, please bring him back, I beg of you . . .'

Jason couldn't continue any further. His heart was now laid bare, wide open for everyone to see.

Journalists began to shout questions. Inspector Ortega leaned in and whispered something to Jason, who nodded, keeping his head down as he wiped tears from his face. Then Jason got up and walked out of the packed room with his head low.

'We can all see how difficult this has been for Jason and the Murphy family,' Inspector Ortega shouted over the din. 'I'll take questions now. Yes, you in the front row . . .'

As Jason reached Kimberly's side, she extended her arms to hold him, and he did the same, holding her tight. For days, they had pushed each other away, believing they didn't deserve solace from anyone. But now they clung to each other like a life raft while they struggled to keep their heads above water. Kimberly wasn't sure they could survive this, but for now all they could do was try not to drown . . .

THEN

July 1983

Kimberly

Hotel Miramar, Barcelona, Spain

As soon as she returned to the hotel after the press conference, Kimberly felt a shift in people's moods. Their faces changed from suspicious to sympathetic. Strangers would call out their support, offer their love and tell her that Robert was in their prayers.

And that helped.

Over the next forty-eight hours, Jason's interview was shared on all Spanish TV channels, but then disappeared from the headlines as new stories unfolded worldwide.

There were some further leads, with sightings of Robert in Alicante, seen in the arms of a dark-haired man, crying and distressed. A false alarm. Then, several sightings of a young blond boy in Barcelona matched Robert's description. It was a rollercoaster as hope soared and fell; a lead was investigated each time, and it came to nothing.

Kimberly folded Lily's clothes that she'd had laundered by the hotel into neat piles in the chest of drawers. Lily sat on a mat in front of the window, playing with a Fisher Price toy. A rap on the door made them both start. Kimberly opened it to Kevin, who stood with a newspaper in his hand.

'I thought you were with Jason,' she said to her father-in-law as he walked in.

'He's talking to a journalist from a local radio station in the lobby. Do you have a minute to chat?'

'Sure,' Kimberly said. They took a seat beside each other on the edge of the bed.

'How are you?' Kevin asked.

'Okay.'

'Jason says you've not been sleeping.'

Kimberly shrugged her shoulders. 'It's hard to switch off.'

'I get that. For me too. Would you take one of your sleeping pills?'

Kimberly looked at Kevin sharply. Was he giving a dig? No, she didn't think so. She only saw concern on his face.

'I'll never take one of those ever again,' Kimberly said flatly.

'Have you seen today's newspapers?' Kevin asked. He had an Irish tabloid in his hands.

Kimberly shook her head. 'I don't read the papers. It's too hard to relive it constantly. Jason tells me if there's anything I need to know.'

Kevin nodded, then flicked open the pages until he came to a two-page spread with several zoomed-in photographs of Kimberly and Jason in the lobby of the hotel, and of Jason at the press conference.

'This paper paid a body-language expert to review footage of you both,' Kevin said. His tone was cold, and Kimberly's heart began to accelerate.

'Jason does not come off well.' Kevin pointed to the first image, which zoomed in on Jason's face. His jaw was clenched, his lips tight and thin. Kevin read a few lines from the article: *'The tightened lips and clenched jaw is often an indicator of anger and annoyance.'*

Kimberly felt a flash of fear run down her spine. Kevin pointed to a series of photographs that captured Jason placing his hand on Kimberly's back and her shrugging it off. Kevin continued to read: '*In these photo sequences, we see Kimberly is hunched forward, which is often an indicator of great anxiety. Although her face is half covered with large sunglasses, and a sunhat, when Jason places a hand on her back, she clearly winces. And her head drops downward. Which could be a sign of fear. When she shrugs her husband's hand off, once again, Jason's lips compress, and his jaw tightens. Another sign of anger.*'

'This is n-nonsense,' Kimberly stuttered.

Further photographs were zoomed in at the most unflattering moments for Jason. She hardly recognised her husband in the stills shared.

Kevin continued to read from the newspaper, his voice clipped.

'*From a nonverbal perspective, there are questions about how the parents have acted. Kimberly seems extremely subdued. She covers her face, never showing her eyes, which indicates that she is wearing a mask. Why? Jason is in pain, but also appears frustrated, which you can see from his clenched jaw and the curl of his lips as they compress. He's defensive. He could be innocent and feel attacked, which is why he's defensive. But he could also be guilty and trying to cover it up.*'

Once he'd finished reading, Kevin dropped the paper between them on the bed as if it were on fire.

'I don't understand,' Kimberly began, feeling confused by the comments. 'I'm not scared of Jason. He's a gentle and kind man.'

Kevin nodded. 'They want a villain. And they've decided that it's my boy. But I won't have it. You and I know that he has done nothing wrong here.' His eyes flashed, and Kimberly felt his hostility move towards her.

'You sound angry with me, Kevin. I've not done anything wrong here either.'

Kevin watched her closely and nodded slowly. 'You need to think about when you will return to Dublin.'

Kimberly was surprised by the change in subject. 'We can't go yet. What if Robert is returned to us?'

Kevin scoffed. 'Do you believe whoever has him will bring

him back? There's been no ransom . . . We have to accept the possibility that we may never find out where he is or what's happened to him.'

'Why would you say that?' Kimberly said, her voice raising. 'Inspector Ortega said Jason's plea could bring the abductor forward.'

'If they were going to do that, they would have by now,' Kevin said sadly. 'It's time to go home. If we stay here, I'm worried that the Spanish police will try to stick this on Jason.'

Kimberly felt as if she'd been given an electric shock.

'Do you think Jason had anything to do with Robert's disappearance?' Kevin pushed further.

'No!' Kimberly replied instantly.

Kevin visibly sagged beside her. 'I needed to hear you say that out loud. Thank you.' He reached over and clasped her hands between his own. 'Will you talk to Jason? Persuade him that it's time to go home. The business is beginning to suffer. A tenant has complained about a leak in his bathroom, and another has given his notice to leave. Mortgages still have to be paid. Life has to continue on.'

Kimberly felt the room shrink around her; the air became dense, and she took several rasping breaths.

'Kimberly? Are you okay?' Kevin asked, his forehead now furrowed and creased.

Kimberly shook her head. She needed to escape, to leave this hotel where she'd spent days doing nothing but waiting for the phone to ring.

'Can you watch Lily? I need to go out, to think.'

Kimberly wasn't even sure where she was going. She pulled her sunhat and sunglasses down low, and sneaked out of the hotel, careful not to let Jason see her. He was still deep in conversation with the journalist, waving his arms around as he made whatever point he was saying.

Kimberly walked along the narrow, cobbled Spanish streets. She passed a lady selling flowers from a basket, and an ice-cream cart, with kids gathered around, waving their money to buy a Cornetto. She kept going until she found herself at Portside, at the water's edge, looking out to a cruise ship that sat in the harbour.

The *Carousel* had long gone, but another group of tourists had arrived on another liner. Carefree, cameras hanging round their necks, faces sun-kissed and sunburnt as they explored.

Kimberly closed her eyes and remembered their first port call in Villefrance. Robert was on Jason's shoulders, Lily in her pram, and the four of them were happy, safe and carefree, unaware that they were days away from this nightmare.

She damned herself for ever agreeing to go on this trip. They should have stayed at home in Ireland. Safe. Hidden from danger.

'I wondered where you were heading,' a voice said, interrupting her thoughts.

Kimberly whipped round to find Inspector Ortega standing behind her, watching her quizzically.

'You followed me?'

'I saw you leave the hotel. I was on my way to speak to you as it happens. You walk fast, Kimberly.'

'What do you want?' She was irritated by his presence. What good was he to her? He couldn't bring Robert back to them.

Ortega gestured towards an empty bench a few hundred feet away. She fell into step beside him, and they both took a seat.

'Do you mind?' Inspector Ortega asked, pulling out his cigarettes.

Kimberly shook her head, then surprised herself by asking, 'Can I have one?'

'I didn't know you smoked,' he replied as he passed her a cigarette, then flicked his lighter on to light it for her.

Kimberly inhaled her first drag, closing her eyes to savour the nicotine. 'I don't. But I had a boyfriend once who did. I used to have the odd one with him,' she answered eventually. 'Thank you.'

They sat silently for a moment as they smoked, watching the tourists move back and forth to and from the cruise ship.

'How are you coping?' Ortega asked.

'I honestly feel like I'm hanging on by a thread.'

'And Jason?'

Kimberly thought about that for a moment. 'You'd need to ask him. I've barely spoken to him in days. He's out searching for Robert practically twenty-four hours a day.'

'Yes. I can see that he's become a little obsessed, even manic. Has he changed?'

'I don't understand the question,' Kimberly said. 'From what?'

'From the man you married? Is this behaviour normal for him?'

'I don't know. We've never had a child taken from us before. He's trying to cope with this like I am.'

Ortega gave a Gallic shrug. 'His actions are interesting to me. This over-the-top and zealous need to search.'

'Surely that's normal for any parent?' Kimberly replied with a frown. Over the past couple of days, she'd seen a new side to Jason – one that was relentless in his need to find Robert. And Kimberly had realised that she didn't know her husband at all.

'Yes, I believe all parents would search the earth for their child. But Jason's behaviour feels almost deranged. Perhaps it's his need to divert attention from the fact that Robert died on the ship.' Ortega's voice was ice cold as he uttered his damning words.

'Jason could never hurt Robert. I told you that already.'

Ortega's eyes narrowed, and his voice dropped until it was almost a gentle caress. 'I believe that you believe that, but something doesn't add up for me.' He paused, then said, 'I think you're scared.'

Kimberly's stomach plummeted at his words.

'Of course I am. I'm terrified you won't find Robert. That he's hurt. That he needs us, and we can't get to him.'

'Maybe,' Inspector Ortega said, but she could see he didn't believe that. 'I have an alternative scenario to put to you.'

'Go on, then. Tell me,' Kimberly said, biting her lip until she felt blood.

'I think you are afraid of Jason. That you suspect he did something wrong.'

Kimberly's mind raced. Her only thought was of Lily back at the hotel. She was safe with Kevin. But then a wild thought snaked its way into her mind. What if Jason took Lily from her? It was clear that Kevin blamed Kimberly for this situation. She could see it in his eyes when he regarded her. Had he turned her husband against her? What if Jason and Kevin were packing their bags right now, ready to leave?

'I want to get back to the hotel. To Lily,' Kimberly said, standing up to leave.

Ortega grabbed her arm, stopping her. 'I want to show you something.'

She flopped back down to the bench.

Ortega reached into his linen jacket pocket and pulled out a photograph. 'We asked everyone on board the *Carousel* to hand over their cameras, and had their photographs developed at our station. This one interests me.'

It was of their family, the day that Robert went missing. He was in her arms, crying, and Jason had Lily in his. His dark eyebrows were knitted together as he glared at Kimberly and Robert.

'You know what I see when I look at this image?' Inspector Ortega said.

Kimberly shook her head, unable to speak.

'I see a woman who is afraid, but also bravely protecting her child.'

Kimberly remembered how she'd felt that day. And she couldn't deny Inspector Ortega's words.

'It's my fault . . .' Kimberly whispered, her eyes never leaving the image of Robert. 'I knew something bad was going to happen. I should have taken the children and run that day.'

Ortega touched her arm again. 'We can help you. I can keep you and Lily safe.'

Kimberly stood up, shaking his hand off her arm. 'I need to

get back to Lily. Thank you, Inspector Ortega, sincerely thank you. But I need to go now.'

'Remember, you can trust me, Kimberly . . .' his voice called out to her.

Kimberly ran back through the streets, all the while thinking of Lily. Sweat dripped down her spine and stained her T-shirt under her arms. She ignored the warm well-wishes of an Irish couple staying in the hotel who had been kind to the family during the week. She pushed the button in the lift and saw it was on an upper floor. The need to see her daughter was overwhelming; she couldn't wait, so she ran to the stairwell and climbed the two floors, her body protesting the assault on her lungs.

When she got to their room, she pounded on the door, praying to a God she wasn't sure she even believed in any more that her baby girl was safe in the room.

Her father-in-law opened the door, but she pushed past him to the bedroom, where she found Lily in Jason's arms.

'Give her to me,' she demanded, tears mixing with her sweat, stinging her eyes.

'What happened?' Kevin demanded from behind her.

'I saw Ortega,' Kimberly said. Then she turned to her husband. 'You were right. He does think you killed Robert.'

Kevin sank to the bed beside his son, a look of horror on his face. He placed a hand on Jason's shoulder. 'It will be okay,' he said, but his face was drawn and grey with worry.

'Do you have the number of that lawyer that the embassy recommended?' Kimberly asked Kevin as she cradled Lily in her arms.

'Yes, I've got his number,' Kevin replied.

'Call him. Find out if there's any reason why we have to stay here. Because, unless they won't let us leave, we have to go back home to Ireland.'

NOW

August 2023

Lily

Phibsborough, Dublin

The rest of the week went by in a blur. Work became a blessing because Lily could forget about Zach when she was with her clients. Or should she say Robert. It was so confusing. After their chat on Wednesday afternoon, she decided two things. One, she liked him. And, two, she believed he was genuine in his belief that he was her brother. So Lily promised him that she would help him discover the truth.

It was Michael who said out loud what they were all thinking. The only way to prove or disprove Zach's theory was to initiate a DNA test. Michael offered to research how to move this plan forward. There were many online options for testing, but Lily felt uncomfortable about that route. After a few phone calls, Michael found a clinic in Dublin they were both happy with. Michael made an appointment for them the following Monday afternoon.

Since then, Lily and Michael had done little else but discuss their next steps. Should they tell Kimberly and Jason? Or wait until the DNA results came in? Both had pros and cons, and neither of them could make a decision.

So Lily decided to visit the one person she trusted as much as her husband. Her grandfather Kevin. Or Gaga as she called him. He lived in a retirement village outside Dublin in the foothills of the Wicklow mountains. Over the past ten years, Gaga had found it increasingly difficult to cope on his own. He was eighty-nine years old. But, in typical Gaga fashion, he had done something about it. He sold his home and bought a two-bedroom bungalow in a gated community that gave him – and his family – the comfort of knowing he was looked after. With twenty-four-hour CCTV and a twenty-four-hour nurse call system, he was safe. But he also had freedom in his bungalow, with all the modern bells and whistles he needed for independent living.

Leaving Ben with Michael, Lily drove to her grandfather's house, where they planned to have dinner together. It was a bright summer evening, and Lily found Gaga watering his window boxes, draped with bright peonies in every rainbow colour.

'How do you get them like that?' Lily said, walking up behind him. 'My baskets at the front door are pitiful in comparison.'

'Pasta water,' Gaga said, putting down his watering can and turning to give Lily a warm hug. 'Next time you make pasta for dinner, keep the strained water and pour it on your flowers. It's full of vitamins and minerals to nourish them – trust me. And free!'

'I'll remember that.' Lily linked arms with her Gaga, and they walked into the bungalow. 'Does that mean we're having your famous pasta bake for dinner?' Lily asked hopefully.

'It sure does. Chorizo, tomato, onion and lots of cheese. It will be ready in forty-five minutes. I've a bottle of Tempranillo breathing out on the patio. Let's have a glass while we wait for the bake to finish.'

'One small glass for me, Gaga. I need to drive home today.'

'I miss the days when you could have a couple of drinks and not worry about the Gardaí pulling you over and bagging you.'

Lily decided to avoid debating the dangers of drunk driving. She'd leave that for another day. She sniffed the proffered glass of red appreciatively. Gaga always bought good wine. Lily took a sip and savoured the plum and blackcurrant notes that danced in her mouth.

'Why don't you cut straight to the chase and tell me what's wrong?' Gaga said.

Lily raised an eyebrow at him. 'What are you, a mind reader?'

'You always visit with Michael and Ben. If you come alone, it usually means you've got something on your mind that needs mulling over.' He pinched the bridge of his nose and asked quietly, 'Is it Jason? Has he gone a bit funny after that TV interview?'

It was a fair question. Lily's dad had form. The highs of the possibility of a breakthrough typically led to a spectacular low when things got quiet again.

'Yes and no,' Lily replied. She'd rehearsed what to say to Gaga all the way over on the drive. But nothing felt right. How did you tell someone news as big as this? 'A man has come forward claiming to be Robert.'

Her grandad's face blanched and his hand shook, sending droplets of red wine falling onto his white T-shirt. He placed his wine glass on the table and said in a voice strained with emotion, 'Tell me everything.'

Lily went through the past few days' events with him, sparing no detail. Her granddad listened without interruption, nodding along as she spoke.

'Are you okay, Gaga?' she asked in concern when she'd finished bringing him up to speed.

He raised his glass of wine to his lips. He took a sip, then put the glass down. 'I never thought we'd see this day.'

'Me neither,' Lily answered. 'We don't know that it's even him . . .'

'But you think it is,' her grandad stated. 'I can see it in your face when you say his name.'

Lily was surprised that he said that, because she wasn't sure she knew what she thought. Most of the time she felt sick with fear when she thought about Zach.

'You came here to know whether you should tell Kimberly and Jason.'

There was little Gaga missed. While his body had slowed down over the past couple of years, his mind was as sharp as ever.

'Should I wait until the DNA test comes back? Or tell them now?' Lily asked.

'It's a tricky situation, but, for what it's worth, I think you have no choice but to speak to them about it. It will be another week or so before you have DNA results. You can't keep them in the dark that long. They won't forgive you for it.'

'What if it isn't him? What if we all get our hopes up again, only for them to be dashed.'

'What if it is, though? I never believed he was dead. I wasn't sure we'd ever find out where he went, but over the side of that ship, no.'

Lily looked at him in surprise. 'Why are you so sure of that?'

'Look at the situation logically. Robert was six months younger than your Ben. There is no way he managed to unlock the cabin door, leave, make his way up to the top deck, climb onto a railing over six feet high and then fall overboard. It doesn't make any sense.'

'But they found his cuddly toy up there.'

'That they did.' He took another sip of wine, then said wearily, 'If Robert drowned that night, then he was murdered. I can't allow myself to think about that. Because if that happened, then Kimberly or Jason . . .' He stopped, shaking his head to throw the thought away.

Lily gasped as she felt fresh dread claw at her insides.

'You know your parents better than anyone. Is there any scenario you can see where they killed Robert? Either on accident or purpose?'

'No!' Lily said without hesitation. Her mother had her neuroses, but she loved her children. And why would her father give his life to finding the truth if he knew it? 'My parents did not kill Robert.'

'Exactly. So it is more likely that someone entered the cabin and took him.' Gaga topped his glass, but Lily held a hand over the rim of hers to stop him from doing the same for her.

'If this is Robert, then we can finally find out what *did* happen that night. And my son can finally have some peace. His life has been on hold for forty years. It's time his pain ended.'

They sat in silence for a moment, each thinking about Jason and the miserable life he'd curated for himself since Robert's disappearance.

'Will you come back to Dublin with me? I could use your support when I tell Mum and Dad.'

'Of course. I'll stay with Jason and make sure he doesn't do anything stupid. You could ask Kimberly to stay with you.' He pulled a face and Lily mirrored it.

'Great,' Lily said, feeling guilty that the notion of being under the same roof as her mum wasn't appealing. 'She'll say no, though. We're too noisy for her and her work. She's always on the phone to clients.'

Her grandfather rolled his eyes. He'd never been a Kimberly fan. 'She had begun to show interest in the business before Robert disappeared. But when we got back from Spain she threw herself into it. And maybe that's good, because Jason lost his way, unable to let Robert's disappearance go.'

'It's understandable that they both threw themselves into something to take their minds off their pain,' Lily said.

'Maybe. But they didn't do right by you. Either of them,' Gaga said gruffly.

'I had you,' Lily replied softly.

'Always,' Gaga replied, and for a moment they locked eyes with each other as they remembered the countless times it had been just the two of them, while Lily's parents hid themselves away from life.

'I'm scared, Gaga.'

'Of what, love?'

'That if this isn't Robert we'll lose Dad too. He's worse than ever, with this over-zealous need to find out what happened. He's lived with all the unresolved trauma for forty years. We *all* have, but for Dad it's developed into an obsession.' Lily ran her hands through her hair, sighing deeply. 'It's robbed him of so much. For his sake, Dad needs to stop searching and start living. He needs Zach to be Robert.'

Gaga put his glass down. 'We've talked about this many times over the years. Jason has always been hard on himself. As a kid he never stopped making lists and was such a perfection-ist. We worried about him, because he put so much pressure on himself.'

'Which is why he succeeded so early with his business. His attention to detail,' Lily added. 'But what was once a manage-able need for order has now taken over his life.'

'Do you have a photograph of him? This Zach fella?' Gaga asked, his brow furrowed with deep lines.

Lily nodded mutely, pulled out her mobile and opened the photo stream. 'Swipe to the left. There are about a dozen photo-graphs I've downloaded from his Instagram account. With his family in Westport, mostly.'

Lily watched her grandfather's face as he scrolled through the images. She could see the wonder and hope in his eyes, which glistened with emotion. He clasped his chest and let out a stran-gled sob. Lily moved around the garden furniture and knelt at Gaga's side.

'It's a lot. I know,' Lily said with understanding.

'It's just . . . I never thought I'd see him again. And I loved that little fella. He might not have been my grandson in blood, but he was in every way that mattered.' He wiped his eyes with the back of his hand and stroked Lily's cheek gently. 'With you, we loved you before you arrived. The excitement of knowing you were on the way. But with Robert it was a little more complicated.'

'How so?'

'When your dad told me that he'd met a woman and they

were getting married, I was shocked and a little sceptical. It all happened so fast. He'd barely mentioned he was dating, and the next minute they were engaged. A single mother from Scotland, that I knew nothing about, and she had a son. I wished your nana was still alive, to get her opinion.'

'What made you so worried about Mum?' Lily asked, sitting back in her chair again.

'I was afraid Kimberly was a gold digger after Jason's money. And I felt she was hiding something from us. She always seemed on edge.'

Lily's throat constricted with emotion at the word 'hiding'. Her grandfather was a good man who had lived in service to his son and, in turn, to his granddaughter. She trusted his judgement.

And Lily had felt more than once that her parents were hiding something. The more she delved into Robert's disappearance, the more frustrated and frightened she became. She hoped with every part of her that Zach *was* Robert so that the truth of what had happened to her brother might end the pain of so many. But she couldn't shift a nagging feeling that this truth could cost them all dearly.

NOW

August 2023

Lily

Phibsborough, Dublin

'So, you see, it's possible that after all this time we've found Robert. Or he's found us,' Lily said gently to her parents, who sat side by side on the sofa.

She watched her mother's mug slip from her hand, crashing to the floor. Her parents looked down at the coffee as it spread across the wooden parquet flooring.

Michael rushed forward to pick up the mug, and this movement ignited the room, which swelled with confusion.

'Son?' Gaga asked, his face creased in concern as he watched Lily's dad. As always, he was ready to catch him if he needed strong arms of support.

'You must have so many questions,' Lily said, her heart hammering in her chest. Her dad reached over to clasp her mother's hands between his own. Her mum looked scared and tearful, whereas her dad looked shell-shocked. He shook his head in disbelief, his knees jiggling nervously.

'I know it's a shock. I'm still trying to process it all myself,' Lily added gently. She watched her parents, waiting for them to say something, worried that she'd made the wrong choice in confiding in them about Zach's assertion before the DNA results.

But then her dad jumped up and fist-pumped the air, finding his voice as he jubilantly shouted, 'I told you! You all thought I was crazy, but I knew someone would recognise Robert from the age progression photographs!'

'I'm proud of you, son,' Lily's Gaga said. 'You never gave up. That says a lot about the man you are.'

'I never thought you were crazy, Dad,' Lily said, her voice trembling. 'I just worried that this search had taken over every part of your life.'

'It did,' her mum whispered, speaking for the first time. 'I think it was the only thing your father has been interested in since Robert disappeared.'

Her dad winced. 'How could I not keep searching for our son?' he asked, looking around the room for absolution.

Lily moved closer to her parents, and said gently to them both, 'You each dealt with things in your own ways. While Dad concentrated on looking for Robert, you threw yourself into work, Mum. You found a way to cope with your grief differently – that's all.'

Lily took a steadying breath, and pushed aside thoughts of her younger self, hurt and lonely, as she vied for her parents' attention.

Her father looked downwards and her mother flushed. Lily hadn't intended for her remark to shame them, but instead to offer them understanding of each other and deflect any bad feeling. She caught Michael's eye and he smiled in sympathy. And knowing she had him in her corner bolstered her.

'Zach doesn't look like the last age-progression image at all. But his childhood photos are almost identical to the ones we have of Robert. And that's what made Zach stop in his tracks when he watched your interview on *Ireland AM*.'

'Can I see what he looks like now?' Her mother's voice cracked as she spoke, too thin to withstand her words.

Michael had gone to the local Fuji camera centre and printed out several copies of each image they had of Zach, which he now passed around.

Silence fell over the sitting room as they looked at Zach's happy face, taken at the cycle run. The only sound in the room that drifted in from next door was Ben's giggles as he watched Goofy chase Mickey Mouse around a garden.

'I can see a resemblance to you, Kimberly,' Michael said eventually. 'Around the mouth. And I think he has Lily's smile.'

'I don't see that,' Gaga said. 'But, either way, we need to call the Gardaí and let them take over the investigation.'

'Zach doesn't want that,' Lily said quickly. 'Not yet, at least. It's difficult for him. If he *is* Robert, then it becomes complicated for his family. He has asked that he is given the time to confront his mother himself, before any authorities are involved.'

'No Gardaí,' her mum said emphatically. 'Not yet.'

Lily looked at Gaga and her dad, who both nodded their agreement.

'That's jumping ahead anyhow. First things first, Lily and Zach will do their DNA test, which is set up for Monday afternoon,' Michael added.

'Good.' Her dad nodded. 'I need to let my friends in *Stolen-Child* know. They will be so excited.' When Lily threw him a warning look, he added, 'Okay, I know. Not until after the DNA results.'

Lily's father moved back to her mother, taking a seat beside her again. Their eyes met and they looked at each other in disbelief.

'What do you think, Kimberly? Is it our boy?' her dad asked.

Her mum's hand touched the face in the image tenderly, then she answered in a voice little more than a whisper, 'It's him, Jason. I'm sure it is. I'd recognise those eyes anywhere.' Tears glistened, and her hand began to shake. 'I've longed to hold him and hug him close, to see the man he must have grown into. And now . . . Jason, I can't bear it.'

And, as was their way, her parents forgot their differences as they clung to each other for support. The room became still and they sobbed quietly in each other's arms.

Lily picked up a box of tissues and handed them to her parents, a lump lodged in her throat as she tried to control her own emotions.

'Call him now. Ask him to join us here,' her dad begged, wiping tears from his cheeks. His eyes glistened in excitement. 'You'd like that, wouldn't you, love?' he asked his ex-wife.

Her mother's face paled, and she didn't answer. Lily had been afraid of this. Her father was moving things along faster than they should.

'Dad, slow down. We've had hundreds of false leads over the years, and each time they have led us to disappointment. I know this must feel so frustrating, but we *have* to wait for the DNA test.'

Her mother whispered something to her father, and whatever it was made him pause. He sat back in the seat, and they leaned into each other again.

'It will be the longest week of our lives, waiting for results,' Gaga said, leaning into the cushions on his armchair. His face was drawn, and Lily could see the strain that this was placing on him. Another stab of guilt hit her as she worried that she'd burdened him with this.

'I'd like to see the family that took him. Do you have any photographs of them?' her mum asked.

'Yes, we do,' Michael said, handing her the photograph taken beside the fire pit of Zach and his parents.

Her mum's hand shook as she reached out to accept it. She closed her eyes for a second or two before looking down at the image. A sob escaped her, and further tears fell.

'They look happy,' her mum finally said.

'Is he tall? I can't tell from the photographs. He was small for his age as a toddler,' her dad asked.

'I'd say about five foot ten. He's a little shorter than me,' Michael answered.

'He looks so handsome,' her mum said, almost wistfully.

'He is,' Lily agreed. 'And clever too, by all accounts. He's done well in his career. He's travelled the world. He's close to his three sisters.'

Lily felt a new lump lodge itself in her throat too. Because maybe Zach had four sisters, not three. And, if so, would she ever have the same relationship with him that he had with the girls he'd grown up with?

'He's had a good life, Mum. He was loved by his mother and stepfather.'

'That's not his mother!' her dad exploded at her words. 'Do not call her that. It's an insult to your mum. This woman, whoever she is, needs to be arrested!'

Her mum trembled beside her dad as his voice rose in anger.

'Hear, hear!' Gaga agreed.

Lily looked over to her grandfather, beseeching him silently for support. She needed her father to remain calm.

Gaga nodded in understanding and cleared his throat before he added, 'Son, your reaction is a hundred per cent normal. I feel the same. But we need to listen to Lily. There's a process to undergo. Let's confirm that Robert is who he says he is. And then we'll have all the time in the world to meet him. And, mark my words, I'll help you get the justice we all deserve for the pain we've endured at the hands of his abductor. I won't rest till they are behind bars. But, first, we have to prove that, beyond any doubt, he *is* our boy.'

Her dad stood up, mollified by his father's words.

Lily watched her parents, her brow furrowed with worry. They'd all waited such a long time to find out the truth. She shivered with the realisation that in a few more days they might finally find out what had happened to Robert.

NOW

August 2023

Lily

DNA Clinic, The Docklands, Dublin

Lily stood outside a tall office block on the quays in Dublin City. The afternoon sun flooded the cement pathway, reflecting on the chrome door of the DNA testing centre. Though they could have ordered an online test, but both had decided that going in person to a clinic felt safer and gave them more control.

'Hey,' Zach said as he approached her. He leaned in as if he were about to kiss her cheek, but Lily panicked and pulled back, almost tripping over her own feet. His kiss landed between her ear and the back of her head.

'Sorry. Awkward,' he apologised, his cheeks flushing pink.

'No, I'm sorry,' Lily quickly interjected, feeling bad for making him feel bad. 'It's that I'm not sure what the protocol is for greeting a client, who may or may not be my missing brother.'

'I've heard a kiss on the ear is the preferred method of greeting. So nailed it,' Zach said with a lopsided grin.

Lily smiled back. It felt less awkward all at once. 'Will we go in and get this over with?'

Zach pulled open the double doors, and she walked before him.

They checked in with the receptionist, and within a few moments they were ushered down a hall into an office.

'Come in – don't be shy,' a woman said, standing up to greet them both. Hands were shaken, and then Lily and Zach took a seat side by side.

'I'm Ciara Shanahan, your technician for today. I see you are booked in for a family DNA test, to confirm if you are siblings. Any questions before we begin?'

Zach and Lily both leaned forward to speak. Zach gestured to Lily to go ahead.

'Erm, I suppose I'd like to understand how accurate the results are?' Lily asked.

'Our DNA tests are conducted in a laboratory with a team of fully qualified scientists. Oh, and naturally we meet the ISO 17025 requirements for testing.' Ciara smiled warmly, saying almost conspiratorially, 'We've done over one million tests since we opened our doors in 2004. They are a hundred per cent accurate. You can trust us.'

Lily exhaled deeply. Ciara had managed to allay her concerns with her speech. She wondered how often she'd rattled that sale pattern off each day.

'You believe you share the same mother, but your mother is not here?' Ciara asked, glancing down at her notes.

'Yes, that's right. And, no, Mum isn't here today. It's just us two. Does that matter?' Lily asked, her stomach lurching. Had they messed up by not bringing her mother with them? But that would have meant introducing Zach to her mum, and it was too early for that.

'We do prefer the mother's sample for the most conclusive result, but it's not mandatory. We should be able to calculate a sibling DNA index with likelihood ratio with your samples.' Again, Ciara flashed her most reassuring smile.

'How long do the results take?' Zach asked.

'Five to seven working days,' Ciara replied.

Lily shifted in her chair before asking, 'And what if we need the results for legal purposes?' Lily flushed as she felt Zach's eyes on her, his body stiffening at the word 'legal'.

'We offer a legal test service. It's slightly different than the family testing service. We can do both today if you like.'

Lily looked at Zach, who fidgeted uneasily in his seat.

'Zach?' Lily asked.

'I'd prefer to do the family testing, and if we need the legal validation later on for any reason we can come back.'

'Okay' Lily said, although she didn't agree. Zach was still in denial about the consequences of him being Robert, for his mother in particular. But he would have to catch up to that soon.

Ciara nodded solemnly, then scribbled a note on her pad. Lily guessed she'd seen all sorts of complex family dynamics in this room. Then she handed them a document and pen each.

'You'll need to fill in a form giving permission for us to use your DNA samples.'

They both took a few moments to fill in their details and sign their permission.

'The test is straightforward. I'll collect cheek cells from your mouth using the cotton swabs. Who'd like to go first?' Ciara said, putting gloves on.

'Ladies first,' Zach said, nudging Lily with a cheeky grin.

'Wimp!' Lily teased back.

It took mere minutes for Ciara to collect the sample and place it in a sealed tube and bag. She pulled a label from the form that Lily had signed earlier, then repeated the process for Zach.

'That's you both all done. We'll be in touch as soon as the results come in. We can send them by email or registered post. Or you can come into the office to collect them.'

'I'd like to collect them together,' Zach said. 'I can't imagine opening mine alone.'

Lily realised she felt the same way. Over the past half hour, she'd begun to feel more comfortable in Zach's presence.

'If they are positive, you're buying lunch,' she said.

'If they're positive, I reckon I owe you a couple of decades of birthday gifts,' Zach replied, and they were back to grinning at each other like idiots again.

'That's nice,' Ciara said in approval. 'I think you have a look of each other, you know. I'm not meant to say that, but there's something about your smiles . . .'

Lily caught Zach's eye, then looked away, feeling shy. Because a new feeling had crept into her that felt a little like hope.

They returned to the reception, and Zach pulled out his credit card as Lily tapped her smartwatch to activate Apple Pay.

'I've got this,' Zach said.

'Let's split it,' Lily countered.

'It was me who brought this to your door, so I think it should be me,' Zach further argued. His jaw was set, and Lily could see he wouldn't change his mind. This was something else she'd noticed about him: he was a determined man who liked to get his way. A trait that he shared with her mum.

'I'll wait outside,' Lily said, and she made her way out into the sunshine. She looked up at the blue sky and searched the clouds for a shape – a silly pastime she'd enjoyed ever since she was a little girl.

'See anything?' Zach asked, looking upwards when he joined her.

'I always see things in the strangest of places. Which incidentally is called pareidolia, some useless information for you! The false perception of seeing faces and shapes in everyday objects. It used to be considered a sign of psychosis,' Lily said in a dramatic voice, as her eyes moved to the left. Then she paused when her eyes rested on a large shape in the clouds – it had a round body, with a smaller head, and two long ears.

'Can you see it?' Lily asked in almost a whisper.

Zach's hand reached out and lightly touched Lily's arm. He gulped loudly, then said in his own whisper, 'It's a rabbit.'

'Like the one you had as a baby,' Lily replied tremulously.

'It's like the universe is sending us signs to confirm I am Robert . . .'

Then they turned to each other and embraced.

NOW

August 2023

Kimberly

DNA Clinic, The Docklands, Dublin

Kimberly adjusted her cap, pulling it lower over her forehead. With her hand against her breast, she watched Lily and Zach gaze upwards at the sky.

She couldn't determine what they were looking at, but she knew Lily had most likely seen something in the clouds, as was her way.

Zach reached out and touched Lily's arm. And then she said something, and turned to him, and they embraced.

As Kimberly watched them, a swarm of butterflies fluttered in her stomach. She had been unable to eat or sleep ever since Lily had told them about Zach. The *possibility* of seeing Robert again made her heart skip a beat.

Could she risk moving closer? Yes, if she was careful. Kimberly straightened her oversized sweatshirt. She had dressed in the most inconspicuous outfit she could find, hoping to blend in with the crowd. But now she felt like a spotlight was shining on her. Check out the middle-aged woman failing to hide in plain sight.

She supposed she could walk over to them and announce herself. Kimberly was a grown woman and in charge of her own actions. But she'd promised Lily she'd stay away from Zach until they knew one way or the other if he was Robert. That was all well in theory. But she could not stay away any more than she could stop the sun from rising tomorrow morning.

Because she *knew* that was him.

They were still hugging, which puzzled Kimberly. They couldn't have received the DNA results already. Kimberly had googled the clinic Lily had booked, and the turnaround time was up to seven days. Had there been a special express service? That didn't make any sense, though. No. Whatever this was, it was not a brother and sister celebrating a DNA match.

She moved closer to them, keeping herself concealed behind the tall building on her left. A woman walking her dog stopped as he sniffed a lamppost before he lifted his leg to relieve himself. Kimberly was grateful for the distraction, and used the moment to move closer unnoticed.

She looked up at the sky, hoping to discern what Lily and Zach had seen, but she couldn't make it out from her new vantage point. She knew the clouds were constantly moving and shifting, so the image must have dispersed.

They began walking towards Clarion Quay, and Kimberly struggled to keep up with their fast pace. Every now and then, she heard laughter drift back to her.

They liked each other. She could tell how Zach moved, half turning so that he looked at his sister as they walked.

His sister. She'd already started to call Lily that in her mind. Because she'd recognise Robert from any line-up. How long she'd waited to see them together.

A pain pierced her chest; she stopped and held on to the brick wall of a betting shop. Was this a heart attack? It felt like one. She couldn't breathe as likely scenarios danced in her brain of what might happen once they received the results raced through her mind.

Lily and Zach approached a busy pedestrian crossing, and as the green man lit up they accelerated. Kimberly, who had been following closely behind them, reached out her hand, almost touching her son's back. However, as the crowd moved forward, Kimberly's feet remained firmly planted on the pavement. People jostled by her, sighing at the annoyance of the silly woman in their way.

Kimberly ached to hold her son in her arms again, to tell him that she'd never stopped loving him, thought about him every day, and was sorry – more sorry than he'd ever know.

But now was not the time or place. Not with Lily by Zach's side, at least. Kimberly knew she had to let them go. She allowed the distance between them to grow until they were no longer in sight, as she formulated a plan.

BEFORE

June 1976

Sally

Doddington Estate, Battersea Park Road, London

Sally tried to block out the shouts that drifted in through the open windows. It was impossible to sleep in the dead summer heat without them open, but the noise of the busy council flats made sleep elusive. A deep voice screamed abuse. It was the caretaker, a large, brutish man who had no joy in his life and wanted everyone else to know.

'No children are allowed to run on the landing. Get them outside or down to the playroom on the ground floor,' he instructed. 'Or, by God, I'll teach them manners.'

In fairness, children had been bounding along the landing all day long. But, like the sound of the trains passing by, Sally had become accustomed to their squeals.

She looked at her watch. It was only ten o'clock. Since returning from her shift at the office block, she'd managed only four hours of sleep. If she had a cup of tea, things might quieten down again on the landing, and then she'd be able to get a few more hours in. Without sleep, she'd be dead on her feet later on and she had plans to go to their local pub, The Grove, with Elsie. It was Saturday, her favourite day of the week, because there was no night work in the office block. She licked her lips at the thought of that cold glass of lager and lime.

Sally got up and walked to the flat window to peek outside. Three young girls were setting themselves up to sunbathe in the concrete courtyard in front of their tower block. They were wearing crochet bikinis, and the sound of Kiki and Elton singing about their broken hearts played in the distance. They swished their long hair and giggled as they lowered themselves into wooden deckchairs.

Sally used to get upset when she witnessed carefree moments like these that she never got to enjoy herself. But she'd learned to harden herself to them over the months. Feeling sorry for yourself didn't pay the rent. Her stomach lurched once more at the thought. She longed for the day when money, or lack of it, was not an issue.

She was now permanently employed by the cleaning company, and Cyril said she was one of his best workers. The problem was that by the time she'd paid rent, electricity and food, there wasn't much left – certainly not enough for crochet bikinis in which to lounge around during this heat wave. Sally picked up her handbag and pulled out her purse, spilling its contents onto the table. By the time she'd put aside money for essentials, it left her with £5 to spend on incidentals. Sighing, she told herself that she'd make it work. She always did.

They'd had thirteen days in a row of scorching sun. Temperatures had reached as high as thirty-five degrees. The caretaker had issued a directive to all tenants stating that they should save water. Shallow baths all around. And at work last night the gaffer repeated Denis Howell's words, who was the Minister for Drought – put washing-up water into the toilet as opposed to flushing. This caused much merriment between the charwomen.

While Sally hated cleaning, she loved the camaraderie of the women there. Her muscles had got used to the hard labour, at least. And her favourite part of the day was the hour Elsie and she spent together before they walked to work. Over the last month since they'd reconnected, they reminisced about their time in the orphanage.

Elsie remained tightlipped about what she'd been up to over the past three years. Sally sensed that there was a story there waiting to be revealed. And that life may not have been kind to her friend.

Dressing quickly in her sundress and sandals, the lightest thing she owned, Sally made her way towards the corner shop to buy some fresh bread.

As she passed the girls, who were now singing 'Save Your Kisses for Me', in time with the radio, she felt their eyes on her. There was little greenery in Battersea, and what there was had now turned yellow from the heat. A musty smell lingered in the air. Sally smiled brightly at the girls. She promised herself that she'd have a garden to sunbathe in one day.

To her surprise, she noted the corner shop had a large handwritten 'Closing Down' sign on the door. She was sorry to see this and said as much to the woman on the till as she counted twenty pence for her bread.

'We've no chance competing against those buggers in the supermarkets,' the woman replied, shaking her head sadly. 'Thirty years we've had this shop. All the good that did us.' Then she pointed to the rack of newspapers that sat beside the counter. 'Did you hear about the ladybirds?'

Sally shook her head.

'There's swarms of them. Twenty-three billion, the paper says, on the hunt. Cos, Lord, save us all, the plants and the bugs that eat them are all dead from the heat, and they are starving. My Ernest said that he'd heard they were attacking humans. Trying to drink our sweat.' She handed Sally one pence change. 'You take care, love. And, if you see any of those ladybirds, run!'

Stifling a giggle, Sally left the shop. The girls in the orphanage would howl at this kind of thing, with Sister Jones giving them the evil eye while trying not to laugh herself. And Sally felt a pang. She still missed them all. Unlike Elsie, who'd left without a backward glance, Sally thought about them often. Without much thought, she ran to the nearest public phone box. She fed the phone fifty pence, and dialled the number, moving from foot to foot as it rang out.

'Good morning, Sunshine House Orphanage. How can I help you?' A Scottish lilt replied.

'Sister Jones!' Sally cried out in delight. 'Hello! It's me, Sally. I wanted to tell you about the killer ladybirds.'

'Slow down, child. How anyone is expected to understand a word you say, the speed you speak! What on earth are you gabbling on about? Honestly, I hoped you'd have outgrown your flights of fancy by now!'

Sally felt a rush of warmth for her old warden. 'Gosh, I miss you telling me off for my nonsense, Sister Jones!'

Sister Jones sighed, and her voice softened. 'And we miss you too. The house has been quiet without you. Are you doing okay? Are you being a good girl?'

Sally thought about the loneliness of life in the Doddington flats, the monotony of her days and the backbreaking work she did every night. 'I don't have much time to be anything but good, Sister. It's not what I thought it would be,' she admitted in a small voice.

'Aye, but life never is, I find,' Sister Jones said. 'But you, young lady, are a force to be reckoned with. Life with all its twists and turns is no match for you.'

'I'm working so hard for a pittance. I barely have enough money to get by.'

'You're young and strong. Hard work won't kill you. But don't settle, Sally. Your head was always full of dreams. Remember them. Chase them with the same gusto you always had when you sneaked out the door after lights out with Elsie Evans!'

'I always wondered if you knew about that or not!' Sally said incredulously.

'Oh, you'd be surprised what I knew.' She could hear the smile in Sister Jones's voice.

'Elsie and I found each other. She lives near me, you know. We work at the same cleaning firm,' Sally gushed.

Sister Jones sighed. 'I've worried about Elsie for years. She had her demons . . .' She paused and left the sentence unfinished. 'Don't let her get you into any trouble.'

Before Sally could question Sister Jones any further, the line beeped, signalling the end of their call.

'I've got to go, Sister. Tell the girls I called and said hello, and tell them about the killer ladybirds too.'

'I will, child.' The nun cleared her throat and said, 'And don't you forget what I said. I believe in *you*.' And then the phone went dead.

She believes in me. It made Sally feel giddy and scared all at once. And then her eyes moved across the busy street to the row of shops opposite her.

Three doors down from the corner shop was a hairdressing salon called Elite. She'd passed it by dozens of times. Sally had been inside it once before, when she'd asked them if they had any vacancies, only to be shown the door with a firm no. Under the large Elite sign, in smaller script font, was a sign that read *Hair styled by Nicola Page*.

Sally's eyes blurred until the name on the sign changed to that of her own, Sally Fox. It was a nice dream. Pulling her shoulders back, she made her way to the salon. She paused for a beat at the door, reached up, smoothed down her hair and marvelled that she had allowed herself to act on a whim for the second time that day. Her hair was still too short, but without the scissor-happy Housemother on the loose, it now fell past her chin. Sally had been experimenting with different styles, and before she went to bed in the wee hours of this morning she'd placed her hair in rags, which gave it a pretty wave today.

The bell rang on the front door as it opened. Inside, two women were getting their hair styled. One had rollers and sat under a giant hairdryer, reading *Cosmopolitan* magazine. The other sat in front of a large mirror as the stylist teased her hair into soft waves.

The small salon shop was spotlessly clean. Painted a bright yellow, it had one chair in front of a sink and two chairs in front of tall mirrors. Behind the till, several framed certificates from the London Institute of Beauty Culture hung on the wall.

'I'll be with you in a minute,' the stylist said as she brandished a tall bottle of hairspray like a weapon. 'Close your eyes,' she advised the client, and then she began spraying. 'There you go. That's rock solid. That won't move anywhere. Just don't go standing near any naked flames.' The two women laughed.

Once money had been exchanged, the stylist turned to Sally. 'Are you looking for a cut and blowdry?' She looked at her diary, running her finger down the entries. 'I'm fully booked all day, but if you don't mind waiting I can squeeze you in after I'm finished with Carol.' She nodded towards the woman under the dryer.

'I'm here because I'd like a job, Ms Page,' Sally said.

'You were in here before,' Nicola said, looking her up and down. 'I remember you.'

'That's correct.' Sally smiled her brightest smile and crossed her fingers behind her back.

'I'm sorry. As I told you back then, I can't afford to take anyone on.' Nicola shrugged and turned her back to walk away.

'I'll work for free!' Sally blurted out.

This stopped Nicola in her tracks. 'Why would you do that?'

'Because I desperately want to learn how to do what you do.' Sally's eyes implored the woman to take a chance on her. 'I already have a job every night cleaning, but I don't need much sleep. I can do both. I'll sweep and mop your floors too. All I ask is that you teach me how to be a stylist.'

Nicola regarded her quizzically. 'Oh my days. That's a lot of work for you. You're only a slip of a thing. How do I know that you won't let me down?'

'I'm small, but I'm strong. And I'm reliable.' Sally pointed to the certificates and said, 'I want to be like you. I want to have my own salon. I want to help make women feel beautiful, like you did with that lady who just left. I saw how she looked at herself in the

157

mirror before she walked out the door. You did that. I want to learn how to do that too.'

Nicola's face broke out in a smile. Sally guessed she was about her mother's age, with fine lines dancing around her mouth and eyes. She had glossy brunette hair that hung in a high ponytail.

'You've got something about you – I'll give you that. Spunky. Tell me more about this cleaning job of yours,' Nicola said.

'I work five nights a week, Monday through Friday, cleaning office blocks. I start at seven-thirty each night and get home by five a.m. So I could be at the salon every morning. If you give me a chance, you won't regret it – I promise you. And if it doesn't work out, I'll go, no questions asked.'

Nicola drummed her red manicured nails on the Formica top of the tall desk. She was going to say no. But at least Sally had tried. And she'd keep on trying, like Sister Jones had made her promise to do.

'I open at nine o'clock every day. How on earth can you come in here with no more than three hours of sleep,' Nicola said, shaking her head in disbelief.

'Please. I want this. Give me a shot, at least,' Sally begged.

'I must need my head tested. On a trial basis, you can work half days from Tuesdays to Saturdays. We're closed on Mondays. You can start at midday, until four o'clock. That way, my conscience is clear that you'll at least get a few hours of sleep every night.'

A wide grin broke out on Sally's face. She could hardly believe her ears.

'You need to wear something smart. And put some make-up on, for the love of God. You're too pale. How in this heat you've managed to avoid a sun tan, I don't know,' Nicola said.

Sally threw her arms round the woman and hugged her tight as she thanked her repeatedly. 'I won't let you down – you'll see. See you on Tuesday!'

Then Sally practically floated home to her flat. As Sister Jones had urged, she'd chased her dreams, and it looked as if she'd finally caught one!

BEFORE

June 1976

Sally

Doddington Estate, Battersea Park Road, London

Sally hummed to herself as she plugged the shower hose into the tap in the bath. Then she squealed as the ice-cold water hit her. They'd announced on the six o'clock news this evening that the water ban was over. Traditional British summer weather was to return this week, with the heat wave finally ending after a thirteen-day streak.

She put on her favourite jeans and T-shirt, then took two rollers from her fringe that she'd put in when she'd got back from the salon, flicking the curls off her face until they fell into loose waves.

She grabbed the gift she'd wrapped earlier that week and left the apartment.

The lifts were out of order again. This usually annoyed her, but nothing could dampen her mood today. She heard the sounds of kids laughing and shouting as she crossed the concrete courtyard to get to Elsie's block. A couple of girls had used chalk to draw out squares and were playing hopscotch. A little boy, no more than three, was peddalling furiously on his tricycle, and another group of boys were kicking a football. Sally wasn't sure she would ever get used to this high-density development, vast

159

and high, with thousands crammed into the small spaces. The flats reminded Sally of Lego pieces stacked on top of each other.

Her butterflies were back as she knocked on Elsie's door. She was unsure how Elsie would take her good news about Elite. Sally knew that Elsie would be happy for her – of course, she would – but she'd noticed a change in Elsie since their time together in the orphanage. A hardness had crept into her friend.

'Door's open,' Elsie's voice called out. Sally walked into the flat, where Elsie sat at her dining-room table, applying lipstick in front of a small vanity mirror.

Elsie's radio cassette sat on the table and a news reporter read the seven o'clock news.

'I'm shattered. I think I might fall asleep into my lager tonight.'

'Me too,' Sally admitted, her ears pricking up when she heard the words 'Yorkshire Ripper'.

The newsreader continued: 'Police investigating the Jack the Ripper-style killings in Yorkshire have issued a warning to women – beware of accepting lifts from strangers. And Assistant Chief Constable Jim Hobson, of Leeds CID, has appealed to prostitutes in the Chapeltown area to report any assaults or threats against them in the past twelve months.'

Elsie reached over and switched the news off.

'It's scary, isn't it?' Sally said. 'Those poor women. Bludgeoned to death with a hammer and stabbed with a screwdriver. What kind of monster does that?'

'Oh, for goodness' sake, must you always be so dramatic?' Elsie snapped. 'We're supposed to be going out tonight. All this talk would depress anyone.'

'I'm sorry,' Sally said, but she wasn't sure why she was apologising.

She passed the small gift-wrapped package in Elsie's direction, hoping it might turn Elsie's bad mood around.

'I got you a gift. A little something to say thank you for all the meals and helping me get that job with Cyril.'

The corners of Elsie's mouth turned up, and half a smile re-appeared on her face. 'You always were an old softie.'

She unwrapped the gift carefully and pulled out two bright purple cushion covers.

'I know it's your favourite colour. And I thought they might brighten the place up,' Sally said.

Elsie's response was to burst into tears. Sally moved closer to her, sitting on the small sofa beside her.

'Hey, what's this all about?' Sally asked, surprised by Elsie's reaction.

'You know, in my twenty-one years, you are the only person who has ever bought me gifts since my mum . . . Well, since she died. Proper got me, this did.' Elsie touched her heart, grinning through her tears. She reached behind her for the two beige cushions, pulled the grim covers off and replaced them with the new ones.

'Regal. Fit for a queen,' Sally said.

'Some queen I am,' Elsie replied with a laugh. 'Put the kettle on. I'm parched.'

Ten minutes later, they were sipping tea and eating fig rolls, laughing at Sally's tale of killer ladybirds and her impulsive call to Sister Jones.

'We didn't know how lucky we was until it was gone,' Elsie stated.

'That's for sure. I feel sorry for the kids in the flats. They've nowhere to play here. We were lucky, weren't we? That big park-land to muck about in, behind the orphanage.'

Elsie nodded towards the front door. 'Up until I found you, I never spoke to anyone. I tried to chat with a few women on this landing when I moved in, but they seem to have little cliques. There's a pensioner down the hall. She's chatty, as long you don't mind listening to her talking about her dead husband.'

'They all keep to themselves on my landing too,' Sally replied. 'Thought I'd made a friend when I got stuck in a lift with a neighbour, but once we got out, she was off!'

'Thank goodness we found each other!' Elsie said. Then she leaned back and looked at Sally a little closer. 'You look different. Your hair is growing out, and you've curled it. It suits you like that.'

Sally swished her hair and smiled. 'I've been trying to do the Farrah flip! I've been practising, but it's not long enough yet. I can do yours for you if you like?'

'It would look stupid on me,' Elsie said, frowning, as she examined her long, straight hair.

'Leave it with me. I'll have you all Farrah'd out before we leave here today!' Sally glanced at Elsie shyly. 'I have some news. I found another job today.'

Sally filled Elsie in on how her chat with Sister Jones had prompted a call into Nicola's salon. She held her breath while waiting for Elsie to respond.

'You probably think I'm stupid, working for nothing . . .' Sally said, doubting herself now as Elsie regarded her quizzically.

'There's one thing you'll never be, Sally Fox, and that's stupid. I told you before you're a shining bright white light. I'm well chuffed for you.'

'Really?' Sally asked, feeling warmth rise into her cheeks.

'Of course I am. Why wouldn't I be? And I'll be expecting free haircuts for life now.'

Sally laughed out loud. 'I think I can manage that.'

'You should ask in the library if they have any books on hair-dressing,' Elsie suggested.

'Why didn't I think of that?' Sally exclaimed. The Battersea Park Library sat on the outskirts of the Doddington Estate and it had become a lifesaver for Sally, who was a regular visitor there, borrowing books, or spending an hour at their record library, headphones on, listening to music.

'You'll be dead on your feet, though,' Elsie said, frowning.

'I know. I'll not do much other than sleep and work for a while. But it will be worth it. I know it.'

'Well, we better make the most of tonight. The Grove won't

know what's hit it when we walk through the door.' She picked up a hairbrush and handed it to Sally. 'Go on, work your magic on my barnet.'

An hour later, they stood at the bar, waiting to order their drinks. Sally felt giddy thinking about the possibilities that lay ahead for her.

Three men were playing darts, and when they glanced over at the girls one of them winked at Sally, making her cheeks flame.

'About time you broke a few hearts,' Elsie said, nudging Sally's side.

'When would I have time for that?' Sally replied with a laugh. 'What about you? Have you found any hunks that you might marry?'

Elsie laughed. 'Chance would be a fine thing. Sure, who'd have me?'

'I would,' a deep voice said from behind them.

They turned round in surprise. Standing behind them, tall, lean, with shaggy long hair that reached his black biker-jacket-clad shoulders was a face from their past. Even though it had been over four years since he'd left Sunshine House Orphanage, he'd not changed a bit.

''Allo, Elsie love. Long time no see,' Reggie said with a goofy grin.

'Hello, Reggie,' Elsie replied, beaming back at her old boy-friend.

NOW

August 2023

Lily

Departures lounge, Dublin Airport

Michael drove into the designated drop-off area at Terminal 1 at Dublin Airport. Lily turned to look at him, her eyes wide in wonder.

'I can't believe I'm doing this,' she said. They both stepped out of the car, and Michael opened the boot to grab Lily's overnight case.

The previous evening, Zach had phoned her to tell her he'd booked a flight to Malaga, Spain. In his words, he was going out of his mind waiting for their DNA results, so he decided to go back to the home he'd lived in with his mother in Ronda. He wanted to ask Señor and Señora Alvarez more about his time there. See if he could unravel some mysteries in his mind by retracing his footsteps.

Lily had wished him luck; she understood his need to keep moving. She felt restless and envious that Zach had something to do while enduring the agonising wait for results. Gaga was with her father, who was beside himself with hope and anticipation that, finally, his quest might be over. Her mother was, as usual, nose down in her ledgers, keeping track of her growing empire of flats and houses. While her father was an open book, his every emotion displayed for all to witness, her mother remained guarded and was harder to read.

It was Michael who suggested that Lily book a ticket. With his eyes on his mobile, he told her that seats were available on the same flight Zach had booked.

'You could do one overnight in Spain and be home to tuck Ben back into bed. Ready for your clients on Monday.'

Lily had rallied against the idea. She'd gone to bed, tossing and turning as she ran through the valid reasons why she shouldn't go with Zach. He was a stranger to her. While she might feel a connection to him, that was most likely her subconscious looking for one. Because she *wanted* him to be her brother. Zach could be unhinged, dangerous even. But she discounted this thought as fast as it came. Her instincts told her that, whether or not he was Robert, his intention was not to cause her any harm.

Over coffee and hot buttery toast earlier that morning, Lily casually asked Michael what time the flight was. And her husband once again surprised her in the best way.

'Flights at eleven o'clock. But you've got lots of time. I've checked you in already.'

'What?' Lily asked, dumbfounded as her heart began to race.

'I knew you would change your mind, so I booked a ticket. We'll need to leave in an hour, which gives you plenty of time to shower and pack an overnight case.'

'I don't deserve you,' Lily said, her heart swelling with gratitude and love for her husband.

'Yes, you do. I don't want you to have any regrets, Lily. What if this *is* your brother? You'll feel so bad that you've left him to deal with this alone.'

And so, here she was, kissing her son goodbye and hugging her husband tight. 'A few weeks ago, I wanted my parents to finally admit to themselves that Robert is dead. And now I am about to fly to Spain with a man who could be him.'

Michael cupped her face in his hands and kissed her lips. 'It's crazy, I know. And while I want you to go, remember that you don't know this guy. Keep your guard up.'

'My gut tells me he's a good guy,' Lily said.

'And I always trust your gut. You read people for a living. But, all the same, be a little wary.'

With one last kiss to her two boys, Lily took her small wheelie case and went to the departure gate. She'd not told Zach she was coming too. Mainly because there was little time, but also because she wanted to surprise him. There was no sign of him in the twenty-minute crawl through security, so she made her way to the departure gate, where boarding was due to begin in thirty minutes. And then she saw him. EarPods in, looking at his phone. Sitting close to the gate, his knee jiggling up and down. He looked stressed. And her heart swelled with something that felt like affection.

'Hey, you,' she said, gently kicking his foot.

He jumped up, startled, and his EarPods fell onto the tiled floor between them.

'What are you doing here?' he asked.

'I thought you could do with the company,' Lily said, feeling a flush run across her face. She'd not considered until this minute that he might not want her to tag along. 'But if you'd rather go it alone, I can go back . . .' She took a step away from him.

A smile broke out across his face, reaching his eyes, which crinkled at the sides.

'This is the nicest thing . . .' He came over and pulled her into a quick hug. 'Thank you. Honestly, I never expected this.'

They weren't sitting together on the flight, but that suited Lily, who was still a little sleepy from her restless night. Three hours later, their flight landed at Malaga airport.

'I've hired a car already,' Zach said as they queued for Passport Control.

Lily pointed to Zach's blue passport. 'It's a little mad to think you might not be a Zach.'

He turned towards her. 'Maybe keep that to yourself as we

walk through, please. Don't fancy being hauled into interrogation for name fraud!' He pulled a face, half grimacing. 'But I've thought about that a lot, too.'

'Zach suits you no matter what,' Lily said, trying to put herself into his shoes. She couldn't imagine having to change her name now, after forty years of living with it.

'I can't conceive not being Zach. But, I have to tell you, Robert doesn't feel wrong either.'

They each passed through Passport Control with little more than a perfunctory wave from the officer in charge, then walked into the busy Arrivals hall. A rush of warm air hit their faces.

'Whoa. That's hot!' Lily said, fanning herself with her passport. 'I'm going to get some water and sun cream while you get the car, okay? I'll follow you over to the car hire area.' She pointed to the sign that hung overhead a few feet away.

Once she'd bought her toiletries and refreshments, she found Zach, who was now ready to collect their vehicle.

'Are you a nervous passenger?' Zach asked as they buckled up into their red Jeep Renegade.

'No. At least I wasn't until you asked that question.'

'I'm a good driver – I've never been in an accident – but the road to Ronda is windy.' He handed Lily his phone. 'I've set the satnav; your job is chief navigator! We're heading for the E15 Autovia first of all, in the direction of Algeciras. Then we'll drive down the coast.'

This was a job that Lily was more than happy to take control of.

'Michael would get lost in a supermarket car park if I'm not there to direct him. You are in safe hands!' Lily joked as she did a quick scan of the route. 'From what I can see, we'll pass through Benalmadena, Torremolinos, and Marbella en route. We could always stop in one of those for a coffee.'

'I could eat. Fair warning: I'm always hungry,' Zach said with his lopsided grin. 'I had a couple of dates with a nice woman from Marbella the summer I lived in Spain. I know a few places we can hit.'

Lily looked at him in surprise. They'd never discussed romantic relationships in therapy, but they were in new territory now. They were moving quickly to the friendship area of town.

'She was Spanish?'

'No, she was Dutch. She was also on a summer vacation. It was one of those flings that spark fiercely but burn out fast.'

'I remember those sparky relationships,' Lily said with a smile, thinking about a year she'd backpacked around Australia after graduating from university.

'Before Michael?'

'One sec. Turn right here . . . yep, either lane will work . . . that's it,' Lily said, her eyes on the map. Then, once Zach was where he should be, she looked up. 'Yep, I had some fun in Australia, before Michael. Who, by the way, was a slow burner instead of a spark. And, it turns out, a keeper.'

'He adores you. That was the first thing I noticed when I met him last week. A blind man could see that.' He paused for a moment and then added softly, 'I envy you both. I've never had that kind of love.'

'We're lucky. I know that not everyone gets what we have, and I don't take it for granted.' She glanced over to Zach. 'You'll find it, though. I reckon you have a lot to offer the right woman.'

'I appreciate the vote of confidence. From your lips to the dating God's ears,' Zach said, a big smile breaking out on his face again. 'Tell me about Oz. With my nomadic tendencies, it's one place I've yet to tick off my bucket list.'

'I fell in love with the country. The people are so friendly. They say the Irish are supposed to be the land of a thousand welcomes. We've nothing on the Australians. I've always thought that it's because they have their work-life balance sorted. They are naturally more chilled and happy.'

'Why did you come home to Ireland, then? Were you not tempted to stay there?'

Lily sighed. 'It's complicated. Family demands, I suppose, is the easiest way to describe it.'

When they saw the first sign for Ronda, he let out a whoop. Zach's excitement was palpable as they drove along the super-highway, and Lily couldn't help but feel a little caught up in it.

'You know, when I spent the summer here, I begged my sisters to visit me. Ronda is so beautiful – I wanted them to experience it too. But family life got in the way for them. Issy nearly came once. But then she met a bloke and cancelled on me at the last minute.' He paused, then glanced over to Lily. 'Weird to think that I might get to show Ronda to one of my sisters after all . . .'

Lily's heart started to flutter. And her breath quickened.

'You okay?' Zach asked. 'Sorry, shouldn't I have said that?'

'I'm fine,' Lily said, feeling anything but. That word – sister – held so much power.

'It's just that when you decided to come here, I figured you would have only done that if you believed me . . .' Zach's voice grew tighter with every word.

'No, it's me who's sorry,' Lily replied, in a rush to make sure that her complicated response to this situation was on her, not on him. 'I *do* believe you. But hearing it out loud . . . that I might be your little sister . . . after all these years of believing I'll never get to find my big brother . . .' Her voice broke off.

It was too much. They drove silently for a while, both lost in their thoughts, but occasionally stealing glances at each other. *Had she made a mistake by joining Zach on this journey?* She had always been careful, always doing the right thing, and now she had thrown caution to the wind. She could only hope she wouldn't regret the first spontaneous thing she had done in years.

BEFORE

September 1976

Sally

Elite, Wandsworth, London

Sally took the dry towels from the line and then pegged the newly washed towels in their place. She moved inside, singing along to the latest *Brotherhood of Man* song, which played on the radio in the salon. Nicola was finishing a perm for Mrs Langton, one of their Friday-afternoon regulars. Another client, a young woman called Hazel, sat underneath a hooded dryer with a hair-net on. Sally refolded the towels into their pile by the sinks, then checked the shampoo bottles to ensure they were all topped up. She tidied the trolley, lining up hair rollers, perm curlers, clips, pins, combs and brushes. Then, once that was all in order, ready for the next client, she swept the salon floor again.

Sally was determined to continue to prove to Nicola that she hadn't made a mistake when she'd taken her on. Her role had progressed over the past three months. Along with cleaning, she had been given the responsibility of shampooing customers. She enjoyed the process, seeing women come into the salon frazzled and then relax as she gently washed their hair, wrapping their hair in a turban-like towel, as she brought them back to their seats for Nicola to do her magic.

'You can take Hazel's curlers out now,' Nicola called over to Sally.

Fridays and Saturdays were busy in the salons, with young women like Hazel in to transform themselves for their nights out. Sally switched off the hooded dryer, then moved it away, ready to get to work. Hazel smiled distractedly at her momentarily, but returned to her glossy magazine again. Sally carefully took the first roller out to ensure the woman's dark hair was dry. She felt Nicola's eyes on her, watching her every move. Sally took a steadying breath, determined not to allow nerves to better her. She took all the curlers out methodically, ensuring she didn't snag Hazel's hair. She'd made that mistake once, and the client's 'Ow!' still rang in her ears. Then she smoothed the curls into soft waves.

'You are a genius!' Hazel was enthused at the finished style.

Sally's chest puffed out in delight.

'That's two pound fifty for the wash and set,' Sally said when they walked to the tills.

Hazel handed her £3. 'Keep the change, love. If this doesn't get my man proposing, nothing will.'

The day went by in a blur of shampoo and sets, colours and perms. Sally kept her eyes on the clock because she habitually lost track of time. She loved her job, but as it didn't pay her a wage she couldn't afford to lose her char work. Sally had thought she was tired before, but now, with two jobs on the go, she finally realised what the saying 'bone tired' meant. She fell into bed every morning after her cleaning shift finished, only to wake when her alarm rang out at eleven o'clock. She lived for Sundays, where she could sleep all day if she wanted, and it wasn't unheard of for her to sleep almost twenty-four hours straight.

Finally, at quarter to four, the salon was empty.

'Take a seat for a moment,' Nicola said, patting one of the salon chairs beside her. She held a folder in her lap, and her face looked deadly serious.

Sally felt a flush rise up her chest. She hadn't messed up; she was sure of it.

'Have I d-done something wrong?' she stammered.

'Oh my days, of course not,' Nicola said. 'You are a breath of fresh air. That's what you are. You've got this place running like clockwork. Look at it.' She waved her hands around the salon. 'Gleaming. That's all you.'

Sally flushed again, but this time with pride.

'I want to offer you a formal apprenticeship. I've got your papers here. You'll do day-release training at a local college every Wednesday. And, while it's not much, I can pay you four pound fifty daily.'

Sally felt her breath leave her body, and she couldn't speak. She wanted to gush her thanks, but she had no words. Instead, she felt hot tears sting her eyes.

'Oh, don't cry. This is good news,' Nicola said, pulling Sally into her embrace. 'There, there. You'll get me started next. And I'm having a particularly good mascara day; it would be a shame to waste it.'

Sally giggled at this, which also set Nicola off. Sally finally found her voice and gushed, 'I never expected this. Thank you.'

'No thanks necessary. I'm happy to do it. Credit where credit is due. And I want you to have your qualifications. Hairdressing can take you around the world if you want it. Now, don't get me wrong. I want you to stay here with me. But, if you decide to move on, this way you will have the papers to take with you.'

Sally could not believe her ears.

'I would like you to give up the char work, though. You look half dead most days. I don't know how you keep going. I'd be done in if I had two jobs on the go, like you.'

Sally couldn't argue with that. Some days, it took all her strength to get out of bed. But every sacrifice had been worth it. She wanted to dance and sing with the pure joy of this news.

'I'll talk to my boss tonight at the office block. Maybe I can reduce my hours? But even with the pay from you I can't afford to give it up.'

'I understand. Well, you can keep your tips. I hope that helps a little too.' Nicola glanced at the clock above the reception area. 'You better get a move on. You'll be late if not.'

With one last hug of gratitude, Sally left, but practically floated back to the flats, peeling her clothes off and jumping onto the bed in her underwear. She usually napped for an hour between her two jobs, but not today. She was too charged up to think about sleeping. Instead, she lay there, eyes closed, and fantasised about some day owning her salon. *Hair by Sally*, she would call it. Maybe she could go to America and get a job in one of the fancy salons in New York. Elsie might even come with her.

She frowned at the thought of her best friend, feeling her good mood dissipate. Elsie and Reggie were dating again. And, while Sally liked Reggie, she worried about him. He was one of life's duckers and divers, and had told the girls that he did errands for one of the gang lords in the East End. Elsie was impressed by the cash that he flashed, but it made Sally nervous.

Elsie had always been easily led, and Sally worried Reggie might take her friend down the wrong path. But they were not kids any more. Sally had to let Elsie live her life.

Sally had to admit to something else too, even if it didn't paint her in the best light: She was jealous. With Reggie back on the scene, Elsie was spending all her spare time with him, rather than Sally. And this only highlighted the fact that Sally was alone, never having a boyfriend of her own. She still had that same dream, of meeting a tall, dark stranger and falling in love. It felt more elusive than ever before.

Sally had never had someone who was one hundred per cent hers, who put her needs before their own, who worried about her and nobody else. She craved that blanket of security that she believed a boyfriend could give her.

But Elsie had promised that they could go to the Grove for a drink this weekend, just the two of them. Maybe Mr Right would walk into the bar, their eyes would lock across the crowded room and they would . . .

The next thing Sally knew, there was a loud banging on her door.

Elsie's voice called in: 'Wake up, you daft ha'p'orth. We need to get going.'

Sally sat up with a start. She'd dozed off dreaming of her handsome stranger and overslept. She rushed to open the door and pulled her char uniform over her head. 'Sorry, Elsie,' she said, zipping herself up as the door opened.

'We've got five minutes – don't worry,' Elsie said, pouring a glass of water for Sally.

'I've got news, Elsie,' Sally said as she ran a brush through her hair. 'Nicola has offered me a hairdressing apprenticeship.'

'Well, about blooming time!' Elsie replied with a whoop. 'She's got a right bobby dazzler with you.'

'She's going to pay me too. Four pound fifty per day.'

Elsie frowned. 'That won't keep the bailiff from the door. You'll have to stay on charring.'

Sally nodded. 'Do you think the gaffer will let me work fewer hours?'

'I don't know. You can ask. He likes you, so maybe he'll agree.'

Elsie held up two slices of buttered bread. 'You'll have to eat these on the go.'

Sally tied her hair back into a ponytail, then grabbed her bag and keys, ready to leave for work.

Once they arrived at the cleaners' room in the office block, nerves began dancing in Sally's stomach. She didn't want to lose this job, but she also knew she couldn't keep up the hours she was working. They found Cyril with a cigarette dangling from his mouth, rubbing his stockinged feet.

'Gout,' he said sorrowfully. 'That's what the doctor said. Right painful bugger it is too.'

Sally cursed his painful feet, which were unlikely to put him in a charitable mood.

'Cyril, can I talk to you about something?'

'Sure.' He nodded to the bench beside him.

'I've been offered an apprenticeship at the hair salon.' Sally said. The charwomen all cheered from behind her.

'Good for you, love,' Cyril said, looking genuinely pleased for her, his eyes crinkling as he smiled. 'Are you giving me your notice?'

'No. I can't afford to give up this job, as I'll only be on apprenticeship wages. But I'm finding it hard to do both.'

Cyril frowned. 'You want less hours?'

Sally nodded, smiling brightly at him, hoping to win him over.

'Can't help, love. I'd like to. But this is a full-time job.'

Sally nodded miserably. She understood and had half expected this response. But then the door opened, and a woman with peroxided blonde hair walked in, eliciting another round of cheers from the charwomen. 'Hallo, Mary!'

She made her way towards Cyril, who welcomed her warmly. 'How's that little wain of yours?'

'Getting big and bold,' Mary replied with a happy smile. She took a step closer. 'The thing is, gaffer, money is tight. And, while I don't want to leave him, I'd like to come back – for a few nights a week.'

Cyril laughed out loud. 'What do you ladies think this is? A pick-and-bleeding-mix? That's two of you looking for part-time work for a full-time job. Well, I never.'

Elsie moved closer and whispered to Sally, 'You need to do the pools this weekend. I think it's your lucky week!' Then she turned to Cyril, 'Even you can see the obvious solution here. Or do I have to spell it out for you?'

Cyril huffed and puffed briefly, then turned to Sally and said, 'A free wash and set for my wife, and I'll allow it.'

Sally threw her arms round him in delight, and then Elsie

orchestrated an impromptu cha, cha, cha train line dance, with Cyril at the head, and the other girls joining in behind them.

With her heart racing for joy, Sally thought, *I'm doing it, Sister Jones. I'm chasing that dream, and you know what? I'm going to get it too.*

BEFORE

September 1976

Sally

Doddington Estate, Battersea Park Road, London

Sally smoothed her hair, then added another slick of lipstick. By the time she'd got home from the salon today, she'd almost cancelled her plans to have drinks with Elsie. Saturdays in the salon were their busiest day and she was exhausted. But now that she'd had a wash and change of clothes she was looking forward to spending the evening with Elsie.

But when she arrived at Elsie's small flat at six o'clock, the door opened to reveal a sullen friend. Sally followed Elsie inside gingerly, feeling tension pierce the air around them.

'How are you?'

Elsie shrugged, flopping into her couch and curling her feel up under her.

'Is everything okay with Reggie?' Sally asked. The question was met with silence. 'If you want him to come along tonight, I don't mind, honestly.'

While Sally didn't relish being a third wheel, she always had a great time with them. Reggie was good company, full of funny stories. Last week, he'd had them both in stitches about an incident with a rabid dog. He was generous too, insisting on buying the rounds for not only Elsie, but also Sally.

177

'I keep telling you, Reggie and I ain't no Romeo and Juliet; we're not tied at the hips. I told him I didn't want to see him tonight,' Elsie announced, picking up a piece of lint from her denim flares.

Sally sensed that Elsie's mood was more complicated, than whatever was going on with Reggie. But she decided not to probe further for now. She knew Elsie. She'd only open up if she decided she wanted to.

Elsie picked up a copy of the *Evening Post* newspaper from the coffee table. Her jaw tightened as she pointed to the glaring headline out loud.

'Killer may strike again' warning.

'Scumbag,' Elsie said. 'I can't stop thinking about those poor women. Emily Jackson left three children behind. Wilma McCann, four.'

Sally's stomach heaved when thinking about what those women had been through. She noticed Elsie's hand shaking and reached over to lay hers on top of Elsie's.

'I know. It's scary. Even the name they've dubbed him, the Yorkshire Ripper. It sends shivers down my spine. But, whoever he is, he's a long way from London.'

Elsie threw a look at Sally, rolling her eyes. 'I bet that's cold comfort for the poor sods working at Battersea Park every night.'

Sally had seen the prostitutes who stood on the corner of the park after dark. 'We can only hope that the police find him. He'll have to slip up.'

'It's the way the press talk about the women. As if they deserved what they got, because they were prostitutes,' Elsie said, her voice laced with anger.

Sally looked at her friend in confusion. 'I know it's unfair. But why are you getting so worked up about this, Elsie? Talk to me. What's going on?'

Sally had felt that her friend had been holding back something from her for a long time. And she knew that if she'd only unburden herself with Sally, it would help. Elsie looked about to say something for a moment, but she remained silent.

Sally tried another tactic, stretching her arms above her head. 'What do you want to do tonight? It's our favourite day of the week – no work tomorrow. Don't know about you, but I plan to sleep until lunchtime.'

Elsie's face remained set like stone.

'Don't be like that,' Sally cajoled. 'I've been looking forward to tonight all week.' She moved closer to her friend and leaned in to tickle under her arm like she used to when they were kids.

'Stop!' Elsie cried out, but her face lightened as she giggled.

'Never!' Sally responded, using both hands to tickle until Elsie begged for mercy. They lay back on the sofa, shoulder to shoulder, laughing together. And the earlier tension, whatever that was, disappeared.

'Let's treat ourselves today,' Sally said. 'We both work so hard and barely get to see each other. So how about a drink in the Grove, then a fish-and-chip supper from the Apollo Café afterwards?'

'I'm broke. I can just about manage to buy two half-lagers. That's it,' Elsie said, her mouth downturned again.

Sally did the maths quickly. She had £1 from tips in the salon yesterday in her handbag. That would pay the 48p needed for two pints of lager and 42p for their chippy supper.

'On me. I had a good day at the salon yesterday,' Sally said. 'Come on. Put some lippy on, and let's go have some fun.'

Twenty minutes later, they were sitting in the corner near the jukebox, with a half pint of lager and lime each. Elton John belted out *Crocodile Rock*, and they sang along to the chorus along with most of the pub.

Elsie's earlier tension disappeared, and Sally thumped the table in front of her, giving herself a drumroll.

'I've got news,' she said in a rush. 'The results of my first exam. I've only gone and got a distinction!'

Elsie punched the air with a fisted hand and whooped out

loud. A group of ladies sitting close to them looked over with interest, one of which was Hazel, her client from the salon. Sally was chuffed to notice that her hair was still perfectly groomed.

'What are you celebrating, Sally?' Hazel called over.

'My best friend is going to be the next Vidal Sassoon! She's got a distinction in her exams!' Elsie boasted.

'I've still got years to go!' Sally exclaimed as the women raised their glasses to cheer her, but she felt happiness spark its way through her. Turning to Elsie, she asked, 'Can you believe it?'

'Yes, I can,' Elsie said, her face now serious as she turned to her friend. 'I am in awe of how hard you've worked this past year. You truly are a wonder. I wish you could give up the char work, though. It's killing you, holding down both jobs.'

Sally shrugged. 'I wish. Unless Prince Charming comes my way, I need the money to top up the apprenticeship wages. But it's helping, only working three nights a week.'

A few minutes later, Hazel approached them and placed two lager glasses on the table. 'Sally love, your hairdo finally brought me luck yesterday. So this is in thanks from me.' Hazel held out a sparkling diamond, and did a twirl and a curtsey as Sally and Elsie gushed their congratulations.

'I've been thinking about doing something new myself too,' Elsie said, once Hazel had returned to her friends. 'Last night, as I sat in the flat on my own – I talked myself out of it, convinced I'd never be able to pull it off – but hearing your news . . . it's inspiring,' Elsie said, almost shyly.

Sally's throat felt tight as she listened to her friend speak. She hated to hear how insecure she was. 'That is the craziest talk I've ever heard. You are the cleverest person I know! Tell me everything.'

Elsie reached into her oversized shoulder bag and pulled out an Avon catalogue. 'One of the girls I knew from . . . well, from before, sells Avon in the evenings. She invited me to meet her manager to discuss me becoming an Avon girl.' Elsie grinned and then sang out, 'Avon calling.' This was the perfect mimic of the Avon adverts that the girls had grown up hearing on the radio and watching on television.

'I cannot think of anyone more suited for this. And I promise you that I'll be your first customer!' Sally said, picking up the catalogue, which had a photograph of the beautiful model Iman on its cover, with the caption – *Perfect care. The Look: Silky Skin.*

'She's so beautiful. Her cheekbones are to die for.' Sally sucked in her cheeks to try to copy Iman's pout.

'You could be a model too if you wanted to be,' Elsie said.

Sally felt a flush of warmth run through her body from the sincerity in her friend's voice.

'Here, I've some samples I can give you of the skin-care cream Iman is wearing,' Elsie said, reaching into her oversized shoulder bag again. She pulled out a couple of small sachets. 'The great thing about it is that I can bring the products to my customer's homes, so they have time to try out the products. We have the biggest beauty range in the world. And I'll be trained to help ladies choose the right skin-care products, make-up, perfumes and toiletries, all at special prices.'

Sally grinned as she listened to Elsie's obvious enthusiasm for her new venture. 'Think of all the potential customers you'd have in the flats. There's hundreds of homes on your doorstep!'

'Exactly. I thought I could hand out catalogues in the evenings.'

Sally smiled as she listened to Elsie laying out her plans on how she'd manage it all. Then she hit the table when a thought struck her, exclaiming delightfully, 'We'll be the queens of cosmetics and hair!'

Elsie placed an imaginary crown on each of their heads, joining the dream. 'We could open our own business one day. We could live together again in a flat over the beauty salon.'

Sally loved the sound of that.

All thoughts of a chippy supper disappeared as they ordered another round of lager and limes. Live music began, with a male and female double act belting out show tunes. The two girls joined Hazel and her friends, and they all danced and sang the night away.

'Last orders!' the barman called out.

'Look, here's our fish supper,' Sally said with a hiccup when the cockle man came in at closing time, carrying a wicker basket full of fish and treats.

The girls each bought a small paper bag filled with cockles, mussels, prawns and winkles laced with vinegar and black pepper. With their last lager and lime of the night, a bag of cheese-and-onion crisps from the bar and their fish treats, it was the best meal that Sally had ever had.

They left the pub, a little unsteady on their feet, clutching each other for support. When Elsie hugged Sally goodbye before they parted for their own flats, she felt tearful. It had been the best night out she'd had since she'd left the orphanage. And the air felt as if it were filled with possibilities.

Ten minutes later, Sally giggled as she toppled onto the bed, unable to keep her balance when she tried to take her shoes off. She opened her handbag and pulled out the Avon catalogue, thinking she'd spend some time in the morning working out what she could afford to buy from Elsie. She could also leave the catalogue in the salon if Nicola didn't mind.

She continued flicking through the magazine, stopping abruptly when she came to the perfume pages. Her eyes were immediately drawn to a cute bottle with a plump peach as its lid.

'Her Pretty in Peach,' she whispered as a memory of her mother spraying that perfume onto her neck and wrists hit her so hard that it took her breath away. She sniffed, sure she could smell the sweet fragrance in the air.

'Oh, Mum,' Sally said, the words choking in her throat.

She'd put her mother out of her mind for years, but it appeared she was not struck from her heart. An ache throbbed inside her so piercingly that it took her breath away.

BEFORE

September 1976

Sally

Doddington Estate, Battersea Park Road, London

Sally awoke the next morning a little before nine o'clock. Her head felt woozy, and her stomach groaned in protest as she tried to sit up. Memories of her late-night shellfish feast and her breath reeking of fish made her stomach heave. She ran to the bathroom, ill from the night's overindulgence. Sally wasn't a drinker, yet she'd drunk more last night than she had in the entire time since she'd left the orphanage. She put the kettle on to make tea.

She didn't regret the hangover, though. They'd needed that blowout. It had been so much fun with Elsie, dancing and singing along to their favourite songs, celebrating and planning for a future that seemed achievable now.

And then she remembered her mother. The image she had burned in her memories of her mother sitting in front of her dressing table, brushing her flame-red hair, pouting her perfect ruby lips, spraying peach perfume liberally onto her neck and her wrists.

Once she'd made a pot of tea and had drunk her first cup, Sally walked out to the small hallway of her flat and picked up the London phone directory from the floor. It sat, gathering dust

183

in the corner, rarely used. Her heart raced as she brought it back to the kitchen table. She laid her hand on the cover, and she could almost feel it throb under her touch.

'She's not going to be listed,' she whispered to herself, trying desperately not to let herself get her hopes up. But her hand shook as she flicked through the pages. Sally's breath came in shallow bursts as she tried to find the courage to move to the 'F' section of the book. Because she knew that there was another possibility, worse than her mother leaving her behind for a new life, unburdened from her responsibilities.

She might be dead.

Sally steadied her right hand with her left, then she flicked through the pages, slowing down when she reached the surnames that started with 'Fo'. She traced her finger down the page, stopping halfway through the second column.

Fox, Lizzie, Ms, 12 Campbell Road, North Islington, London.

The room stilled, her hand stopped trembling and the words blurred as Sally blinked back tears.

That was her mother. It had to be. And, without any real thought of running through the pros and cons, Sally knew that she had to visit her. See her for herself. She caught a sob in her throat as she imagined feeling her mother's arms round her one more time.

What would Sally say to her if she found the nerve to visit her? Her body began to shake as a hidden memory resurfaced. Her mother, clicking the latch on her small suitcase, avoiding Sally's questioning eyes. And then the moment her mother had turned her back on Sally, walking away from her daughter, who sat quivering in the back of Mrs Burton's car.

Why did you send me away, Mum? Did I do something wrong?

Sally shook the thoughts away. If she did go to see her mother, Sally would keep these questions to herself. She wasn't sure she was brave enough to ask them, or to hear the answer.

Sally stood up and made her way to the bathroom. This was

the most critical first impression of her life. Her mother was a glamorous woman – she remembered that much clearly – who spent a lot of time sitting in front of her dressing table, getting ready to go out. So Sally took her time, teasing her hair into place, then applying her make-up carefully. She knew what she was going to wear. High-waisted mint-green flared trousers, a small gold buckle belt that cinched in her waist and a bell-sleeved silk print blouse in creams, with mint-green and light-blue patterns swirling prettily together. She'd bought the blouse for 50p in her favourite second-hand shop and had worn it on her first day of college.

Once she was ready, she looked at herself in her mirror, turning sideways to check her appearance from every direction. Would her mother be proud of her daughter? Would she think Sally was pretty? Her hammering heart told her that, no matter what she might tell herself, she still desperately needed her mother's approval.

Sally made her way to Battersea Park Station and, with the help of a kind ticket agent, worked out her route to North Islington. Her mother's house was only a three-minute walk from the station. Less than an hour later, she arrived at Campbell Road. Had she been living this close to her mother all this time? A mere sixty minutes from the only person to whom she was related in this world?

Sally felt a tension headache begin to pound as she ran through the words she'd practised in her mind during the train journey here. She looked at her small Timex watch, surprised it was only eleven. It felt as if a day had passed since she'd written down her mother's address on the back of a brown envelope. Was it too early to call? She hoped not. Sally paused at a corner shop and went inside to buy a box of Milk Tray chocolates.

'For anyone special?' the shopkeeper asked as Sally paid him.

'For my mother,' Sally replied, and felt a flush of warmth move from her chest to her face. She loved how that sounded on her lips.

My mother.

Campbell Road was an eclectic group of old houses comprising red, grey and white brick, with many of them derelict. A couple of cars were parked up along the street. A group of kids played chase with each other, dodging cars as their drivers honked their horns to move them out of the way. A man wearing a heavy knitted cardigan leaned on his front door, smoking a pipe. He paid her no attention as she passed him by. A stench filled the air. Putrid damp and decay. Several houses had 'Sold' signs pinned to boarded-up windows and doors. Graffiti scarred the facade of a large corner house, painted white. Windows were broken in another.

She counted down the numbers from 103 until she came to 20. Then she slowed to almost a standstill. Her heart raced again as she willed herself the courage to walk the last few feet. Sally noticed a woman with hair in large round curlers. She wore a bright-red housecoat. Smoke drifted upwards, as she took a deep drag of her cigarette. Two more steps and she arrived outside number 12. Pink flowery curtains were closed in the window beside the black front door and grey-brick home. Their bright colour was a lonely but hopeful sight in a grey landscape. A promising sign, Sally told herself, lifting her hand to knock on the door.

She felt the eyes of the woman in curlers watching her as she rapped the brass knocker. The woman said, 'She won't be up, love.' She sniffed, then added, 'She'll have been up half the night.'

Sally ignored her. She knew her type, always watching, judging, gossiping. She had half a dozen neighbours on her landing who were the same. Sally took a step back, preparing herself for disappointment. But then a flash of movement on her left caught her eye. The curtains twitched. Sally knocked a second time, and then she heard the sound of footsteps making their way towards the front door.

Sally crossed her fingers, holding her hands behind her back. *Please, Mum, let it be you.*

And her wish was granted because the door opened to reveal Lizzie Fox.

She was older, but nonetheless impossible to mistake. Her hair was still vibrant red, back-combed high on her head. Dark kohl eyeliner framed her green eyes, and her signature ruby red lipstick stained her lips. But the colour bled into new lines running around her mother's mouth.

Her mother looked at her, and Sally watched her, hoping she would see instant recognition in her eyes. But there was no Hollywood reunion.

'Whatever you're selling, I'm not buying.'

Her voice threw Sally. It was deeper than she remembered it, raspy, as if she had smoked too much. Prepared speeches disappeared as a rush of emotion flooded Sally again.

'Cat got your tongue?' her mother asked again. But her voice wasn't cruel as she surveyed Sally, and she smiled lopsidedly at her.

Sally remembered that smile, and it gave her the courage to move closer again.

'Hello, Mum.'

Her mother's face paled as Sally's words landed. Her eyes drifted up and down Sally, and then, with a quick glance up and down the road, she gestured inside.

'You better come in.'

The house was clean; that was Sally's first thought as she walked down the small hallway into a square sitting room. The heavy scent of cologne lingered behind her mother as she moved. It wasn't Pretty in Peach, though. Something muskier that she didn't recognise. A brown velvet couch and armchair were pushed against the wall. The floor was carpeted, deep red, with a beige pattern running through it. A coffee table sat in the middle of the room, and several magazines were on top. It looked normal, like any mother's home.

'I can't believe it's you,' her mum said as she took a seat in the armchair, her eyes running over Sally from head to toe. Sally perched herself on the edge of the sofa, her body trembling as her heart raced.

'You look well, Mum,' Sally said, clasping her hands on her lap so tightly that her knuckles turned white.

'And you've all grown up,' her mum replied. She smoothed down her hair, licking her lips as she took in Sally. 'How'd you find me?'

'The phone book,' Sally said. 'I thought you might have left England. I was happy to see you are still here.'

Her mother's face clouded, and the lines around her lips deepened as she frowned. 'I should have gone to Australia when I had the chance.'

Sally shifted in her seat as her mother's eyes glared at her. It was as if Sally were to blame for this missed opportunity. 'Why didn't you go?'

'My friend and I applied for the ten-pound passage as part of the Australian Migration Scheme – Ten-pound Poms, they called it. I was all set. But then I got pregnant. I had to stay here while my pal was out in Perth, living her best life. The sun shines every day there, so I'm told.'

Ah, it *was* her fault. Sally didn't know how to respond, so she stayed dumb. An uneasy silence filled the small sitting room.

Ask me how I am, Mum, please.

'I haven't got any money if that's what you're looking for,' her mother eventually said.

'I didn't come for money, Mum,' Sally replied. Her hands felt clammy, so she wiped them on her trousers. 'I have a job. Well, two, actually. I'm an apprentice hairdresser, and I work at night cleaning offices.'

Her mother smiled again, and the tension left the room. 'My daughter is a hairdresser!' She clapped her hands in delight, clearly pleased with this career choice. 'You have pretty hair. I like that style,' she stated, and Sally basked in the compliment.

'The Farrah Fawcett flick is popular in my salon. Nicola, she's my boss, she styled my hair like this. I'm glad you like it.'

Sally passed the brown paper bag to her mother. 'I got you some chocolates.'

Her mother opened the bag and smiled her lopsided grin again. 'All because the lady loves Milk Tray. My favourite. Tell you what, let's have some tea and chocolates now.'

Her mother disappeared, and Sally took the chance to look at the photographs that lined the mantlepiece over the fire as she heard her fill the kettle.

'There's none of you there,' her mother's voice said from behind. 'Too hard to look at you after I handed you over.'

This was the first sign of emotion from her mother, and Sally clung to it.

'I understand.' Sally paused, trying to work up the courage to admit her truth. 'I missed you, Mum.'

There, she'd said it.

Her mother walked to her and held her hands between her own. Bright red nail polish gleamed on her mother's long acrylic nails.

'I can't wear polish because of the cleaning job. It never lasts,' Sally explained, feeling a little embarrassed by her boring, unadorned nails.

'You have pretty hands. Keep putting hand cream on every morning and night. It's the only way to keep age at bay. The lines on her hands are such a giveaway tale about a woman's age.'

'You have pretty hands too, Mum,' Sally said, and she could see that her mother was pleased with that compliment too.

The kettle whistled its readiness, so her mum disappeared again, returning a few moments later with two mugs of steaming tea.

'I hope you like milk and sugar. I made it the same way I like mine.'

'It's exactly as I drink it,' Sally replied as she took her first sip. Another sign, she told herself. They had something else in common. This was going to work out. They'd be friends again, once more

189

in each other's lives. Her mum could come to the salon once a week, and Sally would do her hair for her.

'Tell me about your life,' her mother said.

And so, as they tucked into the chocolates, Sally told her mother about Nicola, Elsie and her flat in Doddington.

'I made the right choice for you,' her mother stated. 'Giving you to the orphanage.'

Sally couldn't bring herself to agree with her mother, even though she knew that was what was expected of her.

'Why did you give me away?' Sally whispered, unable to keep the question in one moment more.

Her mother stood up, her green kaftan billowing out behind her as she walked to the windows. Had she heard Sally? She moved aside the flowery curtains and looked out, her forehead furrowed in a frown.

'Look at those poor buggers trying to pretend that they are having fun as they kick a tin can about. The kids here will never see the ocean. They'll never get to ride a rollercoaster. Or play in a green field. They'll live and die in this dump. I wanted more than that for you.' She turned round, her eyes glistening as the sunlight hit them from the window. Her voice dropped to a whisper. 'Have you seen the ocean?'

Sally remembered a trip when she was twelve years old. With Sister Jones in charge, she'd hired a bus and taken them all to Margate for the day. Most of the girls in Sunshine House had never been outside London before. There had been so much excitement on the bus that it had felt like it would combust, blowing its rusty seams apart. And when they'd stopped at the pier they'd run at full speed towards the sea, pulling their stockings and shoes off. Her toes curled in memory of that first shock as the water kissed her feet. Gulls had cawed in the blue skies, harmonising with the squeals of the girls.

'I saw the ocean, Mum. And it was the most wondrous sight.'

Her mother nodded, wiping under her eyes with the back of her hand. 'It broke my heart that day. Sending you to the orphanage.'

Sally's breath caught in her throat.

'I loved you. But I couldn't take care of you any more. Life was . . . complicated. I had no choice. I had to give you up. But I need you to know that it cost me.'

Sally watched her mother's face crumple as she spoke, decades of hurt and loss etched onto the fine lines of her face.

'It's okay, Mum,' Sally said, desperate to take away her mother's pain.

'You must hate me.'

Sally shook her head, knowing it to be true that she did not. 'I missed you. I was worried for you. I was scared and hurt. But I never hated you, Mum.'

Her mother turned back to the window again, and said softly, 'My daughter got to see the ocean . . .'

'One day, I'd like to live near the water,' Sally said shyly, admitting out loud a secret dream.

'You could open a hairdressing salon somewhere on the coast. Bournemouth is meant to be lovely.' Her mother frowned. 'I knew a man from Bournemouth once. He had the longest fingernails. Off-putting.'

Sally stood up, placing her mug on the coffee table. 'Maybe I could do your hair for you.'

For a moment, happiness sparked its way through her mother, like sunbeams on the window pane, as she smiled in delight at Sally's suggestion. Sally couldn't help herself. She lunged forward and threw her arms round her mother, holding her close. She inhaled her musky scent hungrily as her hands reached up to touch her mother's hair again. They stood in each other's embrace, their breaths moving in synchrony.

'I'm afraid I need to ask you to leave. I have to go to work,' her mother said, pulling apart and stepping backwards until she touched the window frame.

Sally almost stumbled, such was her surprise at her mother's sudden mood change. 'What do you work at?' Sally asked, keeping her smile brightly fixed on as she tried to hide her hurt.

191

'This and that,' was her unsatisfactory answer. 'I'm truly happy to have seen you, Sally. You are a beautiful young woman, and I'm proud of all you are doing in your life. But I'm sorry. I don't have it in me to be your mother – not how you want me to be.'

Sally raised her hands in protest, reaching out to clasp her mother's again. But they fell into a growing abyss between them.

'I don't need anything from you, Mum. Promise. I want to see you every now and then.'

'I don't know. Maybe. But you need to go now.' Her eyes darted to the front door as if expecting someone to come through at any minute.

'Shall I come back next Sunday to talk some more?' Sally asked, her voice coming out in a high-pitched squeak.

'No! Don't come back. Only if we've arranged it beforehand. You can't just show up here.'

Sally's stomach dropped in disappointment. 'Okay, Mum. But can I call you first to arrange it? Do you have a phone?'

'No. When I need the phone, I use the call box at the end of the road.'

'I can write to you,' Sally said, desperate to find a way to keep in touch.

'It's a free world,' her mother replied, her voice now cool, and unyielding. 'Thank you for the chocolates. And good luck with the hairdressing.'

Her mother moved towards the front door, leaving a confused Sally no option but to follow her out.

'Is everything okay?' Sally asked, failing to catch her mother's eyes.

'It's fine. I'm busy, that's all.' Her mother's voice caught as she continued, 'It was good to see you Sally. Goodbye.'

And then she closed the front door softly between them.

'Don't send me away again mum, please . . .' Sally whispered, as she stood rooted to the spot, holding back tears.

But the door remained closed, so Sally made her way home.

NOW

August 2023

Lily

Casa Rosa, Ronda, Spain

They stopped for a coffee and pastry en route. The sugar and caffeine, with the incredible backdrop of the Spanish coastal town of Marbella in the background, broke the tension that had built up when Zach referred to Lily as his sister. By the time they were back on the road, moving onto the smaller serpentine windy A397, their earlier ease with each other had returned.

'The road will get tricky for a bit, so I'm going mute as I concentrate. Enjoy the views, Lily. They took my breath away the first time I saw them.'

The road was a single track, reasonably wide, but it had continuous hairpin bends that made her stomach flip as Zach navigated them. But then she caught sight of the coast, and, as Zach had predicted, the view was breathtaking. She forgot about the road before her, trusting Zach's driving. Sally instead focused on the Spanish landscape. As they climbed higher, she noticed netting had been placed on the reddish volcanic rock face. Presumably, to keep rocks from falling onto the road.

After a particularly large bend, the landscape changed, with the red rock disappearing and white limestone taking its place. She spied a peregrine falcon swooping down over a nearby mountaintop. And they passed a couple of ventas – the local cafés – one of which had dozens of bikers sitting outside, who waved at Lily as they passed them by.

'Almost there,' Zach said as the first glimpse of Ronda came into view.

Whitewashed buildings were carved into the cliff edge, and the Puente Nuevo bridge stood proud against a blue, cloudless sky.

'Ronda is one of the *pueblos blancos* – white villages – of Andalucia,' Zach said.

Lily could hear pride in his voice as he became her unofficial tour guide. 'It's good to be back. There's something about this place that resonates with me deeply.'

He slowed to a crawl as he began weaving their car through the one-way streets, moving towards the older part of the historic town.

'Are you going to tell me where we're staying?' Lily asked.

Zach had reassured her that accommodation was sorted, but had remained tight-lipped about where it was.

'We're here.' He pulled into a small driveway in front of a row of whitewashed villas, which overlooked the gorge below.

They jumped out of the car, and Zach practically bounced up to the villa on the left-hand side. He opened his phone, then punched in a code from an email he'd received into a keypad on the wall. Pulling the key out, he opened the front door.

'Welcome to Casa Rosa,' he proclaimed, ushering Lily in. 'I think you'll like this place. It's over a century old.'

The hall led into a small open-plan living space. Whitewashed walls, terracotta flagstones on the floor and dark wooden beams on the ceiling gave the room a rustic charm. A small galley kitchen ran along one end, with a sitting room on the other. A comfortable green sofa sat beside a log stove, and a rattan rug was on the floor.

'It's lovely,' Lily said. She opened a door off the hall to reveal a small bathroom with a Moroccan feel. Then, opposite that room, was a bedroom with a large double bed in its centre, with pristine white duvet covers and pillowcases. 'Erm, Zach, where's the second bedroom?'

'There's only one. You get the bedroom; I've got the couch. Simple,' Zach said. 'And don't even think about arguing.' He left the room to end the discussion and called over his shoulder, 'Come check this out.'

She followed him onto a small brick terrace. Pots filled with peonies in every rainbow colour sat along its edge, framing the view below. She was speechless as she took in the incredible vista below.

'This brick –' Zach touched the weathered caramel and honey-coloured bricks – 'is part of the city wall of Ronda. Isn't that something? To be part of something so historic. It's one of the best-preserved city walls on the peninsula. It's famed for it.'

'It's stunning, Zach,' Lily said as she breathed deeply the scent of flowers, and birds sang out a welcome. 'I can't believe that this morning I was scraping porridge from Ben's hair and face at breakfast . . . and now this.'

'Wild, right?' Zach asked, grinning. Then he paused, his smile disappearing as a frown deepened into his forehead. 'Lily, this is the first home that I remember. This is the villa my mom and I lived in, in the 1980s.'

Lily felt her breath disappear as the weight of that piece of information hit her.

She looked at Zach, and the years slipped away like leaves in an autumn breeze, until he was no longer a grown man, but a young toddler of two and a half. After decades of wondering where Robert had disappeared to, was she finally standing in the answer? A shiver ran down her spine.

'Were you happy here?' she managed to whisper.

He shrugged his shoulders, his own eyes filling with tears too.

'I don't know. I think so. But, as I've told you before, most of my earliest memories are American ones with Mom and Dad. Playing with my sisters when they came along. All happy there. But I do have fragments of my Spanish childhood locked away in my mind. And when I came here for that summer it was as if the air around me had the key to open them up again. I remembered feelings or moments. Nothing I could cling to, though.'

Lily saw something flash across Zach's face. A shadow of . . . pain, she thought. 'Good memories?' she pushed.

'Not all of them. I remember feeling scared while I was here,' Zach said, his eyes looking downwards to his feet.

'Are you okay?' Lily asked, moving towards him.

Another shrug. Then he walked back into the villa. 'Let's go next door and meet Señor and Señora Alvarez. They are the owners I told you about. I'd like you to meet them.'

They were in luck. A smiling woman with twinkling brown eyes opened the door. She had long dark hair peppered with white streaks, tied in a low bun.

'*Hola, mi querido chico, Zach,*' she said as she pulled him into her arms for a warm embrace.

Zach began speaking fluent Spanish. Lily guessed he was introducing her, and smiled as Señora Alvarez kissed both her cheeks, before ushering them both inside.

The Alvarez villa was larger than their rental next door, but had the same earthy charm and similar decor. They walked to a large patio overlooking a lush green garden and found Señor Alvarez smoking a pipe. They exchanged more hugs, and he kissed Lily on each cheek when she was introduced. Señora Alvarez disappeared into the kitchen momentarily, returning with drinks for them all.

'Tinto de verano is a red wine with fizzy lemonade. It's delicious and addictive, honestly,' Zach said as Lily accepted a tall glass, resembling rosé Prosecco.

Lily took a sip and thanked Señora Alvarez. It was cold, sweet and, as Zach predicted, delicious.

She sat back and watched Zach and the older couple chat, laughing as they swapped stories. Their ease with each other suggested many happy moments on this terrace, drinking Tinto de Verano.

'We should speak English. For Lily,' Señor Alvarez said slowly.

She could see that he was a kind man, and Lily was grateful to him for this concession.

'Your mother, she is well?'

Zach smiled as he opened his phone to show the older couple the screen saver, which displayed a photograph of Zach and his mother together.

Señora Alvarez clapped her hands in delight. 'I like seeing her smile. She not smile enough when she lived here.'

Lily and Zach glanced at each other.

'She was sad?' Lily asked.

Señor Alvarez looked at his wife in silent question, who nodded back.

'She was not sad. She was happy with you, her child. But she was scared,' he said.

'Of what?' Zach asked.

'I don't know. But she would not leave your side, even for a moment, for the first year you lived here,' Señora Alvarez replied.

'She hides,' Señor Alvarez said, shrugging. 'I say to my wife when she arrives with one bag and eyes that never stop looking over her shoulder, that she is running from something.'

'Or someone,' Zach added. 'Mom had just left my father when she got here.' His lips tightened as he said, 'He was abusive to her. So you are right. She was hiding. From him.'

Lily nudged Zach's leg with her foot. 'But we are confused about when that was. Right?'

Zach turned to the Alvarezes again. 'Do you remember what year my mom and I arrived here? It's important to me to find out when.' He licked his lips repeatedly as the Alvarezes debated this amongst themselves.

Señora Alvarez finally turned back to them both.

'Sister Monique from the Benedictine Convent in Ronda drove you here.'

Zach's eyebrows shot up at this information. 'A nun brought us here?'

'*Si.*'

'From the convent here in Ronda?' Lily asked.

'*Si,*' Señora Alvarez replied. 'It was the year before the Olympics in Los Angeles. We all watched Luis Doreste and Roberto Molina win gold. For sailing. Oh, how we cheered! And I remember so clearly your mother saying that it was a double celebration, because it was also the anniversary of when you moved into the villa. And we cheered that too.'

Señor Alvarez nodded his agreement to this.

Lily picked up her phone and googled the Olympics in Los Angeles. She looked at Zach and said softly, 'That was in July 1984.'

'*Si. Eso es correcto,*' Señora Alvarez agreed. 'July 1984.'

'Was I a little baby when I arrived here?' Zach asked, imitating rocking a baby in his arms.

'No!' Señora Alvarez said with a laugh. 'Big, strong boy.' She showed them his height when he arrived.

Roughly the height of a toddler.

'Are you a hundred per cent sure?' Zach asked softly.

'*Si,*' both Alvarezes answered, looking a little bewildered by all the questions.

Zach turned to Lily, his face twisted in worry. 'Why did Mom tell me we got here a year earlier, in 1982?'

PART THREE

Do not overlook negative actions merely because they are small;
however small a spark may be,
it can burn down a haystack as big as a mountain.

Karma: Truth and Consequences, Gautama Buddha

BEFORE

May 1979

Sally

Elite, Wandsworth, London

Nicola hammered a nail into the wall behind the reception desk. Then she picked up a black A4 frame and carefully hung it, ensuring it was straight. She took a step back to stand beside Sally, and together they admired the certificate proudly on display.

Sally Fox
City and Guilds Hairdressing Diploma
May 1979

Over the past three years, Sally had studied and worked so hard that the time had passed by in a flash. But finally she was done. And seeing the diploma, hanging beside Nicola's certificates, made her heart swell with pride.

'I'm so proud of you,' Nicola stated, giving Sally's arm another squeeze.

'I can't believe it,' Sally said. 'Seeing my certificate up on the wall beside yours feels like a dream.'

'Where else would it go?' Nicola asked.

'I'd like to take a photograph of it. I'll take it to Sister Jones at Sunshine House so she can see I did it. I caught that dream.'

'She'll be so happy for you – and rightly so, love. You have to send one to your mum too.'

Sally frowned, unsure if that was a good idea or not. Despite her best efforts, her relationship with her mother ran hot and cold. She'd only seen her half a dozen times since that first reunion in the autumn of 1976. Nicola had been more of a mother to Sally in that time than her own had throughout her entire life.

Nicola nudged her arm. 'Now that you are fully qualified, I've decided it's time to make some further changes around here. We've grown our clientele by over fifty per cent in the past couple of years. So I'm going to open six days a week, starting next month. I thought you could manage Mondays on your own, and then you could take Tuesdays off, where I'll open up on my own. They are both typically quieter days.'

Sally's mind raced with this news. Her dream was to give up her cleaning work and dedicate herself to hairdressing, but she wasn't sure she could afford it, even with an extra day's salary. Would her wages increase?

'Of course, your wages will increase too,' Nicola added as if she could read Sally's mind. She paused, deliberately, to add drama.

Sally wanted to scream, 'How much, how much?' but managed to keep her mouth shut.

'How does forty-eight pounds per week sound? Eight pounds per day, plus your tips are your own, as I always say.'

It sounded incredible to her. Sally began to laugh out loud, then grabbed Nicola round her waist, pulling her into a half dance and half hug of delight.

'I thought that might make you happy. You tell that gaffer of yours that you are quitting. I'm sick of looking at you yawning every other day,' Nicola teased. 'And it's time you got yourself a boyfriend too.'

'Chance would be a fine thing!' But a grin broke out on her

face because Nicola was right. She'd had a few dates over the past couple of years, but they always fizzled out because she was never available for a second date.

'This feels like a dream,' Sally said with a sigh.

'It's no dream. Oh my days, I've not seen a soul work harder than you have. In three years, you've not let me down. The customers love you. You are a born natural, a wonder with those little hands of yours.'

Sally flushed with the praise, feeling giddy and light, ready to take on the world.

'How about we close up for the day and head to the Grove for a lager and lime?' Nicola asked.

Before Sally could answer, the bell sounded at the front door, and a broad man, with brown, shaggy hair walked in. He wore a black leather overcoat, a black turtleneck and black slacks. As Sally's eyes gave him the once-over, she noticed he had cream leather loafers, which seemed in contrast to the rest of his outfit.

'That's the Old Bill, can tell by the cut of him,' Nicola whispered to Sally. She moved towards the front desk. 'Short back and sides, is it?'

The man smiled, and murmured a 'not today'. Then he pulled out his badge, and flashed it in Nicola's direction. 'I'm Detective Sergeant Ian Baldwin.'

Sally moved closer to Nicola in a gesture of solidarity. She had no clue why the police officer was in the salon, but figured he was following trouble.

'We're looking for a . . .' Detective Sergeant Baldwin looked down at a notepad he'd pulled from his jacket. 'A Ms Sally Fox.'

Sally had not expected her name to be called out. She swallowed and replied, 'I'm Sally.'

'Is there somewhere I can have a private conversation with you?' Detective Sergeant Baldwin asked, looking around the small salon.

Sally felt Nicola's comforting hand move round her waist. 'I'll go into the stockroom – you can chat here,' she said.

'No, stay with me, please,' Sally said. She looked at the police officer. 'I'd like her to stay, if that's all right.'

The detective sergeant nodded his agreement, glancing at his notebook again. 'Ms Fox, are you the daughter of Lizzie Fox, of Campbell Road, North Islington?'

Sally nodded, feeling a lump lodge its way into her throat. Her breathing quickened. She felt Nicola's arm tighten its grip round her.

'When was the last time that you saw your mother?' Detective Sergeant Baldwin asked.

Sally chewed her bottom lip as she tried to work it out. 'I called to see her at Easter, but she wasn't in. The last time I spoke to her in person was at Christmas. I called to visit her on Christmas Eve to give her a gift – perfume. She likes perfume . . .' She trailed off, realising she was babbling.

'And you haven't seen her since then?' Detective Sergeant Baldwin asked.

Years of unreturned letters, knocking on an unopened door, and occasional visits that were warm and inviting or cold and dismissive, depending on her mother's whim, cut Sally as memories flooded back to her.

'As I said, I tried to visit at Easter, but she wasn't there.' She inhaled deeply, then admitted with a sigh, 'We're not close. I saw her a couple of times a year at most.' Then, it struck her that there was no good reason why a police officer was asking her these questions. Ice-cold shivers ran down her spine as she asked, 'Why do you want to know? Has something happened to her?'

'Would you like to take a seat?' Detective Sergeant Baldwin asked, ignoring her question and nodding towards the salon chairs.

Sally shook her head and straightened her back, determined to be strong for whatever was about to be thrown her way.

The detective sergeant's voice turned sombre, his face grave, 'I'm sorry to inform you, Ms Fox, that your mother's body was found earlier today at her home in Campbell Road.'

'Oh my days!' Nicola said, her voice coming out in a high squeak.

Sally's ears pulsed as her mind tried to register the detective sergeant's words. He continued to explain the horrific details to her. 'A neighbour called the police this morning, reporting that she'd not seen Ms Fox for several days. And, when one of my colleagues called to check on your mother, they discovered your mother's body.' He paused, locking eyes with Sally. 'She'd been dead for several days.'

This detail made Sally's knees sag, and the breath left her body.

Her mother had died, and nobody knew for days.

That was the saddest thing she'd ever heard in her life. Nicola led her to one of the salon chairs, whispering soothing sounds.

'I d-don't understand,' Sally eventually stammered. 'When I saw her at Christmas, she was in perfect health. She looked the same as she did every single time.'

She closed her eyes for a moment, thinking of her mother in a fitted green velour jumpsuit with her ruby-red lips, looking vibrant and happy.

'How did she die?' Nicola asked.

'There will be an autopsy, but it looks likely that foul play was involved,' Detective Sergeant Baldwin said.

His words hit Sally with such a punch that she felt further winded. She felt his eyes watching her closely; it was as if they were boring holes into her head.

Sally turned away from him, whispering to Nicola, 'Who would want to hurt my mother?'

'I don't know, love, but that's where these lot come in,' Nicola replied, nodding over her shoulder towards Baldwin.

'I'll need you to come to the morgue to identify her,' Detective Sergeant Baldwin said. 'I can take you now, then bring you home afterwards.'

'Okay,' Sally said. 'I need to sort out the towels . . .'

Nicola held her hand up. 'You don't need to do anything, love, but get through this heartbreak the best you can.' She turned to Baldwin. 'I'll go with Sally too. She'll not face this on her own.'

Holding Nicola's hand, Sally found herself in the back of a white Ford Cortina. The traffic was in their favour, and within ten minutes they were at the city morgue being led into a room by a sombre-faced pathologist.

Her legs felt as if they were filled with cement as she looked around the cold, sterile morgue. She moved slowly to the gurney where her mother's body lay underneath a crisp white sheet. Sally held her breath as the pathologist lifted the covering, revealing her mother's face.

It looked as if she were sleeping.

Her face was unmarked, and she looked younger somehow, with her red hair fanned around her – the mother of Sally's childhood, before she sent her away to Sunshine House.

'Is this your mother, Lizzie Fox?' Detective Sergeant Baldwin asked gently.

Sally didn't look up, keeping her eyes locked on her mother's face instead. 'Yes.' She was surprised at her voice's strength because her insides felt as if they were on fire, melting every part of her. 'Can I touch her?' she whispered.

'I'm afraid not,' the pathologist replied. 'It's not permitted before we do the post mortem.'

Sally leaned down close to her mother's face and breathed in deeply. She couldn't smell her musky scent, only the sterile aroma of bleach, and that was all wrong. She reached into her handbag and fumbled until she found her tiny bottle of Charlie perfume.

'Could you spray this on her when you have finished the post-mortem? My mother would hate the smell of bleach. She wears perfume every day.'

The pathologist took the bottle solemnly and promised he would do as Sally asked.

Sally kissed her own fingertips, then held them an inch above her mother's mouth.

'I'm sorry this happened to you, Mum. I'm sorry that your life was cut short. I'm sorry that we weren't closer. I'm sorry. I'm so sorry . . .' Sally finished on a sob.

BEFORE

May 1979

Sally

Doddington Estate, Battersea Park Road, London

As Detective Sergeant Baldwin drove them home, Sally lay her head on Nicola's shoulder, closing her eyes. She wasn't asleep, but couldn't muster any energy for small talk. When they arrived outside the Doddington flats, Baldwin opened the car door for them.

'Are you okay?' he asked, his brown eyes warm, with concern etched on his face.

'Not really,' Sally answered truthfully. 'But I will be.'

'I need to ask you some further questions, but if you are not up to it now, we can wait until tomorrow.'

'I think Sally has been through enough,' Nicola said, her voice firm.

While Sally appreciated her friend's intervention, she could think of nothing worse than continuing this conversation again the following day.

'It's okay. I'd prefer to get this over and done with. My flat is this way.'

Detective Sergeant Baldwin followed Sally and Nicola up the cement walkway towards the stairwell.

'The lifts are broken. Sorry,' Sally said as she began to climb upwards.

'They're always bloody broken,' Nicola grumbled. 'You go on ahead. I'm going to get Elsie.'

When they entered Sally's flat, Detective Sergeant Baldwin's eyes ran over the sitting-room area. Sally supposed it must look small and tatty to him, but she had made the best of the space. She'd replaced the net curtains with vibrant red-and-cream geometric-patterned curtains two years ago, and placed a large shag-pile rug on top of the carpet. Framed posters filled the walls. Two wicker chairs bought in the Camden market, with bright red cushions, sat opposite the sofa. It wasn't much, but it was home.

Sally sat in one of the wicker chairs and motioned for the detective sergeant to sit down too.

'Ask me whatever you need to.'

But, before he could, Elsie ran into the flat, out of breath, with a red-faced Nicola on her tail. Sally stood up and moved into her friend's embrace.

'I can't believe this has happened, Elsie.'

Elsie stroked the back of Sally's head as she whispered how sorry she was.

'I'll make us all some tea,' Nicola said, moving into the kitchenette.

Detective Sergeant Baldwin cleared his throat, and Sally pulled away from Elsie and retook her seat. She heard the hum of the kettle in the kitchen, along with muffled whispers from her two friends.

'I know this has been a shock for you. I'm sorry,' Baldwin said.

'It's fine. Ask me whatever it is you need to know.'

He pulled out his notebook and flipped through the pages. 'Do you know what your mother did for a living?'

Sally nodded. 'Yes. She was a waitress.'

The detective sergeant raised his eyebrows at this. 'Where did she work?'

'It changed a lot. She always got restless. At least that's what she told me. But when I spoke to her last Christmas she said she was working in a new Indian restaurant near the Finchley Road.'

Baldwin scribbled that down in his notebook. 'Do you know the name of it?'

Sally shook her head.

'Are you aware that your mother was arrested several times?'

Sally sat forward as if an electric shock had pierced her. This was news to her. She shook her head, afraid to ask what crime her mother had committed. Shoplifting maybe? Sally could imagine her pocketing lipstick from Woolworths and walking out the door. But nothing prepared her for the next revelation out of the detective sergeant's mouth.

'For soliciting.'

Sally fell back into the chair. Her cheeks flamed red as she repeated his words to herself. They didn't make sense to her.

'There's . . . there's been some mistake,' she eventually stammered.

Sally looked over to Elsie and Nicola, who were hovering close by. Elsie's face went so pale that Sally thought she might faint. Nicola quickly placed a cup of tea in Sally's hands.

'Here, love. Drink this. I've put sugar in for the shock.'

She then placed a cup in front of Baldwin. 'Are you sure you have the right Lizzie Fox?'

'There's no mistake,' he replied firmly. 'I arrested her once myself. She was memorable, what with her flame-red hair.'

Sally took a sip of the hot, sweet tea. It was welcome and needed. And, as much as she wanted to pretend this wasn't happening, Sally knew she had to face this news. Taking a steadying breath, she asked, 'When was Mum arrested?'

Baldwin opened his notebook again and flipped through a couple of pages. 'The first time was in December 1963.'

Sally's mind reeled as she took in the timing. 'My mother gave me up to the orphanage in September 1963. Which was three months before she was arrested.'

Had she been prostituting before she handed Sally over to the home? Or had that happened afterwards?

She heard Elsie suck in her breath and Nicola mutter another of her 'Oh my days'.

'She was arrested a further two times, in 1968 and in 1971. But she's been cautioned half a dozen times too. She was well known to the local bobby. Lizzie worked the corner of Finsbury Park, a popular spot for the women.'

'I d-didn't know,' Sally stammered. Her cup shook in her hand as she tried to lift it to her mouth. She placed it back down on the coffee table, then ran to the bathroom, feeling her stomach heave and turn as she tried to digest the police officer's words. She retched, but nothing came up. Her eyes stung as she splashed cold water on her face.

There was a light tap on the door, then Elsie poked her head in.

'Come here,' Elsie said, again taking her into her arms.

'I can't believe it,' Sally cried as she lay her head on her friend's shoulder.

'Me either. It's a shocker. But how could you know this, in fairness? Will I tell the Old Bill to do one?'

Sally nodded, grateful for the suggestion. She'd had enough questions. She stayed in the bathroom until she heard the bang of the front door closing. A few minutes later, she returned to the sitting room, joining Nicola and Elsie.

'I made fresh tea,' Nicola said. 'But we might need something stronger.'

Sally had never been more grateful for these women; her sisterhood was always here to support her.

'Sit down here,' Elsie said, patting the seat beside her while Nicola searched the kitchen cabinet until she found a small bottle of gin. She poured three shots of it into tumblers, then added a splash of lemonade from the fridge. The women sat in silence for a few moments, sipping their drinks. Sally could feel their eyes upon her, each trying to work out what to say. There was nothing to be said.

'I never knew,' Sally said again.

'How could you?' Nicola asked, shaking her head. 'The poor woman. What a life.'

Sally couldn't bear to think about what her mother may have suffered over the years. What decisions she'd made in her life that had brought her to this final crossroads. It made her head pound and her stomach flip and turn. Then a rush of fatigue passed over her. She stifled a yawn as her eyes stung and prickled.

'You look done in,' Nicola said. 'It's the shock of it all. No wonder. You should get to bed. Get a good night's sleep.'

'How can a day go from being the best one of your life to the worst?' Sally asked. 'One minute we're hanging my hairdressing diploma up on the wall, celebrating your job offer and the next . . .'

'Life isn't fair, that's for sure,' Elsie said. Then she looked at Sally in surprise and asked, 'What job offer?'

Nicola quickly explained their plans for the future. 'We'll celebrate another night.'

Sally smiled weakly.

Nicola downed the last drink and stood up, giving Sally one last embrace. 'I'm going to go, let you get to bed. Sleep is the ticket. I'll call over tomorrow to see how you are. You'll get through this, love, and we'll be right here beside you to help.'

'I'll make you a hot-water bottle before I go,' Elsie said, moving into the kitchen to fill a kettle. 'And I'll call Mary to see if she can do your shifts next week. I know she needs the extra few bob; I think she'll be glad. One less thing for you to worry about.'

'Do you think she'll want to go back full time?' Sally asked. 'I need to give my notice to the gaffer.'

'I'll talk to the gaffer tomorrow night before our shift starts. Let him know about your mother. With a bit of luck, you might not even have to worry about working your notice.'

Sally felt her stomach flip. 'Please don't tell anyone about what my mo—'

Elsie shook her head quickly. 'That's your mother's business. I won't be saying it to anyone.' Then she stepped in closer and lowered her voice to say, 'When your back's to the wall, you don't have a choice.'

Sally looked up at her in surprise.

'Get into bed. I'll be in shortly with your bottle,' Elsie said, gently pushing her towards the bedroom.

Sally peeled off her clothes and slipped into her pyjamas. While her body ached with tiredness, she wasn't sure she could sleep – not without having nightmares, that is. Elsie joined her and slipped a bottle under the bedclothes. Then, taking a look at Sally's pale face, she motioned her to move over and lay on the bed beside her – like they used to do back in the orphanage.

Sally was surprised when she felt Elsie's body shaking beside her. She hadn't expected her to be as upset about her mother.

'Are you okay?' Sally asked gently.

'I'm going to tell you something I swore I'd never tell a soul,' Elsie whispered. 'And you can't ask me about it again. Promise me.'

Sally promised, turning her body, so that she faced her friend.

'Before I started work with Cyril, I'd been out of work for a few months. And, as I told you, I ran out of money pretty fast.' She sighed, deep and long, and her eyes darkened as she spoke. 'It got to the point that I'd not eaten properly in a week. Anything I could sell was gone. I was desperate.'

Elsie's breath quickened and she closed her eyes for a moment. 'I knew that I had to do something drastic, or I'd starve.' Elsie breathed in. 'I'd seen the women on Wandsworth Common. Standing in a row, waiting for a car to pull over.'

Sally's heart began to hammer so loudly that she was sure Elise could hear it. She saw Elsie's jaw clench as she spoke. And Sally could tell how much Elsie's story was costing her to recount. Sally reached over to clasp Elsie's hand under the bedclothes as she spoke, trying to show her that she was on her side.

But Elsie was lost in her memory and didn't seem to notice.

'I wore my best dress and walked to the end of the common, standing a few feet from a pretty woman with long blonde hair and pink lips. She smiled at me when I joined her. I was trembling so much I thought my legs were going to give way under me. And she must have understood that it was my first time, that I didn't know what I was doing, because when a car pulled up in front of me she walked over and spoke on my behalf, telling the punter it was five pounds a trick, and he had to bring me back to this spot when he was done.' Tears poured down Elsie's face. 'You don't need to hear any more. But you need to know that when a person decides to do that, it's not a life choice made on a whim.'

'I'm so sorry, Elsie,' Sally said, squeezing her friend's hand. All those times she'd been sure Elsie was hiding something, Sally had never suspected anything like this. And then another thought struck Sally, that if Elsie hadn't found her at the rubbish bins that day, she herself might have followed in her mother's footsteps.

'I think you are so brave. And strong. And wonderful,' Sally said, desperately trying to find the right words to help take some of Elsie's pain away.

'I wanted you to know so you don't think badly of your mother. To help explain that just because you do a bad thing, it doesn't make you bad.'

'I don't think you're bad, Elsie,' Sally said. 'And, if anything, hearing this about my mother helps me understand her more. I'm glad you've told me. And I'm here to listen to you, any time you want to talk about it.'

Elsie's face darkened. 'I will never discuss it again. I can't, Sally. It's too difficult. The only way I can live with . . . certain parts of my life is to pretend that they've never happened. Promise me you will never ask me about this again.'

'I promise,' Sally whispered as the hairs rose on the back of her neck. What other parts of Elsie's life were hidden? Did she know her best friend at all?

Elsie climbed out of the bed, then kissed Sally's forehead lightly, before tucking the bedclothes in tight around her. 'I know this must feel overwhelming. You've had to deal with a lot of shocks today. But you are the strongest person I know. You'll be okay.'

Sally's head pounded as a tension headache took firm hold. Elsie was right – she *would* find her way through this. What else could she do but continue to move forward, as she'd done her entire life?

But as Sally heard the front door close softly behind Elsie, her only thought was for her best friend.

What about you, Elsie? Will you be okay?

NOW

August 2023

Lily

Ronda, Spain

Zach had been quiet since they'd left the Alvarez villa, refusing to debate the new information they'd gleaned from their hosts. He marched purposefully into Ronda town centre, and all Lily could do was try to keep up with his long strides.

He only stopped when they reached the foot of what looked like a church.

'The Convento de Santa Benedictine,' Zach said, waving towards the building with cream brickwork that was typical in the area. The convent was at the top of a flight of wide steps, lending it an air of grandeur and majesty.

'Do you think this Sister Monique is still here?' Lily asked, using her hand to shield the sun as she looked at Zach.

Zach shrugged. 'There's only one way to find out.' He reached up to rap a brass knocker loudly on the wooden door.

'What are you going to say?' Lily whispered as they waited.

'I don't know. I'll figure it out,' Zach replied.

A few moments passed before the door opened to reveal a diminutive nun, who was no more than five feet tall. She was dressed in grey, from her veil to her long-sleeved blouse and knee-length skirt. She looked up at them both and smiled a welcome.

Lily had to let Zach take control, and how smoothly he could switch to fluent Spanish once again impressed Lily.

'*Estoy buscando a la Hermana Monique,*' Zach said.

The nun's smile broadened, and she pointed to herself, '*Esa soy yo.*'

Zach looked triumphant as he quickly told Lily that the woman in front of them was Sister Monique.

'Hello, Sister,' Lily said, fighting the urge to curtsy.

'English?' the nun replied.

'Irish,' Lily responded.

'Slàinte!' Sister Monique said, saying the Irish term for 'cheers', then cackled laughter at her joke, with Lily and Zach joining in. She then continued her conversation with Zach again, back in her native Spanish. Lily heard the Alvarez name mentioned, but struggled to understand any more.

The smile left Sister Monique's face as Zach spoke, and she watched him guardedly. She responded curtly and waved for them to go, closing the door firmly behind them.

'What was that about?' Lily asked, dumbfounded by how the exchange had gone from friendly to frosty in seconds.

'I need a drink,' Zach grumbled. 'I'll fill you in once we get to the bar.'

He led Lily to a small tapas bar that he had enjoyed during his time in Spain. The bar was once an old storehouse with old-style piping lacing the walls. Lily and Zach ordered nine different tapas dishes and a bottle of Rioja to share.

'Come on, what did Sister Monique say to you?' Lily asked again.

Zach seemed lost in his thoughts as he stared at the brick wall to their left. A waitress appeared with their wine and filled their glasses.

'I have never needed a drink more. I'm sorry for being so quiet. My head is about to explode with everything I've found out today. Did you see Sister Monique's face when I mentioned my mom and I staying at the convent?'

Lily nodded. Even if she couldn't understand the conversation, body language was impossible to misinterpret.

'She clammed up!' Zach said. 'Then swore that she didn't remember us ever visiting the convent. That she had no recollection of bringing us to the Alvarez villa. That they were mistaken. But I could tell she was lying. She practically threw us out, didn't she?'

'It all seemed a little odd,' Lily agreed. 'Add that to the confusion around the dates you arrived here . . .'

Zach sighed. 'Everything points to me being Robert, doesn't it?'

Lily nodded slowly. The evidence kept piling up.

'The timing of your arrival at the Alvarez villa in July 1983, a few weeks after Robert was taken from our cabin, feels too coincidental.'

'What does that make my mother?' Zach whispered. He shook his head as if trying to dislodge the answer that had formed in his mind. 'Can we not talk about it for a bit?' Zach asked, taking a sip of his red wine.

'I'll be too busy eating to talk,' Lily joked as their waitress walked over with several pisto and tapas dishes. Lily went straight for the goat-cheese *croquetas*, which melted in her mouth. 'We'll need another of these,' she joked to Zach, who took her at her word and immediately ordered another.

'I'm not sure I'm ready to share this one,' Zach teased, spearing a piece of juicy meat from the pork-cheek stew.

Lily tried some and groaned in pleasure. It was the perfect contrast to the sweet and pungent cheese dish. But the vermicelli pasta with light garlic butter and sweet wine sauce made her taste buds explode delightfully. 'Worth coming for the food alone!'

'Surprisingly healthy too,' Zach said.

Lily wasn't sure she believed him as she dipped a slice of thick, crusty bread into creamy aioli.

'I need distraction. Earlier today, when we were driving here, you said you had to come home from Australia. I sensed a story. Wanna spill?' Zach asked.

Lily sighed, because, while Zach wanted a distraction from Robert, this question brought her firmly back to him. 'You might not want to hear this. It's about Robert. Dad thought he'd found you.'

'Oh,' Zach replied, his fork hovering in the air as he took that in.

'The thing is, we'd been through that scenario many times. Over the years, when a new age-progression photo came in, we'd lose Dad. He'd dive in again, determined that this time that photograph would lead us all to you.'

'That must have been difficult to contend with,' Zach said, watching Lily closely.

'Yep. I didn't only lose my brother in 1983, I lost part of my parents too,' Lily replied. Her throat tightened, and she felt her eyes sting. She picked up her wine and took a long gulp.

Zach refilled both their glasses. 'We're not driving, so drink up . . .'

Lily played with a piece of chorizo on her plate, then asked, 'Have you heard of the *StolenChild* network?'

'I don't think so.'

'It's an international agency for the parents of missing children. Dad is one of their most active members. They help keep the names and photographs of missing children in the public domain. The members support each other as pictures of the progression of the new age are made.'

'Ah! I remember now. Your dad spoke about an agency on the *IrelandAM* interview,' Zach said. His nose scrunched up a little, and it caught Lily's breath. There was a photograph at her mother's house of Robert cradling Lily on his lap, and he had the exact same expression on his face. It was uncanny. She felt a flutter of excitement ripple through her.

'Australia,' Zach prompted.

'Right. I'd almost finished my year in Australia, and as it was so much fun, I decided to stay on for another year. But then I got a call from Gaga. My grandfather. He's Dad's father, not Mom's father, so he'd be your step-grandfather if you are—'

'Got it,' Zach said in understanding, sparing Lily from further over-explaining.

'Well, Gaga is about the only one who can handle Dad when he gets into one of his spirals.'

Zach raised his eyebrows in question.

'I'll give you an example. I have dozens, but this is one of my favourites.' Lily took another long sip of her wine. 'One spiral happened when Dad heard about a sighting of a kid that matched your description in Germany. He booked a flight and began knocking on random doors, trying to find you. People thought he was deranged.'

'When was that?' Zach asked, his eyes wide as he listened.

'1991. And the reason I remember it so clearly is because it was at the time of my First Holy Communion, which Dad missed because he was looking for Robert. And Mum missed it because she was so angry that he was looking for Robert that she went to bed with a migraine. I'd have been alone at the altar if it wasn't for Gaga.' Lily closed her eyes momentarily, thinking about her lovely Gaga who always saved the day for her, as a child, and still now when she needed him. 'In the end, Gaga had to fly to Germany to drag him home.'

'Oh, Lily. I'm so sorry.'

'I got used to it.' Lily sniffed. 'Honestly, it's fine. And it wasn't all bad. I was loved. In an abstract, distant way.'

There had been many other absent moments in her childhood. She shook her head, refusing to allow herself to wallow in any self-pity. There were plenty who had it worse than her. She glanced at Zach. If he was Robert, well, he'd had it tough, no doubt about it.

'Okay, back to Australia and that particular spiral. As I said, Gaga called me, worried about Dad. Reluctantly, I might add, because he didn't want to ruin my trip. But Gaga had fallen and broken his hip, and he was snookered. Anyhow, a few weeks previously, a guy had landed on Dad's doorstep and claimed to be Robert. Manuel, he was called. But everyone called him Manny.'

'Jesus,' Zach said, raising his eyebrows in surprise.

'Yep. That name might be apt. Because his guy claimed to have had as many miracles as Jesus had had.'

Zach giggled and clinked glasses with Lily, who giggled along with him. It was nice that Zach got her sense of humour.

'Manny said – wait for this; it's a good story – that he'd been found by a fisherman, washed up in a remote Spanish inlet, half drowned. The fisherman took him home and cared for him, returning Manny to health. It took years for the fisherman to admit that he knew the kid was Robert from the cruise ship. But he'd hidden this, because he had nobody to take over his business. He wanted a son.'

'This is wild,' Zach said, taking another slug of wine.

'Oh, it gets better! Dad became convinced that this Manny was Robert. And, to be fair, he was almost identical to the latest age-progression photograph.'

'I get why you are so sceptical about them now,' Zach said, shaking his head.

'The stories I could tell. But, back to Manny, Dad moved him into his home and gave him money. Mum met him, but, to her credit, she was one hundred per cent certain he was an imposter. I mean, the story was too incredulous.'

'For sure. How on earth did they think that Robert, at three years old, was supposed to have gotten over the railing and fallen overboard in the first place?'

'Exactly,' Lily said, spooning meatballs onto her plate.

'What happened? Did they DNA test him?' Zach asked.

'Yeah, but the results took ages to come through back then. And that's when Gaga called me in a panic because he thought Dad would be bankrupt before they found out the truth. This guy was draining Dad's bank account daily.'

'I've heard of romance fraud, but DNA fraud is a new one for me. Wow,' Zach said, sitting back in his chair.

'I've seen it all over the years. Trust me. Anyhow, I had no choice but to come home from Australia. First and foremost, to get rid of the fraudster. And then to pick up the pieces from his deceit. Dad goes up pretty fast, but, like a rollercoaster, he always comes crashing down afterwards.' She demonstrated an explosive drop with her hands.

'They are lucky to have you. Kimberly and Jason,' Zach said. 'I hope they know that.'

Lily shrugged. She wasn't sure they did. 'Gaga says it's easy to take something for granted that's right under your nose. As I said, I know they love me, but I wish they'd show it a little more.' She looked up and caught Zach's eyes watching her thoughtfully. 'You had a happy childhood with your parents, though, didn't you?'

Zach answered immediately. 'The best. It was a charmed life. Which is why this is so difficult for me. Because if I am Robert that means my entire life has been a lie. And I don't know what to do with that.'

Their waitress sidled up to the table and topped up their wines, emptying the last of the bottle.

Lily leaned back in her chair and looked down at her tummy, now swollen with good food. 'Zach, this was an incredible meal – the best I've had in a long time. But I am about to burst. I've eaten too much.'

Zach held up the empty bottle. 'Another one?'

'Could we go for a walk first, and then we can find a bar for another drink?'

With the plan made, Lily insisted that she pay for their meal, as Zach had paid for the car and villa. Then they walked to the Puente Nuevo, Ronda's famous bridge, that Zach had told Lily about. It spanned a narrow chasm that divided the city into the old town, La Ciudad, and the new town, Mercadillo.

Lily looked down into the breathtaking panorama of the gorge and the Guadalevin River.

'It looks like a romanticist painting, from the national gallery.'

'Especially in this light, bathed in the golden sunset,' Zach agreed.

'What does Puente Nuevo mean?' Lily asked.

'New bridge,' Zach said with a smile. 'Which is funny because the bridge was built in 1759. By American standards, that's pretty old.'

'It looks like a fortress, the way the stone is carved into the cliffs,' Lily remarked in wonder.

'Yeah. It's almost three hundred feet high. I feel like I'm in another era whenever I stand here,' Zach admitted. He turned to face her. 'I'm glad you're here too, Lily, that you came with me. Thank you.'

'It's okay,' Lily replied, feeling a rush of affection once more for this man who had been a stranger to her a short time ago, but who was now beginning to feel like family.

'Zach . . .' Lily began as a group of birds flew up from beneath the bridge in synchronised movement. 'Maybe it's the wine, this place, I don't know, but I want you to know that I believe you. I feel it too. You are my brother.'

Zach moved closer and put an arm round her shoulders as they watched the birds continue to swoop and twirl as one beneath them. 'You're trembling.'

'Scared,' Lily admitted.

'Of me?' Zach asked in a whisper.

'No!' Lily answered quickly. 'I'm scared that for the first time in a long time I've allowed myself to believe that Robert – you – could be alive. But if I go to sleep I'll wake up tomorrow, and it will all have been a dream.'

She leaned in closer to Zach, and they watched the birds until they disappeared under their feet once again.

NOW

August 2023

Lily

Casa Rosa, Ronda, Spain

Lily reached over to grab her phone and hit the snooze button on the alarm. She'd forgotten to turn it off from her regular seven o'clock wake-up time. Her tongue felt like it was coated with sandpaper, and her head throbbed. How much had she and Zach put away the previous night? After their walk, they'd visited what felt like every bar in Ronda.

She jumped up, pulling on a T-shirt and jeans over her underwear, which she'd slept in the night before. Lily found Zach guzzling water from the tap in the kitchen. She appeared to be not the only one suffering.

'Shove over,' she said, nudging him. Then she filled a glass of water for herself and gulped it back in one satisfying go.

'How're you feeling?' Zach asked, scratching his head.

'I'm regretting my life choices,' Lily said, collapsing into one of the chairs in the living room. 'I mean, what was I thinking, saying yes to limoncello shots in that last bar?'

'It's the negroni I regret,' Zach said, shaking his head sorrowfully. 'I'll make some coffee. Señora Alvarez always leaves the best ground roast for her guests. And treats too, with any luck.'

He opened a ceramic bread bin and whooped when he discovered a bag of pastries.

He began preparing their coffee in a stovetop moka pot. The rich, fragrant aroma of the coffee beans filled the air and with one espresso and a sweet, flaky almond pastry behind her, Lily began to feel more human.

'Better?' Zach asked, licking his fingertips.

'I'll live. But it's a good job I'm only here for one night. My head and liver couldn't survive another night like that!'

A big grin spread across Zach's face. 'It was fun, though, wasn't it? You, little sis, are good company.' He caught her eye and looked away as he finished. 'It feels like I've known you my entire life.'

Lily understood what he was saying. She felt an ease with Zach that she rarely found with strangers.

'When we get confirmation . . . that we are brother and sister . . . we can catch up on all those lost occasions,' Zach said.

A shiver of unease ran down Lily's spine – not because she didn't want that, but because she was becoming increasingly worried about what might happen when the results came back. Zach appeared to have a simplistic view of their future, and assumed they could all become one big happy family.

'Zach . , ,' she started, then stopped, finding it difficult to break their happy mood.

'Go on. You can say anything to me,' Zach replied, a line creasing his forehead.

'I believe that our DNA test will come back positive. It will be an incredible moment for my family. I can't even begin to imagine how Dad and Mum will feel. But have you thought about what will happen to *your* family?'

His frown deepened, and Lily took no pleasure in upsetting him, but the truth had to be said.

'Zach, your mother stole you. And put my family through decades of horrific loss. I'm not sure that those damages can ever be repaired . . .' She paused as Zach's eyes glistened.

'My mother would never hurt anyone,' Zach said, but his voice was uncertain. 'She's a good person. The best person I know.'

Lily picked up her iPad from the table. She opened YouTube and found a video that she wanted Zach to look at. She'd watched it hundreds of times over the years.

The screen filled with a close-up of Jason sitting beside Inspector Ortega, at their press conference in July 1983. Lily turned the sound up so Zach could hear the pain and anguish in Jason's voice as he begged for information on their missing son.

'Do you see?' Lily asked. 'Your mother will have to pay for what she did to my family. If she took you, there has to be accountability.'

'Mom might be arrested,' Zach said, his voice little more than a whisper.

'I suspect so.'

'She'd never survive prison.' Zach hit the table with his fist, anger sparking from his eyes.

Lily closed her eyes in frustration at his reaction. 'One could argue that my parents have been in their own prison for forty years. You'd be surprised what a body can survive.'

He pushed his seat back, and the sound of the chair scraping on the terracotta floor pierced the air.

'What a bloody mess,' Zach said.

'I know. But it's not our mess, Zach. You can't take responsibility for your mother's actions. You didn't ask for any of this.'

'I need to get out of here,' Zach said, standing up abruptly. 'I'm going for a walk, okay?'

Lily understood. He had a lot on his mind, and the fresh air would do him good. She hated that her words had caused Zach pain, but she wasn't sorry that she had stressed what the repercussions of his reappearance might be.

Once he'd left, her eyes moved to Inspector Ortega, frozen on the screen beside her father. Her parents hadn't said much about the formal investigation at that time, but it was evident that her dad in particular had little love for the inspector, going by the scathing tone he used whenever his name came up.

She googled 'Inspector Ortega' and dozens of online news reports came up. Using the translate button, Lily scrolled through several articles until she came to the most recent one in 2022. She paused when she saw a photograph of Inspector Ortega standing in front of an imposing building. From what she could garner, he had received a distinguished service medal. The auto-translate was tricky to understand, but Lily got the gist.

The inspector had retired from active service. This made sense, because he must be in his seventies now. She did a double take when she came to the final line, which stated that Ortega had retired to the coastal town of Marbella, which they'd passed by on their way to Ronda.

Zach returned within half an hour, but the walk didn't appear to have resolved anything for him. His face was drawn, and his jaw clenched in the way she'd begun to notice was his when he was upset.

'You okay?' she asked tentatively.

He shook his head. 'I've been so busy worrying about myself I forgot to think about my family.'

'I think you can be forgiven for being a little preoccupied. I'm not sure I've won mother or wife of the year these past few days,' Lily replied, feeling a stab of guilt as she thought about her two boys at home.

'Maybe I should call my sisters,' Zach said, almost to himself.

'Before you call your mom?' Lily asked, wondering if that was the right move. 'Would it be better to have all the facts first of all? Only call them when you have proof that you are Robert?'

'Maybe. I don't know.'

'Out of the three girls, who are you closest to?'

He sat down opposite Lily again. 'I'd say Issy because I've seen more of her over the past few years, as she's in London. Ally and Jenny are busy with their own families.'

Lily rubbed her temples as she considered possible scenarios for Zach. 'After the results, call Issy. Or fly over to see her. That gives you some support too, when you confront your mom.'

'Do you think your parents will give me the time to visit my mom before they call the authorities?' Zach's lip trembled.

'I'll make sure they do. They will want this to be as easy on you as possible. They love Robert . . . love you . . .' Lily paused, flustered again as she tried to navigate the complications of how to refer to her possible missing sibling.

Zach looked at her sadly, whispering, 'For the first time today, I wished I'd never seen your dad's interview.'

And Lily realised a truth for her, answering, 'Well, for the first time today, I'm glad you *did* see it, because I've found you again. And I know it's an unholy mess, but we'll figure it out. Together.' She reached over and clasped his hand.

'Thanks,' he whispered back to her. His eyes drifted down to the iPad screen.

'You will not believe where Inspector Ortega lives. Only in Marbella! Isn't that mad?'

'Wild! Let's see if I can find out where in Marbella.' Zach picked up his own phone and began typing away.

Lily tidied up their cups and dishes, but hadn't even begun drying them when Zach shouted out, 'Got him!' as he raised his fist in triumph.

'How on earth did you manage that so quickly?'

'Honestly, you'd be surprised what people put up on the internet. I found his wife's personal Facebook page, and she has no security.' He turned his phone to show Lily, but as it was all in Spanish, it meant little to her. 'She is a member of the resident's society for a square in old Marbella called Plaza de los Naranjos. I know it. We can swing by there on the way to the airport if you like. We've got a few hours to kill before returning the car.'

Lily looked at Zach in surprise.

He shrugged. 'Look, sometimes you have to grab the bull by the horns, so to speak. I did when I booked an appointment with you. Look where that has led us.'

Lily couldn't disagree. Every day they learned another clue, which she believed was bringing them closer to solving this mystery. Within thirty minutes, they had packed up, said their goodbyes to the Alvarezes and made their way back down the twisting road towards the coast.

BEFORE

May 1979

Sally

South London Crematorium, London

Lizzie Fox's body was released for the funeral once the post-mortem was completed. This confirmed that Sally's mum had died from a single blow to the back of her head. Wearing a black skirt and cream blouse borrowed from Nicola, Sally couldn't believe that her mother was finally gone. Only when she arrived at the crematorium with her friends and saw the simple pine coffin did the stark reality of the situation begin to sink in.

Sally trembled and her breath quickened. She wasn't sure she had the strength to get through the service. But then Elsie and Nicola, who had supported her steadfastly over the past couple of weeks, tightened their clasp on either side of her. She'd never needed them more than she did right then.

To Sally's surprise, shortly before the short service began, Sister Jones arrived, followed by Cyril, along with Noreen, Sandra, Carys and Mary. This gesture, knowing that they had each for-gone sleep to be there, made her heart ache, and it was her undoing. Tears she'd promised she would not shed today came thick and fast. She looked around the small room with gratitude.

These people had never met her mother yet were here for her.

Sally would always remember that. And, even though she was

no longer a charwoman, she knew that bond would stay with them for life. She caught Mary's eye and nodded, a thank-you to the woman who had taken over her shifts at a moment's notice.

Sally noticed a woman sitting at the back of the church on her own. She was around her mum's age, in her early forties, Sally guessed. The woman wore a black headscarf, and held a white handkerchief to her mouth as she quietly wept and waited for the service to begin. Sally didn't recognise her, but she smiled in the woman's direction, grateful that her mother had a friend here.

There was no eulogy for Lizzie Fox. But Sally had asked the funeral director to play 'I Want to Hold Your Hand' by the Beatles, which she hoped her mother would have approved of. It had come on the radio once while she was visiting her the previous year, and her mother had sung along to every word, holding Sally's hand as she had done when Sally was a little girl. It was one of Sally's favourite memories of them.

The small group began singing along as her coffin disappeared through the velvet curtains. And, by the time the last note ended, Sally whispered, 'I hope you are at peace now, Mum. Sleep well.'

There was one more surprise for Sally. When she left the crematorium, she found Detective Sergeant Ian Baldwin waiting outside, leaning against his car.

'Will I go with you?' Elsie asked as Sally walked towards him.

'No, it's fine. I'll be with you in a moment,' she replied with a smile of thanks and made her way to him. After the emotional release of the tears she'd shed at her mother's service, she wasn't sure she could take any further blows today.

'Hello, Detective Sergeant Baldwin.'

'Hello, Sally. That's a bit of a mouthful, isn't it? Why don't you call me Ian?'

Sally smiled weakly.

'I can imagine the service was tough,' Ian said. His dark eyes searched hers and Sally felt a shiver run down her back. 'You holding up okay?'

'Let's just say that I'm glad it's over.'

He nodded. 'I came today because I thought you'd like to know this. We've arrested a man for the murder of your mum.'

Sally took a step back, almost stumbling on the street kerb. Ian reached for her arm to steady her. Sally watched a black crow swoop down from a nearby electricity pole to peck the ground near her. And in the distance, a woman's cry echoed towards them. The next funeral cortege had arrived.

'Sally?' Ian asked, his voice laced with concern. His hand remained on her arm, and the warmth of his touch brought Sally back to the moment.

'Who w-was it?' Sally eventually stammered.

'A man called John Fenton. Local.'

'Do you know why he did it?' Sally asked, even though she realised that it didn't matter. It wouldn't bring back her mother.

'He was one of her regulars.' Ian paused momentarily to let that sink in, and Sally was grateful for it. The thought of her mother having 'regulars' was a difficult pill to swallow.

'We had a couple of leads from one of the women who worked alongside your mother. Betty and your mother were good friends and since the string of murders in Leeds and Manchester, Betty said that Lizzie and her had made a pact to keep an eye on each other. They took note of the car regs of their customers, that kind of thing.'

Sally felt nauseous thinking about the women that had been murdered by the Yorkshire Ripper. And the police seemed no closer to finding him since it had all begun five years ago. Visceral, raw headlines appeared in the papers almost daily about the seemingly unsolvable crimes. In the salon, customers spoke about the victims in whispered voices. Most were prostitutes, but some victims happened to be in the wrong place at the wrong time. As each new murder was reported, unease spread from the North to London.

The latest victim, Josephine Whitaker, was only a couple of years younger than Sally. A lovely young woman, walking home from her grandparents, taken from the world cruelly. Now, when Sally, Elsie and Nicola went for a drink in the Grove, Reggie insisted that he walk each of them home. And they clung to each other, each feeling vulnerable as their eyes searched the shadows for the bogeyman who bludgeoned women to their deaths.

Sally's breath quickened because she knew that if she was scared, how must her mother have felt? And Betty too, and other women like her. They must live in constant terror. She looked around, searching for the woman who'd sat at the back of the church, sure she had to be her mother's friend, Betty. But there was no sign of her now. She'd disappeared once the service ended.

'Are you saying my mother's murder is connected to those up North?' Sally whispered.

Ian immediately shook his head and leaned in closer. 'No. Your mother's injuries were not consistent with those women's . . .' He paused, seeing a flash of pain pass over Sally's face again, then continued. 'Betty told us about a punter called John, who had become obsessed with Lizzie. And it was making Lizzie a little uncomfortable. He drove a green Pontiac. A neighbour said that they'd regularly seen a green Pontiac parked outside your mother's house. So we questioned all owners of green Pontiacs in the Greater London area. When we called Fenton's house, it was almost as if he was waiting for us. We pulled him in for questioning, and he caved and confessed.'

Sally wasn't sure how to react to this. Should she be grateful that this John Fenton had a conscience?

'He alleges that it was an accident. He didn't mean to kill Lizzie. They fought when he tried to get her to give up the game. She pushed him, he shoved her back and then she stumbled and hit her head on the corner of the coffee table. Fenton said he panicked and left her there.'

'I can't believe it ended like this for Mum,' Sally said, feeling fresh tears prickle her eyes as she grappled to accept the bitter truth of her mother's demise. She turned to glance at where her friends stood, looking over at her in concern, and she desperately wanted to go back to them, to talk this all through with people who loved her.

'I appreciate you taking the time to come and tell me this, Detective Sergeant. I'm not sure how I'll ever be able to thank you properly for finding out what happened to Mum. I'll always be grateful.'

'Ian. Please call me Ian,' he replied, those dark eyes of his boring into Sally's soul. 'And there are no thanks necessary. Knowing you have some peace, with the murderer behind bars, is enough for me.'

'That does help,' Sally replied. 'Well, I better get going.'

'Maybe you could cut my hair some time,' Ian called out as she turned to walk away.

Sally swung back, her eyes widening in surprise. 'Of course. Call the salon whenever it suits you. You know where I work.'

He nodded, and a broad smile changed his face from broody to handsome. Sally felt her heart quicken in a way it hadn't for a long time. As Ian got into his car and sped off, leaving a trail of dust on the road, Sally knew that this would not be the last time she saw him.

NOW

Lily

Plaza de los Naranjos, Marbella, Spain

'I want to come back to Spain with Michael and Ben one day,' Lily said as they arrived in the old town of Marbella.

Zach swung his car into a space that looked too small for their rental, with the ease of a seasoned driver.

'It's addictive, isn't it? I could live over here. Might be a holiday villa, one of these days,' Zach said. 'Listen, before we head off, when we find this Ortega dude, let's not tell him that we think I'm Robert.'

Lily smiled at Zach. 'You are always so positive. You haven't even considered we might not find Ortega! I like that about you. But why don't you want him to know?'

'If we tell him, he might call it into his buddies in the Policia. And, before we know it, this whole thing has legs, and we've lost control of what happens next.'

Lily could see the logic in Zach's assumptions. She reassured Zach, and they made their way along a narrow cobbled street with tall, whitewashed buildings, all with colourful hanging baskets of flowers, until they arrived at the Plaza de los Naranjos. Ornate terracotta flagstones, with landscaped gardens, tall orange trees and sprinkling fountains were a feast for her eyes.

On a whitewashed wall hung dozens of bright blue flowerpots with red flowers.

Zach told her that Marbella streets were full of pots like these, and Lily couldn't help but take a couple of photos. Zach insisted on a selfie, and she snapped one of them both looking into the camera with matching grins.

'Our first photo together,' Lily said to him. And they shared a look that silently expressed the wish that it would be the first of many more to come.

They made their way across the square to a long row of restaurants with seating outside, perfect for enjoying an espresso and people-watching.

'Let's see if fortune does favour the brave once more,' Zach said. He marched into the first café and began chatting to one of the waitresses.

'She doesn't know the inspector, but I did get her socials.' Zach winked, then dodged a swipe from Lily. They moved to the next café and began the same process, but once again had no luck. Once they'd hit a blank wall for the sixth time, Lily was ready to give up. As they were about to leave, a waitress beckoned Zach over and told him about a small café, hidden on a nearby side street, that Ortega favoured.

Within a few feet of the café, Lily spotted him. Unmistakable, even from his side profile, there was Ortega, sitting at a table outside, cigarette smoke wafting up from behind a newspaper.

Lily's heart hammered so loudly in her chest that she was sure the restaurant would hear it. But only when she cleared her throat did the man in front of them put down his newspaper and regard them both quizzically.

'Señor Ortega? Inspector Ortega?' Lily asked. Her voice was steadier than she felt.

'*Si*,' he replied, flicking ash into an almost full ashtray, and taking another long drag.

'Do you speak English?' Lily asked.

He shrugged, giving little away. He looked them both up and down suspiciously.

Lily licked her lips, wishing she had a glass of water. 'My name is Lily Murphy and this is my friend Zach.' There was no flicker of recognition. But that was hardly surprising. It was, after all, over forty years ago. 'You were the inspector in charge of an investigation into the disappearance of my brother—'

'Robert,' Inspector Ortega butted in. He motioned to the seats before him, so Lily and Zach took a seat each. 'You grew up.'

Lily smiled, feeling a little shy as he scrutinised her.

'I'm retired, so I cannot help you now, any more than I could help your mother forty years ago.' His face clouded for a moment.

Lily cursed herself for not rehearsing what to say to him. Truthfully, she never expected to find him.

Inspector Ortega continued, 'I have looked at the case occasionally over the years. It always pained me that I never found Robert for your mother. How is Kimberly?'

Lily noted that he didn't say he regretted not finding Robert for her dad. Maybe her dad wasn't wrong that the inspector did not like him.

'My mother is as well as she can be,' Lily replied. 'She runs the family business and enjoys that.'

Ortega sucked in air between his teeth. 'You didn't come here to swap idle chit-chat.' He stubbed out his cigarette, then drained the last of his espresso. 'What do you want to know?'

A waitress hovered, so Zach ordered a round of coffees and water for them all.

Lily answered in a quiet voice, 'I suppose I want to ask you about the investigation, and whether you believe Robert is alive.'

Ortega examined his fingernails for a moment before answering sadly, 'No. I believe he died the night before the *Carousel* docked in Barcelona.'

'How?' Lily asked as her stomach flipped and turned in protest. She looked at Zach and saw that he had blanched a little under his dark tan too.

'That I do not know. But I believe your father holds the answer to that question.'

Lily felt the hair on her neck bristle at the inspector's blatant insinuation.

'You think Jason had something to do with Robert's disappearance?' Zach asked. He gave Lily's arm a quick pat of reassurance.

Ortega looked between Zach and Lily. 'Yes. I do.'

'Do you know that my father has not stopped looking for Robert? He's obsessed with finding out what happened to my brother. Why would he dedicate his life to this if he himself had killed Robert?'

Ortega shrugged, drumming his fingers on the table.

Lily blundered on, determined to make the inspector admit that her father could be innocent. 'Dad has admitted it's possible he left the door of the cabin open that night. My theory is that Robert walked out, perhaps sleepwalking, then someone saw the opportunity and grabbed him.'

'Perhaps,' Ortega answered, but he still looked doubtful. 'But how did that person leave the ship? All passengers and crew were accounted for as they left once the *Carousel* docked. Only a handful of staff had left before the alert was raised, and camera footage at the exits showed that none of these had a child with them.'

Lily cursed under her breath. This felt like trying to push water up a hill.

'Does the name Sister Monique mean anything to you?' Zach asked.

Ortega grabbed another cigarette and considered the question. Once lit, he took a long drag while watching Lily and Zach. 'No. I do not recall that name. Why do you ask?'

'My mother mentioned her – that's all,' Lily responded, telling a white lie. 'I think she may have met her while in Barcelona.'

Ortega leaned closer to Lily and asked her, 'What do you think happened to your big brother?'

Lily's mind returned to Ben's birthday celebration, the row between her parents and her mother's breakdown. 'I've spent years puzzling over this. I have changed my mind many times, from his accidental death, to his abduction, but I've begun to believe that he is still alive.' She glanced at Zach quickly, and he half-smiled back at her.

'Maybe,' Ortega said. 'But that leaves me two questions, not only *who* abducted him, but *how*.'

Lily felt unexpected tears rush to her eyes. 'My mother has never got over the loss of Robert. I don't know what she was like before he was taken from us because my only memory of her has been of a broken woman.'

'A parent never gets over the loss of a child,' Ortega said matter-of-factly.

'Yes, but I think it's more than that. She got distraught last week and spoke about guilt. When I questioned her, she clammed up, saying I would never understand. She looked so scared. There's something more to this story. I can feel it.'

'*Dios mío*,' Ortega muttered as the waitress placed their drinks before them. 'You may never know what happened that night.' Ortega waved his cigarette at Lily. 'The truth has been hidden for decades. And I'm not sure it will ever be uncovered.'

Zach's jaw tightened and he said, 'In my experience, the truth always finds its way to the surface.'

Ortega ignored Zach and focused on Lily instead. 'Kimberly was terrified back then. And I'm not only talking about the terror of having your child disappear. There was something else going on. I felt an undercurrent whenever she looked at your dad.'

Ortega's cigarette smoke hit her nostrils, and the smell made Lily gag. She had to escape from this man who was so resolute in his accusations. She stood up, thanking Ortega for his time. Zach left twenty euros on the table to cover the bill. And they left, walking in silence back to the car. No selfies, no chit-chat – just dark thoughts swirling around Lily's head.

She loved her parents.

They were flawed, yes, there could be no doubting that. But they'd done their best with Lily as they'd learned to live with their grief.

Or was it their guilt rather than grief with which they had to live? Lily's mind went back to Ben's birthday again.

Guilt never allows you to let go – that's what her mother had said.

What had her parents done that night?

BEFORE

November 1979

Sally

Elite, Wandsworth, London

Sally gazed at her reflection in the mirror as excitement and nerves bubbled in her heart. Her hair, meticulously styled into soft waves, cascaded to her shoulders. Nicola pinned a delicate white floral headpiece to her crown and stepped back to ensure it was perfectly aligned.

'The prettiest bride I've ever seen,' Nicola declared, rearranging one stray strand of hair on Sally's shoulder.

'Let me touch up your make-up,' Elsie said, moving forward. She opened a large cosmetic case and pulled out powder, dabbing it onto the bridge of Sally's nose. Then she reapplied another layer of pink lipstick. 'Perfection.'

'Thank you, both. I couldn't have done this without you.' Sally's eyes welled with gratitude as she looked at them, dressed in pretty powder-blue dresses specially bought for this day as her bridesmaids. 'And you both look stunning,' she added, her voice filled with affection.

'Between our hairdressing skills and Elsie's make-up artistry, we can't fail to stun everyone!' Nicola said, giving them a little twirl. She pulled a bottle of Cava from behind the reception desk, popped its cork and filled three coupé glasses with the

241

frothy liquid. 'We've got half an hour before we need to get you changed into your wedding dress, so let's have a little snifter here first of all.' She passed them their drinks. 'A toast. For Sally and Ian. A whirlwind love story.'

'Cheers!' they all called out as they clinked glasses.

'Are you sure?' Elsie asked, taking her by surprise.

Nicola made a face at Elsie, as if warning her to stay quiet, but Elsie never listened to anyone else. When she had something to say, she usually did. 'It's only been six months since you met Ian. It's not too late to back out if you're unsure. That's all I'm saying.'

Sally felt a flush of anger at Elsie's comment. She replied in a clipped voice, 'Of course I'm sure. We love each other. Why should we wait to get married?' Her best friend and the woman who had become her surrogate mother looked back at her in silence. 'I wouldn't have said yes when he proposed if I wasn't one hundred per cent sure!'

'Well, that's okay, then,' Elsie finally replied with a smile.

But Sally didn't return the smile. Elsie's question had touched a nerve.

'Why can't you be happy for me?' Sally asked.

As ever the peacekeeper, Nicola said, 'Elsie is looking out for her best friend. That's all.'

'Look, if you are happy, so am I!' Elsie said, holding her hands up as if in surrender. 'Come on, don't be cross with me. Not today.'

Sally took a sip of her drink, her resolve firm. She was determined not to let anything dampen today's happiness, so she let Elsie's comment slide, no matter how much it irked her. Yes, her relationship with Ian had been a whirlwind, but she believed in their love.

When Ian had arrived at the salon the week after her mother's cremation, Sally had felt butterflies dance in her tummy. She knew that his presence was a statement. He waited until Sally was free so that she could wash and cut his hair. Massaging shampoo into a scalp had never felt so intimate before. As she trimmed his long, dark, feathered hair, she felt his eyes watching her every move.

He was the most handsome man that Sally had ever met. His muscular frame made her feel safe and secure. When he asked her to go to the pictures with him after work, she had no choice but to say yes, because all plans of being coy flew out of the window when he touched her hand, sending shivers down her spine. Ian drove them to the Granada Theatre, at Clapham Junction, and they sat on the front row of the balcony, which had a plaque noting that the Duchess of Kent had sat there too, when it had opened. And Sally had felt like a duchess too as she sat there.

They saw *The Champ*, which was the new Jon Voight and Faye Dunaway movie. By the final credits, Sally was weeping and she leaned into Ian's comforting embrace. He passed her his white handkerchief and kissed her hand gently as she dabbed her tears away.

Sally knew, with every fibre of her being, that her future was with this man.

Less than three months later they were engaged, and now, six months after their first date, they were to be married. It was a small civil ceremony, followed by a reception in a nearby hotel. Ian had insisted that he organise it all. And Sally knew that this in part was why Elsie was irked. She'd wanted to help, but Ian had refused all offers. They decided to have an intimate ceremony, with two witnesses each. Ian had persuaded her that it was best to have it this way, as it wouldn't seem right if they had a big celebration so soon after her mother's death. And, when he put it like that, she could understand his logic.

This meant that Sally could not invite Sister Jones and the gang from the cleaning company. She would have loved them to be there, to watch her make her vows. Ian wasn't close to his parents or siblings, so they were not invited either. And, as Sally was an orphan with no siblings, that suited her too.

'Hey, stop daydreaming about your man! It's time to get you dressed,' Nicola said, taking Sally's now empty glass.

Sally entered the back storeroom, where her dress hung from a hanger, waiting for her. It was a vintage lace fit-and-flare long dress with striking bishop sleeves. Nicola and Elsie helped her slip the dress over her head and shoulders. Together, they buttoned up the tiny brocade buttons running down it's back.

'Now you're a bride,' Nicola said, her voice tight with emotion.

She took Sally by the hand and led her back into the salon so that she could look at herself in the mirrors.

'I wish Mum were here to see me looking like this,' Sally whispered when she saw herself for the first time. She'd never felt more beautiful and shivered in anticipation of Ian's reaction.

'She is here. Watching you from up there,' Nicola insisted.

'And she's proud of you too,' Elsie added.

Their taxi arrived, and within a ten-minute drive the three friends arrived at the registrar's office. While it wasn't the wedding Sally had dreamed about over the years, it still felt magical. When she followed Nicola and Elsie into the small room where Ian was waiting for her, with his two friends Declan and Bob by his side, Sally thought Ian had never looked more handsome. He wore a light brown suit, with a white shirt and a wide chocolate-brown tie. He had a white corsage pinned to the lapel of his jacket.

When she reached his side, he whispered into her ear, 'How did I ever deserve to get such a beautiful woman?'

The ceremony only took fifteen minutes, from her entrance to their signing of the register and their long, passionate kiss, amid the cheers of their small group of friends. They walked to the hotel together, holding hands, telling each other how happy they were. As Ian led her into the small private room he'd booked for their wedding meal, Sally had never felt more content.

To her surprise, at least two dozen guests were waiting for them. A loud cheer erupted as Sally scanned the room to see who was there. She recognised about half the people there to be colleagues of Ian's, along with their wives or girlfriends, who she had met at their summer barbecue. She scanned the tables, hoping to see Cyril and the girls, perhaps Sister Jones, also seated there. A surprise from her husband. But there was no sign of any of Sally's friends.

Declan, Bob, Nicola, and Elsie were seated at either end of the top table, where two empty chairs awaited Ian and Sally.

'I thought it was supposed to be the six of us,' Elsie said when Sally sat down beside her. 'I wasn't even allowed to invite my Reggie.'

'It was. I don't understand,' Sally replied, her stomach flipping as she tried to make sense of the situation.

Ian looked over at them, a big grin on his face. 'I hope you're all hungry. We've got a prawn cocktail to start, chicken kiev for mains, and Black Forest gateau for dessert. Nothing but the best for my bride.' He picked up a bottle of white wine from a cooler and poured them a drink, before passing the bottle down to Elsie.

'I didn't know you were inviting work friends,' Sally said.

'The biggest day of my life – I couldn't do it without them,' Ian said, raising his glass to toast the tables before them.

'Clearly, when your husband said invite no friends, he meant no friends of yours, Sally, not his,' Elsie said loudly enough for Ian to hear.

His eyes narrowed as he looked at Elsie, and his jaw clenched. 'I'm not sure what you're getting at. You and Nicola are here. Sally's two closest friends.'

'We are. But Sally has other friends too. Cyril and the rest of the char gang,' Elsie replied, locking eyes with Ian.

The start of a tension headache nipped Sally's temples as her best friend and new husband stared each other down. She'd seen signs of a clash developing over the past couple of months, ever since a double date with Elsie and Reggie had fallen flat.

'It's not your business, but my wife and I discussed why they shouldn't be invited.' He chuckled as if greatly amused by Elsie. 'I mean, Sally no longer even works with them.'

'That doesn't mean that they are not her friends,' Elsie retorted, unwilling to let it go. 'Or maybe it's because they are not the kind of friends you want your wife to have, though. Charwomen.'

'Oh my days, here we go,' Nicola said, throwing her eyes upwards. She put a calming hand on Elsie's arm. 'Best leave it for today, love.' Elsie continued to eyeball Ian, so Nicola whispered, 'Look, you're only upsetting Sally. It's her day. Remember that.'

They all turned to look at Sally, whose face was now flushed with embarrassment. Ian clasped her hand under his. 'The reason I've invited these colleagues is because when you lay down your life with people, as I have done with all of these, you form a bond.' He glanced back in Elsie's direction and said, 'I'm not sure acquaintances formed while mopping a floor are in the same league.'

Sally started at her husband's inference that her friends were not good enough for him. She'd noticed he didn't like it when Sally mentioned her cleaning days. She was proud of how hard she'd worked, for years, until she'd got her hairdressing diploma, and would never want to hide any part of who she was.

Ian's face softened, and he said in a gentler voice as he stroked Sally's cheek, 'I'm sorry if I've upset you. It was never my intention to do that.'

Sally looked at her friends. Nicola nodded encouragingly to her, but Elsie's face was still clouded in anger.

'He's bang out of order,' Elsie muttered.

Ian ignored Elsie and asked Sally, 'Do you want me to ask them all to leave? I will do if that's what you want.'

Sally felt her day unravel before she could stop it, before it was too late to pull it back together again.

'Don't be silly. Your friends are important to you, so they are important to me too. Of course they should stay.'

'That's my girl,' Ian said, and he leaned in and kissed her, which got another rousing cheer from his friends.

Sally had spent her life dreaming of meeting a man like Ian.

Someone who had made something of himself. Someone that she could make a home with. Start a family with. She'd finally done that. And she would not let a silly misunderstanding get in the way. Everything would be okay because Sally would make sure it was.

NOW

August 2023

Lily

Phibsborough, Dublin

Lily looked down at her sleeping son, who lay on his back, two hands above his head. His lips were pursed in a perfect pout while he dreamed. She hoped that for her little Ben they were only happy thoughts.

His vulnerability, as he lay there, caught her off-guard not for the first time. Robert had been almost the same age when he was snatched from their lives. Anger sparked through her as Zach's mother's face formed in her mind's eye. Since her return from Spain, Lily had been unable to stop thinking about her. Before, the abductor was a faceless predator, but now it had taken shape and form in that of a sixty-five-year-old woman living in America.

She'd spent hours scrolling through Zach's Instagram grid, searching for hidden secrets in his parents' faces. Every snap only showed two parents who obviously doted on their children. Their faces were alight with pride as they stood, arms looped round their shoulders, laughing without a care for the camera.

Whether it was at Lake Champlain boating, in their backyard barbecuing, at their daughters' weddings, beside a resplendent

Christmas tree drinking eggnog, every shot showed a happy family life.

Their lives were like the gifts under their tree, wrapped beautifully with a big red bow. While Lily's and her parents' were discarded, broken and not quite right.

Lily backed out of the room stealthily to avoid waking Ben. Michael was waiting for her at the foot of the stairs, his forehead creased in deep lines.

'We've got a visitor. It's Zach. He arrived a few minutes ago in a bit of a state.'

Lily hurried into the large family room, where she found Zach pacing the wooden floors.

'It's all gone wrong,' he said, the second he saw her. 'I kept thinking about what you said in Spain about not blindsiding my family. So I flew over to London yesterday to tell Issy.' He ran his hands through his hair, then turned to face Lily. 'She went ballistic. I've never seen her so angry. I thought she'd be on my side, but instead she rang Ally and Jenny. That was the worst group video chat I've ever had.' He sighed again. 'If you saw them, Lily . . . They were spitting fire at me one minute, crying the next, then back to angry again.'

His tanned face was tinged with splotches of bright red, and he looked so lost as he recounted his update that it made Lily's heart ache.

'Michael, will you get us all a drink? Anything at all. Zach, sit down beside me and take a deep breath. It's going to be all right.'

'It isn't, Lily. Jenny said she'd never forgive me for doing this to our family.'

'Do they believe you?' Lily asked.

Zach shook his head. 'Ally and Issy think I'm raving mad to even think Mom could do such a thing. Jenny kept staring at me, as if I'd murdered someone.'

Lily could only imagine what that must feel like for him. She had spent her entire life as an only child. This was new territory for her. But she wasn't entirely surprised that his sisters hadn't welcomed his news with open arms. Albeit that it was disappointing that they couldn't see through their own fear to notice their brother's pain.

Michael returned with a bottle of red Pinot noir and three glasses. They each accepted a glass and Zach took a deep glug.

'Did you explain about the photographs and what you found out in Ronda?' Michael said once Lily had quickly brought him up to speed on what had happened.

'I tried, but they were not interested in hearing what I had to say.'

Lily shrugged. 'When we are angry, it's hard to listen, to understand. You need to give them time to recover from the shock and adjust to the possibility that you are right.'

Zach took another drink. 'I tried to make them understand. But the thing that hurt me more than anything was that Ally and Issy won't even consider that it's possible that Mom could have taken me.'

Lily could see how hurtful that would be for Zach. Now at his most vulnerable, he'd never needed his sisters more. And she felt another ache twist her heart. Lily knew that there could only be more heartbreaking moments for Zach and his family, if he was right.

'Jenny asked me if I'd had a good life. I said yes, of course I had. She said if that was the case the subject should be closed. If Mom did take me, so what? I should be grateful for the life she'd given me.'

'But what about the life you could have had with me and our family?' Lily whispered, feeling stung by the injustice of Jenny's reckoning.

Zach glanced at her and nodded sadly. 'I keep thinking about that too. I love my family and cannot imagine a world without them, but when I'm with you . . . I feel a connection too. You feel like family to me, Lily.'

Lily's eyes glistened as she reached over to clasp Zach's hand for a moment.

He pulled out his phone. 'Jenny called me an hour ago. She's given me an ultimatum. She said that if I go ahead and collect the results from the clinic on Wednesday, the family will all disown me. No matter what they are.'

'She has no right to do that!' Lily said, feeling her hackles rise in indignation for them and the truth they desperately wanted.

'I've never seen Jenny like that. She's rattled. She conceded that it's a possibility that Mom did take me.'

'She's scared,' Lily said. 'This . . . whatever this is . . . well, it's a threat to your family. Give her time.'

Zach grimaced. 'But what if she's right? If I pursue this and it is true, the consequences could be devastating for everyone. Would Mom face charges? Jenny's worried that Mom and Dad's marriage would be unlikely to survive the fallout too. So their divorce would be on my conscience along with breaking up the family.'

Michael omitted a low whistle. 'That's a lot to land on your shoulders.'

'It's a bloody liberty,' Lily added, feeling her earlier ire at Zach's mother now spread to her daughters too. She had tried to empathise with how they must be feeling, but the strain of this was taking an evident toll on Zach. 'What about *your* feelings? What about the impact of this on *you*? Not to mention our family,' Lily said. She took a deep breath, and tried to calm herself. Zach didn't need her anger on top of his sisters.

'What will you do?' Michael asked, throwing a worried look in Lily's direction.

Zach placed his head in his hands. 'I don't know.'

Lily saw mirrored sympathy in her husband's eyes for Zach. He was in an impossible situation. She tapped Zach on his knee lightly. 'Even if you don't go to the clinic on Wednesday, I still will. We have to know, one way or the other. My family needs to know.'

'The horse has bolted, mate,' Michael said, shrugging. 'There's no point closing the stable door now.'

Zach nodded miserably.

'You could tell your sisters it's out of your hands now,' Michael suggested.

'Yeah. Blame me,' Lily agreed. 'Say I refuse to ignore the results.'

Zach stood up, taking his glass of wine with him. He couldn't sit still, and Lily understood his restlessness. She'd felt the same way ever since he'd walked into her office twelve days ago and blown all their lives up.

'What kind of a brother would I be if I left you to do all this alone?' he said, smiling weakly at Lily. 'I'm Robert. I feel it with every part of me.' He thumped his chest. 'And when we go to the clinic together the results will confirm that.'

Lily, her voice filled with empathy, stood up and moved closer to him. 'I feel that too.' She placed her own hand over his, which still rested against his heart. 'I hate seeing you torn between two families. It's a painful place to be and nobody wants that.'

'If I ask Kimberly and Jason to stay quiet about it all, for me, will they? If I can reassure my sisters that there will be no criminal charges, they'll calm down. I know they will.'

Lily's heart sank because she knew that they couldn't agree to that, nor did she want them to.

She answered as gently as she could. 'Zach, you have to know that you can't steal someone's child and expect to get away with it. Your sisters will have to accept that too. If you are Robert, your mother will have to face the consequences.'

Zach picked up a framed photograph of Lily and Michael, taken on their wedding day, surrounded by their families. He touched Kimberly's face gently, 'By finding my other mother and sister, I stand to lose my mom and family too. How is that fair?'

His voice trembled with sadness and anger, and Lily could find no response to give him.

NOW

August 2023

Kimberly

Ace Funds, Ormonde Quay, Dublin

Tomorrow was the day of reckoning. Kimberly had been marking her calendar with an X every morning, each day bringing her closer to the truth. The wait was agonising, filled with a mix of anticipation and anxiety. Lily had called to see her at the office the day before. She'd not seen her daughter so animated. Nervous energy filled her every move as she stumbled through her tale of trips to Ronda and Marbella, and ultimatums from Zach's family.

Not to mention Inspector Ortega.

Kimberly had not seen him for decades, but sometimes, if she smelled cigarette smoke, it brought her back to that time. He'd been kind to her. At no point had she felt his finger of accusation, not in her direction at least.

Jason's face came to mind, followed by a familiar ache. She missed him, even after all this time. Their love had been a rollercoaster, with moments of intense passion and fleeting togetherness. There had been times over the years when they'd rekindled their love affair. And, for a while, they would be back in sync again. Until Robert's name came up. And then their fragile unity would crumble to ashes between them.

Lily had shared her hope and excitement that when Zach was proven to be Robert doubts and accusations would finally be removed from her father's direction. And Jason deserved the peace that would bring. He'd spent forty years of his life chasing false lead after false lead.

Kimberly's heart ached a little more as she worried about the results and the devastation they would bring. She knew that it was a win-lose situation for her and for Zach's family in America.

Kimberly sighed, her mind clouded with uncertainty. What to do? The decision weighed heavily on her. Should she wait it out until Lily called from the clinic tomorrow? Or should she go through with her plan, which she'd been contemplating for days? She was unsure of the outcome, but driven by a desperate need to see Zach for herself. It was a physical pain, knowing he was in Dublin, so close, but out of her reach.

Kimberly had to move forward.

That's what she had done her entire life when faced with curveballs. She brushed her ash-blonde hair. She wore it short now, in a blunt bob cut above her jawline. Kimberly knew that she looked very different from the woman who'd held Robert in her arms forty years ago – and unrecognisable as the young girl she'd once been.

She smoothed down her cream linen dress and grabbed her handbag as she left her house to take an Uber taxi into the city centre. Twenty minutes later, she stood in Ace Funds' glossy marble reception area. Kimberly felt a smidgeon of pride in her heart at the thought that *her* boy worked there.

'Can I help you?' a pretty receptionist asked as she approached the desk.

'I'd like to see Zach Brady.'

'Do you have an appointment?'

'No, I don't.' Kimberly held her hand up as the receptionist was about to tell her that her request was futile. 'If you tell him Kimberly Murphy is here to see him, I'm sure he will be available.'

The receptionist briefly thought about it, then dialled Zach's number. Kimberly was immediately led to a bright meeting room that sat a few feet from the reception.

Her eyes focused on the sizeable black-and-white clock on the wall above the long mahogany desk. She watched the second hand move, one step at a time. Then the door opened, and Zach was standing there.

Tall, dark, tanned, with eyes that sparkled with emotion beneath black-rimmed glasses, he wore a pair of beige chino trousers with a crisp white shirt. A smartwatch with a brown leather strap flashed on his wrist. His hair was wavy, worn a little long on top but neat on the sides, and he had a manicured beard – one of those trendy ones, not like the one Jason had when he went feral after their divorce, refusing to shave or get his hair cut for years.

Kimberly pushed the thought of her ex-husband from her mind. She knew he would have wanted to come with her if he'd known she had planned this. But Kimberly had to do this on her own. She needed to be with her son, without anyone else taking his attention.

'Hello,' Zach said.

Kimberly had dreamed of hearing his voice again. Now, hearing his deep baritone American accent, she felt a rush of emotion.

This man, this stranger, was her Robert.

She stood, holding on to the table for support. Beyond coming here, Kimberly had not known what she would do next. She'd known only that she must see him. She couldn't wait for any DNA results; she had to see him with her own eyes.

'Hello . . . Robert,' Kimberly replied tremulously.

His steel-blue eyes became glassy as he whispered in awe, 'You believe I'm Robert?'

'Yes, I do. Now that I've seen you, I want you to know that I believe you are my boy, without any need for DNA results.'

And then they moved towards each other.

In one fluid moment, she held her arms out wide, and he fell into them.

They stood as one, reunited again, silently weeping for forty lost years.

BEFORE

June 1980

Sally

Elite, Wandsworth, London

A crash echoed through the salon as Nicola's new apprentice, Andrea, dropped a gallon of shampoo onto the floor, sending a pile of newly folded towels in their wake.

'That girl will be the death of me,' Nicola muttered as she placed Sally's hair into rollers. 'Can I persuade you to come back? Please. For my sanity, if nothing else.'

There had been many moments over the past few months when Sally wished she hadn't resigned from her job here. But Ian was adamant that his wife should be at home, as his mother had been for his father before him. At first it had been a novelty as she turned their new house into a home.

Ian had surprised her shortly before their wedding with the keys to a three-bedroom detached home in a new estate in Harrow. She spent her days cleaning the house from top to bottom each day. Plumping the pillows just so. Polishing the floor till it shone. And making delicious meals for Ian, ready for his return each evening.

But lately the novelty of living in a home that she had dreamed of as a child and young woman had waned. She'd begun to feel bored and constricted. There wasn't time to think about that now, as a wave of nausea rushed over her. Sally placed a hand to her mouth.

'You've gone as white as a ghost,' Nicola said, her forehead wrinkled in a frown. She walked into the back office and returned a few moments later with a glass of water. 'Here, drink this.'

The water helped, and the nausea subsided. 'I'm afraid I wouldn't be much use to you right now anyway,' Sally admitted as another crash echoed through the salon. 'You see, I'm—'

'Up the duff!' Nicola squealed, finishing her sentence for her. 'Oh my days, I'm so happy for you.'

Sally reached for her friend's hand over her shoulder, to squeeze it, looking at her in the mirror before her. 'I've wanted a family of my own for as long as I can remember. And it's finally happened.' She placed her other hand protectively over her non-existent bump. 'I've never loved someone so much in my life. I will do everything I can to keep this little one safe.'

'Course you will. That's a mother's love right there. This is the best news I've heard in a long time.'

'When I think about that day I came here begging for a job . . .'

'I'll thank the stars I said yes that day. You're like my own daughter now, Sally. I don't have a family, so having you in my life has been such a blessing for me.' Nicola placed her hand over Sally's on her stomach and promised, 'Aunty Nicola is going to spoil this little one so much.'

Sally felt her heart constrict with love for her friend. 'I hope that maybe you might be this little one's godmother.'

'Well, that would be my honour, love. But you'll have to get his lordship's approval first. You know what Ian's like. He likes to be the one to make all the decisions.'

Sally was sure she saw a hardening in Nicola's eyes as she mentioned Ian, and her friend's words stung her. Was Nicola intimating that Sally didn't have a voice of her own, that she was under Ian's beck and call? That wasn't true, was it? Yes, he did like things his way, but he was so good to her.

But what about that little voice that niggled her every week when Ian handed over her housekeeping money. She had no control over their finances. He insisted on paying all bills and the mortgage. And when Sally had expressed an interest in sharing this role, he'd smiled indulgently, telling her she shouldn't worry about such matters. And when she'd pushed it, enquiring about their savings, he'd got angry. Accused her of not trusting him. She'd ended up apologising to him, and balance had been restored. But the memory of that still irked her a little.

She wouldn't tell Nicola this, though. She'd made her vows, and loyalty to her spouse was part of that.

Instead, Sally said firmly, 'Ian will want what I want. And I can't think of a better person to be the godmother than you.'

Nicola smiled placatingly, and Sally couldn't help but think her friend didn't buy her protestations. She decided to change the subject.

'How's Elsie doing? I haven't managed to see her for a little while. Is she all right?'

'She's back on again with Reggie,' Nicola said.

The two women rolled their eyes in unison. Elsie's on-off relationship with Reggie had worn thin with them both at this stage. No sooner would they dry their friend's tears, than she'd be back in his arms again. Then he'd disappear for weeks on end, on the run from the Old Bill, for some trouble he'd got himself caught up in.

'I worry about Elsie,' Nicola admitted. 'She always looks on the edge of –' she wrinkled her nose as she searched for a word – 'chaos.'

This surprised Sally. She didn't see Elsie that way at all. Her friend was the strong one. But, unfortunately, Nicola wasn't the only one who doubted Elsie.

'Ian has concerns about her too.'

'Go on,' Nicola urged, leaning in for the gossip.

'You know that Reggie was in prison for forging banknotes when he was twenty. Elsie swears she already knew this, when I told her. But I wonder if she did. And Reggie runs favours for some of London's heavyweights. Not to mention the scams he's always got on the go. Last week, Ian said that he's now a suspect in an armed raid.'

'Oh my days, that's not good, but Reggie always wriggles his way out of trouble, doesn't he? I can't help but like Reggie, though. He's a decent sort.'

Sally agreed. 'I've grown fond of him too over the years. I have no issue with him, as long as he treats Elsie well. But hearing about armed raids . . . well, that's a different matter.'

'Well, all you can do is advise Elsie to take care of herself.'

Sally sighed. 'I'll try. The thing is, Ian wants me to keep my distance from Elsie and Reggie. Especially now, with the baby on the way . . .'

'But Elsie is your best friend, love. How can you keep away from her?'

Sally shrugged. For that, she had no answer.

BEFORE

August 1980

Sally

Hereford Gardens, Harrow, London

Sally unfastened the top button of her jeans as her ever-growing stomach pinched in protest. Almost overnight, she'd gone from a flat tummy to blooming pregnant. But she loved her new shape. It made her feel closer to her own mother too. Because, while Sally could not ignore the fact that her mother had made mistakes – many mistakes – she also believed that Lizzie Fox had loved her, and done her best for her daughter. She had put Sally's needs before her own, giving her up, to ensure she was safe. Maybe Lizzie had cradled her own growing tummy, as Sally did now, when she was pregnant. It was a nice thought that gave her comfort as she grieved her mother's loss.

Ian was excited to meet his son. He refused to believe that he would have anything but a boy. Sally had a feeling that he would get his wish too. Nicola had spun her wedding ring on a piece of string over her bump the previous week at the salon, and declared it was a boy. Time would tell.

Sally decided to make spaghetti Bolognese for dinner. Ian enjoyed that. She would prepare the sauce now, and then cook the pasta once Ian got home. As she chopped onions and peppers into fine slices, the doorbell rang. Wiping her hands on her apron, Sally went to see who it was and found Elsie standing there with a bunch of buttery yellow carnations in her arms.

'If the mountain won't come to Mohammad . . .' Elsie joked.

Sally flushed beetroot red. Elsie had phoned and asked Sally to meet several times and, understandably, had got sick of being brushed off with excuses.

'I'm sorry,' Sally apologised. 'I've been a rubbish friend. It's just . . .' She couldn't finish the sentence. How could she explain to Elsie that her husband disapproved of her? And that he had forbidden her from seeing Elsie any more, saying that he could not have his wife associated with a known criminal's girlfriend?

'I know what it is. Or, rather, who it is,' Elsie replied, rolling her eyes. 'I don't blame you one bit.'

'It's difficult for him . . . He worries about me. And with his job he can't be in the same company as Reggie . . .' Sally tried to explain, but as she heard the words spill from her lips she knew how lame they were.

Elsie guffawed, shaking her head. 'Pot kettle black.'

'What do you mean by that?' Sally asked.

Elsie looked down at Sally's bump, then back up again, replacing her frown with a smile. 'Doesn't matter. Ignore me. I'm here to see how you are, not talk about your husband. Can I come in?'

Sally led her back into the kitchen, glancing at the clock quickly to check it was still early afternoon. It would be hours before Ian got home.

'How are you feeling? Your bump has got so big!' Elsie exclaimed, placing a hand on her friend's tummy.

'I'm huge! I can't close my jeans,' Sally boasted. 'And I'm not due until January!'

'It suits you. You look beautiful. Blooming!'

'That's what Sister Jones said last week. I called in to the orphanage to say hello and tell her my news.'

'How is the old bag?'

'Elsie!' Sally scolded. 'I like her. We've got close. I visit her every now and then. She'd even insisted that I call her by her first name.' Sally let that tidbit hang in the air.

'What is it?' Elsie demanded.

'Guess!'

'Oh God, the pressure of thinking of a Scottish name... Bonnie?'

They both laughed, and then Sally said, 'Ailsa.'

'Ailsa?' Elsie exclaimed. 'That's her name? I would not have got that if you'd given me a hundred guesses.'

Sally nodded. 'It's pretty, isn't it? A Scottish name, apparently, and she told me that she's named after her grandmother.'

'Goodness, you *are* chummy now!'

'I like her,' Sally replied truthfully. 'Anyway, enough about me. Tell me all your news. How's Cyril and the girls?'

'Mary's up the duff again. Cyril said us women would be the death of him.' Elsie started to cackle with laughter.

'Ah, that's lovely news. Please give her my best. And Reggie, how's he?'

'Lying low,' Elsie said, then leaned in closer to whisper, 'He did a job for you-know-who, and the Old Bill are everywhere, trying to pin it on someone. Probably won't see much of him for a week or two.'

'That worries me,' Sally admitted with a frown. 'I like Reggie. You know that. He's a fun guy. But you deserve someone who can give you more than that. Don't you want that for yourself?'

Elsie looked around the modern semi-detached home, from the half-prepared food on the countertop, to Sally's bump. 'Like you have here?'

'Yes. Or a version of this,' Sally said, smiling. 'Do you remember all those nights we'd whisper to each other, our hopes to marry two brothers, and live next door.'

'Not sure I want that any more,' Elsie replied sadly.

'Why?' Sally demanded, feeling her stomach sink at Elsie's comment.

'I don't know. Maybe I wouldn't be a good mother. Not every-one has the maternal gene, like you do,' Elsie said as a shadow passed over her face.

'You would be a great mother, Elsie. You took me under your wing the first moment you met me. I would never have survived Sunshine House without you.'

'Yes you would. I keep telling you, you'll always be okay. You're a bright light that will never go out.' Then she frowned as she asked, 'Is Ian good to you? Does he treat you right?'

Sally nodded immediately. 'He loves me. I'm happy, honestly. Ian *is* good to me.'

And, in the main, this statement was true. She pushed aside the nagging thought that followed – that Ian was good to her as long as she did as he demanded. On the occasions she resisted, Ian did not respond well.

Elsie raised an eyebrow as she searched Sally's face. Then she shrugged, and said, 'Look, it doesn't matter what either of us think about our boyfriends or husbands, as long as we're happy, right?'

'Exactly!' Sally replied.

'We might not get your dream of living next door to each other, though. Not if I stick with my Reggie, that is. Can you imagine Ian and Reggie cutting the lawn, side by side?' Elsie added, with a cheeky wink, making Sally snort with laughter.

And that's all it took for them both to regain their equilib-rium. Friendship was restored. But, as they caught up with each other's news, Sally forgot the time. She only realised that it was six o'clock when the creak of the front door opening announced Ian's return.

'Damn it, Ian's back and the dinner isn't cooked,' Sally said, holding a hand to her face.

'You can get a takeaway,' Elsie said reassuringly. 'He will understand.'

Ian didn't understand, though. His face turned to thunder when he saw the two friends sitting side by side at the kitchen table.

'All right for some, sitting on their backsides all day gossiping, while others are out working hard.'

Sally jumped up and kissed him on the cheek. 'Dinner will be ready in fifteen minutes, darling.'

'I called unexpectedly. Sally didn't know I was coming,' Elsie said, locking eyes with Ian. 'And I'm leaving, so don't worry – your precious dinner will not be delayed a moment longer by me.'

'You should call in advance the next time. Some would say turning up unannounced is bad manners,' Ian said. Then he turned his back on her before Elsie could respond.

Once Sally had said her goodbyes to Elsie, apologising for Ian's rudeness, she returned to the kitchen. She had to make Ian see that he could not speak to her friends like that. But before she had a chance to relay this to him, she felt a sharp blow on her cheek. Stunned, she turned to see Ian lowering his hand.

'You . . . you slapped me,' Sally stammered, feeling heat rush to her cheek as it throbbed from the impact.

'It was a slap in *my* face to return home to *my* wife, who couldn't be bothered to cook her husband a meal. Who would rather ignore my express wishes to not spend her free time with a criminal. Now you know what it felt like to me.'

'But . . . but Elsie isn't a criminal. She's my oldest and dearest friend,' Sally said as she trembled in shock.

'How do you know that? Can you honestly say Reggie hasn't got her mixed up in his work? For all we know, she's knee deep in it all. Her kind always are.'

'Her kind? What kind is that?' Sally asked. 'Because whatever kind that is, it's what you married!'

Anger flashed over Ian's face again and he raised his hand.

'You can't hit me!' Sally protested, holding her arms up in front of her bump to protect the baby.

'I can and I will do as I see fit. And, as my wife, you better learn to accept that,' he replied. 'Keep away from Elsie Evans and anyone else from the orphanage. That part of your life is no longer relevant.'

Sally looked at him in surprise, then her eyes narrowed as understanding dawned. 'You are embarrassed by my background. That I grew up in care. That my mother was a prostitute. That I was a cleaner.'

Ian took a step closer, picking up a strand of Sally's blonde hair. 'I took you in. I gave you all of this . . .' He waved his hand around the kitchen. 'And you should be bloody grateful. Leave the past where it belongs. Now make my dinner. I'll have it in the sitting room on a tray.'

Then he walked away, leaving a shell-shocked Sally in his wake.

To her growing horror, in the days that followed, Ian showed no remorse. He felt justified in his actions. It was as if an alien had abducted her kind and charming husband, replacing him with a man she did not recognise.

That had been the end of their honeymoon period. And the start of a new phase in their marriage.

Life with Ian could be peaceful and loving for weeks, but then a transgression would occur – an act of disobedience from Sally for which she would have to pay the price. He restrained himself to ankle kicks, vicelike pinches and slaps – all sharp and painful, but manageable for Sally to endure.

And each time Sally swore that she would leave, because she was not the kind of woman to stay with a man who hit her. But then she'd look at her growing bump and think of her baby.

Where would they go?

What would become of her child?

Alone, would she follow in her mother's footsteps, unable to manage, and forced to give her child up?

So Sally told herself that when the baby came it would soften Ian. It would make him see how much he had to lose if he continued his bullish behaviour.

And each day she stayed, a little bit more of her bright white light dulled.

BEFORE

July 1981

Sally

Hereford Gardens, Harrow, London

Sally held a pack of Birds Eye frozen peas against her cheek. The ice stung for a moment, but it was a welcome relief from the pain in her jaw. A gift from Ian before he'd left for work this morning.

She still struggled to understand how it had come to this.

She cocked her ear to listen for sounds from the nursery upstairs. No, all was quiet still. Her heart swelled, thinking about her baby boy taking his morning nap. So much had changed since his arrival six months ago. Her life was a continual contradiction of light and dark.

Light when it was her and the baby, every moment of being his mother a joy. Dark when Ian was home, sucking every inch of happiness from her with his mood swings and temper.

This morning, Ian was disappointed in a crease he'd found in his white shirt that she'd ironed the evening before. Sally was careful with his clothes, knowing he liked to be just so. He'd been in a mood since arriving home late the night before, grumbling that he had been overlooked for a promotion.

Sally returned to the freezer and replaced the frozen peas. She sighed as she pondered what she could do to change her situation. Over the past year, she'd tried everything to make their marriage work. She'd pleaded with Ian. She'd argued back and held her own when he attacked. She'd threatened to leave. She'd cried pitifully as he backed her into a corner. But no matter what reaction she gave him it seemed to fall on deaf ears. Ian would watch her with a half-grin as if he were enjoying her reactions.

Sally looked at the clock and decided it was time to wake Zach. She went upstairs to the nursery, smiling as she heard her son's happy gurgles. 'Hello, Mama's special little boy.'

She reached down and picked him up, holding him close in her arms, nuzzling into his soft, downy blond curls. He smelled like baby powder and vanilla. Sally didn't think there was a more addictive smell than his. She brought Zach to the changing unit, put a fresh nappy on him and dressed him in his outdoor Baby-gro. It was time for their morning walk.

This was her favourite part of the day and one that Ian encouraged. He liked Sally to keep her figure trim. Luckily for her, their home in Hereford Gardens had direct access to the Pinner Village Gardens park. As she walked towards the Rose Garden, her favourite spot in the parkland, she pointed out the trees and wildlife pond to Zach, who regarded his surroundings with interest. A group of teens flew kites on the green, and echoes of children's happy squeals drifted towards them from the playground.

'You'll be old enough for the swings in no time, Zach,' Sally promised, looking forward to the day she could take him there too. She sat on a bench in the Rose Garden and leaned back to let the warmth of the summer sun bathe her face.

'Hello, Sally,' a voice said as a shadow appeared from behind her.

Sally looked up in surprise. Elsie sat down beside her on the park bench. Sally's heart ached at seeing her best friend for the first time in almost a year. She looked well. Her hair had changed colour and was now blonde and fell in long waves past her shoulders in a style almost identical to Sally's.

Sally felt a flush of shame. She'd been a rubbish friend, and her guilt at disappearing from Elsie's life weighed heavy on her.

'I'm sorry . . .' Sally began.

'Hush now. I'm not here for you to apologise. I'm here to see this little one. Oh, Sally, he's beautiful,' Elsie said, her eyes hungrily taking in Zach.

'Almost six months old now. And the sweetest boy. He's my whole world.'

'Can I give him a cuddle?' Elsie asked.

'Of course you can. I've told him all about his auntie Elsie.'

Sally watched her oldest friend pick up her son and hold him close. Elsie kissed both his cheeks tenderly, and her eyes glistened with emotion as she nestled him in close to her.

'Hello, little man. I'm so happy to meet you. I'm sorry it's taken so long.'

Zach reached a chubby hand upwards and touched Elsie's face. Then he grabbed a handful of her blonde hair and gave it a yank.

Elsie's laugh bellowed out, and Zach giggled along. 'He's a little belter!'

'I can't wear earrings any more or he'll yank them out!' Sally said.

'I'm not sure I'll be able to let him go. He's perfect,' Elsie said wistfully. 'He reminds me of Bertie . . .' She didn't finish the sentence.

'Bertie?' Sally asked, in surprise. She'd never heard that name before.

'A kid who used to live on our road . . . before I moved to the orphanage,' Elsie said quickly. 'But I don't think I've seen a bonnier baby than this little man.'

Sally basked in the praise. She'd had visitors to their home since his birth, but they were all Ian's friends. Nicola had been granted permission to come and had visited a couple of times each month. But Ian had refused to leave them alone for more than a moment. He was afraid Sally would confide in her friend about how unhappy she was. But he needn't have worried. She didn't think she was brave enough to tell anyone her shameful secret.

'I called to the house a few times. Not sure you knew that,' Elsie said softly, her eyes not leaving Zach's even for a moment. 'But Ian wouldn't let me in.'

'I didn't know. I'm so sorry,' Sally said. 'I wanted to visit you too, so many times . . . but . . . it's been difficult.'

Elsie bounced Zach on her lap and then swivelled round so that she faced Sally.

'I'm worried about you,' Elsie said.

Sally's head went through half a dozen possible responses – all denials of trouble, with assurances that she was living a happy life. Instead, Sally replied simply, 'I'm worried about me too.'

'We used to tell each other everything. But now I feel like I don't know you. Or your life.'

Sally understood. It was a fair comment. 'It's complicated.'

'Talk to me now. There's nobody around to hear you.'

It was clear to Sally that Elsie had had suspicions about Ian for some time. Nicola too. But she wasn't sure that either of her friends could ever understand what it was like for her behind closed doors.

Sally looked around her, ensuring nobody was nearby and could overhear them. Then, satisfied that they were alone, she began to speak. 'Ian likes things done a certain way. And, if I stray from that, he gets angry.'

She glanced at Elsie and was relieved that her friend remained silent, allowing her to reveal her secrets at her own pace. She touched her cheek, still tender from this morning. She felt heat rise from her chest upwards towards her face.

Shame that she'd allowed herself to be in this situation.

Shame that she hadn't found a way to stop the rising tide of abuse from her husband.

'He hits you too,' Elsie stated, her eyes resting on Sally's swollen cheek.

Sally knew there was no point in denying it, so she nodded. 'I'm in such a mess, Elsie. I don't know what to do.'

'It's a good job I'm here to help you figure that out,' Elsie replied, patting her hand. 'You can't go on like this. It's not right for you or for little Zach. Because, trust me, growing up in an unhappy home isn't what you want for this precious little boy.'

Not for the first time, Sally thought Elsie was hiding secrets from her childhood. 'Like you had at your home?'

Elsie shrugged, tightening her arms round Zach, then she did what she always did when Sally brought up a subject she didn't want to talk about – she diverted her.

'Reggie and I split up. For good, this time.'

'Oh, I'm sorry,' Sally said. 'Are you okay?'

'I told you years ago that we ain't no Romeo and Juliet. We gave it a good go, but we don't love each other. Not how you're supposed to. We'd become a habit. We were both lonely.' She sighed, then admitted, 'He'll end up back in prison or found dead in an alleyway somewhere, someday. I don't want to be here when that happens.'

Sally was surprised at how honest Elsie finally was about their relationship. 'You've never wanted to talk about Reggie's criminal past before.'

'I know. But I've done a lot of thinking over the past couple of months. Looked at my life, square on. And I didn't like a lot of what I saw,' Elsie said firmly.

'That takes great courage, Elsie,' Sally said, her voice full of admiration.

'Maybe. I'm glad that we've ended things amicably, all the same. Reggie was always good to me, but I can't turn my back on his life choices any more. I've told him that I want more from my life.'

'Good for you,' Sally said, smiling her approval. 'What's next for Elsie Evans, then?'

'Time to move on, Sally. It's not possible to start afresh here. Too many ghosts from my past remind me of the bad times.'

Sally realised she was not the only one who had experienced a lot of change over the past year. But those changes had been good for Elsie. She seemed far more together than she'd ever been.

'You sound so strong.'

'I'm trying to be,' Elsie said. 'I've saved a bit of money up from my Avon work. I seem to have a knack for running my own business. When Reggie and I talked about leaving London, he suggested we go to Spain. He's got contacts there. And it was tempting to go together, give it one more chance, but I've decided to go alone. Maybe manage a bar. Be my own boss.' She sighed, then looked up shyly. 'I've finished charring, said goodbye to Cyril and the girls.' Tears filled her eyes, and she blinked them away. 'But I couldn't leave without seeing you again.'

Sally looked at her friend closely and was relieved to see excitement on her face as opposed to any lingering sadness.

'I'm so proud of you. And I know you'll get where you need to be, Elsie. I'm sure of it. Imagine what new things are in your future.' Sally looked at her watch. 'Crikey, I need to get back. Ian calls every day at one o'clock, once I'm back from my walk.' She reached over and took Zach back into her arms.

Elsie's eyes flashed with irritation, and she shook her head as she spluttered, 'You know that's not normal. Your husband checking in on you every couple of hours.'

'I know,' Sally replied softly, 'but I can't get into that right now.'

'When? I told you I'm off soon, Sally. And before I leave I need to tell you something that's been playing on my mind.'

Sally's heart began to accelerate as she surmised what Elsie might want to tell her. 'Go on, then.'

'Have you ever wondered why Ian forbade you from seeing me?' Elsie asked.

'We know why. It's because he's a police officer, and his wife can't be in the company of known criminals.'

Elsie rolled her eyes. 'That's not it. Ian was afraid that Reggie or I would spill the beans on who *he* is, more like.'

Sally frowned, 'I don't understand.'

'Remember that night in the Grove when the four of us went on a double date?'

Sally nodded. It was early in their romance, and she'd been excited to introduce Ian to her friends. Also, it was their *only* double date. It hadn't been a success.

'Ian's face when he clocked eyes on Reggie. I'll never forget it. It was like he'd seen a ghost. I asked Reggie about it, later that night, but he told me to leave it.'

Sally exhaled, trying to understand where this was going.

'When you guys got married, Reggie laughed when I told him he wasn't invited. He said he wasn't surprised, but wouldn't tell me why, other than to say, "You wait and see. Baldwin will stop Sally seeing us both next." Well, he was right about that, wasn't he?'

Sally flushed, hating the fact that she was the topic of conversation with her friends. 'Why are you telling me all of this now?' She looked at her watch again, sweat prickling under her armpits.

'Reggie finally told me last week why Ian was so hot and bothered about him.' Elsie's eyes narrowed. 'Your Ian was worried that Reggie would out him.'

'Out him for what?' Sally asked.

'Ian is on the payroll for Reggie's boss. He's corrupt.'

Sally's heart began to race as she tried to compute Elsie's words. 'That doesn't make sense. Ian always does things by the book.'

Elsie raised her eyebrows, then asked, 'Have you ever wondered how he managed to buy that house of yours on a DS salary?'

Sally frowned. 'He did what most people do. He got a mortgage from a bank.'

'Or he paid for it in cash,' Elsie said pointedly. 'You ever see how much money he has in his bank account?'

Sally felt alarm bells ringing in her head. She'd given up asking Ian about their finances, because it invariably caused an argument.

'Look, I know Reggie ain't no angel. As I told you, that's why I decided to move on from him. But he's not a cruel man. I trust him.' She breathed in deeply and her voice softened. 'When I told him that I was worried about you, he said that I should be worried. That Baldwin is a nasty bugger. I believe him, and you should too.'

Sally pulled Zach into her arms again, taking comfort from his soft body as he nestled close to her. How could something so beautiful as Zach come from someone as horrible as Ian? Her head swam with it all. 'Thank you for telling me this, but I've got to go, Elsie.'

'Think about what I said, Sally. Be on your guard – that's all I'm saying.'

Sally squeezed her friend's hand quickly. 'I'm happy I saw you today. More than you could know. I've missed you so much.' Her mind began racing through possibilities of how she might see Elsie before she left for Spain. 'I'm going to Nicola's for a wash and blow-dry on Saturday. Ian and I are invited to a work dinner dance. Could you be at the salon for two o'clock? It would give us a chance to continue chatting. I'd like to say a proper goodbye before you leave.'

'A great idea. It will be like old times, back in the salon with you and Nicola again.'

Sally stood up, clipping Zach into his pram, then rearranging the soft blue blanket over his legs, tucking it in tightly. He was forever kicking it off.

Sally turned to Elsie, a frown creasing her forehead. 'I'll try to get the bus, but Ian might insist on dropping me over. And if he sees you at the salon, he'll come in and wait for me there. We won't get to chat.'

'No problem. I'll hide in the back room until he's gone.'

With one last hug, Sally hurried home. And she didn't feel so alone any more. Elsie would find a way to help her.

NOW

August 2023

Kimberly

Gardiner Street Apartments, Dublin

Kimberly's apartment looked completely different from how it used to when she and Robert lived there in 1981. After her divorce from Jason, they sold their family home. Jason bought his fixer-upper in Phibsborough, and Kimberly decided to return to her first home in Dublin, the flat in Gardiner Street. Jason and she still owned the complex, and Kimberly had felt compelled to move back in. She'd gutted it, knocking walls down and making one large reception room with a stunning primary suite.

And now, for the first time in forty years, her family were reunited again in this apartment.

Kimberly surveyed the room, taking in Jason, Lily and Zach, who sat on her L-shaped cream sofa. Kimberly had insisted that it be only the four of them. Jason's father, Kevin, was so objectionable, always finding fault with her. While she adored her little grandson, she didn't want any distractions today, so Michael and Ben stayed home too. Just thinking about Ben made Kimberly smile. He was her happy place. When he was in her arms, every worry and stress melted away.

'Your home is so elegant,' Zach said.

Kimberly accepted the compliment with a gracious nod as she

laid a tray of refreshments on the coffee table – a jug of elder-flower tonic water and four crystal glasses, perfect for the warm day. Kimberly had finessed her unique and understated style dec-ades before. She knew what she liked and had the budget to pander to her expensive taste. The room had a soothing palette of creams with gold accents. White oak floorboards ran through the entire space, giving it uniformity. She'd meticulously curated exquisite pieces of art and sculpture to which the eye was drawn but by which it was never distracted.

Her home had become her haven.

And, sometimes, she even managed to find some peace within these four walls.

'I'm always half afraid to let Ben loose in here. His sticky fin-gers would have a field day,' Lily joked with her dad and Zach, who laughed with her.

'That's what wipes are for,' Kimberly said. 'Ben can come here to stay any time, you know. I don't mind a little mess.'

Lily smiled sceptically at her mother and Kimberly felt a flush creep into her cheeks. Had she been such a bad mother that her own daughter doubted her so? She made a mental note to arrange a sleepover here with Ben soon.

Kimberly took a deep breath and said to Zach, 'I asked you to come here because this was our first home in Dublin when it was the two of us. And it was where I met and fell in love with you, Jason. And where we brought you home from the hospital, Lily.'

Jason smiled at Kimberly and said, 'I can still remember the moment I saw you for the first time. You had Robert in your arms, and he was playing with your hair. I'd never seen a more beautiful woman in my life.'

Kimberly blushed at his compliment. Why was it that, after all this time and so much water under their bridges, Jason could still make her feel like a giddy sixteen-year-old?

'I wish I could remember living here,' Zach said.

'You were too young. We moved into a house on Shandon

Road a few months after Lily was born,' Jason said. 'But we sold that after the divorce . . .'

The room was quiet momentarily as tension began to creep into the air. Kimberly didn't want that. She wanted today to be another happy memory to add to the ones formed forty years previously. She sat in her favourite mid-century armchair, with its solid ash frame and soft cream upholstery, and turned to address them.

'I asked you all to come here today because while my flat is small, so much love and happy memories are infused into its walls. It's why I choose to live here. It's where I was happiest in my life. And I wanted the four of us to spend a little time together here before things get crazy tomorrow when the results are back.'

Kimberly sighed with pleasure when she saw that her words had readdressed the balance, and her family visibly relaxed as they sat back in their seats.

'You see, I don't need a DNA test to prove that Zach is Robert,' Kimberly said, touching her chest. 'I can feel it here.'

'It's the same for me too,' Jason added, patting Zach's knee beside him.

And, for a moment, the four Murphys, reunited again for the first time in forty years, sat in silence, shyly looking at each other, as they tried to adjust to this new normal. Kimberly looked at each of them in silent and grateful wonder. And she wished with all her heart that she could lock the front door, and keep them all here with her, safe from the outside world and its nasty truths.

'You okay, Mum?' Lily asked gently. She reached for a tissue from her handbag and passed it to her.

Kimberly smiled as she patted away her tears. 'I'm being a silly old sentimental mother, aren't I? Happy tears, I promise you.'

'You're allowed,' Jason said. 'If anyone is allowed to cry, it's you, my love.'

A shiver ran down Kimberly's back as she thought about her son's other family. Menacing and dark, ready to pounce and threaten her family again. But they were in America, thousands of miles away. Robert . . . or Zach . . . was here with his family. Kimberly was determined to only focus on that.

'I want us to have a happy time together. That's the only rule for today. And, with that in mind, could you help me get something from my bedroom, Jason?' Kimberly asked.

Together, they left and returned a few moments later with a large cardboard box.

Lily half smiled, half sobbed. 'Robert's gifts.'

'This is only one of the boxes. There're another two in the bedroom,' Jason said with a grin.

'I am so sure that you *are* Robert that I want you to open these, please,' Kimberly said, pushing the box towards Zach. 'There's one for every birthday and Christmas since you disappeared.'

Zach looked over to Kimberly, his face softening with emotion. 'I'm overwhelmed.'

'These are the gifts bought over the past twenty years. We thought you'd prefer to start with them. I'm not sure you have much use for the toys we bought during your childhood,' Kimberly said, blinking back tears. She'd yearned for this day for so long that she could scarcely believe it was finally here.

Zach opened the lid, reached into the box and pulled out a small package wrapped in bright green paper. He read the gift card aloud, 'Happy fortieth birthday, Robert.' He ripped open the box to reveal a set of AirPods. 'Wow! Would you believe that I have misplaced my EarPods? I think I left them on the flight coming home from Ronda. These are great!'

Kimberly pointed to another package. 'Will you open that one next?'

Zach ripped the bright paper off, and groaned when he saw what was inside. 'My Peter Rabbit.'

'I thought it was time it went back to its rightful owner,' Kimberly whispered.

'You kept it all this time,' Zach said, shaking his head.

'I knew you'd come back for it one day,' Kimberly replied.

Then, wiping tears from her eyes, she pointed to the box. 'Go on. Keep opening!'

Twenty minutes later, there was a pile of wrapping paper on the floor beside an even more enormous pile of gifts – shirts, an Ireland rugby jersey, cufflinks, an Ed Sheeran CD, aftershave, and a framed family photograph taken at Ben's christening, amongst the favourites for Zach.

Kimberly never took her eyes off Zach as he opened each gift. She revelled in his joy at each item.

'I'd like to take you to your first Irish rugby match. You can wear that jersey,' Jason said. 'Ben and Michael can come too. It will be a boy's day out!'

Zach stood up and pulled the jersey over his white tee shirt. It fitted perfectly as he declared, 'I'm ready! Come on, Ireland!'

Kimberly caught Lily's eye and saw her daughter fight back emotion. Lily had always been an open book, wearing her heart on her sleeve.

'You okay?' Kimberly asked quietly, reaching out to touch Lily's arm.

Lily smiled through her tears. 'It's hearing Dad talking about doing something fun with his family, with his grandson . . . I didn't think I'd ever hear that.'

And Kimberly felt a sharp pain between her temples as she reflected on that sad statement. Another of her damn migraines threatened to scupper the day. But she would not allow it. Kimberly excused herself and walked into the bathroom to grab some painkillers, swallowing them dry. She looked up into the large round mirror and took in her appearance.

Kimberly had spent as much effort and time cultivating her own look over the years as she had with her decor at home. She chose her make-up, jewellery and clothes carefully.

To her, elegance was simplicity and effectiveness.

But, to her surprise, her eyes blurred, and for a moment she disappeared. A young orphan girl, scared and alone, stared back at her.

A tap on the bathroom door brought her image back to sharp focus.

'You've been in there a while. Do you need anything, Mum?' Lily asked, her eyes round with concern when Kimberly opened the door.

'No thank you, Lily. It's all a little overwhelming, isn't it? But know that I'm happy,' Kimberly replied. Then, impulsively, she pulled her daughter into her arms and held her. She felt Lily stiffen at first, but Kimberly didn't let go until she relaxed into her embrace.

Kimberly wasn't so stupid that she hadn't realised how difficult Lily had it at times. She'd spent her childhood in the middle of her parents, trying hard to broker peace or add joy when things got overwrought.

'You are a good daughter, and I'm sorry for all I've put you through,' Kimberly whispered. 'All I wanted was to be a good mother to you, but I know I have let you down. When things were difficult for me, I let that pain get in the way of you and me.'

Lily pulled back and looked at her mother in surprise.

'You had it worse than any of us, I think,' Kimberly added. 'And we often forget that. Can you forgive me?'

Lily nodded, her lips quivering as she desperately tried to fight back tears. 'I love you, Mum.'

'And I love you,' Kimberly replied. 'I hope you remember that, no matter what happens tomorrow. Everything I've done has been for our family.'

Lily nodded silently.

Kimberly watched her daughter trying to process her words. And Lily, with her kind-hearted nature, was already forgiving her mother for the many transgressions she'd endured.

'I truly am sorry for all the mistakes I've made . . .'

'We've all made mistakes, Mum,' Lily said, interrupting her. 'I want you to stop being so hard on yourself. We've been given a chance to start over, as a family, back together again. You said earlier that you wanted this to be a happy day. And it has been. One of my happiest, truly.' Lily wiped her eyes with the back of her hand, as she used to do as a child. Kimberly grabbed a tissue from the bathroom, and dabbed her daughter's cheeks lightly.

'How did I get to be so lucky to have you?' Kimberly whispered. Then she kissed Lily's cheek one more time, before saying jokily, 'We'd better return to Jason and Robert before they plan a boy's only trip to New Zealand to see the rugby without us!'

Kimberly knew she had to call him Zach out loud, but in the privacy of her own mind he would always be Robert to her. Holding Kimberly's hand, Lily led her back to the living room.

Zach had now opened all his gifts, and he seemed reflective as he looked down at them, scattered at his feet on the floor. 'I've never had so many gifts in my life. And Santa was always generous!'

'Don't expect this every year at Christmas, son,' Jason replied with a wink.

They all laughed and Kimberly's heart swelled as their family teased each other.

But then Zach's face clouded and he turned to face Kimberly and Jason. 'I'm sorry this happened to you. I'm sorry that Robert was taken from you. I'm sorry that my mom hurt you like this,' he blurted out.

The room quietened as his words bounced between them and their memories of a life lived with the ghost of a stolen child.

Silent Christmas mornings, escaping to a locked bathroom to cry, coming out with a bright smile as she and Jason tried to make the best of it for Lily. Until one of them would say Robert's name out loud, and a fight would follow. Accusations slung about how they each dealt with Robert's absence. Jason searching, always searching. Lily mediating. And Kimberly hiding her pain in her work. Until one Christmas Jason got up and left, slamming the front door so hard that it almost came off its hinges.

That was the end of the Murphy family.

Kimberly looked at her ex-husband and daughter and saw the pain she felt mirrored on each of their faces.

'We missed you so much,' Kimberly whispered. A tear trickled down her cheek, and she dabbed it away with the back of her hand. 'But you are back now, and I do not want any sad thoughts today. This is a celebration! I have a beautiful meal prepared for us. I hope you are all hungry! And I've managed to get a bottle of Amelia Park 2015 Museum Reserve Cabernet Sauvignon. It's always been a favourite.'

'You're giving us the reserve wine?' Jason asked.

'You've cooked?' Lily added incredulously, making Jason and her laugh.

'Yes! I do cook occasionally,' Kimberly replied, giggling, and admitted, 'Oh, okay, I may have used a caterer.'

As everyone giggled together, Kimberly felt overwhelming joy and relief. Her headache had vanished.

'Will I get the childhood toys?' Jason asked, with a twinkle in his eyes.

Lily raised her hands in the air. 'Before you do, I have a confession to make. When I was six, I sneaked into the attic of our old house and opened all of your childhood gifts.'

Zach laughed, playfully shoving Lily's arm. 'You little monkey! Well, did I get anything nice?'

'Yeah, lots of decent stuff. I particularly liked the train set. Mum and Dad found me up there in a sea of wrapping paper. Dad thought it was funny, but Mum went berserk! She rewrapped it all up. But Dad insisted that I get to keep the train. He bought another one for you.'

'I did not go berserk. You make me sound like a crazy woman,' Kimberly rebutted.

'Maybe a little berserk,' Jason teased, and Kimberly couldn't help but grin, conceding this.

As she hoped it would be, that day, having her family in their first home, back together again, was one of the happiest days of Kimberly's life.

'Memories banked forever,' she whispered to herself in satisfaction. No matter what happened following the fallout of the DNA results tomorrow, she'd always have today.

NOW

August 2023

Lily

DNA Clinic, Docklands, Dublin

Lily arrived fifteen minutes early for their clinic appointment at 12pm, but it was clear she wasn't the only early bird. She found Zach pacing up and down the quayside, scrolling through his phone. His shoulders were rounded, and his eyes darted up and down the street, looking out for her, she assumed. And when he spotted Lily his face broke into the lopsided grin, she now associated with him. He jogged towards her, pulling her into a quick hug.

'Am I glad to see you! Every nerve is on edge,' Zach said.

Lily could sympathise. She'd only managed a couple of hours' sleep the previous night.

'I know! But wasn't yesterday lovely? I've never seen Mum and Dad so happy and relaxed.'

'I'll never forget it,' Zach agreed, then held up his AirPods. 'Best present ever!'

Lily looked up at him and frowned. 'I feel like everything is about to change, Zach.' Her stomach flipped and turned, as it used to before she was due to sit her exams in college.

Zach face crumpled. 'I think it already has changed.'

'What's wrong?' Lily asked. 'I mean, other than the obvious.'

284

'Jenny called again and demanded that I not collect the results.'

'I do sympathise with her. It must be scary, waiting to hear the news,' Lily replied. 'But it's unfair of her to blame you for something you have no control over.'

'She doesn't see it like that. And when I told her that it didn't matter if I stayed home today, you would come in for the results anyway, she started to cry. She said she'd never forgive me for bringing this to them all.'

A bike whizzed by on the cycle lane, and the sound of cars moving along the busy road filled the air. Lily shrugged off her light denim jacket. The sun had exploded into the blue sky from behind the clouds hanging low all day.

'That's a good sign.' Lily said, pointing upwards. 'It will all work out. You'll see.' But she felt a shiver run down her spine as she spoke.

Zach's phone beeped, alerting him to a text. He paled as he read it. 'It's from Jenny.' He cleared his throat and then read the text out loud.

'Zach, it's clear that you have no intention of doing what's right for your family. I don't know what you are looking for, but I hope you don't lose everything in pursuing this crusade. You left me with no choice following our call yesterday. Ally and I called to see Mom and Dad. We've told them both about what you are up to. Mom crumbled in front of us. That's on you. And, for the record, she said emphatically that she did *not* steal anyone else's child.'

Lily winced as Zach's voice trailed off. She could only imagine how distressing this was for him.

'Well, your mother would deny it all, wouldn't she?' Lily said.

'I suppose. What a bloody mess!' Zach replied. Then his phone rang, the sound piercing the air between them. 'It's Mom!'

They both looked at the phone ringing repeatedly, unable to take their eyes off it until, mercifully, it finally went to voicemail.

But, less than thirty seconds later, it rang again. This time it was Zach's stepfather, Dom.

'Put it on silent,' Lily advised.

Zach did as she suggested, and then they stood looking at the doorway to the clinic.

'I suppose we should go in,' Lily said, making her way inside, with Zach following behind. Once they'd given the receptionist their details, they took a seat and waited.

'Dad's still ringing,' Zach said, holding up his phone. 'Hang on, there's a text from Mom now.' His jaw tightened as he read, 'Zach, stay away from the Murphy family. I need you to trust me on this. Call me back urgently – Mom.'

Lily felt a flash of anger at this woman again. How dare she tell Zach to stay away from *them*? As if it were they who were the dangerous ones. 'Your mom has some cheek.'

'It makes me even more sure that I'm right,' Zach said, his face flushing with anger.

Ciara Shanahan poked her head out of her office and down the corridor. 'Zach, Lily, you can come in now.'

'You ready for this?' Zach asked.

'Nope. Yes. Maybe.'

They both giggled nervously at Lily's words. But then Lily stood up and held her hand out to Zach.

'We've got this. Together.' They walked side by side into Ciara's office.

'I won't ask how you're both doing. I can see by the matching looks of fear on your faces that you are not in the mood for chit-chat. So I'll get straight to the results,' Ciara said. She picked up a brown folder and opened it, taking out an A4 sheet.

Lily watched her face, looking for a clue as to what she was reading, but it was impassive, giving nothing away.

'We wanted to determine if you both share one common parent. In a sibling test, we calculate a sibling index, and if this

286

is less than 1.00, then it indicates that you are not related. If the index is greater than 1.00, then you are related, either as half or full siblings, depending on the number.'

Zach squeezed Lily's hand so tightly that she winced in pain. 'The number is less than 1.00. You are *not* siblings.'

PART FOUR

And, after all, what is a lie?
'Tis but the truth in masquerade.

Lord Byron

NOW

August 2023

Lily

DNA Clinic, Docklands, Dublin

The air sucked out of her body, and Lily's ears buzzed.

She'd misheard Ciara – that must be it. But the sound of a gasp from Zach on her left-hand side made her doubt herself.

'We are *not* siblings?' Lily asked.

Ciara shook her head. 'No.'

'We never thought we were full siblings. Half siblings,' Zach said hurriedly, and Lily smiled at his words.

'Yes, we have different fathers!' Lily added.

Ciara looked down at her brown folder again and shook her head. 'We have taken that into account,' she said.

Lily looked at Zach in disbelief. He was Robert – she was sure of it. 'Could there be a mistake?'

'There has to be,' Zach agreed. 'I want you to double-check. Redo the test.'

'And we can get my mum in to do a test too, and cross-check against us both,' Lily added.

'That would conclusively confirm if you were both her children,' Ciara said. 'But I do not want to waste your time or money. In my opinion, the chances of you being siblings are extremely slim.'

And so, with nothing else to be said, they got up and left the DNA clinic.

'I was sure I was Robert,' Zach whispered as he leaned against the brick wall.

'Me too,' Lily replied as her body shook with the news.

Lily had got so carried away with the idea of having her brother back that she'd been blind to the possibility that Zach was perhaps nothing more than a mixed-up man with an over-active imagination.

'What now?' Zach asked.

'We go to my house as planned. Mum and Dad are there waiting for us, with Michael, Ben and Gaga,' Lily replied in a low voice. 'Although how we tell them this . . .'

Zach winced. 'I can't bear to break their hearts. I never wanted this. To be another one of the false leads you've all had to deal with. I would *never* have pursued this if I didn't one hundred per cent believe it to be true.'

'I know,' Lily said.

'I was so sure I was Robert,' he repeated again, then glanced down at his phone, pressing the end button on another call. 'It's Mom again. At least my family at home will all be happy to get this update.'

'Every cloud and all that . . .' Lily replied as she fought back tears.

The happiness yesterday at her mum's apartment would fade when the news broke, and soon it would disappear forever. They'd go back to the same splintered, broken Murphy family.

'Maybe you should take that,' Lily said, pointing to Zach's phone. When he shook his head fervently, she added, 'Okay, but you can't ignore her forever. Let's grab a taxi and go home. I think we both could do with a coffee.'

Twenty minutes later, Lily turned the key into her front door, where she found Michael waiting for her. A quick shake of her head, and his face fell in understanding. He pulled her into his arms and kissed her forehead, and for a moment she allowed herself to stay there, regaining strength to face her parents and their inevitable disappointment.

Her dad was pacing the floor, with Lily's Gaga hovering close by. Her mum bounced a giggling Ben on her knee, a smile lighting up her face as she played with her beloved grandson.

'It was positive?' her dad asked in a desperate voice as he walked towards them both.

Lily and Zach glanced at each other, and then, with a sigh, Lily answered, 'I'm so sorry, but Zach and I do not share enough DNA to be considered siblings.'

The weight of this swung back and forth between them all like a pendulum on a grandfather's clock.

'I was sure. I have champagne in the fridge waiting for us to pop open.' Her dad's shoulders slumped as he grabbed the side of the sofa to support him.

'I don't understand. Everything pointed to you being Robert,' Gaga said, shaking his head in disbelief as he reached over to place a hand of comfort on his son's shoulder.

'I'm sorry, Dad,' Lily said, her stomach flipping as she watched the anguish on his face. She looked over to her mother, but she kept her head down low, avoiding all eye contact.

Lily walked over to her mum and held her arms out for Ben, needing to feel his soft body in her arms. His arms wrapped round her neck as he sighed, 'Mama . . .'

Lily's mum finally looked up as her grandson spoke. She pulled herself up from the sofa and walked over to Zach, caressing his cheek gently.

'I don't care what the DNA results say. You are Robert and I—' But her mum's thought was interrupted by a loud rap on the front door, which echoed down the hallway into the kitchen.

'I'll go,' Michael said. 'Probably the postman.'

Lily heard the muffled sounds of a conversation at the front door, followed by footsteps.

Michael made a face at Lily when he returned, thumbing behind him as a woman followed him into the room.

Lily's mother gasped, and she held on to Zach's arm in support as she trembled beside him.

'Who is that?' her dad asked, moving closer to his ex-wife.

Zach shook his head in surprise. 'This is my mom, Sally.'

Lily couldn't believe her eyes as she stared at the woman that she'd been obsessing over for days now. Sally was dressed casually in loungewear and bright white trainers. Her blonde hair was tied back in a low ponytail. She looked as wholesome as apple pie.

Zach walked towards his mother, and they embraced. 'What on earth are you doing here?'

Lily heard her mother omit an anguished groan as she watched them hug each other, and Lily quickly rushed to her side, along with Michael, her dad and Gaga.

The Murphy family, united, ready to protect each other.

'I've been calling you, trying to tell you that I was on my way, but you haven't taken my calls,' Sally said. 'I came straight from the airport.'

'How did you get this address?' Lily asked, feeling vulnerable again. Michael placed a protective arm round her and took Ben into his arms.

'Zach's secretary gave it to me,' Sally replied, then she looked up to Zach. 'You had it in your online diary. Don't be cross with her; you know how persuasive I can be.'

'Why are you here?' Zach asked in a low voice.

'I was worried about you. When Jenny told me what you were going through here, on your own . . . I had to come over. I caught the overnight flight, and arrived this morning.' Her mouth turned down at the corners and it looked as if she might cry. 'I've been so worried, thinking about you dealing with this on your own. Have you been to the clinic yet?'

'Yes. I'm so sorry for making you worry so much, Mom . . .'

Sally's face blanched as she clasped her son's hand,

interrupting him. 'You have nothing to be sorry about. None of this is your fault.'

Before Zach could continue, Lily's mum called out, surprising them all, 'You need to leave, Sally. We don't want you here.'

Sally's only response was to raise an eyebrow in her direction.

'Mom, this is Kimberly and Jason Murphy. They are the couple whose child was abducted. I thought . . . I thought I was their son, Robert, and I'll never forgive myself for getting their hopes up. We've come back from the clinic. The DNA results were negative. I'm not Robert.'

Sally's face fell, and her eyes glistened, 'I'm sorry, Zach. You shouldn't have had to go through that without me.'

'You're not angry with me?' Zach asked.

'Of course not. You were searching for the truth. I understand that,' Sally replied.

'I think it's best you both left,' Gaga said, taking a step forward, leaning heavily on his walking cane. 'It's been a distressing day for my family. We need to get our heads around the results. In private.'

Sally looked over to the Murphy family again, but focused her eyes on Lily's mum. 'Not before I say hello to an old friend. How are you . . . what is it you call yourself now . . . *Kimberly*?'

NOW

August 2023

Kimberly

Phibsborough, Dublin

The air thickened with tension as Kimberly and Sally locked eyes with each other. Kimberly's mind raced as she tried to think of something . . . anything . . . to say to Sally, to get her to leave, without ruining everything.

Sally took several deep breaths, then turned to face Zach. 'I never wanted you to find out like this. I still can't believe you found your way to the Murphys. But you have, and it's clear that I have to tell you everything.' Sally paused, as the room held on to her every word. Kimberly's breath caught in her mouth and she felt her knees buckle. Jason caught her arm on one side, and Lily caught the other. 'You were right about all of this, Zach. You *are* Robert.' The room silenced again, in shock and confusion at Sally's words.

'I am Robert?' Zach asked softly, looking over to Lily in confusion.

'Yes. I'm so sorry you had to find out like this,' Sally replied, eyes glistening as she watched him.

Lily took a step forward, closer to Zach. 'Does that mean that the DNA test was wrong?' Her voice sounded unsure.

'It must have been faulty, Lily!' Zach said, his voice rising with excitement. 'I knew I was right,' he ended triumphantly. Then he paused, his face frozen in horror. 'But that means you . . . you took me! How could you do that to them, Mom?' He gestured behind him to the Murphy family, who huddled together in one group. His voice went up an octave and he screamed, 'How could you do that to *me?*'

'She wants locking up,' Kevin exploded, moving forward, waving his cane in the air.

His words ignited them all. Jason rushed forward too, his nostrils flaring as he spat out the words, 'You. Stole. Our. Son.'

Sally flinched, pain passing over her face, but then she looked over to Kimberly, and lifted her chin defiantly as she replied, 'No, Jason. I didn't steal your son.'

'Oh, for goodness' sake, you've contradicted yourself! You said Zach is Robert. So admit what you did to us. You stole my brother,' Lily cried out.

Lily reached back and put an arm round Kimberly's shoulder, who could only watch the drama unfold mutely. She contemplated leaving, running away from it all, but Kimberly had spent over forty years running from this moment. It was time to confront her past.

Sally looked around the room sadly, taking in each person, finally resting her eyes on Zach. 'I did not steal anyone!'

'You are not making any sense!' Zach cried back desperately.

Then in one damning sentence, Sally ended everything.

'I didn't steal you, Zach, because it's impossible to steal a child that is already yours!' Sally cried.

NOW

August 2023

Kimberly

Phibsborough, Dublin

And that's when the chaos truly began. Lily and Jason shouted at Sally to explain what she meant. Michael held Ben in his arms, but hovered by Lily's side, ready to protect her if she needed it. But it was Zach that Kimberly's gaze remained fixed on.

He looked stricken, his eyes flicking between Sally's and Kimberly's, back and forth, and her heart splintered into a thousand pieces again. Because she'd caused all this pain and she wasn't even sure how it had happened.

Tears began to fall, thick and fast like a river down Kimberly's cheeks. She'd never felt old before, but in this moment she was every part of her sixty-nine years.

'What does she mean, Mum?' Lily asked.

'I was trying to help – that's all,' Kimberly replied, her eyes downcast.

Jason slumped on to a chair, and he too looked as tired as Kimberly felt. Lily sat down beside him, and they held hands. She had always been a daddy's girl – thank goodness for that – because once Kimberly shared her story they would need each other.

Sally walked towards Kimberly. 'It's time to tell your family the truth. Who you are. You can't keep this hidden any longer, *Elsie*.'

Kimberly had heard people report about their lives flashing before their eyes, in a near-death experience, but it wasn't death that her moment of reckoning came – it was now.

Safe and loved with her family, before her world ended and turned dark at only six years old. Light returning when little Sally arrived at the orphanage, only to extinguish again when Elsie's tentative steps as an adult left her broken and alone. But, miraculously, she and Sally found each other again, and her friend shone a bright light over both of them.

Until Elsie sent them both into the darkness, once and for all.

Kimberly felt Jason's hands on her shoulders, shaking her as he demanded, 'Who is Elsie?'

'I'm sorry,' Kimberly whispered, her heart racing, because she knew that, after all this time, she had no choice but to tell her family the truth. And she knew what that would cost her.

'My real name is Elsie Evans. I became Kimberly Blair in 1981.'

'I don't understand.' Jason's voice was filled with disbelief.

'Me either, Dad,' Lily replied tremulously.

Kimberly felt her gut twist again, and acid burned its way to her mouth, knowing that she was about to break both their hearts.

'I've known your mother for sixty years. We met in the Sunshine House Orphanage in London,' Sally said.

'But Mum had a family. In Glasgow. I don't understand,' Lily said, her voice uncertain. 'Are you sure you mean my mum?'

Sally nodded and replied in a trembling voice, 'I'm sure. Best friends forever we always said.'

'I still have the card. And the mood ring,' Kimberly whispered.

Sally scoffed, then continued, 'I would have done anything for you, Elsie.'

'And I for you, Sally. What I did, I did for *you*!' Kimberly's voice cracked with emotion as she cried out, her words a desperate plea.

'Don't you dare pretend this was for anyone but you!' Sally responded, two dots of pink appearing on her cheeks.

'Oh, Mom,' Zach said, his voice filled with anguish.

Kimberly turned to him.

But it wasn't Kimberly that Zach was calling out to.

It was Sally.

How had Kimberly got so much wrong? She'd been hiding from the truth for so long, but deep down she always knew that one day it would catch up with her. And the only way to make Zach and her family understand what had happened on the *Carousel* was to go back to the summer of 1981, in London.

BEFORE

July 1981

Sally

Elite, Wandsworth, London

'Why you must insist on coming all the way over here when there are perfectly good hairdressing salons in Harrow, I'll never understand,' Ian grumbled as he parked in a spot a few feet from Nicola's.

'I know how important these work dinners are for you. As a detective sergeant, you have a standing. I want my hair to be just right. And Nicola knows how you like it, Ian,' Sally replied meekly.

Like a proud peacock, he puffed his chest at Sally's words.

'You never let me down.' He leaned over and kissed her cheek. 'I am fond of Nicola, and I suppose it's the decent thing to do. Support her little business.'

'She's ever so grateful,' Sally said, smiling sweetly. She thanked the stars that Nicola had never rubbed Ian up the wrong way – not like Elsie, who had never hidden her disdain for him. Sally reached back to touch her son's cheek. 'He looks so handsome in green, doesn't he?' she said.

'Like his daddy,' Ian said with a wink.

Sally wished with all her heart that her sweet baby boy would never grow up to be anything like his father. As Ian looked back

301

tenderly to their sleeping boy, she could see the man she fell in love with. A man who she admired and respected, who made her feel safe. He'd hidden his cruel nature from her, but now that it was out there was no escaping it.

Yet her fears for herself were nothing compared to those she felt for her child.

'Off you go and pamper yourself. How long do you need? An hour?' Ian asked, interrupting her thought.

'Two hours I would think, Ian.' Sally held her breath, hoping Ian would not question that.

His eyes narrowed. 'For one hair style. I hope you're not planning on running away on me.'

'Of course not. Where would I go?' Sally replied, desperately trying to keep her voice even and her face passive, because the truth was that *all* Sally thought about these days was how to escape the brute she'd married.

'Okay. Look, I tell you what, I'll go visit Dan. I'll take Zach with me.'

Sally's stomach clenched at the thought. How could she protect Zach from his father if she wasn't there too? She would have to feign a headache and tell him to bring them both home, forget about her hair appointment. No matter how desperate she was to see Elsie and Nicola.

But then a sour stench filled the car as Zach dirtied his nappy. His timing had never been more perfect because Ian didn't change nappies or feed bottles. That was women's work, he always maintained. She watched Ian pull a face as he wrinkled his nose.

'You know what? It's best you take Zach with you. He'll only fret and it's not fair to inflict that racket on Dan.' He reached into his pocket and pulled out a five-pound note from his wallet. 'Get a taxi back home. I'll see you there this afternoon.'

'Whatever you want,' Sally said, then kissed her husband on his cheek. She got out and took Zach and his changing bag from the back seat.

'See you in a couple of hours.'

Sally stood on the path and waved her husband off, all the while thinking to herself what a fraud she was – playing the dutiful and happy wife when the truth was so much darker. She walked into Elite, where Nicola and Elsie were waiting for her.

'I thought he'd never go,' Elsie grumbled, and then her face broke into a warm smile as she took Zach into her arms. 'Oh, he's ripe! Give me that bag, and I'll change him for you.'

'I've tea made,' Nicola said. 'I've sent Andrea on her lunch break, and we've nobody booked in for an hour, so we've got the place to ourselves.'

Sally's shoulders dropped in relief as she sank into one of the salon seats. She watched her two friends fuss over Zach as they changed his nappy. But her mind was on the previous evening.

'How's everything at home?' Nicola asked, handing Sally a mug. 'You've got dark circles under your eyes. Is Zach keeping you up at night?'

'No. He's a good boy. Sleeps right through now.'

That was a lie.

'How's his lordship?' Elsie asked as she rocked Zach in her arms.

'Fine,' Sally said.

A second blatant lie. She was getting good at them.

Nicola stood up and put the CLOSED sign on the salon's front door, then turned the key in the lock.

'Nobody is going to bother us here. Think of the salon as a confessional. Come on, love, get it off your chest. Whatever it is, it's weighing you down.'

Sally looked at the two women, whose faces were drawn tight with worry. She wished she could find the words to reassure them that they need not fret, but she'd gone beyond that.

'I thought I could handle him. Handle his moods,' Sally said quietly. Her eyes moved to Zach, who was playing with one of Elsie's long curls. 'But I'm scared for Zach.'

A sharp breath from Elsie made Zach start. She leaned down

and kissed his soft downy head, murmuring soothing endearments.

'I think he's jealous of him,' Sally admitted. 'Ian doesn't like me holding Zach when he's home. He gets irritated if Zach cries, and I want to pick him up. At first, it was sighing and muttering under his breath about me spoiling Zach. But last night . . .' She paused, unsure if she could say the words out loud.

'What did he do?' Elsie asked, her tone venomous.

'Zach wouldn't settle. And Ian wanted . . . he wanted me in bed with him.' Sally blushed, unsure how to finish that statement.

'Oh my days.' Nicola said, understanding Sally's embarrassment.

'I could hear Zach's cries getting louder, and his breathing sounded ragged like he couldn't catch his breath between the sobs. I pushed Ian off me and ran to him, afraid that he was choking.' Her eyes filled with tears, and she began to shake. 'He wrenched Zach from my arms. Too hard. Too damn hard . . .' Sally went on. 'He threw Zach back into his crib. And he landed with such a thud. I thought . . . I thought . . .' Sally couldn't continue, the horror of the night before too much to articulate out loud.

Nicola pulled Sally into her arms as Elsie declared that she would kill Ian.

'That's not going to solve anything,' Nicola said, glancing at Elsie, irritated. 'What happened next?'

'I screamed at Ian to get out, and I frantically checked Zach. He hadn't a mark on him. I've looked dozens of times. I didn't sleep for one second last night. I brought him down to the sitting room, and he slept in my arms on the couch. My eyes never left his, not for one second,' Sally said, her eyes searching Nicola's for absolution.

'You did the right thing,' Nicola said.

'This cannot continue,' Elsie said firmly. 'He'll not stop till he kills you. Or the baby. I told you, there's a cruelty in that man.'

Sally took a breath, steadying herself. 'I know. I thought about this all night, as I watched Zach. Ian will never leave, so that means that we'll have to. I need to work out where and when.'

'I've given notice on my flat. I'm supposed to leave in two weeks for Spain,' Elsie said, frowning.

'You can come to me,' Nicola said. 'I know the flat is small, but we'll make it work. You and the little 'un can have my bedroom, and I'll sleep on the couch. Until you get sorted.'

'Thank you,' Sally said, her lip trembling. 'I hoped you might offer. I'll go home and pack while Ian is at Dan's, then I'll tell him when he gets home that it's over. I'll get a taxi back here this evening.'

Elsie butted in. 'Don't wait to tell him it's over. Pack up and come here straight away. Don't give him a chance to try to worm his way out of this.'

Sally thought about this for a moment, but in the end decided against it. 'There's nothing he can say that will make me stay, but if I don't tell him I'm going he'll only come here to look for me.' Sally stood up, pushing her shoulders back resolutely. 'I've got to face him. Make sure he understands that we are over.'

BEFORE

July 1981

Sally

Hereford Gardens, Harrow, London

Two large suitcases and Zach's pram and crib sat by the front door. Sally had booked a taxi, and it was due in thirty minutes shortly after Ian was due home.

Every noise outside made her jump, the sounds amplified, along with Sally's nerves. Zach slept silently on the couch beside her, propped up by several cushions. Finally, she heard the roar of the car pull into their driveway, then the bang of a door and the turn of the key.

'What the . . .' Ian called out as he entered the hall and spotted the luggage.

Sally stood up, clenching her fists tightly by her side until her nails pierced the soft round of her palm. Her husband appeared at the door of the sitting room, his face masked and unreadable.

'Going somewhere?' he asked, almost pleasantly.

'Yes,' Sally replied in a voice stronger than she felt. 'I'm leaving you, Ian.'

She lifted her chin and forced herself to look him square in his eyes. Sally would not cower, not today.

He nodded his head as he mulled over these words, then once again, in that agreeable tone, replied, 'Okay.'

Sally's knees almost buckled. She'd not expected him to capitulate so quickly. 'I'm going to Nicola's and will stay there until I find somewhere more suitable.'

'Fine,' Ian said, then he walked over to the couch and picked up Zach, holding the baby close to his chest. 'But he stays.'

Sally's eyes widened, and she felt a trickle of sweat move down the small part of her back. 'No, Ian. Zach comes with me. You said yourself earlier that a baby needs his mother.'

Ian tenderly kissed his son's head as he replied, 'A decent mother, yes. But not the daughter of a prostitute.' He tutted several times, all the while smiling at Sally.

'Give me, Zach,' Sally said, moving closer to her son. 'If you think I'd ever leave him in your care. You could have killed him last night . . .'

Ian sat down, still cradling Zach, and then the smile disappeared. 'It was a shocking night. When I found you shaking our baby so cruelly, throwing him forcibly into his crib, I was horrified. So much so, that I confided in my colleague today. And Dan was so shocked he insisted I call my solicitor. Which I did. She, like me, is worried about Zach's safety.'

Sally was speechless, and fresh terror began to surge through her. 'You can't . . . you . . . you . . . you can't do this.'

'Oh, I can, and I will. You leave today, but you will never see your son again. I will get full custody. I have the weight of the law behind me. And what do you have? Let's see. Your mother was a prostitute, your father is unknown – let's face it: he could be anyone – you were brought up in an orphanage, where you befriended known criminals.'

'You won't get away with this,' Sally spluttered. 'It's *you* who is the criminal.' She took a deep breath then threw her own grenade. 'I know you're on the take.'

Ian smiled coldly again. 'So Elsie did tell you that. I wondered if she had. Lies of course.' Then he winked. 'Oh, and I will get away with this. I have already. And you know it. So, unless you want to walk away from your son, I suggest you unpack those cases, then pretty yourself up and be ready for our dinner dance. I expect a happy wife on my arm, so no tears or tantrums.'

Sally felt rage rise, and she stepped closer to Ian. 'If you think I'm going to go anywhere with you and pretend we're a happy couple, then you have another thing coming.'

Ian's smile dropped. 'That's your problem right there. You can't pretend. I've seen how you look at me. I knew it was only a matter of time before you tried to run, so I've always been two steps ahead of you. Never underestimate me, Sally. That will be at your peril, I promise you.'

The doorbell rang, shrill, cutting the air between them.

Ian raised an eyebrow. 'Expecting someone?'

Sally looked out of the front window and saw a black cab parked behind Ian's car. Her mind raced as she tried to work out what to do.

Wrestle her baby from Ian's arms? No, that might hurt Zach. Ask the taxi driver to help her. But to what end? Ian had blackened her name. He was ready for her.

Ian walked to the front door, still holding Zach, then opened it with a big smile, saying to the driver, 'Hello, mate. I'll let the missus know you're here.' He turned to Sally. 'Darling, it's for you.'

Sally walked to her husband's side, pulled a one-pound note from her jeans pocket, and handed it to the driver. 'I'm sorry to have bothered you, but I don't need a taxi after all,' she said.

'That's a good girl,' Ian said smugly when she closed the front door.

'I need to call Nicola,' Sally said.

'Don't worry about that. I'll take care of it,' Ian said, finally handing Zach over to Sally.

Then he opened the small black address and phone book on the hall table, looking for Nicola's number. He dialled the salon. Nicola answered within two rings as if she had been waiting by the phone for it to call.

'Hello, Nicola, it's Ian here. Sally won't be joining you. We had a silly row, but it's all okay again now. And she feels embarrassed to have worried you.' Silence as Nicola responded. 'No. She can't talk right now. She's with the baby.' Silence again. 'I'll let her know. Goodbye.'

He hung up and then reached over to gently cup Sally's chin in a way that used to make her shiver with pleasure, but now filled her with dread. 'Let that be the end of that nonsense.'

As he walked away, whistling like he had no care in the world, Sally felt anger replace her fear. Ian might have won this battle, but he wouldn't win the war.

Sally leaned in close and whispered into Zach's ear, 'Don't worry, baby boy. I'll find a way to get us out of here. I promise.'

BEFORE

July 1981

Elsie

Elite, Wandsworth, London

Nicola and Elsie had spent hours preparing the flat above the salon for Sally and Zach's arrival. While Nicola had prepared a supper for them, Elsie ran to the supermarket to buy baby essentials, because she wasn't sure if Sally would have the time to bring formula and nappies. It had felt good doing something at last other than being silent witnesses to a situation, that became increasingly dangerous daily.

But Sally did not arrive as planned.

As the minutes ticked on, Elsie knew something had gone drastically wrong. As Nicola and she decided to call a taxi and go to Hereford Gardens themselves to collect Sally, the phone rang.

Baldwin.

He relayed a cock-and-bull story about a silly row being resolved. As Elsie's temper flared, and she tried to grab the phone from Nicola to scream at him, Nicola had proved herself to be quick-witted and strong, holding Elsie at arm's length.

'I'm so pleased to hear that. As I always say to Sally, she is so lucky to have you, Ian. You are such a good and decent man. I knew it would blow over. Give Sally my love and tell her that I'll see her next week.'

When she placed the phone's receiver down, she turned to Elsie to explain. 'I had to pretend I'm on his side, so he doesn't stop Sally from coming here. Our only chance to help her is if we make sure she's not further isolated from us.'

'Clever,' Elsie said, understanding immediately. 'I should have gone with her. I knew that bastard would find a way to keep Sally at home. What has he said to her?'

'Who knows?' Nicola replied, her brow furrowed. 'I just hope he hasn't hit her again.'

'Or charmed her into forgiving him,' Elsie muttered bitterly. She felt irritation grow at that thought. 'If she's stupid enough to believe his bull—'

'Eh! Settle down,' Nicola replied. 'You will never understand what Sally is going through. Not unless you've walked in her shoes.'

Elsie sighed. She may not have walked in Sally's shoes, but she sure as hell had walked in the shoes of a child at risk. And there was no way she was going to let anything happen to Zach.

On Saturday afternoon, Elsie asked Reggie to drive her to Hereford Gardens. And, despite the fact that they were no longer dating, he dropped everything to help. They parked a few doors up from Sally's house, and watched, hoping that Ian might leave, giving Elsie a chance to check in on Sally. But the front door remained firmly shut.

Reggie grew angrier by the minute as Elsie told him what Ian had done to Sally and Zach.

'Someone needs to teach Baldwin a lesson,' Reggie growled.

But Elsie remembered Nicola's words and knew that, for now, she had to wait and bide her time. They finally drove away, worried that if they knocked on the front door, they'd make things worse.

The rest of the weekend passed without contact from Sally. Watching the second hand on the clock, tick and tock, at an excruciatingly slow speed, almost drove Elsie to distraction. She was sleep-deprived and anxious, but she couldn't rest until she knew Sally and Zach were safe. Her mind raced with all the possibilities of what Baldwin might have done to them or what he might plan to do yet.

After a restless night, Elsie awoke on Monday morning with fresh resolve. She would go to the park near Sally's house, at midday, in the hope that Sally had kept her daily routine. If Sally wasn't at the park, then Elsie would call at the house and demand to see her. And, if Ian refused, then Elsie would call the police. Or let Reggie and his friends sort Ian out.

At a quarter to twelve, Elsie sat at the same bench where she had met Sally only a few days earlier. She couldn't relax and felt uneasy, constantly scanning her surroundings, searching for her friend. She felt too exposed, sitting out in the open, and her instincts urged her to move. So she concealed herself behind a large, leafy oak tree a few feet from the bench. Her heart jumped with relief when she saw the familiar sight of Sally pushing Zach's pram. Only to fall when she noticed a tall, stocky figure walking beside her. *Baldwin.* Elsie watched them take a seat on the bench, and her skin crawled when she saw Baldwin's hand move up and hold on to Sally's neck in a vicelike grip. It took all Elsie's power not to lunge at him, claw his face, eyes and skin.

Sally looked around her, and her eyes rested on the oak tree. Ensuring Baldwin's head was facing forward, Elsie stepped out from behind her shadowy hiding spot. Sally nodded once, and Elsie scanned her face, thanking the heavens that there was no outward sign of injury. Then Sally turned back towards her husband. Elsie quickly hid again and waited anxiously, her mind whirling with possible scenarios of what she should do next.

Her instinct was to confront Ian, but Elsie thought of Nicola's wise counsel on Saturday. And knew that she should remain hidden. Her heart pumped so hard that she felt it thudding against her chest. Sally rocked the pram. Baldwin stood up and put his arms on his hips as he looked around. Then Sally stood up to join him.

But, as they walked away, Elsie noticed Sally drop something onto the bench. That was deliberate, Elsie thought, praying that the wind would not whip up whatever it was. Once they'd disappeared from view, Elsie raced over and retrieved an envelope with her name scribbled on it.

Elsie,

I have no idea if you'll come to the park or if I'll even get a chance to get this to you, but I have to try.

I'm trapped.

Ian was two steps ahead of me. He's been to a solicitor and reported me for abusing Zach. He will get full custody of Zach if I leave. As he said, it's his word, as a police officer, or mine, someone who was brought up in care, the daughter of a prostitute.

He swears I'll never see Zach again. And I believe him. So I can't go. Yet.

I need your help, Elsie.

I have to run, as far away as I can from Ian. Because when we go we have to disappear forever.

Please help us,

Sally x

BEFORE

July 1981

Elsie

Elite, Wandsworth, London

Elsie went back to the park every day that week, but when Sally did turn up, Ian was with her. It was clear that Ian did not trust Sally, and was watching her closely. He called Nicola to cancel her Saturday hair appointment, claiming Sally had a tummy bug.

But Elsie kept her faith, because she knew that Ian would eventually turn his eyes away from his wife and son. In the meantime, she had work to do, preparing for their escape.

Elsie turned to Reggie again, who was more than happy to come through for them. He quietly took over and devised a plan for Sally and Zach. And, as Elsie had already decided to move on from London, it made sense that she would disappear with them both.

It would be a fresh start for them all that Elsie couldn't wait to begin.

Reggie asked for photographs of Sally and Zach, which Nicola was able to provide. He used his contacts to create two new identities for them.

They would leave on Wednesday.

Reggie would take them to Liverpool port on Wednesday morning, where they would travel onwards to Dublin, hidden in the back of a lorry. Reggie had found a flat for them and paid the rent for a month, so that they could lie low there. Then he would be in touch again, with details of how they would move onwards to Spain, using his network of contacts again.

'Maybe we should go to a small village somewhere in Ireland rather than Dublin?' Elsie asked, surprised by the arrangements.

'Trust me, getting lost in a busy city is easier than standing out like a sore thumb in a rural location. I know what I'm doing.'

Over the years, Reggie had disappeared on several occasions to lie low following some misdemeanour, so she trusted his judgement.

Now, they had to get Sally and Zach away from Ian.

Elsie had shared the bare minimum about the plans with Nicola, as Reggie had been adamant that nobody should know the details.

'What Nicola doesn't know, she can't tell,' he'd declared.

Nicola accepted this with her usual grace. 'I'll miss you all. When you are settled and safe, you get in touch. But let me see if I can get Sally and Zach here on Wednesday.' She picked up the phone and dialled Sally's number.

'He won't let you talk to her,' Elsie said.

'It's Ian I want to talk to,' Nicola said.

The two women leaned in to listen, as Ian answered the phone.

'Hello, Ian love, it's Nicola here. How's Sally? Is that tummy bug better?'

'She's good as gold again, Nicola. Thank you for checking in,' Ian said.

'Can I have a word?'

'She's upstairs with Zach, giving him a bath,' Ian replied without missing a beat.

'That little fella is lucky to have you both. Best parents a child could wish for. Can you remind Sally that she's got an appointment here on Wednesday?'

'Oh, I didn't know that. She never mentioned it,' Ian replied.

'That wife of yours would forget her head if it weren't stitched on,' Nicola joked, and Ian laughed in response. Then her voice became serious and she said, 'If Sally doesn't turn up on Wednesday, I'll think there's something up with her. That you're hiding her from me, Ian.'

Ian whistled softly, then responded, 'Nobody is hiding anyone. Sally will be there. What time?'

Elsie whispered, 'Eleven o'clock,' and Nicola repeated that to Ian. 'Ta-ra, love,' she said, then hung up.

Since then, Elsie had kept herself busy, packing up her things from the flat. Most of her belongings went to a charity shop, where she'd bought them in the first place. Then she gave two suitcases to Reggie, who assured her they would be in the car waiting for them on Wednesday.

'I've cancelled all my appointments. Given Andrea the day off,' Nicola said when Elsie arrived on Wednesday morning, a little before eleven. 'Oh my days, I'll be in an early grave with all this worry. I hope you know what you're doing, Elsie.'

'I trust Reggie. He'll be here at quarter past. I'm going to wait in the storeroom, in case Baldwin walks in with Sally.'

'What do we do then?' Nicola asked, biting her lip.

'I've no idea,' Elsie said.

A few moments later, the door opened. Despite it being the summer, the heavens had opened up with a heavy downpour of rain. Sally pushed the pram into the salon, and Elsie could have whooped with relief when she saw that she was alone. Until she took in her friend's complexion. Sally was pale, had dark circles under her eyes and looked as if she had aged over the previous couple of weeks.

Nicola took the pram from Sally, wheeling it beside the front reception. Then she locked the door to the salon. Elsie ran over to the pram and pulled back the blanket to double-check that Zach was okay. He smiled up at her, a big goofy grin, and his blue eyes sparkled with mischief. It still caught her off guard how alike he was to her little Bertie. She cursed herself for allowing him to jump into her mind, and pushed his face away from her again.

Elsie touched Zach's cheek gently, amazed at her love for this little boy. She turned to Sally and said, 'It's going to be okay. I've got a plan. We're going to run today, in a few minutes.'

Sally's eyes filled with tears, and she shook her head. 'We can't go today. I told you, he's always one step ahead of me.'

'What do you mean? What's happened now?' Elsie asked.

'This morning, before he left for work, Ian told me that he has eyes all over the city. He said that if I was ever stupid enough to try and escape, he'd find me. Then, when he did, he'd have me arrested for abduction.'

'The bastard,' Nicola said. 'He can't get away with this. We need to call the Old Bill. Report him.'

Elsie looked at Nicola with disdain. 'Oh, for God's sake, Baldwin *is* the Old Bill. We can't call them. They all look after each other. Did he drive you here?' Elsie's eyes darted to the window of the salon.

'No, I got a taxi.' Sally ran a hand through her blonde hair, and the sleeve of her blouse fell down, revealing a purple bruise on her forearm.

Elsie caught Nicola's eye. She'd seen the bruise too.

'That's a new one,' Elsie said.

'Ian didn't like my tone when I asked him to increase my housekeeping. I thought if I could get extra cash, it would help when I run.'

'Don't worry about money; I've got that sorted. Everything is in place. I told you, we have to leave. Today,' Elsie said firmly.

Sally's face turned ashen. Her voice trembled as she said, 'Not today, Elsie. I told you that Ian is watching me. He suspects I might try something while I'm here, so he has a squad car parked down the road. I clocked it when I got out of the taxi.'

'Reggie will be able to lose the Old Bill. Won't be the first time he's had to shake them off,' Elsie said, unwilling to admit defeat. She'd put too much into this to let it go without a fight.

'We wouldn't get further than the end of Battersea Park Road.'

'Let me see if the car is still there,' Elsie said. She pulled a poncho-style rain mac from a peg behind the desk and put it on. Her face disappeared into the voluminous hood when she pulled it over her head. She picked up Nicola's cigarettes, lit one, walked to the salon door, unlocked it, and walked outside. She stood for a moment, puffing her cigarette, then stubbed it out on the path, returning inside, shaking the wet mac off, and placing it back on the peg.

'It's still there. Parked outside the corner shop,' Elsie said.

'I told you. He'll never let me get away, will he?' Sally said, her hands trembling as she wiped tears from her face.

'He can't watch you twenty-four seven,' Nicola replied. 'You'll find a way.'

Zach whimpered in his pram. Elsie walked over and rocked him until he settled.

'Sally, listen to me. I can feel it here –' Elsie thumped her chest – 'if you don't leave today, he's gonna kill you both. That man ain't right. There's a violence in him that scares me.'

'You think I don't know that? I want to leave, but I have to know that it's safe to do so. That there's no chance it will fail. Because, if it does, I'll lose Zach.'

'We can disappear before Baldwin even knows we're gone. I know we can,' Elsie insisted.

Nicola looked outside the window again, frowning. 'I don't know, Elsie. That squad car is only a few feet from here. I think let the dust settle for a few weeks, then when Ian's guard is down, Sally and Zach can get away safely. I'm sure Reggie can rearrange things.'

Elsie sucked in her breath as anger sparked inside her. Nicola and Sally didn't get it.

Waiting got you killed.

She knew that better than anyone else.

'I'm supposed to leave for Spain today. I've given up my flat,' Elsie said.

'That's the answer. You go to Spain, find a place over there for you all, then Sally and Zach can follow in a few weeks,' Nicola said. She led Sally to the sink. 'Come on, love, let's get your hair sorted. You can't go home without a blow-dry and set, or he'll be suspicious.'

Elsie was stunned as Nicola ran the water over Sally's hair. Was Sally stupid? Or too scared to do the right thing? Did it matter which? She didn't suppose it did.

Sally began to cry as Nicola wrapped her hair in a towel once she'd finished washing it. Her body rocked and reeled as she sobbed in Nicola's arms. It was as if, once she'd started, she couldn't stop.

'Let's go upstairs to the flat for a cuppa. Tea always makes things a little easier to bear, doesn't it? And maybe a sandwich. You're skin and bones. I bet you've not eaten a bite with the worry.'

Sally nodded, then made her way to the pram to get Zach.

Nicola steered her towards the stairs. 'Elsie can get Zach. You concentrate on yourself for a few minutes.'

Elsie smiled reassuringly at Sally, as she picked up the infant. 'We'll follow you up.'

Zach looked up at Elsie, his blue eyes wide in question.

'What's wrong, little man?' Elsie asked, cradling him close to her. 'What horrors have you already been witness to?'

She felt tears sting her own eyes as a memory pierced her.

The silence, deafening, slicing cruelly through the air. The smell, like rotten eggs, making her nose wrinkle. She gagged, as her eyes moved around the room. Brown hair, fanned across the white tiled floor. Still, so still.

'I won't let anything happen to you, Zach. I won't,' Elsie promised.

Her body trembled as her mind rallied with what to do next. And then she heard a car pull up in front of the salon.

It was Reggie. He wound down his window and peered out, beckoning to her to join him.

As if moving in a trance, Elsie picked up Zach's changing bag, slinging it over one shoulder. A sheen of sweat lined her face as she looked out of the salon window, up and down the street, checking for any sign of Baldwin, or his cronies.

The squad car was still there.

Elsie walked behind the reception desk and grabbed Nicola's rain mac again, pulling it over herself and Zach, the hood covering her face. Her legs felt leaden as she went to the salon door, but they still moved, one foot at a time. She slid the lock across, unlocking it in one fluid movement, and for a moment Elsie waited for a voice to call out to stop her.

Sally or Nicola would come down, looking for Zach. She'd turn back, and that would be that.

But no voice came.

Zach's little hand reached up and touched Elsie's face. Those eyes looked at her again, pleading with her to help him. As another little boy's had done, a long time ago.

She had to do this. She had to save *him*.

She leaned in and whispered into his soft, downy hair, 'If I take you now, then your mummy will have no choice but to follow us. She'll leave your bad daddy behind her. Reggie will tell her where to find us. I couldn't keep Bertie safe, but if I take you with me now I can make sure that nothing bad ever happens to you.'

And then, in a move that would change everyone's lives forever, Elsie slipped out of the salon and got into the back of the car.

BEFORE

July 1981

Elsie

Gardiner Street Apartments, Dublin

One week had passed since Elsie had left London.

Reggie had driven her to Liverpool. It took a little bit of time to make him understand why she'd taken Zach on her own. He was angry, and this made Elsie doubt herself. She told Reggie to turn round and bring them home. But he refused, saying they'd both be locked up for abduction. They had no choice but to go on.

They met the forty-foot lorry driver a mile from the port. His name was Lloyd, and he wasn't chatty, barely giving her or Zach a quick glance. A duvet, water and snacks had been placed in the back of the lorry. Elsie suspected she wasn't the first fugitive Lloyd had secreted away across the Irish Sea. She made Reggie promise again that he'd get in touch with Sally, and help her follow on too.

There wasn't a moment that Elsie didn't fret about Sally and what she might be dealing with. She imagined Sally's shock when she discovered Elsie and Zach had disappeared. Nicola was clever, though, and would understand the bigger picture. She'd make sure Sally saw why Elsie had no choice but to take Zach. Because Elsie knew better than anyone else what happens when action is not taken.

This way, Sally's hand would be forced. And Elsie pushed

down any guilt she felt. She was doing this out of her great love for Sally and Zach.

Zach had been a dream on the journey. Easy to comfort when he cried, with either a cuddle or a bottle. They'd both fallen asleep at some point in the night, waking in the early morning hours, not long before arriving at Dublin port. Lloyd warned her that they couldn't make a sound as they departed the ship and passed through customs. While Zach sucked on a bottle, she rocked him gently in her arms.

Luck was on their side when they docked. They passed through customs without issue, and twenty minutes later, the truck came to a shuddering halt. Lloyd carried her suitcases, and brought her to the block of flats that would be their home for the foreseeable. A key had been left under a stone and, once Lloyd opened the front door, and left her cases in the hallway, he left with a gruff, 'Good luck.'

The flat had two bedrooms – a double and a box room. It was fully furnished, and a crib was already set up in the corner of the living room. The cupboards and fridge were all fully stocked. Reggie had thought of everything.

He'd also insisted that she could not call anyone in London, including him, but that he'd be in touch when it was safe to do so about moving them on to Spain. So she spent the days playing with Zach, caring for his every need. She sang to him the same song she'd sung to his mummy, when Sally had arrived at the orphanage all those years ago. And her heart weighed heavy as she promised him that his mummy would be with them both soon.

There was a TV in the sitting room, but it only had two Irish channels, RTE One and RTE Two. Elsie watched the news every day, terrified that she'd see her face on the screen. But there was no mention of her or a missing baby over here in Ireland.

It was a strange feeling for Elsie, having so much time on her hands. Her long hours of charring, coupled with the Avon business, meant that she rarely had time to think.

Now, all she did was think.

Elsie knew that when Sally arrived she would need a back-story to go with her new identity. So Elsie rehearsed one for her, ready for Sally when she came. She tweaked and turned it many times until Elsie believed it to be airtight.

Sally's new name was to be Kimberly Blair, a single mother. Elsie thought it sounded glamorous, and she was sure Sally would like it too. She had wanted Zach to keep his name, but Reggie felt it was best that he also had a new identity. So Zach was now Robert Blair. And Elsie couldn't help think that this name suited him so much better. She had already stopped calling him Zach. Because the sooner the little boy got used to his new name, the better.

The rumble of a truck outside the flat made Elsie run to the window. *Please let it be Lloyd back with Sally this time.* But it was another false alarm. Elsie returned to the kitchenette and prepared a bottle for Robert, sighing as the scoop scraped the bottom of the can. She was running low on formula, and she needed fresh bread and milk for herself too, but Elsie was afraid to leave the flat. The news on RTE might not have covered the story, but what about the newspapers? For all she knew, their faces could be plastered all over the tabloids, and they'd be instantly recognised if she walked into a shop with Zach.

She shook her head in annoyance at herself.

Elsie walked over to Robert and scooped him up into her arms from his crib, giving him his bottle. He was a good boy, so easy to love. And Elsie's heart had grown in ways she didn't think were possible, every moment in his company. Her waking moments were in service to this little boy, who was now in her care.

'Do you know Robert is a special name?' she whispered to him. 'You are named after a special boy that I loved dearly. As much as I love you now. Would you like to hear a story? Yes, I knew you would. Well, let's start by telling you all about your mother – a woman called Kimberly, who is from Glasgow.'

Elsie chuckled, knowing Sally would appreciate this humorous touch, making Kimberly Scottish – like her beloved Sister Jones.

Sally would have to practise her accent when she got here. Elsie could teach her that. Grinning to herself, she continued her make-believe story about Robert's new family history in a lilting imitation of Sister Jones. She was happy with the story she created, believing it to be rock solid, and it would work for any nosy parkers who asked difficult questions.

Elsie heard movement along the corridor outside the flat. Even though she knew it was likely to be her neighbours, coming and going, her heart began to accelerate. And then she heard a rap on the front door.

Sally!

Or the police!

Elsie held her breath and tried to work out what she should do: ignore it, open it, ignore it, open it. A second rap and Robert cried out in response to the sound, which meant she could no longer pretend she wasn't here.

Elsie prayed to a God she wasn't sure she believed in that it would be Sally standing outside the flat. That she had found the strength to escape Ian, and that she was ready to join them in a new life.

Opening the door, with Robert in her arms, she came face to face with a tall, dark man. He had wavy brown hair, dark eyes and a lean physique that his tight jeans and blue denim shirt showed off. Elsie felt a shift inside her as she took him in. A reaction to him that she'd never felt with another man before.

'Hello. You must be Kimberly. And you, young sir, must be Robert,' the man said, his face breaking out into a smile. He held several plastic bags in each hand. 'I'm Jason. And I'm your landlord.'

Elsie frowned. What did he want? Money?

Jason grinned reassuringly. 'When your friend booked this flat for you last week, he also arranged for me to deliver another load of groceries for you today. I've more bags in the car. I'll run down and get them if I can drop these in first.'

Elsie offered a silent thank-you to Reggie, who'd once again proved that he thought of everything. She moved aside to let Jason enter. He placed the bags on the small round dining-room table. Then he ran out, returning a few moments later with more packed bags.

'If anything is missing, let me know. I'm back and forth to the flats most days, so I'm happy to grab things for you if you need them.' He cocked his head to one side, looking at her quizzically. 'You don't say much, do you, Kimberly? I won't bite, promise.'

Elsie laughed briefly in response. She was afraid to speak. Would her cockney accent give her away? What if the newspapers had said a Londoner had taken Zach?

Elsie watched Jason unload the groceries onto the kitchen counter. His movements were lithe, and his energy seemed to exude goodness.

'You said you own the flats?' Elsie asked, and to her surprise Sister Jones's lilt came out. It must have been because she'd been mimicking it whilst practising Kimberly's story for Robert. She waited for Jason to laugh at her put-on accent, but he didn't bat an eyelid.

'Yeah, I was lucky. This was my grandparents' house, and they left it to me after they died. It's three stories, so I decided to convert it into flats and try my hand at being a landlord. It turns out I'm good at it. I've gone on and bought a few more properties since then too.'

'You're young to be an entrepreneur,' Elsie said, impressed by him.

He shrugged. 'Maybe. As I said, I got a lucky start. What brings you to Dublin, Kimberly?'

Elsie paled. She'd not paid much attention when he'd called her Kimberly earlier. Her mind raced as she tried to work out how to respond. Should she say she was Elsie and that Kimberly wasn't here yet? Or would that raise an alarm bell? Why would she have Robert? It could be best to pretend she *was* Kimberly, and when Sally got here she could take over the name. They'd be moving on to Spain soon enough anyhow.

'My parents were Irish. I wanted to show Robert his roots.'

'That's nice,' Jason said. 'Well, welcome home, so.' He eyed the kettle and asked, with a twinkle in his eye, 'Don't suppose a cuppa's on the cards? My throat feels like it's been cut.'

Elsie laughed, delighted that Jason had suggested prolonging his visit. She had been starved of company and realised that she didn't want him to go. She picked up a packet of fig rolls and waved them in his direction. 'I think, as you have saved the day by delivering my groceries, I can manage tea and biscuits.'

'Thanks, Kimberly,' Jason said, taking a seat at the kitchen table. 'If this isn't too cheeky, is there a Mr Blair?'

Elsie felt a flush rise into her cheeks, and butterflies danced in her tummy. Was Jason flirting with her? She thought that maybe he was.

'No, there's no Mr Blair,' she replied, trying to keep her voice steady. 'Just me and Robert. I'm a single mum.' Then, lowering her eyes, she added shyly, 'Robert's father is not in the picture.'

Jason responded by smiling at her so brightly that it made her heart skip a beat. The warmth of his gaze made her feel special in a way that Reggie had never managed.

She made their tea, and they sat side by side, chatting about their lives. Of course, all Elsie's stories were from her imagination. She spoke of a fairytale childhood in Glasgow – an only child, adored by her parents, who sadly died in a tragic car crash, leaving Kimberly on her own – until Robert came along, the result of a sad fling with a one-night stand, who she's never seen since, but she would never regret, because it gave her the greatest love of her life.

Her life in the orphanage, her prostitution, her charring – all erased in an afternoon spent in the company of a handsome Irishman who made her feel beautiful, elegant and desired.

Although it wasn't planned, by the time Jason left, with promises of calling back the next day, Elsie had disappeared behind a new mask, and she had become Kimberly.

NOW

August 2023

Lily

Phibsborough, Dublin

The room was heavy with stunned silence as Lily and her family tried to process the shocking revelations her mother and Sally had outlined.

Lily's mum wasn't Kimberly, but instead a woman called Elsie. Who used to be Sally's best friend. This new information made Lily's head spin as she struggled to comprehend what else might have been hidden.

'You were supposed to come to Ireland with me,' her mum said to Sally accusingly. 'If you'd come with me, none of this would have happened.'

'How dare you!' Sally replied, her eyes flashing fire. 'I told you it wasn't safe to leave in that moment. I had to do what was best for Zach! For my child.'

'I know you believe that, Sally, but I had to protect him from Baldwin. He would have killed you both.'

'I would never have allowed that to happen. I was always going to leave, but you never gave me the chance. You took matters into your own hands, leaving me behind to deal not only with the horror of my son's abduction but my husband's anger too.' Sally's voice trembled with the accusation.

Lily's head spun as both women screamed at each other, about how they'd done what was best for Zach. How could they think, for one second, that any of this was okay? She looked at her mother in disbelief.

Who was she?

'How could you do this to your best friend? Snatch a child from her like that? It's barbaric,' Lily said, her voice quivering with emotion.

'You don't understand,' her mum replied, her eyes pleading with Lily to see it from her side. 'I was sure if I took Zach it would force Sally's hand to follow me. And then we could go on with our plan – the three of us – together. Reggie was supposed to tell Sally where to find me.'

Zach stepped forward, his face ashen and his upper lip beaded with sweat. 'Why didn't you follow her, Mom? What happened after Elsie left?'

The tension in the room was palpable as everyone waited for an answer.

Sally turned to her son, 'I went back down to the salon a few minutes later, wondering why Elsie and you hadn't joined us upstairs. I don't think I can ever explain the horror when I saw your empty pram. At first, we thought Elsie had taken you for a walk. But it became clear as the minutes became half an hour, that wasn't the case. Nicola explained what little she knew about Elsie and Reggie's plan, and we eventually put two and two together. I was dumbfounded that Elsie had taken you. And I had no clue where she had disappeared to.'

'Why didn't you ask this Reggie fella?' Lily asked.

'Oh we tried, but he disappeared too. Nicola asked some of Reggie's friends from the Grove, and they said Reggie had had to go into hiding. Word on the street was that he was about to be nicked for aggravated burglary,' Sally said. 'It was as if Elsie and Zach had disappeared into thin air.'

'Call the Gardaí. Let them sort all this out,' Gaga said suddenly. He reached into his pocket and pulled out his mobile phone. 'I want it on record that my son had nothing to do with this.'

Zach reached for Kevin's arm and laid a hand on it. 'Please, sir. Not yet. I need to hear what happened next. Once we've heard it all, you can do what you want.'

Lily felt her head swim. All this time, they'd thought her mum was the victim when all along she was the perpetrator.

Sally looked at Lily's grandfather. 'For what this woman did to me, she deserves to be locked up for life, but Zach is right. It's time for answers that I've waited over forty years to hear. How could you do that to *me*, Elsie? We were as good as sisters. And yet you never got in touch, not a postcard or a phone call to let me know Zach was okay.'

Lily's mum could only hang her head, at a loss for words.

Zach held the bridge of his nose as if in pain. Lily understood. An ache pierced her temples as the revelations kept on coming.

'What did my father ... this Baldwin man ... do when he found out I was taken by Elsie?' Zach asked.

Sally's face darkened, and she bit her lip as she steadied herself to respond. 'I wanted to tell him and the police that Elsie had taken Zach, but Nicola talked me out of it. She insisted that Elsie had a plan and we should trust her. I had no choice but to go along with that, figuring that if I gave the police her name it might jeopardise my chance to follow Elsie and Zach. So I placed my trust in the person I was closest to.' Sally laughed without merriment. 'What a fool I was.'

The room was silent, save for the laboured breaths from Kimberly.

Lily looked over at her father, who was quiet – too quiet. Surely, he had something to say about this? He had to be angry, because Lily felt fury begin to dance its way through her.

'Nicola and I told Ian and the police the truth, that we'd gone upstairs for a few moments, but when we returned Zach had gone. We left Elsie out of the story. The assumption was that someone had sneaked in and snatched the baby. Ian accused me of being an unfit mother, leaving Zach on his own in the salon. A nationwide search was put in place, but of course Zach was nowhere to be found. Meanwhile, I was vilified in the press. Every newspaper raked through my past, from the orphanage, to my prostitute mother and her murder. Nobody cared that I was grieving and heartbroken.' Sally wiped tears away and continued, her voice trembling. 'I didn't have to worry about leaving Ian after all, because he disowned me. My sordid past, which he'd worked so hard to hide from everyone, was now public knowledge. He wanted nothing to do with me.'

Zach wiped tears from his eyes as he listened to his mother speak. Lily's heart constricted, watching the pain he was obviously in.

Sally's voice dropped to a whisper. 'Ian left me with one last gift before he – literally – kicked me out of our home. I was lucky to leave alive.' She lifted her long blonde hair to reveal a faded scar.

'You said that was from a childhood accident – that you fell off your bike,' Zach whispered.

Sally shook her head sadly and for the first time since she'd arrived she began to cry.

'You should be ashamed of yourself,' Gaga angrily shouted at Lily's mother, his face bright red. He pointed to Sally's scar. 'You might as well have struck her yourself. What you did to that woman . . . I'm ashamed of you.'

Zach pulled his mother into his arms and held her close. She lay her head on his shoulder as he gently stroked the back of her hair. The tenderness of the moment brought a lump to Lily's throat. The love between them was undeniable and starkly contrasted to Lily's relationship with her own mother.

Yesterday, when her mum had held her in her arms, it had taken her breath away. She'd not been embraced like that in years. And now she wasn't sure she would ever want to be ever again.

Lily's mum walked to her side, as if she sensed that Lily was pulling away from her. 'I swear when I left London it was a spur-of-the-moment decision. I didn't plan any further than getting Zach away from Baldwin. Then, when your dad assumed I was Kimberly, I was afraid to correct him.'

Lily desperately wanted to understand her mother's motives as genuine. But she shook her head in denial at these words. 'No, Mum! When Sally didn't arrive in Dublin, did you attempt to check if she was okay? Were you not worried that her crazy husband, that you had no choice but to save Zach from, had killed *her*?'

'Excellent question,' Gaga said in approval.

Her mum's face flushed and she looked over to Lily's dad, her face softening with affection. 'I wanted to. Of course, I did. But the thing was I fell in love with your dad.' Her mum offered this as if it were an acceptable explanation.

This finally sparked a reaction from Lily's dad. He looked up, as if he were awakening from a dream.

'Was any of it true?' he asked, his face ashen and grey.

'Of course, Jason. The way I felt about you . . .'

Lily scoffed in response. 'All those stories of a childhood spent fishing at Loch Lomond with your parents. The house in Glasnevin that used to be our grandparents' before they moved to Glasgow.'

'I made that all up,' her mum admitted, tears now filling her eyes.

Lily's head continued to throb as she tried to push aside the things her mother had shared.

Somewhere, hidden beneath the murky words, was another dark truth.

She could feel it.

Michael hovered close by, and Ben reached for Lily, saying, 'Mama.' He quietened at once when Lily took him in her arms.

'All this time, we've been searching for my brother when he wasn't ours to lose in the first place,' Lily said, feeling nauseous at the thought.

'I loved Robert like he was my son,' her mother whispered.

331

Then she moved to her ex-husband and took his hand in hers. 'Our son.'

'You should have told me,' her dad replied, and then to Lily's shock he placed an arm round her mum. 'And while I'll not condone what you did, taking Zach, I know you would have done it from a place of love.'

Lily felt anger prickle her forearms. How could her father still be excusing his wife? Why wasn't he angry with her?

Then a terrifying thought struck Lily and she said, 'When Robert went missing from our cabin, you must have at least suspected that Sally took her son back.'

Her mother's face blanched even further. She ignored her daughter and turned to her husband again, looking for his reassurance. 'I couldn't say anything to Inspector Ortega because then he would have known about what I'd done. And I was so scared I'd lose you and Lily. You understand, don't you?'

Her dad's arm dropped from round her mum's shoulders.

'What if Inspector Ortega had arrested my son? Would you have spoken up then?' Gaga asked, his voice like ice, slicing through the tension in the room.

'Of course,' her mum answered. 'I told Ortega repeatedly that Jason was innocent.'

'She did,' Jason said. 'And if Kimberly had known for sure that Sally had taken Robert she would have told me that. Wouldn't you, love?'

Her mum nodded mutely.

However, none of this added up for Lily. Zach, too, seemed to be struggling to make sense of the pieces.

'You are saying that you didn't know that my mom took me from your cabin?' Zach asked accusingly.

Lily watched her mother and Sally stare at each other. Lily's mum was the first to break eye contact, when she finally answered Zach.

'If I'm honest, I did suspect it for a little bit, but I didn't know for sure. I mean, I hoped it was Sally that took you, rather than the other horrifying option, that you'd fallen overboard.'

'Lies drip from your mouth so easily. How can you sleep at night?' Sally said.

'I don't sleep,' her mum replied sadly. 'I lost so much forty years ago and I'm begging you not to take the crumbs of my life now.'

But Sally wasn't listening to her old friend.

'The time for secrets is over, Elsie. It's time to tell them everything.'

And then Sally brought them all back to 1983 for one last time . . .

BEFORE

July 1983

Sally

The Carousel, *Spanish Coast*

Sally stretched her arms above her head. It had been a busy morning in the salon. Tonight was one of the formal captain's dinners, so she'd had a packed day of appointments in the salon. Ladies who all wanted their hair teased into an up style, ready for their formal photograph with the captain. Up styles were one of Sally's strengths, and she always enjoyed seeing the women's reactions to her creations when she revealed the finished style. She glanced at the clock and saw she had five minutes until her next appointment.

Before her client arrived, Sally needed a caffeine boost, so she moved into the small office behind the salon and put the kettle on. A few minutes later, she sipped her Nescafé Gold Blend and sighed in pleasure. Some days, it felt as if she ran purely on caffeine.

She opened her small spiral notebook, and flicked through the pages until she came to the Barcelona section. Last time they were docked here, she'd focused on Ciutat Vella, the old town in Catalan. She planned to trawl the south area of Montjuïc this time. Sally had no idea if Elsie had ever gone through with her plan to start afresh in Spain, but she had to keep looking, so she used all her spare time at ports searching for her son. Nicola told her it was like looking for a needle in a haystack, but the thing was that Sally knew the needle was *somewhere*. She'd been searching for Zach for more than two years and she wouldn't stop looking till she found him.

She heard the salon door open, signalling the end of her brief reprieve. Sally snapped her notebook shut. She'd get back to her plans this evening.

'Be right with you,' Sally called out, then took another sip of coffee before placing it back on the countertop.

'There's no rush,' a soft Scottish lilt responded.

But Sally knew better than to leave her ladies waiting. She immediately walked back into the salon and saw a tall woman with shoulder-length blonde hair sitting down, her head bent low into a magazine. The woman screamed sophistication, wearing a cream linen sundress, leather sandals and gold jewellery.

'Hello. You must be my three o'clock, Mrs Murphy? I'm Sally, your stylist today.' She smoothed down her uniform, feeling a little scruffy beside the elegant lady.

The woman looked up, and her eyes rounded in disbelief when they locked with Sally's. Sally's breath quickened, and her heart rate beat so fast that she thought she might black out. She blinked three times, not trusting what was right before her. She'd changed, almost unrecognisable from the last time she'd seen her, but there was no doubt.

'It's y-y-you . . .' Sally stuttered.

Kimberly's face blanched, and a sheen of sweat appeared on her upper lip. Then her eyes darted to the salon door. Sally instinctively moved to stand in front of it.

'Sally, I can't believe it's you,' Kimberly whispered. She stood, picked up her handbag and circled round Sally, moving closer to the door.

'Where's my son?' Sally screamed, clenching her hands beside her thighs into tight fists. When she didn't get a response, Sally continued, 'You tell me where my son is right this minute, or I'll kill you. I swear to God, I will kill you with my bare hands, Elsie.'

'I've not been called that for a while. I'm Kimberly now.' She licked her lips repeatedly and stepped an inch closer to the door.

But she'd have to physically get through Sally first before she'd let her leave this salon. Sally glanced at the phone on the reception desk. Should she run to it and call security for help? But would Elsie run if she did?

'Wait,' Kimberly replied, following Sally's eyes towards the phone.

Sally realised that it wasn't only Elsie's name that had changed. Her London cockney accent was gone. She was groomed in a way that Sally had never seen before. While her sundress was simple, Sally knew money when she saw it, from the gold watch on her wrist to the delicate diamond earrings in her lobes. Every fibre of Sally was insulted by this. While she'd been living a life in constant sorrow without her son, Elsie was thriving.

'You have till I count to three to tell me where Zach is. And don't think about running. There's nowhere to hide this time. We're on a ship in the middle of the ocean.'

Kimberly nodded, again licking her lips. 'Robert is with my husband and daughter.'

Sally was confused. Who the hell was Robert? It took her a beat to realise that not only had Elsie changed her name, but her son's too. What else had changed in the last two years? Sally's body began to shake as thoughts of her son's safety flooded her. Elsie would never hurt her baby, would she?

'Is Zach okay? Please tell me he's okay,' Sally begged, her voice cracking as she asked the question that had haunted her for over two years.

Kimberly's face softened, and she quickly responded. 'He's thriving. Happy and safe. I promise you.'

Sally's shoulders slumped, and she grabbed the door frame to steady herself. Taking a deep breath, she looked up and said firmly, 'Take me to him right now.'

'Wait,' Kimberly said, holding her hand up. 'Just wait a moment. Don't you want to hear about him first? About where we've been?'

Sally desperately craved every single detail, but she didn't trust Kimberly not to bolt.

'You said yourself there's nowhere for me to run. Sit down. Please. Let me explain. I owe you that much, at least.'

'I'll give you five minutes, but I'm fine standing,' Sally spat back at her.

Kimberly returned to the sofa and sat down again, crossing her legs elegantly. Sally could hardly fathom that this woman was the same person who once had been her best friend – her sister in every way but blood.

'You must hate me,' Kimberly said. 'And I don't blame you. I hate myself.'

'Save me the theatrics.' Sally replied acidly.

Kimberly sighed. 'You have to believe me. I didn't plan it. When you refused to leave, I knew I had to save Robert.'

'Would you stop calling him that? His name is Zach!' Sally shouted. She'd never felt rage like this before, and it took all her strength and willpower not to rush at Kimberly, as she'd threatened only a few moments before.

'Okay. Zach it is.' Kimberly smiled pleasantly. 'But you need to know that he answers to Robert now. He has a little sister, Lily. She's six months old. And he has the most wonderful father. Jason. Who adores him as if he were his own child. He has the life that you always wanted for him. But that he could never have with Ian Baldwin.'

Sally could not believe her ears. 'Are you telling me that my son is better off with you, in some fantasy make-believe world, than with me, his mother?'

Kimberly didn't respond, and Sally said incredulously, 'You genuinely believe that, don't you?'

'You left me no choice but to run. For Rober . . . I mean Zach's sake, I had to leave. I was scared for him . . . for you too.'

Sally had heard enough. She needed to see her son, and hold him in her arms. 'I'm done listening. I'm going to the captain and he can call the Spanish police. And I am taking back my little boy!'

Sally opened the door of the salon, but before she could leave she felt two arms pull her from behind, dragging her forcibly back into the room.

'I can't let you do that, Sally. You're going nowhere. Not until you hear me out.'

BEFORE

July 1983

Sally

The Carousel, *Spanish Coast*

Sally's breath quickened as she listened to Kimberly go through all that had transpired since that fateful day at Elite in London. She began to clap slowly when Kimberly finished her account.

'You fell in love. You met a man and decided to play happy families with him. With *my* child. That's your explanation of why you abducted my son.'

'You make it sound so sinister,' Kimberly replied, her face flushed with affront.

'It *is* sinister. You can try and dress that up as much as you like, but the bottom line is this irrefutable fact. You abducted a child, Elsie.'

'I love him,' Kimberly said, her eyes glassy with tears. 'Robert is my world – him, Lily and Jason. We're a family. We love each other. And, I told you,' her voice hardened, 'I'm Kimberly now.'

Sally clenched her fists by her side, her nails pinching her palms. 'He is not yours, though! And what about me? Your oldest friend from childhood. Do you even care about the devastation you left in your wake? The hell you put me through?'

Kimberly's breath quickened, and she raised a hand to her temples as she listened to Sally.

'When we found Zach's empty pram, Nicola stayed in the salon, in case you came back, and I began running up and down the streets, searching for you.'

'You were supposed to follow me to Ireland!' Kimberly said, her voice rising an octave in accusation. 'I knew you'd never leave Baldwin!'

'Oh, I left Ian. But how could I follow you when I didn't know where you'd gone?' Sally cried. 'You disappeared off the face of the earth!'

'Reggie . . . Reggie was supposed to tell you so you could join me,' Kimberly stammered.

Sally scoffed. 'Well, that didn't happen. Reggie disappeared too. I half suspected that he'd gone with you, but Nicola heard a rumour a year ago that he'd been killed.'

Kimberly paled and groaned softly, 'Poor Reggie. So that's why I never heard from him again. I always thought his life choices would catch up with him.'

Sally looked at her old friend in disbelief. 'I couldn't care less about bloody Reggie. He helped you take Zach from me. And I'm done talking to you. I want my son back *now*. Call your husband and tell him to bring Zach here immediately.'

'Wait!' Kimberly's eyes darted to the phone, and then she turned back to Sally, her lips quivering. 'How did you find me? And end up working here?'

Sally raised a hand to her temple, and felt the outline of the ragged scar that she hid behind her blonde hair. 'While you were living your best life, I lost everything. Ian threw me out when the world discovered my past. The daughter of a prostitute, brought up in care, who was so negligent of her son, that she left him alone in a busy hair salon where he was snatched. Made for great headlines in the papers for a few weeks.'

'The bastard! You were a good mother,' Kimberly protested.

'I know I was! I don't need you to tell me that! You don't get to say anything to me, because you lost that right when you stole my baby.' Sally breathed in deeply, then added, 'Once Ian threw me out on the street, bloodied and broken, with only a black sack filled with my clothes, I had nothing.'

'What did you do?' Kimberly whispered.

'I couldn't go to Nicola's because the press relentlessly pursued her too. For a few weeks at least, until we became yesterday's news, and they moved on to something else. So it was Sister Ailsa Jones who took me back to Sunshine House and gave me a room in the staff quarters to regain my strength.

'Eventually, I went back to work at the salon. The only clue we had was that you'd planned to go to Spain, so I went to Spain whenever I could afford it, to search for you. Alicante, Barcelona, Malaga, Valencia . . . Sister Jones – Ailsa – and Nicola both chipped in some money to help pay for the airfares. But, as Nicola said, it was like looking for a needle in a haystack. Sister Ailsa kept saying that I must have faith. But I was slowly losing my mind, let alone my faith.' Sally sighed. 'I decided I needed a private detective, but I didn't have that kind of money.

'Nicola came to the rescue again. She has a friend who manages the salon here on the *Carousel*, and she pulled in a favour, getting me a three-month contract. The money is good, but the tips are even better. I've been saving every penny. And as the ship visits several Spanish ports it means I can search for you here too.' Sally laughed mirthlessly. 'And to think I fought Nicola when she suggested this; I didn't want to accept the position because I was afraid it would take me further from my little boy. But Sister Ailsa was right all along. I *did* need to have faith, because this job has led me to you and Zach.'

'Sally, I'm so sorry. You didn't deserve any of this.' Kimberly sighed, and half smiled at Sally. 'I shouldn't be surprised that you found us. You are the most determined woman I've ever known. I've never seen anyone fight for what she wants more than you.'

Sally threw a look of disgust at Elsie. For the past two years she'd thought about what she might say to her when she found her. Because Sally had never been in doubt that one day she would do just that, and get her son back. 'You said to me once that I was a pure bright white light, but you'd had to step back from me so you didn't spread your darkness to me. Well, I have wished every day since you took my baby that you had stayed away, because you managed to send me to pitch darkness in the end.'

Elsie or Kimberly or whoever she was, began to cry as she kept repeating how sorry she was, but Sally didn't believe her crocodile tears. Seeing Kimberly get just desserts for what she'd put her through was the only apology she would accept.

'You know, at least with Ian, there was an honesty about his cruelty. He showed me his true colours with his fists.' Sally spat at her.

Kimberly winced at Sally's words, but Sally wasn't done yet. She continued, her voice cold and resolute, as she finally said the words that had been bubbling up inside her.

'But you . . . you were sly, making me believe that you were on my side, that you were there for me. I often saw signs of your selfishness as we grew up in Sunshine House, but I never believed you could be this cruel.' Sally strode to the telephone and picked up the receiver to call security. 'I lost everything: my child, my home, my reputation . . . Well, now it's *your* turn to face the consequences.'

BEFORE

July 1983

Kimberly

The Carousel, *Spanish Coast*

Kimberly's heart raced as she sprinted across the salon floor, her handbag nearly causing her to trip. She called out desperately, 'Wait, please. Wait.'

Having spent so long pretending to be someone she wasn't, Kimberly had lost touch with her true identity. Now, standing face to face with her past, her mask finally dropping, she felt panic sweep over her. The thought of Sally calling security filled her with dread. If Robert was taken away from her, she knew she'd also lose Jason and Lily.

Sally's expression was now hard and cold, unlike the kind and warm face Kimberly had known for years. But Kimberly knew she was to blame for this change in Sally's demeanour.

But the thing was she wasn't Elsie – not any more. She'd spent the past couple of years redefining herself. And she liked Kimberly in a way that she had never liked Elsie.

So, was it fair that she be held accountable for the part of her past that she'd left so far behind?

She needed to come up with a plan before it was too late and she lost everything.

'You can't call security,' Kimberly said firmly, her hand shaking as she held it over Sally's.

'Give me one good reason,' Sally countered.

And in that desperate moment, as Kimberly tried to buy some time, the perfect answer came. 'Ian Baldwin.'

Sally's face blanched at the mention of his name, understanding beginning to dawn.

'If you call security, then he'll be notified, won't he?' Kimberly continued, her voice going stronger as her thoughts crystallised. 'And you said yourself he damned you publicly, stating that you were a bad mother. He'll take Robert . . .' She corrected herself when she saw Sally's face flinch. 'He'll take Zach. You know I'm right. You will get your son back, only to lose him again. Do you think a judge will allow you to keep him?'

Sally collapsed onto the couch in the reception area, her body shaking uncontrollably. The weight of Kimberly's words had crushed her, leaving her feeling vulnerable and helpless.

'You could leave Zach with me . . . with Jason and his little sister, Lily.' Kimberly held a placating hand up when Sally yelled out an immediate no. 'You could come to live in Dublin with my family. We bought a new house a few months ago. It's got four bedrooms. I'll introduce you as my long-lost sister. You'll be Robert's godmother. And, this way, you can see him every day.' Kimberly smiled encouragingly. 'My husband and I have money. We have our own business, and it's doing well. Since working with Jason, I've transformed it, doubling our revenue. I can pay you too, give you a lump sum, so you can open that salon you've always dreamed of . . .'

Kimberly saw she had made a mistake mentioning money when anger flashed over Sally's face at the clumsy attempt to bribe her.

'You think I'd give up my son for money?' Sally's voice was high-pitched in its incredulity. 'You are delusional, Elsie Evans, if you think I'd ever agree to that.' She stood up and moved close to Kimberly, their noses an inch apart. 'I want my son back. And there is no other solution here than that. So you can forget your fairytale nonsense of me living as a second-class godmother.'

Kimberly nodded along, her mind racing again as she tried to work out her next move, anything but allowing Sally to finish placing her call to security – her hand still hovered over the receiver.

'You need to understand that in the same way that you can't lose Zach I cannot lose Jason and Lily,' Kimberly stated as she felt terror snake its way around her body, making her tremble. For the first time, she truly understood the horror through which she'd put her best friend. But they'd reached a stalemate, and they both knew it.

Then an idea came to Kimberly, and she knew there was only one thing they could do so they both got to keep their families.

'You have to take Robert. Abduct him. Then disappear forever,' Kimberly said, her voice barely above a whisper.

Sally's hand fell limply to her side. Kimberly led her back to the couch, and they sat side by side, as they'd done hundreds of times throughout their childhood. Sally listened as Kimberly made a plan to get them out of trouble – as she'd always done.

BEFORE

July 1983

Sally

The Carousel, *Spanish Coast*

Sally closed her rucksack. She was packed and ready to leave when the ship docked at Barcelona port.

She'd made two phone calls yesterday once Elsie returned to her family.

Her family. What a lie that was. In truth, every part of the life that Kimberly had created was a facade, from the phony Scottish accent to the clothes and mannerisms. Elsie had replaced every part of her warm, cockney friend with someone Sally didn't recognise.

How could Elsie try to justify the horrific thing she'd done? And pretend it had been in Sally's best interest? When it was, without doubt, the most selfish thing any person could do to another. And then to try to bribe her? Sally felt anger nip at her again, but knew she had to keep that bay. She needed all her wits about her to pull this off.

The first call Sally made was to a stunned Nicola. But, as always, her surrogate mother came through for Sally. She called her friend, Sally's manager on the *Carousel*, and tearfully explained that Sally's grandmother was terminally ill and that she had to return to England immediately.

When her manager called Sally to her office to break the sad news, Sally didn't need to pretend to be shaken. And Sally was granted permission to leave the *Carousel* as soon as they arrived at Barcelona port, which they expected to be at four o'clock in the morning.

The day passed at a snail's pace. Sally listened to clients chit-chat about their holiday as her mind whirled with what she had facing her.

Her biggest issue had been staying away from Zach. On her lunch break, she'd gone to the pool area and watched the Murphy family together from afar. When Zach lifted his arms upwards and called 'Mama' to Elsie, it felt like a knife was gutting her.

And she almost charged at them.

But then she remembered why she was doing things this way. Yes, it helped Elsie, but that wasn't important. All she had to focus on was that this way she got to keep Zach – and herself – safe. It wasn't enough that she got him back. She also had to protect him from his father.

Finally, it was time. It was almost three thirty in the morning, and the ship was quiet. Passengers and staff were asleep, save for the crew on the night shift. Sally slipped out of her cabin and went to deck eight, using the stairwell rather than the lift. As she'd hoped, she didn't meet anyone.

Sally knew she should be scared, but knowing she was right and taking back what was hers made her bold. She moved swiftly, taking a longer route than necessary to avoid the areas with security cameras of which she'd taken note earlier that day.

And then she finally reached Cabin 1812. Sally reached for the key that Elsie had dropped into her earlier at the salon whilst pretending to buy some hair products. Sally listened at the door momentarily, but it seemed quiet inside. So she slipped the key into the lock and opened it, pausing for a moment to ensure the click hadn't woken anyone up.

She pulled a small torch from her jacket pocket, flicked it on, pointed the small circular light towards the floor and went inside. She heard snores from the bed – from both Elsie and Jason, who were unconscious. The waft of stale lager lingered in the air. Jason had clearly had a few drinks too many. But she ignored all of that, and instead, her eyes scanned the room until the outline of a small body underneath a soft white duvet appeared.

Sally's heart stopped, and she couldn't help herself: she gasped out loud. Holding a hand over her mouth, she ran to Zach's side and sobbed as she saw her baby for the first time in two years.

He'd grown so much – from a tiny infant to a toddler. His blond and curly hair was damp with the heat of his warm bed. His face was pink and flushed. She reached down to touch him, scared that he was running a fever. Relief made her shoulders sag when she felt him, and found his temperature normal.

Sally scooped him up, pulling him close to her, and it felt as if it had only been minutes since she'd last held him.

'I'm so sorry. I'm so sorry I lost you . . .' she whispered into his ear.

He stirred a little in her arms, but then snuggled in closer to her, fast asleep as Elsie had promised he would be. She had placed allergy medication in his bottle, which acted as a sleeping draught. Elsie said it would be enough to make him sleep through the next crucial hours.

Sally had rallied against the idea at first, scared it might be harmful to Zach. But Elsie had calmly explained that he'd taken it before, prescribed by their doctor, for his hay fever. It hurt that she didn't know this about her little boy. She'd missed so much. But, no matter what happened next, she vowed to herself that she would not miss another day of his life.

Sally reached under the small bed and found a long canvas bag. Elsie had done as she promised, lining the inside with a long, soft pillow and a small blue-checked blanket. A makeshift bed for her darling boy. Sally lay him inside the bag, and, yes, it was the perfect size as Kimberly had said it would be. She grabbed his soft Peter Rabbit toy and placed it in his arms. Then she zipped the bag up, leaving a small gap at the top to ensure air could freely flow in.

Also packed in the bag were enough nappies and bottles to get Sally through the next twenty-four hours. With one last look around the room, Sally left, holding the canvas bag tenderly, as if it were precious cargo.

Sally returned to her own staff quarters, but with one quick pit stop on the way. She exited deck eight at the end of the corridor, and went outside. Taking the stuffed bunny rabbit from the sleeping Zach, she threw it behind a nearby lifeboat, as Elsie had instructed her to do.

This cost her more than anything else she was doing: the deliberate red herring that her son might have fallen overboard, knowing the pain that would cause many innocents. Sally didn't know Jason or the little infant Lily, but she knew that, like Sally and Zach, they were victims in this lie that Elsie had created.

Waiting for the ship to dock at Barcelona was torturous. Twenty minutes felt like an eternity, until she finally heard the familiar pull and tug as the ship manoeuvred into port. Sally had made arrangements the previous day for an immediate disembarkation when they docked, so that she could catch the first flight back to the UK. So at four in the morning, with a rucksack on her back and the canvas bag with the most precious cargo she'd ever carried hanging over her shoulder, Sally made her way to the exit. Zach's weight made her back ache, and she felt sweat trickle into pools under her armpits. But she gritted her teeth and kept moving.

The disembarkation crew were seated at the gangway, reading the morning newspapers. A rope cordoned off the exit, which stopped anyone from leaving.

Sally passed her crew badge to them. 'I've been given permission to leave early as I have a family emergency. My grandmother is dying,' Sally said tearfully, her hand underneath the canvas bag, carefully balancing it as she waited. She prayed that Zach would not take this moment to awake.

'Sorry to hear about your troubles,' the crew member said, passing her a slip to sign, and once Sally had done so, with a quick nod of thanks to the two crew members, she exited down the gangway.

The Customs Hall was empty at this early hour, save for one officer, who was half asleep. She held her crew badge up, and he waved her through without a second glance.

Every step she took, Sally worried that it would jar Zach awake, but he continued to sleep. And as soon as she was clear from the eye-line of the ship, she paused, placing the bag gently on a bench. She looked up and down the street, making sure that there were no CCTV cameras. Then, satisfied that there were no watchful eyes, she reached down to open the canvas bag fully.

Sally held her breath as she looked down at Zach's face. It was red, and he was sweating. But his chest rose and fell, and he didn't seem distressed. She desperately wanted to hold him, but knew she had to keep moving. Sally picked up the bag again and doubled her speed, desperate to escape Portside.

If Jason had awoken early, he may have already raised the alarm. She might only have minutes to disappear. And now Sally could only hope that the second call she'd made yesterday had come through for her.

'I'm holding on to my faith a little longer,' she whispered.

When she reached the Ronda del Litoral, she took a left onto a smaller cobbled street, then she took another left and a right. Every part of her body was on high alert, but the streets were empty. She could have wept when she turned her final corner and saw a familiar sight a few feet from her.

Wearing a grey skirt and white blouse, with her grey veil flapping behind her, Sister Ailsa leaned against a small red Fiat Punto. She held her arms stretched open as she ran towards Sally and Zach.

'I found him . . . After all this time, I finally found him,' Sally cried as she fell into Sister Ailsa's arms.

BEFORE

July 1983

Sally

Port of Barcelona, Spain

Sally carefully lifted Zach from his crude makeshift crib and cradled him tightly. In the back seat of Sister Ailsa's car, she held him close, fastening the seatbelt securely round them both. In the rearview mirror, Sister Ailsa watched Sally.

'You haven't taken your eyes off him, not even once,' she remarked, her voice soft with admiration.

Sally's face was wet with tears as she looked down at her little boy. 'I'm afraid if I do he'll disappear again,' she confessed. 'I'm not sure I'll believe he's back with me, and that this is not a dream, for a long time, if ever.'

'I told you to hold on to your faith, didn't I? I knew he would find his way home to his mother. I prayed for this day,' Sister Ailsa replied. She glanced upwards as if offering a silent prayer.

'You were right, as you usually are,' Sally whispered. 'Where are we going?'

'Let me navigate this bit, get us out of Barcelona, then I'll fill you in.'

Sister Ailsa exited a roundabout heading towards the B20. A little traffic was beginning to enter the city as people woke up to start their days. Sally listened acutely for the sounds of sirens in

351

the distance that might be coming for her. But so far all was quiet. It wasn't until they'd left the city limits of Barcelona behind that Sally's heart began to slow down.

'What happens if the police stop us?' she asked, her voice trembling with fear.

'We tell them the truth – that you are Zach's mother,' Sister Ailsa said calmly. 'I have Zach's birth certificate for you, as you requested.' She nodded towards her handbag on the passenger's seat. 'It was where you said it would be.'

Sally had left several bags of clothes, along with important documentation, with Nicola when she'd left for her three-month job on the cruise ship. She'd asked Sister Ailsa to pick up Zach's birth certificate. Sally had her own passport with her, of course, but now, with Zach's birth certificate with her, she could apply for a passport for him too. This gave them options on where they could go.

An image of her mother came to Sally. Lizzie with her striking red hair, talking about her unfulfilled dream to escape England for sunny Australia. Maybe Sally would go there, for her mother – far from Ian's reach.

Sally knew that none of this would have been possible had it not been for Sister Ailsa. Taking several steadying breaths, Sally struggled to articulate her gratitude to her old guardian.

'When I saw you standing there, waiting for me . . .' Sally's words ended on a strangled sob. 'I'll never be able to repay you.'

'I'm glad you called me. Nicola helped me pull the plan together too. She paid for my flight and the car hire. She's a kind woman and loves you. And promises to visit you as soon as you are settled.'

Nicola had in fact immediately offered to come to Spain herself, when Sally had called her asking for help. But Sally needed her to stay in London. If Sally's manager called, to double check Sally had arrived home in London, Nicola would cover for her. Sally would hand her notice in, at the end of the week, stating that she had to take care of her grandmother.

Sister Ailsa turned the car radio on, turning the dial until she found a news channel.

'Best listen in case there are any reports of an abduction.'

Abduction. Sally's hand trembled as she stroked Zach's head. Her poor baby boy had gone through that horror twice now. He stirred in his sleep, but instead of waking up he stretched his arms and snuggled closer to Sally. His vulnerability overwhelmed her, and the love she'd felt from the moment she'd discovered she was pregnant rushed at her again in one torrential force.

But then another image came to mind.

Another mother who had cradled Zach at the poolside yesterday, with such tenderness it had felt palpable.

'Am I as bad as her?' Sally whispered. 'Snatching him from the only mother he remembers and loves?'

'No! You have committed no crime, Sally. I will never understand how Elsie could have done that to you. She is lucky that she is not behind bars right now,' Sister Ailsa declared.

'Trust me, I wish she were,' Sally said bitterly. 'But she was right about one thing. Ian would find a way to take Zach from me if he knew I'd found him.'

'I must admit that keeping the fact that we found Zach from his father cost me sleep last night.'

She reached forward to squeeze the nun's shoulder. 'I'm sorry for dragging you into this. I'm lucky it was Sunshine House my mother sent me to. I want you to know that.'

'You were always special. I've always tried not to form attachments with my girls, but some, like you, become family,' Sister Aisla said, catching Sally's eye in the mirror. 'And I saw firsthand what Ian did to you and what Elsie took from you. While I don't agree with all the lies, I understand the need for them. I reckon the boss would understand too.' She looked upwards again with a grin.

Sister Ailsa increased the volume as the five o'clock news began on the radio.

'No mention of Zach,' Sister Ailsa reported a couple of moments later.

'You speak Spanish?' Sally asked in surprise.

'Yes, it's a little rusty because I've not spoken it for a while, but enough to get us by.'

'I think we have a little more time before the Murphys wake up. Elsie told me that it's normally seven before the children stir. So hopefully they don't know that Zach is gone yet.'

Sally's stomach cramped and pinched as she tried to imagine the fallout when it was discovered that a child was missing from the ship. There would be a full-scale search. And the need to hide and stay out of sight, away from eagle-eyed citizens who might report that they'd spotted Sally, became overwhelming.

'It feels too exposed here on the motorway,' Sally fretted, her eyes wide with fear as she watched cars pass them by.

'I agree. But I want to get as far away from Barcelona as possible before anyone starts looking. We'll move to secondary roads by seven, where it will be harder for anyone to spot us. As for where we are going, we are en route to a Benedictine convent in Ronda. A village that sits high on a mountain, remote enough that I am confident you will be safe. I have friends there who will take care of us. It's a long drive, but, God willing, we'll get there by this afternoon.'

'A convent,' Sally repeated, surprised, but found she was not upset by the suggestion.

'Yes, I hope this is the last place the police will go looking for a stolen child. There is a community of twenty nuns there. It was where I spent my early years as a noviciate. I lived in that convent for almost ten years after I took my vows, before I settled into my life at Sunshine House.'

'Do the nuns there know what I've done?' Sally asked, her voice rising an octave at the thought that she might arrive in Ronda to a trap, with the police waiting for them.

'They know the truth, most of it at least. That you were in my care in Sunshine House and that now you and your baby son are hiding from an abusive husband. As far as they are concerned, you arrived here on the same flight as I did last night.'

How little Sally knew of the woman who had, without a moment's hesitation, agreed to help her. Who was capable and brave beyond Sally's wildest imagination. She needed some of Sister Ailsa's courage, because a new fear had begun to snake its way into her mind.

'What if Zach wakes up and doesn't remember me?'

Sister Ailsa sighed. 'It's unlikely that he will, Sally. He was six months old the last time he saw you. So, he'll need some time to adjust to your care. But he's young, and he's where he should be. As long as you love him and show him that, with your actions and your words, he will soon know only you as his mother. What do I always say?'

'I need to have faith,' Sally said, smiling as she stroked Zach's cheek gently. His face was no longer flushed, now that he was out of the warm Spanish sun. And then he began to stir again, but this time he opened his eyes wide as he took in his surroundings. Sally whispered endearments to him, but he jerked in her lap, looking around him for clues as to where he was.

'There, there, it's okay, my darling,' Sally said, feeling tears sting her eyes as he worried and fretted in her arms.

'Mama,' he cried out, wriggling fiercely as he tried to escape her.

'Give him a bottle,' Sister Ailsa suggested. 'That will settle him.'

'He's scared of me,' Sally said tremulously as tears threatened to fall.

'Stop that now, girl,' Sister Ailsa admonished. 'You're his mother, and it's up to you to be strong for the wee bairn now. Give him his bottle. Show him he has nothing to fear from you, and he'll respond to that kindness. It's all I could ever do for the girls when they arrived to me over the years. You included.'

Sally sucked in deep breaths until she had control of her emotions again. Then, grabbing one of the prepared bottles Elsie had stashed in the canvas bag, she shook it and gently placed the teat in Zach's mouth.

'I'm your mama. I've always been your mama. Kimberly, well she was your other mother. Just for a little while. But you are back now with me, where you are meant to be. And I love you so very much.'

Zach watched her with those big blue eyes, and the comforting taste of his milk and her soft voice soothed his tears away.

Sally had ached for the chance to feed her child again, to feel the weight of him in her arms and hear the gentle sucking of the teat as he hungrily drank. The wonder and majesty of this simple moment took her breath away. Zach's hands reached up to clasp the bottle.

Sally swore to herself that she would not stop showering him with love until he realised he had nothing to fear from her – that he was loved more than any other child could be.

Zach napped again in her arms, lulled by both the bottle and the gentle movement of the car. Despite herself, Sally dozed off too, waking a few hours later when she felt the car grind to a juddering halt.

'That did you good. You were exhausted,' Sister Ailsa said approvingly. They were parked in a supermarket car lot, underneath the shade of a tall oak tree. 'We need to stretch our legs. And we need to eat. It's past nine now. How about I go into the shop to buy us some breakfast? Because I suspect the wee fella might have a present for you.'

Sally wrinkled her nose as a smell drifted towards her. Laughing at her joke, Sister Ailsa left Sally to change Zach's nappy. He kicked his legs with delight, feeling the air on them.

Sally thought that by now the Murphy family would be awake and have discovered that Zach was gone. To her surprise, she felt only sadness at this. Any satisfaction she'd felt yesterday had now dissipated. It appeared that having her son back in her arms again had mellowed her anger.

While they awaited Sister Ailsa's return, Sally took Zach for a walk to stretch his legs. His eyes lit up with delight when a small starling bird landed a few feet from them. He began to run towards it, laughing as it flew away.

'You're fast!' Sally said, running after him. 'You have to hold my hand. Okay?'

He looked up at her, and nodded his assent as he placed his little hand in Sally's. 'Let's go find some pretty leaves,' Sally suggested.

And together they happily began searching the ground underneath the tree for nature's treasures. When Sister Ailsa returned, she confirmed that there had been no mention of Zach on the news yet either. After a hearty breakfast of freshly baked baguettes, cheese and Parma ham, followed by a gooey custard pastry, washed down with freshly squeezed orange juice, they all felt much better. Sally laughed joyfully, seeing her boy tuck into solids for the first time – for her, at least. Sister Ailsa had bought him many choices, but he clearly loved bananas and yoghurt more than anything else.

'Can you be parted from him, for a little bit, to take a turn driving?' Sister Ailsa asked, smiling indulgently, while she watched Sally make *choo-choo* train noises as she spoon-fed Zach.

Sally frowned. The thought of letting Zach go, even to the arms of Sister Ailsa, whom she trusted with both their lives, pained her.

'I feel revived after our food,' Sister Ailsa continued. 'I'll drive for another hour or two. But you'll have to take a turn at some point. I'll need to take a nap. I'm afraid I've not slept much since you called.'

'I think Zach would like a cuddle from Sister Ailsa, wouldn't you, darling?' Sally asked him.

'I'm Robert,' he replied, his eyes wide with confusion.

Sally's stomach flipped. She hated causing her little boy any further confusion. 'Yes, Robert, but you have another name too . . . Zach!'

Sister Ailsa took the mashed fruit and said, 'And I have another choo-choo train . . .'

'Again, again!' Zach squealed with laughter as he swallowed another spoon of banana.

In the end, they continued their journey, this time with Sally at the wheel. Sister Ailsa sang Scottish lullabies to Zach about a bonnie wee lassie, and his laugh made Sally's heart sing.

'He looks like my mother now,' Sally said, her heart lurching as she watched them play together through the mirror. 'When he was born, everyone said he was Ian's doppelgänger, but the past two years have changed him. He has the same lopsided grin my mother had.'

'Isn't that a wonder,' Sister Ailsa said knowingly. 'You've got your son back, and he's brought a little bit of your mother too.'

At lunchtime, they stopped for another picnic at a small park with a playground. As Sally pushed Zach on a swing, she fought back another wash of tears. She'd daydreamed about this simple pleasure for so long. After he was born, as she'd walked through Pinner Village Gardens park, pushing Zach in his pram, she'd promised he would be big enough for the swings one day. And, finally, that moment had come.

'We need to get going,' Sister Ailsa said, joining them. So they continued their drive, this time with Sister Ailsa behind the wheel, expertly navigating them along the twisty road to Ronda. The road was winding with dangerous bends that made Sally's stomach flip when she peeked over the high ridge.

They arrived at the Convento de Santa Benedictine a little after four o'clock in the afternoon, hot and tired from the long drive in the small car. Despite their weariness, Sally was grateful that the journey had passed without incident. The convent was an imposing three-storey building with a magnificent bell tower that caught the sunlight and shone like a beacon. It had rich creamy brickwork and elaborately carved granite arches above the windows and doors.

Sister Ailsa glanced at Sally and Zach and said, 'Most nuns here don't speak English, but a couple do. Follow my lead.' She opened the back door, and Sally and Zach stepped out of the car.

Zach was wide awake now, and looked around in fascination. Sally kissed his cheek tenderly and smiled at him. He didn't flinch or move away. He regarded her with his big blue eyes, and she thought there was less fear in his face now. She continued murmuring soothing words of love to him as she gently bounced him in her arms.

As they approached the heavy wooden front door, Sally's heart pounded with anticipation. She had no idea what to expect inside the convent walls. The door opened, revealing two women dressed in formal nuns' black habits. They greeted Sally and Sister Ailsa with warm smiles.

'Hola, Sister Monique. Hola, Sister Teresa,' Sister Ailsa said, and they kissed each other on the cheek.

'Hola, Sister Ailsa,' they chorused. And then their faces lit up with delight as they saw Zach. They ushered Sally and her Zach inside the convent walls and closed the door behind them.

Sally had done the impossible.

Against all odds, she had not only managed to find her stolen child, but escape to safety too. Looking at her son's beautiful face, she knew she would never let Zach go again.

NOW

August 2023

Lily

Phibsborough, Dublin

Zach listened intently as Sally spoke about her incredible reunion with her son and their escape from the *Carousel*, his eyes never leaving his mother's face.

The air was heavy and silent, with long-held secrets finally being revealed – their vice-like grip loosening at last for the first time in more than forty years.

Lily stood silently, her eyes darting around the room as she tried to make sense of it all. Her mother's face was impassive, and her father still seemed completely bewildered. He looked over to Lily, his eyes begging her to help him understand.

But Lily was as lost as her father. How do you come to terms with a lifetime of lies and deceit? How could any of them move forward when everything you thought to be true turned out to be untrue, leaving destruction in its path?

'We always thought it was impossible for someone to abduct a crying child without notice,' Lily said.

'You're right, Lily. It would have been impossible without your mother's help. Now you know how.' Sally turned to Zach, and said softly, her brow furrowed, 'You're quiet. I know this is a lot to process. And you've every right to be angry and upset.'

Zach finally broke his silence, his voice barely above a whisper as he said to Sally, 'All I want to say is thank you.'

'For what?' Sally replied, her eyes wide in surprise.

'For fulfilling that promise you made when you took me back. That you would spend your life showing me how much you loved me.' His voice trembled as he told her, 'Well, you did that. I've lived a life of love – from you and Dad. And the girls.'

A strangled sob escaped Sally, and she held a hand to her chest as she struggled to contain her emotions.

'I am in awe of your bravery and strength,' Zach added, his voice stronger now. 'What you endured . . . it was monstrous.' He threw a look of disgust in Kimberly's direction.

Tears glistened in Sally's eyes. 'I would do anything for my children. And now you know why Sister Ailsa and Nicola were like family to me.'

'I wish I'd known. All those times they visited us at Lake Champlain, but I never understood how deep your connection to them was.'

'They loved you,' Sally said. 'I wish they were still alive, because they would both get peace, knowing that the truth was finally free.'

'Does Dad know about all this?' Zach asked, his brow furrowing.

Sally nodded. 'We have no secrets. Before I accepted Dom's proposal, I told him everything. We had a small wedding in the chapel in the Benedictine convent in Ronda, then we left for America shortly afterwards.'

'Why didn't you tell me about this before, Mom?' Zach asked, his voice low.

Sally shrugged. 'We thought it was better you didn't know. That it would be easier for you. Boy, did we get that wrong! I can see that now. Secrets always find a way to reveal themselves.'

Sally then turned to Lily, Jason and Gaga. 'I can't imagine what you are all thinking right now. And I truly am sorry for my part in the pain that you have all endured.' She took a deep breath, then said softly, 'I never wanted this to be a secret, Jason. I wanted you to know that Robert was safe, and loved by his own mother. I gave Elsie the option to let you say goodbye to Zach before I disappeared. But she was insistent that I leave in the dead of night, without your knowledge.'

This was too much for Lily. She slumped in the chair, feeling hot tears fall. The betrayals kept coming.

'Despicable,' Gaga cried out.

'I couldn't risk losing you, Jason, and I was terrified that you'd take Lily from me. Don't you see? I loved you both so much, so I had to lie,' her mum cried out, two dots of colour flooding her cheeks.

'All you've ever done is lie to us,' Lily said to her mother. 'All this talk about love is a convenient excuse to hide behind. Love isn't manipulative or cruel. Love doesn't take, and twist and turn a truth to suit oneself!'

Her mother retreated to a corner of the living room, curling into an armchair with her legs tucked under her, and began to rock back and forth like a wounded animal.

Zach walked closer to Lily. 'I never thought I'd bring this to you all. I just wanted to understand the truth. I'm so sorry, Lily.'

'None of this is your fault, Zach,' Lily said, then she touched his cheek briefly. 'But it's such a mess. I am ashamed that my mother did this to you and your mom.'

Zach shook his head emphatically. 'Do you remember what you said to me in Ronda, when I worried about what would happen to my mom when the DNA results came back?' he asked, moving closer to Lily. He repeated Lily's words to her now: 'You said that I couldn't take responsibility for my mother's actions. The same goes for you.'

Lily smiled back wistfully. 'Even though you were never truly ours, I'm so glad we've found you again. My big bro.'

'My little sis,' Zach replied, clasping her hand for a moment.

Then Lily turned her focus to her father, who sat beside

Michael and Ben on the sofa. Lily rejoined him and placed an arm round his shoulder. She felt his shoulders shake beneath her hand, and her heart constricted in love and pain for him.

'It's a lot to take in, isn't it?' she asked gently.

'She knew all along, Lily. Your mum let me spend forty years looking for Robert when she knew where he was. I can't . . .' His eyes drifted across the room to Kimberly, but he pulled back from her.

Zach walked over to her dad's side and held out his hand. 'Can I give you a hug? To thank you for caring enough to look for me all this time. I'll never be able to express how much that means to me.'

Her father looked up at the little boy he'd once loved as his own, and stood now to face him. 'I always believed that you were alive, so I had no choice but to keep looking for you.' His lip quivered, and his shoulders sagged.

Zach placed a hand on his shoulder. 'You can stop looking now, Jason.'

Lily felt her fractured heart begin to form together again at those words, and then the two men embraced.

'What do we do now?' her dad asked when they broke apart.

'I don't think that's up to us,' Lily said. She turned to Sally. 'Do you want to press charges against my mother?'

Before Sally could answer, Jason finally allowed his anger to come through. 'Kimberly or Elsie or whoever the hell she is, deserves to go to hell for what she put our family through. Call the Gardaí.'

Her mum jumped from her seat and rushed towards them, 'You can't do that to me. Not after all this time. It's cruel.'

'Cruel?' Lily cried out. 'What you did was not only cruel – it was evil! You can't expect to get away with that scot-free!'

'You don't understand. None of you do. I had to take Zach. I had to!' Kimberly's eyes were frantic as she looked at each of them. 'I had to save him!' She walked over to Jason and pulled at his shirt, desperately pleading with him to forgive her.

Jason pushed her aside and said, 'We are done. I don't want to hear it any more.'

Then Kimberly turned to Lily, and begged, 'Please, Lily. I shouldn't have taken Zach, but you would have too if you had been me back then. I had no choice.'

Lily was sick of hearing the same excuse over and over and batted her mother away.

But it was Sally who came to her old friend's rescue, moving closer as she watched her quizzically.

'What aren't you telling us, Elsie?' she asked softly. 'What have you been hiding all these years?'

'He died. And I couldn't save him,' she answered on a sob.

'Who died?' Sally asked.

Everyone moved closer to Kimberly, forming a circle around her as she finally revealed, 'My baby brother.'

NOW

Kimberly

Phibsborough, Dublin

Kimberly was sixty-eight years old. And for sixty-two of those years she'd worn many different masks, each one masquerading a different version of herself. But who she was now was her favourite. And she'd sworn to herself that she'd never go back to any of the previous versions of herself. Part of that promise was to deny her baby brother ever existed – always pushing away all thoughts of him when they crept up on her.

But today the masks were free-falling, and Kimberly couldn't see a way to stop them. The life she'd worked so hard to curate for herself was crumbling away to nothing.

Her daughter's face, and that of the man she'd loved for four decades, betrayed the truth – they thought she was an evil woman because of her actions that day in 1981. Her last throw of the dice was to reveal the original Elsie to them all.

'He was only six months old. I adored him from the moment my mum brought him home from the hospital. I was his big sister, and I couldn't wait to take care of him,' Kimberly explained. She closed her eyes and breathed in deeply. 'He smelled like talcum powder. His skin was so soft.' She opened her eyes again. 'I know everyone thinks their child is beautiful, but he really was. A mop of dark hair and big blue eyes.'

'I never knew you had a brother,' Lily said, her eyes widening.

'That's because I never talked about him.'

'What was his name?' Sally asked.

Kimberly sighed. 'Robert. But I shortened that to Bertie by the end of his first day at home.'

'You named Zach after your baby brother?' Sally asked, incredulously.

Kimberly held her hands up to ward off everyone's comments. She had to tell them what happened first.

'I realised that there was something wrong with Mum pretty fast. She went into the hospital with her big bump, happy and smiling, loving and kind. But returned with Bertie, withdrawn and snappy. My dad had done a runner, a year after I was born, and I never knew who Bertie's dad was, so we were on our own.' Kimberly sighed, then added, 'I had no choice but to take over.'

'What age were you?' Lily asked.

'I'd just turned five.'

Kimberly closed her eyes again as she tried to remember Bertie's face, and it came back crystal clear, but, try as she might, she couldn't picture what *she* looked like back then. That image was grainy in her mind.

'I loved taking care of Bertie. Bathing him, rocking him to sleep, giving him his bottle. He liked it when I sang to him.' Kimberly softly began to sing, 'You are my sunshine,' stopping when a lump formed in her throat.

'Oh, Mum,' Lily whispered. 'You used to sing that to me.'

'Yes I did. And I sang it to Sally and Robert too.' Kimberly closed her eyes again, and she was back in that small terraced home in London. 'Mum kept forgetting to feed us. She was never hungry herself, so food wasn't important, I suppose. We all got so thin. I began missing school because I was afraid to leave Bertie alone with Mum. I knew she wouldn't hurt him on purpose, but she'd forget he was there sometimes. Nowadays they'd call it post partum depression. But back then there wasn't anyone to spot that Mum was having problems. Except for me, and I didn't know what to do about it.'

'You were five. How could you?' Sally said softly.

Lily walked back to Michael and Ben. They huddled together on the sofa, Michael's arms moving tight round his wife and son. Kimberly envied them. She'd had similar family love to theirs, for the briefest, most magical time of her life. And now she would do anything to feel her grandson's comforting arms around her. But she wasn't sure she would ever be allowed that privilege again. Sighing, she continued her story.

'The school called and threatened social services if I didn't return, so Mum forced me to go in. Bertie was six months old by this time. I'd turned six. I was so worried about leaving him on his own. Because, even though I was little, I knew my mum wasn't well enough to take care of him.'

Kimberly pulled at her hair, the sharp pain on her scalp a welcome diversion from the pain piercing her heart. Her bones ached and she felt so tired. She wasn't sure if she could finish this story that she'd buried deep inside of herself for more than sixty years.

But then she caught Lily's eye and saw her daughter's beautiful face clouded with worry and heartache. She knew that the only chance they would ever have to repair the damage she'd caused was to be honest, no matter the cost to herself.

'I went to school that day, worrying constantly about what was happening at home. When the rest of my class ate their lunches at break time, my teacher, Mrs Joyce, called me up to the top of the class. She'd seen that I had no packed lunch with me, and she gave me a ham sandwich. I can still remember how good that tasted. I was hungry a lot of the time back then.'

Sally made an anguished sigh and they locked eyes, remembering another time in both their lives on the Doddington Estate when each of them had been driven to desperation with hunger. And Kimberly thought to herself that no matter how many mistakes she'd made her children had never gone hungry.

'Mrs Joyce asked me what was wrong, told me that I should tell her if there were problems at home, that she would help ensure Bertie and I were safe.' A tear escaped and trailed its way down Kimberly's cheek. 'I wanted to tell her. Let her take the responsibility that was crippling me. And I'll always regret that I didn't confide in her, because maybe then . . .' She paused, unable to finish the thought. 'I was too scared, so I kept my secrets, insisting that everything was perfect at home.'

Kimberly looked around the room again and smiled. 'And it was perfect in here.' She tapped the side of her head. 'I had such a good imagination, and I created a world where Mum was happy, like she used to be when it was the two of us. And Bertie and I were bathed in love and smiles, all day long.'

Kimberly half groaned.

'I went back to school the next day, looking forward to it, even, because Mrs Joyce had promised she'd bring me lunch again. And I desperately wanted that soft white bread with butter thickly spread, and salty ham. As soon as it was break-time, Mrs Joyce asked me again if all was okay. And I swore we were fine.'

Kimberly felt her body begin to tremble as the final, horrific memory had to be relayed.

'But it wasn't fine.' Kimberly brushed tears away from her face as she spoke. 'I thought Bertie was sleeping when I got home. But I couldn't get him to wake up. His skin was cold, so very cold. The air smelled like rotten eggs. And I had to wrap my school scarf round my face to try to block it. I ran to Mum, but she was asleep too. Lying on the kitchen floor, her hair fanning out on the tiles. I shook her and begged her to wake up, but the smell was so bad I couldn't breathe.'

Kimberly wiped away tears that cascaded down her cheeks as she wept for the first time in decades for her beloved mother and brother. 'I ran outside because I was coughing so much, and I retched on the grass. Then I banged on our neighbour's door for help.'

Kimberly heard Lily sob from across the room, and her stomach twisted, knowing that the final part of her story would cause her more pain.

'While I was at school happily eating my ham sandwich, Mum forgot to turn the gas stove off. She was heating some soup for herself. Bertie and Mum both suffocated from the fumes.'

Kimberly felt arms move round her. She couldn't stop shaking. Her whole body trembled and swayed as she revealed her secret. Then she felt those arms tighten round her, steadying her. Jason. Her constant. Her safe harbour.

When they pulled apart, Kimberly said, 'Do you see now? It was my fault that Bertie died. If I'd done something, if I'd said something to Mrs Joyce . . . Bertie would be alive today. But I pretended all was okay.' She turned to Zach now. 'I couldn't do that to you, Robert. I had to save you, unlike my little Bertie . . .' Her voice broke on a sob as she looked around the room, desperate for their understanding.

They didn't answer. Each watched her with echoing looks of sympathy and sadness. Even Jason's father had stopped glaring at her. But none of them spoke up, none of them reassured her by saying that she was right to do what she had.

Kimberly cried out, her voice strangled, 'You must understand. I had to save Bertie!'

'It wasn't your fault that Bertie died. Or your mum. You were a child yourself. You have to know that now,' Sally said, her face pinched with worry. 'But Zach wasn't your brother Bertie. Nor was I your mother, unable to take care of him. I would have laid down my life for Zach.'

Jason stepped away from Kimberly then. He looked so tired as he wearily said, 'I understand why you took Zach now. I'm glad you told us. But I'll never understand how you let me spend forty years searching for a little boy when you knew where he was all along. I can't forgive what you did to our family. To me.'

Kimberly turned to Lily. 'And you?'

Lily's answer was to move to her father's side and hold his hand.

'What now? You call the Gardaí?' Kimberly asked in a shaky voice.

'No!' Zach stated firmly. 'There's been too much pain. I want it to be over.'

'I've spent decades waiting for the moment when Elsie was arrested for what she did to us all back then.' Sally said. She reached over to clasp Zach's hand. 'But maybe it's time that we all learn to live with the truth. If we can find a way to accept the past, maybe then we can find a new future. So I agree with you Zach. This ends here today.'

Kimberly's shoulders sagged with relief and when she saw Lily make her way over to her she smiled. It was going to be okay. But her smile froze when she heard her daughter's words.

'I'd like you to leave, Mum. You are not welcome here any more.'

Kimberly felt everyone's eyes on her. She almost crumpled in front of them all, but then she remembered who she was, so she squared her shoulders and lifted her chin. She'd been through worse storms than this. And she had not only survived, she'd thrived.

She walked over to the sofa and leaned down to kiss Ben gently on his forehead. Then, picking up her handbag, she walked out of the room.

ONE YEAR LATER

July 2024

Zach

Lake Champlain, New York

Jason and Dom wore matching black aprons and chef's hats. They stood by the barbecue, their laughter mingling with the sizzling and spitting of steaks. They had formed an instant bond when they'd met the previous week. Zach's three sisters, Jenny, Ally and Issy, lay side by side on sun loungers, their giggles filling the air as they caught up on gossip. Jenny and Ally's children played tag with Ben, who joyfully toddled around. They were captivated by their new Irish cousin, their laughter echoing through the backyard.

Zach's mom and Michael, their wine glasses glinting in the sunlight, stood at the lake's edge, voices intermingling with the children's laughter. Then Lily emerged from the house, a small infant nestled in a sling against her chest. She walked up to Zach, and he gazed down at his new niece, her tiny features a perfect reflection of innocence. Only two months old, but already a source of boundless love. Her rosebud lips pouted as she slept, a picture of serenity against her mother's warm embrace.

'I still can't believe this, you know,' Zach said, his voice filled with a mix of wonder and gratitude. 'When I walked into your office a year ago, I could never have dreamed any of this.'

'Me neither,' Lily replied. 'The year was full of surprises . . .' She nodded towards her little girl.

'The best one of all,' Zach said, his voice filled with emotion, leaning down to kiss the baby's soft head. 'I feel like –' he paused, a lump forming in his throat – 'that with Lexi here, it's a chance to get things right. You and I didn't get to grow up together, and I didn't get to be your big brother, but Ben can do that for Lexi.' He stopped, his heart swelling with love and longing.

Lily nodded and he was glad she understood his sentiment. 'I thought something similar too. And you know what else, Zach? While we didn't grow up together as kids, we're making up for it now.'

This was one of the things that made him happier than anything else. His relationship with Lily, Michael, Ben and Jason grew stronger daily. And, no matter what the DNA said, he *felt* like Lily's older brother.

They'd banked many happy memories over the past year, but one of his favourites was going to an Ireland rugby match with Jason, Michael and Ben, who looked so cute, wearing a pair of ear muffs. Zach knew that technically he wasn't Irish, but he felt a connection to Ireland in the same way he had always felt one to Spain. Both were early homes for him and markers for who he was and who he'd become.

'Michael and I have been planning Lexi's christening,' Lily said. 'We've set the date for the first of September.'

'Oh, that's nice,' Zach replied.

'We wondered if you would do us the honour of being Lexi's godfather?' Lily asked, looking up at him from under her lashes.

Happiness burst out of Zach in a delighted laugh. 'I'd love to. I'd be honoured. Jeez, thanks, Lily. Means a lot to me.'

'It means a lot to me too,' Lily replied. She leaned her head on Zach's shoulder, and they stood side by side, watching the sun begin to set over the blue waters of Lake Champlain.

'Do you think she's okay with you all here?' Zach asked.

There was no need to elaborate on who *she* was. Kimberly remained the elephant in every room they were in.

Lily sighed. 'Mum will be fine, doing what she does best – working. When I saw her last week, she had received the deeds for a new property she plans to convert to flats. She never stops.'

Zach whistled softly. 'She's a powerhouse.'

'I think it's more than that. I don't think she *can* stop,' Lily said in a low voice. 'Work helps her quieten the nagging voice of truth. When she's at work, she can keep pretending she's living her perfectly curated life.'

'Has your dad spoken to her yet?'

Lily shook her head. 'Nope. He's not said a word to her since that day at my house, when all our dirty washing came tumbling out.'

'I thought they might get back together, you know,' Zach said, nodding towards Jason, who was popping the caps on two beers. 'He was so gentle with her after she told us about Bertie and her mother.'

'Their relationship has always been complicated. They never could get over the trauma of losing the future they'd hoped and dreamed of for their family.' She sighed, then added softly, 'Lost in the blink of an eye, not once, but twice.'

'I sometimes think I've dreamt all of this. It feels too incredible that Kimberly ever did that to my mom. And to your dad.' Zach replied.

'I think I could forgive her for taking you. Especially knowing about Bertie. But I'll never forgive her for not telling dad. And me. Betrayal and guilt found its way into our family decades ago, courtesy of Mum.'

Zach nodded towards Jason, whose head was tilted back as he roared laughter at something Dom was saying. 'It's good to see Jason beginning to move past it all now.'

Lily looked over to her father, and a smile lit up her face. Jason looked younger, relaxed, and that frantic energy he'd always exuded had finally been put to bed. With so much spare time on his hands, he now devoted himself to his dad, and to Lily, Michael, Ben and Lexi.

'Dad says that he'll never forgive Mum for the years he lost. And, to be honest, Zach, I don't think he should. Mum did a terrible thing – there must be consequences.'

The words hung heavy in the air, a testament to the deep wounds and the long road that still lay ahead of them before they could ever reach a place of forgiveness and reconciliation.

Then Ben ran towards them, shouting excitedly as he held his arms up: 'Uncle Zach, bring me to the boat! I want to see the fishies.'

With a quick wink to his sister, Zach scooped his nephew up into his arms and made his way to the lake.

Thousands of miles away, Kimberly stood in a bright, open-plan flat, holding a glossy brochure in her hand. She pointed out the spacious wardrobe and en suite of the primary bedroom to a young couple who hoped to rent it. They were a handsome duo, excited about renting their first home together.

'We could put the crib over there,' the young woman said, holding a protective hand to her tummy.

'You're pregnant.' Kimberly said, smiling. 'Congratulations. It's such a special time.'

'Do you have kids or grandkids?' the man asked as he slung his arm round his wife's shoulders.

The gesture brought a lump to Kimberly's throat. These two were united in love, as Kimberly and Jason once had been. But it had been nearly a year since she'd last spoken to her ex-husband. Even during their most challenging times, they never went longer than two weeks without contact. Lily was barely civil to her, and she felt lucky to be allowed to visit her grandchildren, Ben and Lexi, once every two weeks. Michael kept telling Kimberly to be patient, that she must give Lily time, that she would come round. And Kimberly was trying hard to do that.

As for Zach and Lily, they were as thick as thieves. From

what Kimberly could see on their Instagram accounts, they spent most weekends in each other's company. The relationship that Kimberly and Sally had dreamed of for their children, all those years ago in the orphanage, had finally happened. They were as close as siblings.

Her heart ached as she thought of Zach, because he, like Jason, had refused all efforts Kimberly had made to contact him. He'd sent her a letter, handwritten on exquisite white notepaper, embossed with his name, asking her never to contact him again. Zach said he couldn't forgive her for what she'd done to everyone, but especially for the pain she'd inflicted on his mom.

Sally.

Thinking of her hurt more than anything. Too much pain had passed between them to ever return to the closeness they'd once had. And that was okay, because Kimberly didn't want to be Sally's friend any more.

Sally had been Elsie's friend, not hers.

And Elsie hadn't existed for more than forty years. She was as dead as her mother and Bertie were.

Kimberly wondered if Sally was gloating now. Because, if this was a game, Sally had won, fair and square. And the final blow was that Kimberly's family were all with Sally in America. Her pure light still shone so brightly that they all couldn't help but circle her, like moths to a flame.

'Are you okay?' the young pregnant woman asked, bringing Kimberly out of her reverie. 'I keep telling my husband that he shouldn't ask people such personal questions.'

'I'm sorry,' he said, grimacing an apology.

Kimberly flicked back her hair and smiled brightly. 'No, it's me who is sorry. I got lost for a moment, thinking about my family.'

The couple beamed back at her, and Kimberly had a good feeling about them. 'You know, you both remind me of my husband and me. We've been married for more than forty years! And would you believe it was in this block of flats that we met? Jason was my landlord!'

Kimberly chuckled when the couple made appropriate surprised gasps.

'We have two children, Robert and Lily. All grown up now! Robert is the clever one, and very handsome. Everyone says he looks like me. Oh, and that's not to say that my daughter isn't beautiful and clever too. She has made me a grandmother – twice! We are so close. She leans on me heavily, with two little ones, who are my everything. But I don't mind. My favourite thing to do is spend time with my family. Let me show you a photograph of little Ben and Lexi . . .'

Kimberly felt no guilt for her masquerade – she never intended to deceive. Many times over the years she'd walked in shadow, relying on others to bring brightness to her life. But Kimberly had found a way to live in light even when there was only darkness around. *And it was glorious.*

Acknowledgements

Thank you to my agent, Rowan Lawton, for always believing in me and for listening when I say, 'I have this great idea for a new book . . .' It's been quite the twelve months, and I wouldn't want to have anyone else by my side. Thank you to Eleanor Lawlor and the rest of the team at The Soho Agency, the rights team at ILA and Tara Timinsky at Grandview LA.

This is my first book with Headline, and it's been joyful since day one. And that's down to my publisher, Jennifer Doyle, who loved my book and understood what I wanted to achieve with the story from our very first 'bonjour' (inside joke). Thank you to the talented team at Headline who have worked on *The Stolen Child*: Hannah Bowstead, Caroline Priestley (my absolute favourite cover yet!), Inka Melson, Alara Delfosse, Alexia Thomaidis, Sam Stanton-Stewart and Nikki Sinclair. Thank you to Hachette Ireland for the warm welcome – Jim Binchy, Breda Purdue, Elaine Egan, Siobhan Tierney, Ruth Shern and Ciara Doorley. Thank you to the international team Eleanor Wood and Ellie Walker.

Thank you to Hazel Gaynor, who is a genius at creating titles and came up with what I believe is the perfect title for this novel. Thank you to Catherine Ryan Howard for listening to my passioned pitch for this story about a missing child and responding by saying, 'If you don't write it, I will.' And then, once I did write the story, for reading an early draft and giving me an endorsement that I'll forever be grateful for. In case you missed it, it's worthy of repeat – 'One of the greatest twists I have ever read.' I know, right?! There's so much more that I'll always be grateful for, but Hazel and Catherine know that already, because we three never leave anything unsaid.

Thank you to Cristian Font Calderón at the Embassy of Spain

Acknowledgements

in Dublin, Freda Yague and Davnet Murphy, who all helped ensure my Spanish phrasing and details were correct. Please forgive any errors if you find them. They are all mine.

Thank you to the hugely supportive writing community in Ireland and the UK, who inspire me daily. Thank you to the book retailers, media, bloggers, podcasts, reviewers, libraries, book clubs and festivals whose passion for putting books into readers' laps helps authors, including me, every day.

To my friends, not only for the WhatsApp chats and gossipy fun dinners with cocktails, but for always supporting me in this somewhat different career I've chosen: Ann Murphy, Sarah Kearney, Davnet Murphy, Fiona Deering, Siobhan O'Brien, Maeve Tumulty, Gillian Jones, Liz Bond, Siobhan Kirby and Maria Murtagh.

To all the O'Grady and Harrington family, thank you for another spin around the sun. There's a lot of love and fun in our families, which I never take for granted. Tina and Michael O'Grady, Fiona, Michael, Amy and Louis Gainfort, Shelley and Anthony Mernagh, Sheryl O'Grady, John and Matilda O'Grady, Ann and Nigel Payne, Eva Corrigan, Evelyn Harrington, Adrienne Harrington and George Whyte, Evelyn, Seamus and Paddy Moher, Leah Harrington: as I always say, *all that matters is family.*

As always, an extra thank you to my first reader, my mum Tina. She rereads my backlist multiple times, and every time I send her a new book, she tells me it's my best yet. I am forever grateful.

Thank you to my husband, Roger, and my children, Amelia and Nate, for being my biggest cheerleaders. I love how excited you all are for me when I finish a new book. I get to live with my favourite people in the world, and I still pinch myself that I got *this* lucky. And George Bailey, I'm not forgetting you – my little shadow and constant companion. Please don't scratch our new front door.

Last but not least, my final thank you goes to my readers. Many of you have been with me right from the beginning. I want you all to know that every day I sit at my desk and write new words, I do that for *you* all.

Carmel

Author Note

Readers often inquire about the inspiration behind my novels, and the truth is that each one has its own unique starting point. Sometimes it begins with a theme, but more often the plot and characters take the lead equally, both vital in each story I craft.

However, *The Stolen Child* has a particularly poignant genesis, sparked by a chilling 'what-if' moment that our family experienced when our children were young. This real-life event became the emotional cornerstone of the story's development. It all began with a holiday in Orlando. Amelia and Nate were five and six years old. And while we were sleeping, our nightmare *almost* began . . .

We were exhausted from our transatlantic travel the night we arrived in Orlando, so we fell into a deep sleep as soon as we checked into the hotel. Our bedroom had two double beds, side by side. The children slept in one, and my husband Rog and I in the other.

At 3 a.m., we awoke to hear someone banging on the door to our room. Rog went to ring reception while I looked through the peephole on the door, which revealed an empty corridor. Even though we couldn't hear any voices, I became convinced that Nate was outside. This made no sense because he was asleep only a few feet away. Rog went to check on the sleeping children, but I didn't wait for him to report back, and I opened the front door immediately.

My maternal instinct was right – it rarely lets me down – because I found Nate crying hysterically in the hotel hallway. I remember falling to my knees to gather him into my arms, and we both stayed on the ground, crying for some time. I cannot express the horror of seeing our vulnerable young child on his own, outside the safety of our hotel room.

It took a while to figure out what happened, but we eventually pieced it together. Nate had begun sleepwalking and had managed to leave our hotel room, only awakening when he reached the elevator at the end of the long hallway. He had no memory of leaving the room, and was so scared when he realised where he was. Thankfully, earlier that night as we exited the lift, I had pointed out to the kids that we'd always remember which was our room because it was right at the end of the long corridor. Nate remembered this fact as he ran towards our room and back into our arms.

While Nate was shaken, he was otherwise safe and unharmed. But I found it hard to let go of the horrifying 'what-ifs' that continued to run through my mind for days.

What if he'd knocked on the wrong door?

What if someone had taken him?

What if he'd gone outside and fallen into the swimming pool?

It was terrifying to contemplate the many scenarios that might have happened that night.

Rog also commented that if someone *had* snatched Nate, and we'd awoken the next morning to find him missing from our shared bedroom, who would believe us that we hadn't heard a thing? What parent could sleep through their child disappearing from a few feet away? It was a sobering thought that the finger of suspicion would have pointed at us, Nate's parents.

And, of course, eventually my author brain began to kick in, and these questions became the beginning of the inspiration for what would become *The Stolen Child*.

This story does not end here though! I'm lucky my children have always shown huge interest in my books. When they get home from school, they ask me about my word count and love to hear about the characters I'm writing.

A couple of years ago, it felt like the right time to explore a story about a missing child. But the motivation for one of the characters eluded me. Until I shared the plot outline with Nate, who, of course, had a particular interest in this story. As I posed my dilemma to Nate, he thought about it for a moment, then replied, 'What if . . .'

His answer gave me goosebumps, because it was so clever and ultimately revealed the devastating and shocking twist that is at the heart of *The Stolen Child*.

You won't be surprised to learn that I've dedicated this book to Nate!

This book would not have been possible if it were not for my son. I don't think I'll ever again have such a special inspiration story for one of my books. Nate has mentioned a few times that he should get half my royalties. We've settled on a new bedroom – I did manage to write 107,000 words all by myself, after all!

As I created the Murphy family, their individual backstories took me to many unexpected places. From a children's home in 1960s London to the bustling suburbs of Dublin, then to the picturesque Andalucian mountains of Spain. And my characters kept surprising me. The masks they wore to hide their past traumas began to fall. Heroes and villains revealed themselves to me, and the novel evolved from a story about the horrifying disappearance of a child to one about the far-reaching consequences for those left behind.

This book is very special to me, and I can only hope that my readers will fall in love with it, too.

Thank you all for reading,

Carmel

A Note from Nate

I can remember the night I began sleepwalking really well. But I don't remember how I got out of our hotel room. I only woke up when I heard the lift make a noise. I was really scared, but remembered Mam saying that we would never forget our room, because it was at the end of the long corridor. So I ran as fast as I could to the end. But there were two rooms, so I had to guess which one was ours. When Mam opened the door, I was so happy and I remember crying in her arms. She was crying too, but I could see she was trying not to. After that night, Mam and Dad always set traps at the doors and windows, to make sure I couldn't sleepwalk outside again! And Mam slept in my bed with me every night, too.

I like chatting to my mam about her books. And when she told me that she was writing a story about a missing child, inspired by me, she said she needed to work out why one of her characters did something. I had an idea, and when I told her she said it was a really clever one.

I'm really happy I helped my mam with this book, and I hope everyone likes reading it.

Nate (aged 12 and three-quarters)

Book Group Questions

There are many strong women in *The Stolen Child*. Of the leading ladies, Sally, Elsie, Lily and Kimberly, which character did you relate to the most? What was it about them that you connected with?

Did any of the events leading up to the reveal of what happened to Robert in 1983 take you by surprise? Did you see each of the plot twists coming?

Location has always played an essential role in Carmel's novels. Do you enjoy travelling to new destinations in a story? Would you like to visit any of the locations Carmel described?

There are difficult themes explored in the novel, including child loss, abandonment, poverty, prostitution and domestic abuse. Were there any moments in the book that made you see things differently?

The bond between Sally and Elsie, formed in the Sunshine House orphanage, is evident throughout the story. Discuss their friendship and the role they played in each other's lives. Did you understand their actions?

How did you feel about the ending for each of the characters? Were you surprised? Would you change the ending for any of them?

What three words would you use to describe the novel?

The novel is an emotional read at times. Which part moved you the most? And have any parts of the story stayed with you since you closed the final page?

If you enjoyed *The Stolen Child*, don't miss
the next gripping novel from Carmel Harrington

THE NOWHERE GIRLS

Coming 2026

Read on for a sneak peek . . .

Prologue

December, 1995

Then

Pearse Station, Dublin

The station master took a moment to readjust his tie, then stepped back onto the busy thoroughfare at Pearse Station. He was late back from his lunch break for the first time in his forty-year career at the train station. But today was a special day. President Bill Clinton and his wife Hilary had just addressed eighty thousand people in College Green. The station master hadn't planned on going along to the event, but as the commuters arrived early in the morning with Irish and American flags, he was swept up in their excitement.

It turned out to be one of the best decisions of his life. He looked down at his hand in wonder. Because thanks to his last-minute whim to join the well-wishers at College Green, he'd shaken the President's hand. Humming The Star-Spangled Banner, the station master placed his arms behind his back and began his regular patrol up and down the platform, his eyes darting from side to side to ensure that all was well. His forehead creased when he noticed something not quite right.

Holding hands, two little girls sat on a bench near the public toilets.

Their lilac floral smocked dresses with starched white collars caught his eye. Reminiscent of a bygone era, he had not seen kids dressed like that for a long time. The smallest of the two sucked her thumb. Her hair was so blonde, it was almost white. The poor little mite didn't look more than a toddler. The elder of the two, with dark brown hair, watched him warily. Her eyes glistened with unshed tears as she wrapped a protective arm around her little companion. He took in their long braids with lilac ribbons tied prettily at the ends. These girls were well looked after, he decided. So why were they on their own?

He moved closer and cleared his throat to gently say, 'Hello.' He pointed to his uniform and added, 'I'm the station master here. Where are your parents?'

They watched him silently, eyes wide with distrust. The younger of the two buried her face into the older girl's chest.

He kept his voice gentle, then crouched down low. 'It's going to be okay. Don't worry. I'm here to help.'

The younger girl began to cry and snuggled further into the embrace of the elder girl, who answered bravely, 'Mammy told us to stay here and that we shouldn't move. We haven't.' Her jaw tightened as she looked at the station master defiantly, ready to battle if he should insist they leave their spot.

The station master nodded approvingly. 'You are very good to do as your mammy said. What age are you?'

'I'm four, and my sister is three,' the dark-haired girl replied, her eyes darting around the platform, back and forth, searching for her mother.

They were sisters, despite their different colouring. It was clear he needed to gain the trust of the elder girl so that he could help them. 'I bet you are a great big sister. How about I make an announcement asking your mammy to come to my office? We'll have you back with her in no time.'

They didn't respond, shrinking back from the question. So he left that for a moment and asked instead, 'Can you tell me what your mammy is called?'

The dark-haired girl looked him up and down, deciding

whether she could trust him. Finally, with a sigh, she responded, 'Her name is Star.'

'That's a pretty name. And what is her surname?'

The girl shrugged, biting her lip.

'That's okay. Let's leave that for now. And where do you both live?'

'We live in the woods.'

'Do you know where the woods are?' he asked.

'Mammy says it's in the middle of nowhere,' the girl replied.

And as she spoke, the strangest sensation overcame the station master. He felt a shiver of unease run down his spine and shuddered inexplicably. Whatever was going on with the girls, his instincts warned him that they were in trouble.